To Debbie,

(You have a delightful hubby.) :)

Sihler
08/26/16

Wild Heart on the Prairie

Jan Thoresen came to tame this vast land —but will the prairie conquer him?

A Prairie Heritage, Book 2

VIKKI KESTELL

Faith-Filled Fiction™

www.faith-filledfiction.com | www.vikkikestell.com

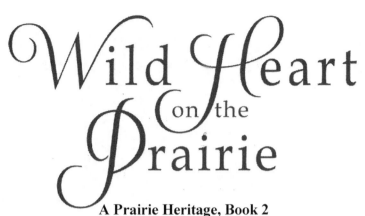

A Prairie Heritage, Book 2
©2014 Vikki Kestell
All Rights Reserved
Also Available in eBook Format

BOOKS BY VIKKI KESTELL

A PRAIRIE HERITAGE

GIRLS FROM THE MOUNTAIN

NANOSTEALTH

WILD HEART ON THE PRAIRIE

Copyright © 2014 Vikki Kestell
All Rights Reserved.
ISBN-10: 0-9824457-6-8
ISBN-13: 978-0-9824457-6-1

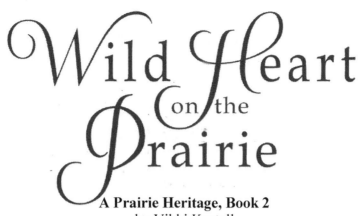

Wild Heart on the Prairie

A Prairie Heritage, Book 2
by Vikki Kestell
Also Available in eBook Format from Most Online Retailers

Brothers Jan (Yahn) and Karl Thoresen have left their native land of Norway and braved many perils and hardships to bring their families to America—the land of freedom and hope. Like thousands of others, Jan and his wife Elli long for the opportunity of a better life and future for their children.

After enduring an ocean crossing and the arduous journey west, they encounter a land so vast and wide that it defies mastery. Jan finds that his struggles are not only with the land, but with a restless and unmanageable heart. Will Jan find a way to overcome this wild land or will the prairie master him?

Wild Heart on the Prairie is chronologically both the prequel and the companion to *A Rose Blooms Twice*.

TO MY READERS

This book is a work of fiction,
what I term "Faith-Filled Fiction™,"
intended to demonstrate how
people of God should and can respond
to difficult and dangerous situations
with courage and conviction.
The characters and events that appear in this book
are not based on any known persons or historical facts;
the challenges described are, however,
very real, both historically and contemporarily.
I give God all the glory.

PRONUNCIATION GUIDE

Amalie .... Ah´-ma-lee
Gjetost .... Yay-toost
Jan .... Yahn
Kjell .... Chell
Sigrün .... Sig´-run
Søren .... Soor´-ren
Thoresen .... Tor´-eh-sen
Uli .... Yoo-lee

The dialogue spoken in this book contains occasional non-English words set in italics. Non-English words set in italics may be Riksmaal (Norwegian), German, or Swedish, depending on the speaker. Some words sound the same from one language to another but are spelled differently, such as the English word "nay" which is spelled *nei* in Riksmaal and *nej* in Swedish and the English words "mama" and "papa" which are spelled *mamma* and *pappa* in Riksmaal.

Dedication

I dedicate this book to two of its characters,
Amalie Thoresen and **Fraulein Adeline Engel**,
who exemplify the many selfless women in the Body of Christ.
These women live their lives, not for themselves,
but for the care and benefit of others
—because they love Jesus.
Lord, bless all women such as these.

Acknowledgements

With each book I write,
I value my proofreading team more and more.
I want to publicly thank
Cheryl Adkins, **Greg McCann**, and **Jan England**
for the many hours of work poured into this manuscript.
I also thank you for our fellowship and shared learning!
I simply cannot do this without you!

Cover Design

Vikki Kestell ©2015
Background image:
Tallgrass Prairie at Sunset
Sean Crane/Minden Pictures

PART 1

No man who demonstrates
an exemplary Christian walk
begins his journey
in an exemplary manner.
Through the furnace and the fire
his life is tried, tempered, and purified.
It is only through
faithfulness to God in these times
a wild heart can be tamed.

—Vikki Kestell

CHAPTER 1

MAY, 1866

Jan Thoresen, heedless of angry shouts, clambered up the wall of crates stacked along the docks. When he reached the top he stared at the crush of humanity surging below and beyond.

O Lord! I have never seen so many people in one place, he marveled, *or such buildings and ships!*

He turned in a circle, trying to absorb the breathtaking view: the docks of New York City, the thousands of rushing, clamoring people, and the towering buildings.

Another angry bellow, one Jan recognized, roused him from his reverie. He grinned and saluted his brother Karl, whose forbidding expression was so familiar.

Jan laughed with the sheer joy of the moment and stretched out his arms to embrace it all. *We have arrived, Lord God!* He took a deep breath and a last glimpse of the panorama before him. *Never again will I see such a sight,* he realized.

Tearing his eyes from it, he climbed down the crates and leapt the last six feet, landing next to Karl. Karl's frown was matched by the threatening scowls of two dock workers advancing on Jan.

As the men pushed their way through the crowd toward him, Jan drew himself up—all six-foot-four-inches of rock-hard muscle. Karl shook his head. As irate as he was with Jan, they were brothers after all. He turned and stood shoulder to shoulder with Jan.

The longshoremen slowed a few yards away. Sensing the crackling tension, the crowd pressed back, leaving space between the Thoresen brothers and the enraged dock workers.

The longshoremen were no strangers to hard work and hard living. They directed menacing glares toward the blonde giants. Jan and Karl, arms folded, stared back, unfazed.

One of the dock workers, a bit wiser than his companion, thought better of wading into a fist fight with the two behemoths—perhaps they weren't as easily intimidated as most immigrants. He shrugged his shoulders. "Well, no harm done after all," he muttered. Placing a restraining hand on the other man's arm, he backed away and they melted into the crowd.

"Come, Karl!" As though they hadn't avoided a brawl their first day in America, Jan shoved toward the line where he and Karl had left their families. Their objective was one of the larger buildings—the Castle Garden rotunda and immigrant landing depot of the United States. The lines, several of them, wended toward the immigration stations at the entrance to the Garden.

Jan already missed the cleaner air he'd breathed atop the heap of crates. The fumes of the creosote-soaked timbers under their feet coupled with the rank odor of many unwashed bodies enveloped them.

After a two-week ocean journey, from Christiana to Liverpool then Liverpool to New York, the Thoresens' fellow shipmates were weak and weary. Sounds of retching along the lines were not infrequent as disembarked families coped with empty bellies, disorientation, and the anxiety of the coming inspections.

Jan, with Karl grumbling behind him, waved to his wife Elli. She was relieved to see the two brothers returning and pointed them out to her sister-in-law Amalie. The women were struggling to keep their places in line and also keep children and baggage together.

Karl scowled but said nothing more about Jan's impetuous climb up the mountain of crates. They helped their wives gather and move their possessions farther up the line and then settled down to wait until the line inched forward again.

Ach! This waiting is so hard, Lord! Jan complained. *I have energy to spare and no good thing to spend it on.*

Jan reached around Karl and pinched his unsuspecting niece, Sigrün. When the girl rounded in indignation, Jan was facing the other way, his hands in the pockets of his homespun trousers. Four-year-old Sigrün's eyes narrowed as she glanced from her distracted father to her seemingly innocent uncle.

Jan winked at Elli, and she winked back. *Oh, it is good to have a little humor to get us through this trial.*

Jan's thoughts returned to the upcoming medical inspections. He knew his children, eight-year-old Søren and six-year-old Kristen, were strong and healthy and that he and Elli presented no health problems.

But Karl, behind his neutral expression, was concerned about little Sigrün. She had been coughing for days. In this line, a cough attracted unwanted attention.

Lord, you have brought us so far. You will not fail us. I trust you, Jan prayed.

America's War Between the States was over; now thousands of Jan and Karl's fellow Norwegians were immigrating every month, hoping America would offer them a brighter future. Jan and Karl were no different—they, too, sought a new life with better opportunities.

The lines moved forward in spurts as families passed through registration stations, medical inspections, and into the spacious rotunda of the Garden. Between 700 and 1,000 new arrivals would spend the night inside. American officials who could read and speak their language would help them retrieve their cargo from the ships and assist them on their way in the morning.

The Thoresens had traveled steerage class, a level below the main deck of the ship. As steerage class passengers, they had spent most of the crossing confined below in an open, shared cargo hold.

Like others in steerage, the Thoresens had cooked their meals at designated times and slept together on wide, wooden berths. The berths were temporary platforms knocked together for steerage passengers, easily removed to accommodate a different sort of cargo on the ship's return voyage.

Jan and Karl and their families had borne the uncomfortable crossing well, but not all had. Some of their traveling companions had come aboard with not much more than their tickets. They carried all they owned on their thin, bowed backs. Their children, with eyes too big for their faces and shoulders too weak for their rucksacks, were too weary to run and play with other shipboard children.

Watching these families, whose flight to America was a last, desperate effort to avoid starvation, had saddened Jan. He and Elli had discreetly shared their food when little ones with hungry eyes had wandered near them at mealtime.

Jan thought of the money he and Karl had scrupulously saved and brought with them, and he thought of their other belongings still in the hold of the ship. The Thoresens would begin their new lives in this country with more than most immigrants would.

Jan was proud of his family and proud of his heritage. He and Karl were broad, thick, and hardened from a life of demanding work and good food. Every Thoresen standing in line was hearty and well fed.

We come from good stock, he reflected with pride.

It was obvious at a glance that Karl and Jan were brothers, but there were also differences. Karl's shaggy hair was light sand in color while Jan's was as white as ripe wheat. Karl's body was a bit more compact than Jan's, too, and he spoke in a rich baritone; Jan was taller and his voice deeper than Karl's.

We will do well in America, Jan assured himself. *This cough of Sigrün's will pass; it is nothing to worry about.*

Jan saw Karl gesture with his chin. Amalie, Karl's stout wife, pulled a small jar of honey from her deep pockets and administered a spoonful to Sigrün.

Søren and Kristen frowned. They longed for a taste of honey, but the families would not eat until they passed the inspections and could sit down together for a bite of bread, stale though it might be.

Kristen cleared her throat and managed to produce a raspy cough, politely muffling it on her sleeve. Jan and Elli both bent stern looks on her, although Jan had to swallow hard to keep from chuckling.

Ah, my little Kristen! You are the most beautiful thing I have ever seen, Jan rejoiced. *I will never stop being amazed that you and your brother came from your mamma's and my love.*

Kristen smiled sheepishly, swished her skirts, and leaned against her mother, resignation written in the slope of her shoulders. Elli sat upon one of their suitcases, the rest of their bags piled near her.

"It will not be much longer," Jan assured Kristen, caressing her cheek with the back of his fingers. She looked up at him from under dark blonde lashes.

You have your mamma's eyes. He shook his head in wonder.

Jan let out a deep breath. He winked at Søren, then reached around Karl and tugged Sigrün's braid. This time the girl was ready for him and pounced. "I knew it was you, *Onkel!*" she squealed, jumping up and down. Søren and Kristen laughed heartily and Jan grinned.

Sigrün's excited outburst ended in a spate of coughing. Karl held her against his leg until she was able to catch her breath. He fixed his disapproval on his brother.

"Jan," he hissed. "Do not provoke this *barn* of mine. Sometimes you are worse than a child yourself." He frowned. "Behave like an adult, eh?" he added.

Jan, still grinning for Søren and Kristen's sake, sauntered out of line to see how far they had to go. Jan's smile faded and he shook his head.

Ah, Karl! Jan had been on the receiving end of his *bror's* and his *far's* reprimands for as long as he could remember.

"You are too impulsive, Jan," his father would declare in a stern tone.

"That temper is going to get you in trouble, Jan," his brother would lecture.

"No one trusts a jokester," his *far* would add.

"Be serious, Jan! Grow up!" Karl would reprimand, and Jan would receive a disapproving frown.

The lectures and sibling rivalry had begun when Jan was a boy. Karl, who was two years Jan's senior, had sprouted up and into a man's body by the time he was fourteen years old! Jan, on the other hand, had been sickly in his early teens and slow to get his growth.

Where Karl was taciturn, Jan was naturally good-humored like his mother. When Karl had bragged on his size and ribbed Jan about his, Jan had plagued his brother with practical jokes.

Their father had not helped. He needed a third man on their farm and regularly told Jan he wished him to be more like Karl—steady, dependable, able to do a man's work. Jan had rebelled at the comparison and provoked his brother further whenever possible.

Then came Jan's seventeenth year. In six months he shot up six inches! The following year he grew another five. His mother, amazed and somewhat in awe, slipped extra food to him between meals, for Jan complained continually of being hungry. Every few weeks the good woman was obliged to let down his trousers or make him a new shirt.

By the time Jan was nineteen, he was an inch taller than his brother and two inches broader in the chest. The competition between the brothers grew fierce as they strived to outdo each other in whatever chore their father assigned.

As Jan grew into a man, years of crop failures across Norway kept him bound to his father's small farm. He longed to escape the narrow life of a second son, but opportunities to learn a different trade—one that would allow him to branch out on his own and support a family—were scarce.

Besides, I am a farmer, Jan knew. *It is in my blood and in my bones.* Like every young farmer in Norway, he dreamed of having his own farm, but land in Norway was scarce and grew more expensive each year. With each year that passed, Jan grew more dissatisfied with his lot in life and more resentful of living under his father's and brother's authority.

Even in this line today, Karl seemed to have forgotten that Jan was a thirty-seven-year-old married man with children, when in fact Jan had married and fathered a child before Karl had!

Of course, marrying before Karl had been a sore point.

The men of their district typically married between ages twenty-five and thirty. Jan, at twenty-eight, had already waited three years to marry Elli Mostrom—all because Karl had been slow to select a bride.

When Jan had first laid eyes on Elli she had been tall and gangly, with a crown of honey-and-wheat colored hair and eyes as deep and blue as a fjord. By age eighteen, Elli had lost her coltish charm; she had grown into a poised, stately woman, the image of a Viking queen. Jan told his parents he would wait no more—he was certain he would lose her if he waited another two years!

Karl was only beginning to court Amalie when Jan and Elli married, and he had been disgruntled. Ten months later, just before Karl and Amalie finally tied the knot, Elli had given birth to Søren. Karl had not been pleased.

That had been Karl's fault for dragging out his courtship, Jan told himself. *Now that we are in America, things are going to change. Once I have my own land and my own home, our relationship will be better!*

He smiled in relief as he looked down the line. *Only three families ahead of us!* Many of the families in line had been on the ship with them. He walked forward, greeting the men and wishing them well.

Betta Harvath, a newborn in her arms and a toddler leaning against her legs, sagged with fatigue. Their family was at the head of the line, and her husband was presenting his papers to the official.

"We will be through this soon," Jan encouraged her gently.

Ah, Lord, he prayed, *I thank you that Elli is not pregnant during this difficult journey. But when we finally have our land, could you please send another little one? It has been a few years now since we had a new baby.*

He paused as the conversation between Per Harvath and the official reached him.

"Did you come to America with any money?" the man asked in passable Riksmaal. "We cannot have immigrants living on the streets, you know."

It wasn't the question that caught Jan's attention; it was the way the official glanced casually to each side before he asked it.

Again the official checked on the location of the supervisors and, not seeing one near, lowered his voice a bit. "I see you have a sickly wife. How do you expect to get her through the inspection?" The official noticed Jan and turned a suspicious eye on him.

Pretending he had heard nothing of their conversation, Jan leaned away from *Fru* Harvath and waved to Søren, several yards down the line. Søren offered a weak, confused wave in return.

After a moment, Jan backed a step closer as the exchange between the official and Mr. Harvath resumed.

"I have money!" Harvath protested. "We have family in America, too. We will not be on the street. We will not be a problem!"

He leaned toward the official. "You don't think the doctor will turn her away, do you? She is only tired. She had a baby just a month before we left."

The official pretended to think. "I don't know . . . but perhaps I should see if you truly do have money and will not be a burden to our country. Show me what you have."

Jan slid his hands into his pockets and nonchalantly angled toward Mrs. Harvath again, but cut his eyes toward the official's table. *Herr* Harvath, obviously anxious, opened his wallet and withdrew a thin stack of currency. The official took the money and rifled through the bills. Jan saw as he slid two of the notes under his book.

"You may pass," the official said at his normal volume. He stamped the entrance papers and waved the man on.

"But, but, you, you took my money!" Per protested, his face reddening.

The official fixed him with a cold eye. "You may pass, I said." He dropped his voice and added, "Do you wish me to alert the doctor of my concern about your wife?"

Per's flushed cheeks turned white as he looked about him in anger and frustration. Reluctantly, he gathered his papers and shouldered his family's belongings. Turning to his wife and children, he shepherded them on to the medical inspection. The next family in line moved up.

Jan had already returned to Karl's side. "Let me go first," he muttered.

"What? Why should I?" Karl shot back. "I don't want you joking with the official and causing us any problems, Jan."

Jan's temper sparked. "*Karl!* Give me your papers and let us go first."

Karl sighed. When his brother got his back up, it was useless to argue. Jan spoke quietly to Søren and to Elli, who cradled a dozing Kristen. They gathered their luggage and moved ahead of Karl, Amalie, and Sigrün. By then all the Thoresens had noted the change in Jan's mood and had become quietly observant.

When it was Jan's turn in line, he handed papers for both families to the official. The official looked down the line, counting heads. Just then Sigrün coughed, and Jan saw the sly look slip across the official's face.

"Have you money to begin your new life in America?" he asked, his voice low and solicitous.

I am glad this man understands Riksmaal, Jan thought. He leaned close to the official's face. "What I have is no concern of yours. We are not poor immigrants without property, nor are we ignorant or stupid. *I saw* you take money from Per Harvath."

Jan leaned closer. "You will not do the same to me. I will call your supervisor, if need be. You will lose your position."

The official's jaw dropped in shock and fear. Jan pointed to his papers. The official gave them a perfunctory inspection and hurried to stamp them. Avoiding Jan's stony glare, he gathered the papers up and handed them back.

Just before Jan stepped away from the table, he reached out and nudged the official's book to the side. Without a word, he scooped up the currency he found there and shoved the bills into his pocket. He stepped out of line and gestured to Elli and Søren to join him.

Karl looked from Jan to the official and back. The official jerked his head, indicating that Karl should follow Jan, but he would not meet Karl's eyes.

Karl, his brow furrowed, gathered up their things and steered Amalie and Sigrün toward Jan. "What was that all about?" he whispered.

"*Ja,* I will tell you, but first we must find *Herr* Harvath."

After they passed—without incident—through the medical inspections and entered their names into the immigration logs, they were herded into the rotunda.

"Oh, my," Elli gasped.

They were standing under the dome of the largest building they had ever been in. Across the wooden-planked floor of the great, round hall, families stacked their belongings and arranged makeshift beds.

Jan looked for Per Harvath and his little family. "*Herr* Harvath!" Jan shouted. His words were caught up in the din and carried away.

"What is it?" Karl asked. He had to shout to be heard.

Jan put his mouth near Karl's ear. "The official! He stole money from Per Harvath. I took it back. I must find him and give it to him."

"Stole!" Karl's expression was shocked. Jan knew that Karl was just as shocked by Jan taking back the money as he was by the official stealing it in the first place.

Jan braced himself for a lecture but made an attempt to distract Karl first. "Do you not remember the warnings?"

Karl and Jan had read all the literature they could lay hands on regarding immigration. The brochures and newspapers included cautionary tales—how newcomers were bilked during currency exchanges, overcharged for goods and services, extorted by officials, and even led into dark alleyways to be set upon and robbed.

The most concerning warnings told of unscrupulous men who managed to separate young women from their families and, under cover of the teeming crowds, spirit them away. As Jan and Karl read those accounts they had exchanged long, grave looks.

Sadly, the literature disclosed that many of the perpetrators of these crimes were people of their own country—men who had been in America long enough to know best how to defraud their own countrymen upon arrival.

"Per Harvath!" Jan shouted again. He may as well have been spitting into the wind, but at least he'd distracted his brother.

Karl leaned close to Jan. "Let us get our families settled. Later you and I can walk around and find him, eh?"

The two men spotted a small open area and led the way toward it. Within a few minutes the women had arranged their baggage to form the three sides of a "u" shape. Elli and Amalie unpacked a few blankets and laid them out.

Toward evening as the crowded rotunda began to settle for the night, Karl and Jan split up and searched for the Harvaths. Jan had been looking for half an hour when he spied Karl and Per Harvath making their way toward him.

"*Herr* Thoresen! Your *bror* tells me you have my money! How can I thank you enough?" The relief in the man's weary eyes was thanks enough for Jan.

"It is nothing. I am glad you will have it back," Jan replied. He pulled the folded notes from his pocket and handed them to the man.

"But, but this is more than he took from me!" Per remonstrated.

"It is?" Jan rubbed his chin. "Then he surely stole from others, too."

"But what shall I do with it?"

The three of them thought for several minutes. It was no small thing, having in one's possession money or property that did not belong to you. Per held the extra bills in his open hand as though their owners might claim them on sight.

"We have no way to return these," Karl said at last. He was nervous, and Jan knew he was concerned that the official would somehow point them out and make trouble for them. Karl sighed and gazed out at the throng spread throughout the hall.

Per followed his gaze. "Someone like me is in sore need of this money."

"I suppose," Karl suggested slowly, "we could just divide the bills between us?"

Jan shook his head. "I would not feel right, would you?"

"No," Karl admitted. Per nodded in agreement.

Jan rubbed his chin again. "So! I have an idea. How much is there?" He explained himself in a few words. Karl and Per thought for a moment and nodded.

Their eyes again turned to the mass of people within the rotunda. Jan motioned to Per who separated the three extra bills, giving one to each of them.

Per looked uncomfortable. "I'm not a good pretender," he confessed.

"Watch me," Jan said. "It should not be hard." He wound his way along the perimeter of the hall until he reached a family he knew from the ship and greeted them.

"*Hei.* Hallo." Jan nodded to the young man, Sänder. His wife, Pergunn, huge with child and worn, could not raise her eyes. Jan knew this family had exhausted their resources just to make the trip. Their three small children had eaten from Elli's hand several times during the passage. Even now, their hungry eyes stared at Jan with undisguised hope.

Jan squatted near the man. "Sänder, look here. We found this; I think you must have dropped it," Jan handed him the bill.

The young man stared at it. "*Nei,* I thank you, but I did not."

Jan stared back. "I assure you, *this is yours,*" he insisted. His hand stayed outstretched until the young man, hesitating, took it and blinked his eyes against the sudden moisture that filled them.

Jan returned to Karl and Per. "See? It was easy."

The other men shook their heads and both of them handed him their bills. "You are good at this, Jan." Karl grinned and punched his brother on the arm. "It is that impulsiveness of yours, *ja?* Come. I will point out the family I have chosen."

"I have one picked, too," Per added, eager now.

The three of them paused, suddenly serious. Karl struggled to put what they were feeling into words. "It is a right thing we are doing, a good thing, *ja?*"

"*Ja,*" Per slowly agreed. "It was wicked that someone stole this money. But God has shown us a *good* use for it." He scrunched his face, thinking. "Is there not some *Skriften* that says this?"

Jan nodded. "*Ja, Herr* Harvath. I think it reads, *They meant it for evil, but God meant it for good.*"

ℰHAPTER 2

Just after dawn the crowded hall began to stir. Jan stretched, trying not to disturb Elli who was asleep in the crook of his arm. He glanced at Kristen snugged against Elli's back. On the other side of Jan, Søren slept on his back, his mouth agape, one arm thrown above his head.

Jan watched his *sønn* with pride. Søren was no longer a "little" boy. Intent on becoming an American, Søren had already learned a few English words and used them whenever possible.

Jan and Elli were not as eager to learn a new language. They were taxed enough keeping track of their children and belongings and managing the day-to-day concerns of traveling without also worrying about new words.

Jan thought ahead to this day's challenges. Today the shipping agents would release their property, the cargo they had shipped with them from Norway. Then the immigration officials would help arrange transportation across the river to the rail station and explain how to ship their belongings by train. Some officials, their Norwegian ship captain had assured them, would speak Riksmaal and would not defraud them.

Yes, Jan and Elli would worry about learning the English later.

Jan was most concerned about the five weaner pigs from his father's Landrace herd. He and Søren had fed and watered them before leaving the ship, and they appeared healthy. But a long train ride was still ahead of them and many more miles by wagon.

An hour later, after eating a simple breakfast and grooming themselves as best they could, the two families knelt in prayer. "Thank you, *Herr*, for bringing us safely to America," Karl prayed. "Lead us this day in paths of righteousness for your name's sake. Amen."

The adults looked at each other. They were far from their destination but they were together, healthy and whole. Sigrün's cough seemed to be subsiding. They had much to be grateful for.

They packed and shouldered their belongings. Joining the long lines, they passed through the exits and onto the docks where they were released onto the teeming streets.

The Thoresens again stacked their belongings into a pile, this time on the other side of the immigration lines. Karl left Jan with the women and children and went to stand in line for the shipping agents.

Hundreds, perhaps thousands of new arrivals were doing the same as they. Jan watched fathers and mothers with anxious faces juggle their possessions and herd their children in one direction or another. He shook his head and checked that their three little ones were safe nearby.

He realized Elli was watching him, her eyes calm and understanding. Kristen's sash was wound about Elli's hand; Søren sat, still and obedient, on her other side.

Jan sighed and smiled. *Ah, my Elli! You know my heart so well, don't you?* He smiled at Elli until she blushed under his knowing gaze.

Jan glanced over to Karl's family. Amalie gripped Sigrün's hand and they sat atop their belongings. Satisfied, Jan turned back. He spotted another family they had crossed with, Oskar and Marta Forgaard.

He watched, curious, as Oskar turned in a complete circle, scanning the crowd. His wife clawed at his arm, fear etched on her face. Oskar shook her off, calling something that Jan could not hear.

What? Where was their *datter,* Freda? He swept his gaze over the crowd, recalling the sweetness of Freda's young face. He was suddenly worried for the Forgaards.

I must get up high as I did yesterday, Jan realized, *where I can see over this crowd!*

He strode toward an immense stack of barrels and clambered to the top. He heard shouts, but ignored them as he scoured the crowded docks and street for a glimpse of Freda's strawberry blonde hair. His expression was fierce as he cast about for the girl.

There!

He spied two burly men, one on either side of a limp Freda, hustling her toward the street. A third man standing in the driver's seat of a covered cart gestured for them to hurry.

Jan leapt from the barrels and ran toward the cart. He plowed through the crowd, tossing aside anything or anyone impeding him, keeping the cart's covered top straight before him.

The man on the cart noticed the stir as Jan bulled his way through the throng. He caught a glimpse of Jan and called for his companions to hurry.

Just before the two men holding Freda's arms reached the cart, Jan caught up to them. He grabbed their shirt collars and jerked them backwards. In a single motion, he slammed their heads together. They crumpled to the ground, unconscious. So did Freda.

The man from the cart rushed at Jan. He "ran into" Jan's left fist and dropped to the cobbled pavement.

Shouts and police whistles sounded all around Jan. The crowd parted, revealing Jan standing above the felled men and unconscious girl.

Four police officers, taking in the scene, confronted him with billy clubs. They shouted orders. Jan yelled back in Norwegian, but they did not understand. Many in the crowd, however, did.

As the battered thugs began to stir and get up, other Norwegian men crowded forward, shouting and gesturing to the police. The police, waving their clubs, warned them to stand back.

The indignant men in the crowd grew more incensed and the mood turned ugly; several bystanders managed to reach the three men. As the thugs resisted, the men who had grabbed them landed punches on their heads and chests.

The police whistled for reinforcements and used their clubs to push back what was becoming an angry mob. One of the policemen landed a blow across Jan's shoulder and gestured for him to kneel. Jan did so, but he realized he only had a moment to stop a riot.

"Who here speaks the English?" he shouted.

A young man, his head and shoulders topping most in the crowd, pushed forward. "I do."

Jan called out to him. "Tell the police I have something to say!"

The boy yelled to the police who were guarding the three thugs and Freda from the crowd and keeping Jan pinned down. Wary and with one eye on the threatening crowd, the policemen turned toward Jan.

Jan explained to the boy what had happened, pointing to Freda. As Jan spoke, the boy translated to the policemen.

At that same moment, the girl's father and Karl broke through the crowd. Karl's face turned red when he saw Jan in police custody. Jan sighed. Surely another lecture would be coming his way soon.

"Freda!" Oskar Forgaard looked about, frantic.

"Here!" Jan replied. To the boy he added, "This is her *far*."

As Oskar and Marta knelt and cradled their *datter* in their arms, the police reassessed the situation and grabbed the three men they had been protecting.

To the crowd's amazed satisfaction, the policemen turned their billy clubs on the would-be kidnappers, landing several blows on each of them before hauling them away. The crowd cheered in wild approval.

But Karl stared down at Jan, his mouth set in a thin line. As Jan got to his feet, Karl started to say something. Before he could utter a word, however, Jan poked him in the chest. *Hard.*

"Do not speak to me of this, *Bror*," Jan warned.

Karl opened his mouth again but did not say anything. Jan's expression counseled him not to. Oskar Forgaard embraced Jan; Marta, with many tears, thanked him. Jan only nodded to them and strode away.

Instead of feeling happy that things had ended well for the Forgaards and their daughter, Jan was livid. Some of the cheering crowd recognized the dark expression on his face for what it was and backed away, letting him through.

Jan knew his actions were not at fault, yet he had no peace. Instead, his heart was in turmoil. Every beat of it seethed with anger toward the men who had tried to steal an innocent girl. With that anger, long-buried resentment toward his brother and father boiled toward the surface.

"Jan." Karl finally caught up to him. "Jan, wait."

Jan rounded on Karl so quickly that they nearly collided. "What? What do you have to say, Karl? Eh?"

Karl backed away a step, confused. "I, I only wanted to say how glad I was, how *proud* I was, that you saved Freda Forgaard." He scowled. "I couldn't believe it when I saw that policeman hit you—how could they have not seen what those men were trying to do and that you were saving the girl?"

As Karl talked, his face settled into the same angry lines Jan had witnessed while on his knees surrounded by the police.

Jan blinked. Karl had not been angry with *him*?

"I thought . . . I thought you were going to lecture me on my temper," Jan stammered.

"*Nei*, brother! Why would you think that?" Karl expostulated.

Jan stared at Karl for a few moments. *Ah, Lord, what has this shown me about my heart? Maybe . . . maybe what I have allowed to fester inside is the real reason I am angry?* Letting out a long sigh, Jan clasped Karl on the shoulder. "I am sorry."

Karl just grinned and punched Jan in the arm. Jan punched him back.

It took the shipping clerk and immigration official more than two hours to clear their cargo through customs. The official exchanged their Norwegian currency for American and helped Jan and Karl to hire a freight wagon. Its driver would haul the Thoresens and their cargo to the ferry and then the rail yard.

Jan stacked the crates holding the weaners in the shade of the clerk's awning and instructed Søren to water the piglets and stand watch over them while the rest of their goods were being loaded. When the wagon was loaded and ready, Karl strapped the piglets' crates to the wagon while Jan and Søren left to get the women and girls. When they returned, the Thoresens seated themselves atop their freight, and the teamster set out for the ferry.

The teamster drove the wagon onto the steam-powered ferry. Jan had seen ferries in Norway; it would not be a long trip to the shore they could see across this river. Once across, the wagon driver would take them on to the trains.

Hours later they were met at the rail yard by other immigration officials. One of them pointed Jan and Karl to a boardinghouse where they could rent rooms. Jan and Karl left the women and girls there to bathe, wash clothing, and arrange some hot meals.

The freight manager pointed out a box car on a siding. With an immigration official's help, Jan paid for the use of the car and its transport to Council Bluffs, Iowa. There they would disembark the train, unload their freight car, and ferry across the Missouri. On the other side of the river they would be in the city of Omaha where they would board another train.

Jan and Karl had read all they could find about the audacious *Pacific Railroad*—some were beginning to call it the *Transcontinental Railroad*—and its progress. Three railroads were racing to build a single line that would connect the eastern and western shores of the United States!

One railroad would build the line from Oakland to Sacramento, California. The Central Pacific Railroad would build the next segment from Sacramento eastward to Utah Territory. The third line, built by the Union Pacific, was to start at Council Bluffs, Iowa, on the eastern shore of the Missouri, and run west until it met and connected with the Central Pacific Railroad.

Building a bridge across the Missouri from Council Bluffs to Omaha, however, had proven too difficult, so the Union Pacific began their segment in Omaha and had laid a few hundred miles of track along the Platte River from Omaha deep into Nebraska Territory.

Jan and Karl intended to ride that track until they reached the northernmost point of the Platte River. The land they had determined to claim lay farther north.

The immigration man tore a piece of paper from his notebook. He wrote "district land office" on it in Riksmaal and opposite it the same words in English. He did the same for "ferry," "homestead claim," "please," "thank you," "hotel," "buy wagons," "lumber," "how much?" and a few other useful words and phrases.

"*Takk*," Jan replied gratefully. He shook the man's hand and handed the paper to Søren. The boy studied the paper for a minute and then folded it carefully and placed it in his pants pocket.

Karl and the teamster were already unloading the wagon into their freight car. The men stacked Thoresen crates and boxes tightly against both ends of the car. When all the boxes and crates were stacked in the car, Jan and Karl tied ropes across the cargo to keep crates from shifting.

When they were finished, a wide area remained open in the middle of the car. This was where the Thoresens would ride as the train moved west in the morning.

Jan and Karl bought six bales of hay and hauled them into the car. They stacked three bales end-to-end, making a row of seating against one side of their belongings. They made a second row against the other side. Several feet remained in the middle between the two rows of bales.

One of the yard men, at the direction of the freight manager, hefted another bale into the car and cut the twine holding it together. He spread it out on the hard wooden floor of the car and pantomimed sleeping.

"*Tanks you*," Søren told the man for his *far* and *onkel*. Jan grinned at Søren. He and Karl shook the man's hand and nodded their gratitude to the freight manager for his thoughtfulness.

The crates containing the weaners went into the freight car last. Karl placed them where Søren could feed and water the piglets during their journey. Jan stood back and marveled at how much they had managed to bring with them all the way across the ocean—and soon would take across the United States.

Finally, Jan and Karl slid the doors closed. Jan fastened a heavy lock on them and pocketed the key. Weary, hungry, and filthy, they tramped across the rail yard to the boardinghouse.

"I just want a hot bath," Karl sighed.

"*Ja*, you need one," Jan shot back.

Both men slugged the other in the arm and laughed. Søren, trudging along beside them, only wanted some good, hot food. He definitely did *not* want a bath!

Jan glanced at Søren as if reading his mind. "*Ja*, you need a bath, too." Søren sighed.

Late that afternoon, Jan, Elli, and Søren, freshly bathed and wearing clean clothes, went out to buy food for the next leg of their journey. They left Kristen napping with Karl, Amalie, and Sigrün.

Søren studied the prices in the small grocery store and asked a few questions of the clerk. He was inquisitive, determined to learn, and not embarrassed to ask.

When they returned to their rooms, Søren asked his *far* to show him his money. Søren laid out a dollar on the table and then four quarters beside it. "This is the same," he said pointing to the dollar and stack of quarters. "Four of these are one *dollar*."

Jan mouthed the word "dollar."

Then Søren rearranged some of Jan's change into two quarters and five dimes. "Ten of these," he said, pointing to the dimes, "are one dollar, too. Five are *one-half* dollar or two of these," pointing to the two quarters.

Jan nodded. They played with the money for a while, moving it into different stacks of change equaling a dollar, and distinguishing between one-, five-, and ten-dollar bills.

Søren pulled out the paper with the English words on it. "So," he showed his father, "*hvor mye vil det koste?* is *how much?* in English."

"Howw much," Jan repeated. He ruffled Søren's hair, proud of his *sønn*.

Early in the morning they rose, gathered their drying clothes, and repacked their bags. Elli and Amalie wrapped and stowed fruit, butter, fresh bread, pickles, cheese, crackers, cookies, and boiled eggs while Karl went downstairs and filled a large can with water.

When they trekked across to the rail yards, their freight car had been moved off the siding. The freight master pointed to it far down the line, already coupled onto the train.

"I wish you well," the man told them. "God bless you."

"*Mange takk,*" Jan and Karl answered, shaking his hand for the last time. "*Farvel.*" Many thanks. Farewell.

"Tanks you," Søren said confidently.

They walked down the rail line and up onto the station platform, all of them marveling at the American trains, their mighty engines belching soot and steam. They passed passenger cars with curious faces looking down on them and a few luxurious private cars.

At the end of the platform they stepped down onto the ground and followed the rails, passing a line of freight cars until they reached their own. Jan unlocked the car and Karl clambered up. He turned and helped the women and girls into the car and then jumped back down.

Karl, Jan, and Søren handed the bags up to the women. Elli and Amalie, chattering happily about the arrangements, unpacked some coverlets and spread them on the hay bales. They hung their still-damp laundry across the crates to dry.

Jan climbed back up and Karl handed him the heavy water can. He stowed it between a bale and the wall of the car. Elli asked Jan to move a crate that sat alone behind one of the bales of hay. He placed it atop another and then climbed up and pushed it back. He retied a rope to keep it from sliding.

Where the crate had been, the women tacked up a sheet, making a tiny water closet. Jan grimaced. It was uncomfortable using a chamber pot in such close proximity to his brother and his brother's wife. He was sure they had to feel the same.

Jan, Karl, and Søren stood outside watching the activity in the yard until the conductor's call of "allll aboooard!" echoed across the rails. Down the line the yard men walked, checking that the freight car doors were closed. The men and Søren climbed into their car and slid the door shut behind them, latching it on the inside.

The car was dim and cool. Just a little light and air came in through slats in the door.

The train shuddered, rocked a bit, and jerked forward. The engine's piercing whistle cut the air. The train began to move, slowly, slowly, a little faster, faster, and faster. The Thoresens, all of them, crowded against the door, peering through the slats, watching the station drop away.

CHAPTER 3

The rhythm of train wheels flying over the tracks lulled them to sleep. All but Jan. He could not sleep now—his pulse had quickened until it matched the clacking cadence of the swaying train.

Jan leaned his forehead against the door and peered through the slats, studying the land passing by. He liked what he saw—large green fields that lay like a patchwork quilt as far as the eye could see. He knew the geography would change considerably by the time they reached their destination, but the size of this country already amazed him.

What will the land be like where we are going? he asked himself for the thousandth time. He had heard that it was like a vast sea with no shores to be seen, that tall grasses danced in the wind like the waves and billows of the ocean.

The newspapers had described the low, rolling hillocks and wide, nearly flat miles as "prairie," something like the lowlands of Norway and Sweden but much wider and broader, all of it open and uncultivated. "Perfect for farming," the papers had read. However, the words that fired Jan's heart and imagination were "160 acres per man" and "free."

Land for free! He and Karl would file for adjoining claims and work them together. All they had to do was build homes on the land and work it for five years. Then it would be theirs.

Jan was restless, ready to begin. And so he studied the terrain as they flew by, taking note of the farms, their barns and houses, and what they had planted. He mentally listed their first priorities and ticked off the items they would need to buy when they left the train.

Their journey would take them across two of America's great rivers. He frowned and recited the rivers' names: Mississippi and Missouri. Just across the Missouri they would stop in the city of Omaha.

In that city they would seek a district land office to file their homestead claims. It would be a risky time. They would need someone—*someone honest*—to help them because of the language barrier.

Jan snorted. Karl would likely *again* bring up their joint decision to go west rather than north to Wisconsin or Minnesota, states that bordered the great lakes of America. But Jan had been adamant.

"Do you wish to be only a dairy farmer, Karl?" Jan had demanded. "Do you wish for an area where the land has been picked over so that we must settle for what is left? Ja, many of our people have established communities in Illinois and these states. That would be nice, eh? To have others who speak our tongue and know our customs?

"But we would have to pay for that land. I want the *free* land—a parcel big enough to plant all the wheat and corn we can handle and raise cows, goats, and our father's hogs. I want space for our sons and their families, too."

His last argument had been the most effective. Yes, their *far* owned land in Norway, but it was a small piece completely surrounded by land owned by others. No matter how well they and their father managed, his ten acres would never support Karl and Jan's families as their children grew. And no more land in Norway was to be had.

Karl, as the elder son, would eventually inherit their father's farm. Even so, their father and mother were still strong and, God willing, had many years ahead of them.

If Karl stayed on his father's farm he would have to work for his father until he died, always doing what his father asked of him. Until his parents died, Amalie would not have her own house. Then Karl's sons would be in the same position—living on and working their father's land with no prospects of their own.

For Jan, and for Karl, the possibility of owning their own land *now*— more land than they had ever dreamed of—was too enticing, the idea of freedom too intoxicating. Land for themselves and land for their sons and their families? The opportunity could not be passed over.

And, Jan knew, he was weary of being dependent on his father. He was a grown man who did a grown man's work every day. If he stayed in Norway, he would always be subject to another man's orders—first his father's and then his older brother's.

In this new country, he and Karl would be equals. No more "little brother" and "elder brother."

Jan longed to put his feet under his own table each night after working his own land each day. Elli wanted her own kitchen and wanted to run her own home.

Was it wrong to want these things? Jan did not believe so, and his heart yearned for them.

Was the free land America offered in Wisconsin or Minnesota? No. It was west—to the Dakotas, the Nebraska Territory, or the territory of Colorado. These territories had much free land open to homesteaders.

How Jan wished he could see a map of the available homestead plots north and northwest of this Platte River. Jan could scarcely contain the restive spirit within himself. His eyes burned to see *his land* for the first time. His fingers itched to work the ground and tame it.

But how many claims were already filed? What land was left? This could only be determined once they arrived in Omaha and visited the claims office.

Jan had searched for and found an anchor that seemed to ease his anxieties. It was found in a passage of the *Bibelen* he had read before they left Norway. The verse had leapt from the page, as though underscored and with the words *Jan! I am speaking to you!* scrawled in the margin.

By faith Abraham,
when he was called to go out into a place
which he should after receive for an inheritance, obeyed;
and he went out, not knowing whither he went.

God was calling him to a place! Jan knew this deep in his being. But where? What place? He had determined to trust God as Abraham had trusted God. His trust in God's leading kept the fears, anxieties, and restlessness of his heart at bay.

God and *Elli* . . .

Back home, in the nights when they should have been sleeping, Jan and Elli had lain abed, twined together, talking . . . and dreaming. Elli, so tall and slender, fit perfectly in his arms.

Her love for him was like that, too. She "fit" him and completed him, touching and healing him in his deepest parts.

"Elli, you know when we go to America life will be hard, even harder than here?" he breathed into her silky hair. "We don't know what we will face. Will you regret it, my love? Will you regret leaving your parents and *søster* so far behind? Our children never seeing their grandparents?"

She snuggled closer to Jan. "You know, my *ektemann*, my husband," she replied softly, "that I love you *more* than my life. I, I am like . . . Ruth! And you," she giggled, "are my Naomi."

He chuckled and kissed her forehead. She was quiet and still in his arms for so long that Jan thought she had slipped away into slumber.

But then she whispered again, her words raw with tears. "Jan, this is truth: Where you go, I will go; and where you live, I will live: your people shall be my people, and your God my God. And where you die, my husband, I will die, and there will I be buried." She lifted her face to him. "This is truth."

Jan kissed her deeply and then buried his face in the warm crook of her neck. "My dear wife! You are God's greatest blessing to me in this life."

With God to lead him and Elli to love him, Jan found strength and hope each morning.

The clacking of the train over the tracks brought Jan back to the present and, as he had learned to do every time he began to fret over their coming journey, he took a deep breath and prayed.

Lord, again I place our journey in your hands. I trust you. Where you lead us, we will go. You have promised to never leave nor forsake us.

Then peace came again to his heart.

He must have dozed off. The sound of vomiting and coughing woke him. Karl sat across from them, staring ahead, his forehead creased a little. He sighed.

"*Mor* has a bad tummy," Sigrün confided in her loudest whisper. Karl shushed her gently.

Jan crooked an eyebrow. "Should we congratulate you?" he asked his brother under his breath.

Elli 'tsked' and pinched his arm. Karl just shook his head and rubbed his tired eyes. A few moments later Amalie reappeared from behind the curtain. Elli silently handed a dampened cloth to her.

"Ach! I am sorry," Amalie muttered.

"Maybe this one will be a boy, eh, *Søster*?" Jan said with a straight face.

Amalie blushed furiously and Karl shot him a dark look.

"This one what?" Kristen asked innocently.

Elli shook her head at the girl, but Jan could not help himself. He quivered with laughter, even though he tried to hold it in. Grinning at Karl and Amalie he made an attempt to apologize, but sniggered instead.

Perhaps it was the strain of the past weeks, but it felt good to laugh, to rejoice in what was ahead. He was happy, and was not a new baby something to rejoice over?

So he laughed. Karl tried to be serious and quell him with a look, but it had the opposite effect. Jan laughed so hard he could not catch his breath. Then Elli giggled and hiccupped, which only caused Jan to laugh harder. Tears leaked down his face.

Karl could hold out no longer. He chuckled, burst into laughter, and slapped Jan on the leg. The children, knowing only that their parents were laughing uncontrollably about something, joined them.

Amalie smiled, too. "Perhaps so, *Bror*," she relented. "It would be nice for a little Karl to be the first Thoresen born in America, *nei*?"

"*Pappa*, can we sing?" Kristen looked at him with hopeful eyes.

"What? Are you tired and bored from riding on this train?" Jan teased.

"Oh, yes, *Pappa*! Please! Can we sing?" she wheedled, batting her wide blue eyes at him.

Jan laughed and Elli shook her head. Karl rolled his eyes.

"You have no idea what is ahead with your little *datter*, *Bror*," Jan teased him.

He placed Kristen on his lap and smoothed her long braids. "*Ja*, little one. We can sing!" He started a merry folk song best sung in a round. Karl began the song again at the right place. Elli and Amalie added a third part. Søren joined his *pappa*, and the girls added their voices to their mothers'.

When that song ended, Karl and Jan jumped into another brisk tune, and then another and another. As the wheels of the train sang against the rails, the enclosed car rang with laughter and song. Finally, Jan began a hymn. They sang hymn after hymn until their hearts were full and their voices well used.

"*Pappa*, I love when our family sings," Kristen whispered, yawning and burrowing into her father's chest.

I love that when I look at you I see your beautiful mamma, Jan thought, his cup running over.

The train stopped every so often that day to take on coal and water. When it did, Jan and Karl slid open the car door. Everyone clambered down to stretch their legs and breathe fresh air. Along the way they emptied the necessary and refilled their water can. Where available they purchased hot food.

As the sun was sinking, stealing their light away, Karl pulled out the Thoresen family Bible and began to read aloud. Jan always thought of his father and mother when he saw the thick book. They had tearfully presented it to their eldest son as both of their children prepared to leave them, probably forever.

"I never imagined our *familie Bibelen* would leave our country, but it must go with you and your *sønns*, Karl, and you must faithfully record our family's history in it," their *far* had instructed, a catch in his voice.

Karl and Jan, with their wives and their children, had knelt on the wood-planked floor of the old farmhouse and received their father's blessing. "*Jeg ber til Gud om at han gir dere sin velsignelse og sitt vern.* I fervently pray our merciful God will extend his blessing and protection on you."

Why is life like this? Jan pondered. *I have spent much of my life trying to leave my parents and their home, but now I am looking back, already missing them. Will Søren someday leave for far-off adventures? And will Kristen marry and move away? How will I feel if my children leave and I am never to see them again? Ah, Lord! This is hard to think on.*

Three long days later their train steamed into Council Bluffs. All were weary of traveling, but perhaps Karl and Jan the most.

After situating Elli, Amalie, and the girls in another boardinghouse, Karl and Jan, with Søren in tow, went to investigate how to ferry their families and belongings across the river.

Using the words "ferry" and "please" written by the helpful immigration man, they soon arrived at the bustling crossing. They found a good place to study the process and watched for half an hour, observing how others made their arrangements, how the workers loaded the ferry, and how long the crossing took.

Jan poked Karl. "Look there."

Karl squinted and looked in the direction Jan was pointing. A large Swede sat atop a loaded wagon. The three Thoresens circled around until they found a path to reach the man.

"*Hei! God ettermiddag!*" Jan called to him.

The blonde, raw-boned man flashed them a smile. "*God dag! Norsk?*"

"*Ja,*" Jan replied. "It's good to hear a familiar tongue." Swedish and Norwegian languages were close enough that they could understand each other.

"I am sure it is! I'm Olafsson. Are you just arrived?" He climbed down from his wagon and shook their hands. He clapped Søren on the shoulder. "So! This young *Norsk* wants to become an American, eh?"

Søren grinned and bobbed his head.

"This is my *sønn* Søren. I am Jan Thoresen," Jan introduced them. "This is my brother, Karl. Our train got here a few hours ago. Are you going across yourself?"

They stepped into the shade of the wagon bed. "*Nej,*" Olafsson answered. "I live in this town. I own many wagons and we help unload the railroad cars and load the ferries." He laughed. "Until they build a bridge for the train here, I will have plenty of work."

Jan couldn't believe their good fortune. "So! We wish to cross tomorrow. Maybe you can give us some good advice, eh?"

Olafsson looked toward the ferries. "*Ja*, sure. I will be in line for an hour more, I think. Tell me, where are you going after you cross?"

Karl spoke up. "We wish to file our claims and take the railroad north until it starts to turn west again. Then, we think, we would get off and drive wagons north."

"Ah! There is still much good land that direction, from what I hear. But where will you get off the train, do you think?"

Jan and Karl looked at each other. "We are not sure yet, perhaps past Fremont."

"And you will need wagons, oxen, supplies?"

"*Ja*," Jan answered. "And lumber."

Olafsson grinned. "It is good we are talking. Let me tell you something. When you get to Fremont and beyond, it is very hard to buy the things you will need—wagons, oxen, and such. And there is no lumber to be had. The railroad takes all there is. I have seen some men return to Omaha because they had no way to haul their belongings from the train to their land."

Karl and Jan raised their eyebrows in understanding. "So," Karl said. "Did they buy what they needed in Omaha and then drive the whole way to their land? It would be a long, hard trip, *nei*?"

Olafsson nodded. "Some do, but if you have the money there is a better way."

"We are listening," Karl replied.

"Omaha has all you need at the best prices west of the Missouri. Not cheap, but best. You already have one freight car?"

Jan nodded.

Their new friend rubbed his chin. "If you can pay for another car, that is the way. Load your oxen into one side of the car. Break down the wagons and load them into the other side. Then when you wish to get off, you reassemble the wagons, load them, and go straight north."

"It may cost a lot," he concluded, "but paying for a car is not more than paying the costs of things farther north—and you do not run the risk of not finding what you need for sale when you get off the train."

Karl looked at Jan and back at Olafsson. "And what of land offices? Do you recommend we file our claims in Omaha or farther on?"

"You can file in Fremont. You will have to pay to have your cars taken off the train and then put back on, but the land you want will be listed there."

Karl and Jan walked away from Olafsson deep in thought.

"We can get everything we need in Omaha," Karl thought aloud. "But can we get it all in another car?" He was thinking of the four head of oxen they would need to pull two wagons.

"We can put more in our car. We can stack things higher." Jan was thinking of what Karl was thinking: the list of what they needed to buy and how much two wagons could hold.

"I am thinking we could use a third wagon, Karl," Jan stated. "But six oxen?"

Karl nodded. "*Ja*. A third wagon would be good. We could buy more lumber."

"Perhaps Elli could drive one of the wagons," Jan suggested.

Karl mulled it over. "We will ask her. You know, I am thinking that we do not need six oxen on our land, eh? But after we get settled, we could sell two of them. If they are scarce, as Olafsson says, then they are *better* than cash money where we are going. We could trade them for other scarce things."

They thought silently for several minutes before Karl concluded. "We will go across and talk to the freight master on the other side about another car, eh?"

Olafsson arrived with a wagon the next morning to unload their freight car and take the Thoresens and their belongings to the ferry.

"Look for my friend Svens Jensen on the other side, Thoresen," Olafsson told Jan. "Tell him Jakov Olafsson sent you. He will treat you fairly."

CHAPTER 4

Jan and Elli, keeping a tight hold of the rail and their children, watched the shore of Council Bluffs disappear, while ahead Omaha drew closer. The city was the capital of the Nebraska Territory, but Jan and Karl had read things in the Norwegian papers about statehood coming, perhaps soon, for parts of this vast land.

Elli looked down and shuddered. The river churning beneath their feet was a thick, muddy brown from upstream runoff. As placid as the wide river appeared on the surface, they had been told of its treacherous currents. A man falling into the river might be sucked down into the silty waters and not resurface for miles. Elli gripped Kristen tighter.

When they reached the other side, the ferrymen herded them off and began the task of unloading the ferry's cargo into a holding enclosure. Jan and Karl made sure everything of theirs was stacked together and that nothing was missing. Over the rails of the enclosure, wagon masters clamored for their business.

"Is there a Svens Jensen?" Jan hollered in Riksmaal.

"Here!" A wiry man with sandy colored hair and a great beard pushed his way toward them. "I am Svens Jensen. Are you Norwegian then?"

"*Ja*," Jan returned. He introduced Karl. "Olafsson told us to look for you. Said you were a good man."

Jensen stroked his beard and laughed. "*Ja*; I treat my customers well and my friends even better. Come! What do you have for me to haul?"

The Thoresens and Jensen began to shift the Thoresens' cargo to his wagon.

"*Pappa*." Søren's crestfallen face peered up at Jan.

"What is it, *Sønn*?"

"*Pappa*, the pigs. Two have died." Tears stood in his eyes.

Jan and Karl quickly ran to the pigs' crates. Sure enough, two of the weaners lay dead inside their crates. The other three looked fine and squealed, hoping to receive some food.

Karl took one of the dead pigs out of its crate and looked it over. "I cannot tell why it died," he muttered darkly, "so now we must keep the rest separate from each other."

Jan nodded in agreement. If the pigs had died of something infectious, their best chance of keeping any alive was to keep them from each other.

Jan noted that one of the dead pigs was a male. Their hope to establish a herd of their father's Landrace pigs in America depended on keeping at least one of each gender alive. They now had two females and one male remaining.

While Søren disposed of the dead piglets, the men washed their hands and separated the pigs' crates from each other. When the cargo was reloaded into a new freight car late that afternoon, Karl and Jan took pains to place each crate as far from the others as possible. They both carefully washed their hands after handling one crate and before touching another.

Karl secured a second car from the freight master before leaving the rail yard. Then Jensen drove them past a hardware store and gave them directions to the stock yards before delivering them to a boardinghouse.

"This store is owned by Petter Rehnquist, a Swede," Jensen told them, pointing to it. "If you have questions, he will help you. Tell him I sent you!" He scratched under his beard. "Maybe he will let his boy, Sauli, take you around. He speaks English and could help you a lot."

"We thank you, *Herr* Jensen, for all of your help and kindness. God bless you," Jan said.

He and Karl shook Jensen's hand with real gratitude as they parted. They would remain in Omaha until they had bought and loaded everything into the two freight cars. It would be an arduous undertaking.

In yet another boardinghouse not far from the rail yard, the two Thoresen families bathed and rested that night. Jan and Karl worked on the list of supplies and other necessities to buy on the morrow. Elli and Amalie composed a list of staples and other foods the families would need for their journey and after they reached their land.

Over breakfast, Karl and Jan planned their day. "We should go to the hardware store first," Karl suggested, "and introduce ourselves. It would be good if the hardware man's *sønn* comes with us to the stock yards, don't you think?"

Jan agreed. He, Karl, and Søren walked into town and toward the hardware store. The bell on the door tinkled, announcing their entrance. Both men immediately liked what they saw.

The store was large and well stocked; out a side door was a fenced yard filled with cut lumber. The owner greeted them pleasantly. Jan and Karl introduced themselves and Søren, saying that Jensen had sent them.

"We must buy wagons and oxen today and then come back to make our purchases. Would your *sønn* be willing to come with us? We do not know the town or the language. He would be a great help to us."

Sauli, a thirteen-year-old boy, was pleased to be asked to help. Although five years separated them, Sauli and Søren grinned and began chatting away, some in Swedish or Riksmaal, some in English.

Jan was glad for it. *Søren could use some time with another boy*, he thought. *And, who knows? Maybe he will learn more English today.*

Even with Sauli's help, it took most of the day to find three good wagons and three sound yoke of oxen for sale. And the purchases were more expensive than Jan or Karl had imagined.

"So!" Karl allowed grudgingly. "They will be worth that much more when we get off the train, *ja?*"

The wagons they bought were not covered like "prairie schooners." They were large, plain boxes with high sides. Jan and Karl did not expect the trip from where they left the railroad to their land to take more than three days, if that. They planned to cover their goods with canvas tarpaulins during the trip and sleep under the wagons at night.

The men tested the wagons and the oxen for an hour, driving up and down a worn track outside the stock yards. Karl was concerned about one of the oxen that had a particularly surly and unpredictable temperament. Jan and Karl gave both boys sound warnings not to stand within reach of any of the oxen's horns or hooves, especially the temperamental one's.

They then looked for and found a wagon repair shop and purchased two spare wheels and a spare axle and tongue. When Jan and Karl were satisfied with their purchases, they allowed Sauli to drive one of the empty wagons to his father's store.

The boys rode together, Sauli pointing out interesting things to Søren as they wound through town. With every hour he spent with Sauli, Søren picked up new English words.

The three wagons pulled to a stop in front of the Rehnquists' store, spanning the full length of the storefront. It was past three o'clock in the afternoon and they had not stopped to eat at midday.

Each driver set the wagons' brakes; Jan and Karl tied the first team to a thick post. They tied the second and third teams to the wagons in front of them. Jan left Søren with the wagons with orders to keep the oxen calm.

"Mind their hooves and horns, *Sønn*," Jan reminded him yet again.

Karl produced the list he and Jan had worked so hard on and began to read it off to Mr. Rehnquist: *Two plows, two sickles, an axe, two hatchets, a whetstone, a pickaxe, a pry bar, a shovel, two hoes, a rake.*

"May I suggest that you also buy a sod cutter?" Mr. Rehnquist explained the sharp, plow-like tool's use in cutting through prairie grass and removing blocks of thickly rooted sod.

"Even if you do not use the blocks for building, you will want to cut the grass and its roots out so you can plant in the soil beneath."

"*Ja*, one of those," both Thoresen men spoke at the same time.

Two hammers, a saw and extra blades. Two sizes of nails, one keg each.

Mr. Rehnquist pointed out smaller tools. "Will you need a rasp or an auger? Chisels? A planer?"

"My brother is a woodworker," Karl replied. "We brought his finer woodworking tools with us."

Candles and matches. Lamps, wicks, cans of kerosene. A cask of grease. A washtub. Two large cast-iron cauldrons. Cast-iron skillets, pots, and Dutch oven. Grain grinder.

The items stacked up; Mr. Rehnquist had Sauli fetch some boxes and crates. Sauli and Jan packed the items in them as tightly as they could.

Two iron bedsteads. Yards of ticking and burlap. A dozen spools of thick, cotton thread. Waterproof canvas tarpaulins and yards of oilcloth. Lengths of rope, twine, and wire.

Buckets and tin pails. Boxes of jars and paraffin. Another strong lock and key. Oats, seed corn, and hard wheat seed.

"Will you not plant a green garden? It is not yet June," Rehnquist suggested, pointing to his selection of seeds.

"*Ja*, we will," Karl answered. "We have brought many seeds from home with us."

Chicken wire. A bag of feed. A dozen chicks.

Sauli lined a box with flannel and lifted the chicks in one at a time. He tacked on a slatted lid, but lightly so it could be easily removed.

As they packed the items and loaded them into the middle wagon, Mr. Rehnquist listed them and their cost on a piece of paper. "Your wives, will they wish to buy dishes also?" he asked.

"*Nei*," Karl replied. "We have brought much of that with us. Even my sister-in-law's cookstove! But we will need a second stove since we will build and live in our barn first. One for heating. And some stove blacking."

He and Jan looked over the stoves. "This one, I think." Karl pointed to a square one with a large burn box. Jan agreed. Mr. Rehnquist selected pipe for it while Jan and Karl started to break down the stove.

"Do you have a gun?" Mr. Rehnquist asked. "Do you need shells?"

Karl and Jan looked curiously at the hardware man's selection of guns and at each other. "Our father has guns we hunted with, but we did not bring any," Karl answered.

Rehnquist raised his brows. "Ach! You cannot be without guns out on the prairie! You both must have one—perhaps even one for the boy. To hunt, yes, but also for protection."

"So? Protection from what? Indians?" Karl and Jan both frowned. They had not anticipated this need.

"No, no, that is not likely, but you will surely have coyotes and wolves sniffing around your animals. Those you *must* shoot. Foxes and weasels, too, although you might trap them and rabbits."

"And you will want to shoot antelope and quail for meat. You might even see buffalo! Good meat and a very good hide."

After a long discussion between the two brothers, they selected a shotgun and a rifle. Mr. Rehnquist added bullets and shells for the guns.

Karl pulled at his bottom lip. The costs were piling up—even after eliminating some items on their list. Things were more expensive than they had thought they would be.

Then Jan and Karl began on the lumber. They told Mr. Rehnquist how much of each type of board they wanted and how much black tar paper. After Mr. Rehnquist wrote the order down, Sauli started pulling the lengths. Jan and Karl stacked and carried them out the yard's gate and laid them into the last wagon in the row.

The lumber wagon was full. The front wagon was nearly so. Karl studied Mr. Rehnquist's numbers and told the total to Jan.

"And still we need to buy food supplies, eh?" Jan remarked wryly.

"Ah! We almost forgot!" Karl tsked. He turned to Mr. Rehnquist. "Can you recommend a good grocer to us?"

"Surely. Go around that corner two blocks. You will see the sign. It is owned by a German, Evard Koehler. An honest man. You will like him."

Karl paid the man and thanked him for his excellent service. Jan and Karl took turns shaking hands with Sauli and his father.

Jan cleared his throat. "Your *sønn* has been a blessing to us, Herr Rehnquist. He is a good boy, a good man already." Jan said this in front of Sauli because he wanted the young man to hear what he said.

Jan turned to Sauli. "You have earned a good wage today." Jan placed a quarter in Sauli's hand. "We thank you."

The boy glowed under Jan's praise and clasped the coin eagerly. His father smiled with pride.

"Come, Søren!" Jan called. "We'll take all this to the train now, eh?"

Søren was glad to get underway. He had spent two hours in the late afternoon sun minding the oxen. Now he took up reins—his *far* had said he could drive the empty wagon behind them to the rail yards! In reality, his wagon's oxen were still tethered to the wagon in front of his.

Karl pulled ahead of them in the lumber wagon and set a sedate pace. Jan followed after him. Søren waved goodbye to Sauli and called to his oxen. They moved out smartly behind Jan.

The Thoresens labored for another two hours unloading the wagons and packing their purchases in the freight cars. They stacked much of it into the first car atop their other cargo.

All the lumber went into one end of the second car except for some lengths Karl kept back. Jan found the crate with the tools and nails and kept it back, too. Then Karl and Jan set to work building a sturdy fence across the car separating the lumber from the rest of the car.

The fence was nose high to the oxen, high enough and strong enough to keep the lumber on one side and the oxen on the other. The six oxen would have two-thirds of the car to travel in.

Finally, they unhitched the oxen and led them into a pen. Jan paid a man to feed and water the beasts. The freight master assured them that the oxen and wagons would be safe overnight.

It was dusk when the three Thoresens dragged themselves back to the boardinghouse, exhausted and hungry. Even after eating a hearty dinner, Jan closed his eyes against a bad headache.

Elli saw him frown and rub his eyes. She stood behind his chair and gently massaged his temples. "Amalie and I have our list ready," she whispered, nuzzling the back of his neck.

"*Ja*, that's good," he replied. He leaned his head back and rested it on her bosom, breathing in her sweet scent. "Don't fret, my love. I will be better in the morning. It has just been a long day."

CHAPTER 5

The next morning began a more leisurely fashion. After a large breakfast, Karl read to them from the family Bible. But when they thought Karl had finished reading, he turned to Proverbs and read aloud:

Trust in the Lord with all thine heart;
and lean not unto thine own understanding.
In all thy ways acknowledge him,
and he shall direct thy paths.

They all knew that the most challenging times were still ahead. "Lord, thank you for directing our paths," Jan prayed. "We trust you and lean on you."

Jan and Karl felt refreshed when they walked back to the rail yard. They opened the pen and led two of the oxen out. Together they placed the yoke across the beasts' muscular necks.

When the team was hitched to one of their wagons, Jan and Karl drove it back to the boardinghouse. Karl helped Elli, Amalie, and the three children into the back, and they set out for the grocer *Herr* Rehnquist had recommended.

An hour and a half later the last of the foodstuffs had been loaded in the wagon: *Burlap bags filled with wheat, dried beans, dried peas, dried corn, onions, potatoes, and cabbages. Crocks of butter, jars of honey, jugs of vinegar. Cans of lard. Bags of salt, sugar, and coffee beans. Cans of baking soda, cream of tartar, and yeast cakes. Jars of pickles, peaches, and tomatoes. Wheels of cheese wrapped in clean cloths. Ropes of sausages and a great log of bologna. A crate of eggs padded in sawdust.*

Jan and Karl wrestled a heavy barrel into the wagon. Packed inside it were two hams. Packed above the hams were carefully wrapped slabs of bacon.

Back in the store, Jan asked, "What are these?" He had spied half dozen green sprigs, not even eight inches high, their roots tied up in damp burlap.

"*Apfel baum,*" Mr. Koehler replied.

Apple saplings! Jan stared at them. "Søren?"

"They are fifty cents, *Pappa*. Half a dollar each."

"So much!" Jan was torn. Their money was dwindling quickly.

"I tell you what," Mr. Koehler said, "You are a good customer. You are buying a lot from me today, *ja*? I sell you two of them for the price of one."

Søren wasn't sure he understood. "Two?" When Mr. Koehler nodded, Søren answered Jan. "*Pappa*, two for fifty cents. A blessing!"

Jan, with a great smile on his face, thanked the grocer. Karl frowned, but when the wagon pulled away, Elli cradled the saplings in her apron.

Back in the rail yard, Jan and Karl packed the foods into the first car while Søren tended the pigs and oxen.

While they worked, Jan's mind was busy. *We finally have everything we need!* Except their claims, of course. But tomorrow they would leave Omaha and arrive in Fremont to seek out the land office.

"*Pappa*." Søren tugged on his sleeve. "*Pappa*, come look at this pig. He is sick, I think."

With sinking hearts, Karl and Jan both followed him. Karl removed the piglet from its crate. It was easy to see that the piglet was in distress— its breathing was labored and watery sounding; it lay without struggle in Karl's hands.

Karl, without being asked, said, "A female."

Jan was careful not to touch the pig or its crate. "Søren, have you tended the other pigs?"

"*Nei, Pappa*. I only touched this one. When I saw it, I came to tell you."

"Good boy. You will go back to your *mor* and wash your hands and arms with hot water and soap, *ja*?"

Karl gave a knowing nod to Jan. They would ask the freight master where to take the dying piglet and its crate, so that the disease did not infect the yard.

Jan finished caring for the last two piglets. They seemed healthy and active—but so had the dying pig two days ago.

Lord, you know these are our last pigs, eh? A male and a female. I know they are not beneath your notice. You care about sparrows, Lord. Will you care about our pigs and keep them healthy? We are leaning on you, Lord.

They had one last task to complete this day. Jan and Karl began breaking down the wagons. As they removed the pegs, pins, and nails, they placed them in a canvas bag. Søren helped stack the boards and roll the wheels to their car.

Karl and Jan stacked all the wagon pieces atop the lumber. Jan hung the sack with the pegs and pins on a nail on the wall and put their tools away.

Very early the following morning, while the sky was still dark, Karl, Jan, and Søren arrived in the yard. The freight master and two of the yard men were waiting to help them load the oxen into their lumber car. The animals had been well fed and watered overnight.

The men rolled a sturdy ramp up to the car. The ramp had sides on it, so the oxen could only see forward. Jan and Karl opened the pen and led an ox to the ramp. As soon as the ox started up the ramp, they removed the rope, slapped the ox's backside, and it ran up the ramp and into the car.

All the oxen went up the ramp easily except the temperamental one. It took the men more time to get him into the car. They had to tie a rope to each horn and stand on either side of the ramp, pulling him up it. Finally, he went in, and Jan closed and locked the door.

They were ready. The freight master would have their cars moved off the siding and onto the track now. He would have the yard men couple their cars to the train.

Karl, Jan, and Søren returned to the boardinghouse and ate a simple breakfast. The women had repacked their belongings. With everyone carrying something, they trekked back to the yard to find their cars.

They were leaving Omaha at last.

The train ride to their next destination took less than two hours. Fremont was a rough settlement with a much smaller rail yard. The railroad had only reached Fremont in December. The track beyond Fremont was all new, having been laid in the months since then.

A ferry crossed the Elkhorn River at Fremont. Before the coming of the railroad, settlers traveling by wagon or on foot crossed the Elkhorn at Fremont, following the Mormon Trail west along the north bank of the Platte River.

The Thoresens disembarked when the train stopped. Karl refreshed their car's water supply. Søren and Jan fed and watered the oxen and pigs; Elli and Amalie took the girls to a small market and bought milk, bread, and fruit. Karl spoke to the freight manager, asking him to move their cars to a siding and reconnect them in the morning.

Then Karl, Jan, and Søren set out to find the land office.

Søren handed the clerk a note that read, "Looking for land north of the Platte." Sauli had scrawled the words for them. Søren managed to tell the clerk they had come from Omaha on the train.

"I hear the railroad will reach Columbus by next month," the clerk replied. "Not much between Fremont and Columbus, and Columbus is mighty small."

Jan and Karl did not understand what he said, and Søren only recognized a few words, but he nodded so the clerk studied the map. "There's a water stop about halfway between Fremont and Columbus. A few folks live farther north in the bend where a little river turns."

He pointed to the map. "We got claims open north and west of there." His finger circled an area.

The two Thoresen men studied the map the claim clerk had laid before them. Jan traced a small river north from the penciled-in rail line and then followed a feeder creek west. Søren looked over Jan and Karl's shoulders.

"These claims front this creek, Karl," Jan murmured.

Karl nodded. "*Ja.* What kind of a creek?"

They looked at Søren. Already they were dependent on the little bit of English Søren was quickly picking up.

Søren licked his lips and asked. "Please. This?" He didn't know a word for creek, so he pointed. Jan traced it for him."

"Yes. That creek flows right into this-here river." He pointed to the river Jan had already noted on the map. "Good little stream. Flows all year round."

"*Far*, he says it is good all the time," Søren reported.

Karl and Jan looked at each other and silently agreed. "Which one do you want, *Bror*?" Jan asked. "You pick; I will take the other, *ja*?"

"*Takk!* I will take this one, on the north," Karl answered eagerly.

"*Sønn*, tell him we will take these two claims," Jan told Søren.

"This one," the clerk pointed to Karl's, "Was homesteaded four years ago. The man went bust; didn't stay."

Søren's forehead puckered, trying to figure out what the clerk had said. "Bust, please?"

"This claim," the clerk tried again, pointing at it on the map.

Søren nodded.

"A man. Claim."

Søren nodded again.

"No stay." The clerk shook his head. "He go away. Bust."

"Ah!" Søren thought he had it. "*Pappa*, he says someone had *Onkel's* claim but, but, I think he says the man did not stay."

Søren pointed to the plot again. "Two claims? Yes?"

"Yes," the clerk replied. "That'll be $18 filing fee for each claim, please."

Jan was dazed with excitement as they left the claims office. He studied the paper in his hand, understanding little of the words printed in ink on it, but he saw his own name printed there beside his signature. He held the paper as if it were made of gold.

He and Karl looked at each other. They grinned. They laughed. They grabbed Søren and danced around in a circle.

Sobering, Jan and Karl carefully folded their claims and each placed his in the breast pocket of his homemade vest. As they started back to the rail yards, Jan patted his claim several times, just assuring himself that it truly was there.

They slept aboard their car in the rail yard that night. It was uncomfortable and crowded, but a light breeze flowing through the half-open door kept them cool.

At dawn a rap sounded on their car. Jan closed and latched the door, and their cars began to move from the siding back onto the main track. A while later the train jerked forward and began moving. Within minutes the tracks were bending west, following the Platte River.

Jan cracked open the door and stared along the curving length of the train ahead. He could see down to the river. In a few hours they would disembark and begin the last leg of their journey.

Ah, Lord! I feel like Abraham today. You are calling us to a place and an inheritance.

CHAPTER 6

Midmorning, the train stopped in the middle of nowhere. The conductor ran down the line and smacked the door of their car.

"Open up," he hollered.

Karl unlatched the door and slid it open. He and Jan jumped down. They saw nothing up and down the line except the train and a water tower, for the train blocked their view of the other side. When the train left they would get their first look at what lay to the north. Two men were busily filling the train's water tank.

The conductor motioned to them. "Unload here." He gestured for them to hurry.

"Here" was simply a flat area to the side of the track. At least the tracks were not on a steep embankment. Jan and Karl unlocked their second car. They would have to unload the oxen first.

The conductor and another railroad man climbed into their first car and began tossing out the bales of hay. Amalie, Elli, and the girls, not knowing what to do, tried to keep out of their way.

A few seconds later Karl and Jan heard Elli crying, "*Nei, nei!*" and turned to see the railroad men tossing their food out of the car, too. A burlap bag of wheat hit the ground, split open, and began pouring grain into the dirt.

Jan ran back to the car and shouted to the men to stop. They ignored him. Jan clambered into the car and grabbed the conductor's arm. The conductor shook Jan off, yelling at him. The other railroad man pushed Elli out of his way and reached for Jan.

Jan did not think; he only acted. His left fist swung in a tight circle. The railroad man bounced off the wall of the car and sank to the floor.

The conductor snarled at Jan. He jumped out of the car and drew a whistle from his pocket. The high-pitched, urgent repeating of his whistle filled the air. In response, a stream of railroad workers, on their way to the end of the line where new track was being laid, poured from a car forward of them. In less than a minute, a swarm of rough-looking men, spoiling for a brawl, surrounded them.

"Jan!" Karl's mouth was tight with concern. He shouldered his way through the twenty or so laborers. They were standing on or walking on the foodstuffs thrown from the train.

46

Jan, with his arm around Elli, stood in the door of the car, waiting. He could feel her trembling within his arms. *Oh, Lord! My quick temper has gotten us into a terrible situation.* He was not unmindful of how badly things could go.

The angry conductor shouted something to the men, pointing from the prostrate form on the floor of the car to Jan. Some of the men reached up to drag Jan down. He let go of Elli, fearful that she would be hurt.

"Well, now. What's goin' on here?" a cool voice drawled. Everyone heard the distinctive "click" of a rifle being cocked.

The laborers jumped aside as a tall, wiry-built man looked around, sizing up the situation. He rested the buttstock of his rifle on his thigh, pointing the barrel toward the sky, but his eyes conveyed a challenge.

Then he glanced down. "What is this? What in tarnation do you boys think yer doin' tramplin' these folks' food?" His eyes narrowed and he stared at the conductor. "Mister, did you toss these things out in the dirt?"

The conductor, drawing himself up, sputtered a reply. "We have a timetable to keep here, Bailey. This is none o' your concern."

"Weeell," the man drew the word out, "I'm sure they paid their fare. 'Sides, you ain't got no right t' be treatin' newcomers like this, so I guess I'm makin' it my concern."

"You men there," he gestured at a knot of laborers to the right. "You think it right t' throw a man's food and things in the dirt? And then *walk on them*?"

The workers, getting a better picture of the situation, began to mutter and shoot dark glances at the conductor. One of the mob piped up, "No sir! Didn't think that was what was happening." He cleared his throat and said to Jan and Elli, "Mighty sorry, sir, ma'am."

"Well, since Mr. Chance is so concerned with keeping his 'timetable,' how 'bout you men give these newcomers a hand unloading their things? *Respectful like.* And pick up their food here."

The men did as Bailey directed. The conductor and another man dragged their unconscious friend from the boxcar and laid him out on the prairie grass. Others began to unload and carefully stack the Thoresens' belongings alongside the tracks.

While some of the men were unloading the first car, several others helped Jan and Karl drag a crude ramp to their second boxcar, unload the oxen, and hobble them. A few more handed down wagon parts.

Jan and Karl set to work assembling the wagons. When the men saw what they were doing, they pitched in to help.

In the meantime, Amalie looked for and found her sewing kit. She stitched a neat seam up the split in the sack of wheat.

Elli and the girls picked through the dirt, salvaging every kernel they could find. They placed the dusty wheat in Elli's apron.

After she and the girls had retrieved all the wheat, Elli asked for the sack in which Jan and Karl had kept the pegs and pins for the wagons. She had Kristen hold the sack open while she poured the wheat into it.

Within an hour the three wagons were assembled and the men had loaded the lumber onto one wagon. Atop the lumber, Karl strapped the new stove and piping and stacked the bales of hay.

The conductor, not willing to wait any longer, signaled the engineer to blow the whistle.

"Guess we gotta go," one of the workers said.

Jan made a point of shaking hands with each man. "Tanks you," he said tentatively. He felt silly, but his efforts earned him a proud smile from Søren. Some of the men clapped him on the shoulder.

All the while, Bailey watched, his face noncommittal, rifle held casually at his side.

When the train pulled away, the Thoresens stared across the tracks. They saw a small clearing and a tiny cabin built into the side of a low hillock.

Beyond that spread the open prairie as far as they could see.

The ground undulated over swells and mounds; the prairie grasses shimmered in the midday sun. Jan's breath left him as he stared.

"You folks all right?" It was the man with the rifle.

Jan and Karl walked over to him. "Tanks you," Jan said, hoping his firm handshake and solemn face expressed how grateful they were.

"*Tusen Takk*," echoed Karl. He pointed to himself. "Karl Thoresen." He pointed at Jan. "Jan Thoresen."

"Robert Bailey. Pleased t' meetcha." Bailey was a little younger than both Jan and Karl. He pointed. "I keep th' water tower filled."

Jan called to Søren. When the boy stepped to his side, Jan put his hand on Søren's shoulder. "*Jeg sønn, Søren.*"

Bailey shook the boy's hand. "You-all have a lot to do still." He pointed at their things spread along the track. "Would you like some help?"

Jan asked Søren what he said. "I think he would like to help, Pappa," Søren replied.

"*Ja,* tanks you!"

A woman emerged from the tiny shack. She walked swiftly toward them, wiping her hands on her apron as she hustled over. "Land sakes, Mr. Bailey! You shoulda tol' me we had comp'ny!"

He grinned at her. "They jest got off th' train, missus. Name o' Thoresen. I think they're brothers. Come meet 'em."

Mrs. Bailey, weatherworn and feisty, was as plainspoken as her husband. She shook hands all around. They were all a little awkward with the language barrier. "Would ya like sumpthin' t' eat? Got some soup on th' back o' th' stove and some biscuits."

"My woman do make good biscuits," Bailey said proudly.

Søren looked at his father. "They said 'eat,' *Pappa*." His stomach growled.

"*Ja*, tanks you!" Jan accepted. He was getting more comfortable with the two words he'd learned. He and Karl unhobbled the oxen and led them to a trough under the water tower. Jan hobbled them again. Karl spread a tarpaulin over their food supplies before turning to the Bailey's cabin.

On the shaded side of the Bailey's cabin, in a small pen, the Thoresens spotted two cows and a calf. "Karl," Amalie whispered, "Look! They have cows!" Karl looked speculatively at the cows and calf. He nudged Jan, who nodded.

Inside, the Thoresens exchanged many comments on the cabin's construction. They were especially impressed after they went inside and found that the back six feet of it was dug into the low hillside.

They enjoyed the soup and quick breads offered to them, but conversation was stilted. Mrs. Bailey chatted on to the women who listened attentively and nodded politely, not understanding a word.

Jan asked Søren to thank the Baileys again, and to say they needed to load their wagons and move on. They likely had four hours of daylight ahead of them but it would take an hour or two just to load the wagons.

Søren did the best he could. "Tanks you, food. We go wagons." He pointed to the northwest.

"Gotcha a claim over there, eh?"

"Claim—*ja!*" Søren nodded vigorously. "Yes."

Søren aided conversation among the men when he suggested that his father show Mr. Bailey his claim paper. Jan and Karl both did so.

"Why, I'm pretty sure thet's Han Gloeckner's old claim," Bailey announced, pointing to Karl's paper. "Ain't seed it m'self, but he described it t' me."

He looked at Karl and Søren and tried to communicate. "Mr. Gloeckner. Mr. Gloeckner's claim," he said, pointing at the paper.

When Bailey spotted a bit of alarm in Karl's eyes he added quickly, "Gloeckner, no." He shot a look for help to Søren. "Gloeckner, gone. Good-bye."

"*Herr* Gloeckner?" Søren asked.

"Yes," Bailey answered but quickly added, "He is gone. Good-bye."

"Good-bye? Go?" Søren was struggling.

"Yes! He go, er, *went*."

"I think he means what the land office man told us, *Onkel*," Søren told his uncle. "A *Herr* Gloeckner had this claim but did not stay long enough to prove it up."

Bailey insisted on helping Karl and Jan to load the remaining two wagons. The men covered the three wagons with tarpaulins and roped them securely.

"Say," Bailey said when they were ready to go. "You goin' t' need all them oxen when ya get to' yer claim?"

The only words Søren caught were "oxen" and "claim." He shook his head and looked at his father. Bailey placed his hand on one of the oxen. He held up a finger. "One." He pointed at the other ox and held up a second finger. "Two."

He pointed down the line and held up a total of six fingers. "Six," he said, pointing again at the oxen. Jan and Søren both nodded, and Jan suddenly smiled.

He pointed to Bailey's two milk cows and the calf and held up one finger and then pointed at one ox.

"An ox fer a milk cow, eh?" Bailey scratched his chin and muttered to himself. "Could use an ox, maybe lease him out. Could sell him, too. Fer cash money."

Bailey held up his hand and strode quickly toward his cabin. Jan and Karl looked at each other.

"Missus! Missus!" Bailey called. "I'm thinkin' on tradin' Molly fer one o' these folks' oxen. Whatcha think o' that?"

"I'm thinkin' we ain't got no use fer two milk cows, thet's what," she called back, "an' they got little ones what need milk. It's all right with me."

It took some time and imaginative communication, but another thirty minutes later, Mr. Bailey hopped aboard one of the wagons and took the reins. Søren rode with Mr. Bailey; his horse and the Thoresens' new cow, Molly, walked along behind them, tied to the back of the wagon.

Bailey had offered to go with them to their claims and then return on his horse, leading one of the oxen. Since he knew best how to reach their homestead claims, Jan and Karl asked him to lead the way.

The sojourners had made five miles when Mr. Bailey stopped atop a knoll and gestured to the river below them. Then his finger tracked far up the river and pointed to where a creek could just be seen joining the river.

Jan and Karl knew immediately that this was "their" creek. It would guide them the rest of the way to their land.

❧ ✳ ❧

CHAPTER 7

Jan stood on a low rise and surveyed the land before him. *My land,* his heart sang. His and Karl's two claims ran side-by-side, the plot Karl had chosen just to the north and *mine right here under my feet,* Jan wanted to shout to the sky. From the small creek west of them to the low, rounded hills in the east, this was their land.

In every direction the prairie grasses danced, an ever-changing kaleidoscope of pale green and silver. He closed his eyes and lifted his face to the sun and waited. He waited in utter stillness for the land to speak to him.

He could hear the morning breeze run its fingers over the grasses, rising and falling, rising and falling. A meadowlark warbled. In the distance the children laughed and called to each other. But right here, in this moment, with his eyes squeezed shut, Jan listened only to the sound of the prairie wind—gentle, undulating, soothing, eternal.

Eyes still tightly closed, Jan inhaled deeply. He smelled sage and cedar mixed with the earthy scent of moist soil. It had rained last night, a late spring shower. A perfect, soaking rain.

He reached down and, grasping a clump of grass with both hands, pulled free a chunk of soil. He examined the soil thick with the roots of prairie grasses. *Sod* they called it. He knew that six inches under the prairie sod ran a layer of dark, rich, fertile earth.

Lord, I thank you, his heart rejoiced. He struggled to contain his emotions, and Jan knew he would remember this moment until he died.

He turned and gazed to the west. Their nearest neighbors were on the claim across the creek. *Anderson,* their new friend *Herr* Bailey had said. Jan studied the low bluff, a few hundred yards beyond the creek. The bluff curved gently, creating a wide hollow between it and the creek.

From this distance Jan could see a plowed field atop the bluff already glowing with the green of newly sprouted corn. A green garden was marked out in the hollow below. He saw a woman going in and out of a door built into the bluff. A small child played close by.

They dug into the bluff, Jan realized. Something like what the Baileys had done. Jan and Karl had read of dugouts and soddies back in Norway. He glanced again at the thick clump of sod in his hand.

They had read how homesteaders cut thick, root-filled sod blocks, a foot wide and two feet long, to build prairie homes. From what he could see at this distance, his neighbors had burrowed into the hillside and used sod bricks for the outside wall.

He watched for a few minutes, his imagination captured by the picturesque curve of the bluff. He easily envisioned a house built there someday, nestled in that hollow and facing the creek. For an instant he wished he had arrived a year or two earlier and filed claim on the acreage across the creek before his neighbor had.

Thou shalt not covet thy neighbor's goods, the Holy Spirit reminded him.

Yes, Lord!

He looked again across their land and his heart swelled. He turned east and saw his family and their wagons. He and Karl had many decisions to make and much work to do—and soon, as quickly as they could manage.

"*Fader*, I am so grateful," he whispered. "I want to build our home right here, on this spot where we have talked this day." Jan looked around him, in his mind seeing the foundations of the house on this gentle rise.

The oxen had been slow and the wagons heavily laden. Because they had left so late in the afternoon their first day on the trail, they had arrived at their claims midmorning on their third day—yesterday, the first day of June.

On the trail to their land Bailey had built their first fire. He showed Elli and Amalie how to gather dry weeds and roots for starter and something else for fuel in place of wood—a dry, flat, gray patty. It had been an interesting moment when he managed to convey to the women that they were collecting buffalo "chips" for firewood.

Bailey had told them it would take him less than a day to return home on horseback, and had headed back immediately. "Got t' keep thet water tank filled," he grinned. "I'll be home 'bout nightfall." He held his new ox on a lead.

Jan and Karl had again thanked him. Amalie was especially appreciative for the trade, and they were already enjoying their fill of milk.

Their new friend started his return home shortly after reaching Thoresen land. Before he left, Bailey had warned them of snakes.

"You be trampin' or cuttin' th' grass down, b'fore y'all lay down t' sleep," he said, demonstrating with a stick and with vigorous stomping. They hadn't followed his words, but they had clearly understood his pantomime.

As soon as Bailey was out of sight, Jan and Karl had rigged their families a temporary shelter while the women watered the chicks and pigs. First, Jan and Karl cut the grass and stomped out the ground around them. With Søren's help, they maneuvered two of the wagons until they were side-by-side with some room between them. Then they unhitched the oxen and hobbled them nearby.

They unloaded the lumber wagon and sorted and stacked the wood. They did not unload the other wagons; many of the things still packed in them would remain crated up until they were under a roof.

With some of the lumber, the men hammered together two benches and a serviceable table that they placed between the wagons. They strung tarpaulins over the table and benches and secured the sides and corners of the canvas sheets to the outside edges of the wagons.

Karl and Jan nailed two tall, upright boards to the ends of the table. They nailed a third board across the tops of the two. The boards lifted up the center of the tenting over the tables.

The families now had a dry shelter under which to eat. They would continue to make their beds on the ground under the wagons as they had done on the journey from the train to their homestead.

Amalie's reaction to the tent had concerned Elli. "I knew we would not have a house for a while," she whispered to her sister-in-law, "but I have never been without a roof over my head . . . and the sky here is so vast and, and this place they call the prairie so . . ." Her voice caught at the end. "I am sorry. I am being silly."

She swallowed. "I could hardly sleep the nights we were coming from the train. The grass is so high and we heard so many strange sounds."

"Maybe you are a little low because of the baby, *ja*?" Elli suggested. "You know how our emotions act when we are pregnant!"

Amalie nodded her agreement, but her eyes were already shadowed from lack of sleep. Elli observed new worry lines around Amalie's eyes.

Elli told Jan about their conversation. "I do think it is the baby, but perhaps not *just* the baby. I worry that she is taking all these changes too hard."

Jan snatched a covert look at Amalie and thought about what Elli had told him. *The tent and wagons provide shelter in fine weather but . . . but perhaps we should think about something better soon, Lord*, he prayed as he pondered all they must do on this new day.

After rigging the tent, Jan, Karl, and Søren built a temporary chicken coop and pen for the pigs. The chicks raced around their coop and gobbled their feed, and the two piglets, allowed to run free within the pen, seemed healthy enough.

As for the hobbled oxen, they would be content to stay near as long as they had grass and water. The men would remove the hobbles and move them to fresh grass each day; Søren would water them twice a day.

The wellbeing of their livestock was a great concern to Jan and Karl, especially the animals' safety from predators. Leaving the oxen in the open at night was not what they wanted, but until they built a barn, it would have to do. They kept the two guns loaded and hanging upon one of the wagon walls—within easy reach.

Jan's reverie was interrupted by Søren's appearance. "*Pappa!* Come see what I have found!"

Søren led the men a distance from their camp, crossing over onto Karl's property, to a slough nestled behind a low hillock. They explored the low, marshy bog, finally locating where water seeped from the ground and pooled. Reeds and a few saplings grew along its edges. A snake slithered away as they cautiously pushed through the rushes.

Jan and Karl were delighted to find a natural source of water on their properties. Eventually they could dig down to the spring, build a dam, and divert the water to a holding pond for their stock. Until then, they could bring the ox and their cow to the slough each day to water them. It was closer than the creek.

"This water will attract much wildlife," Karl warned. "Venomous snakes, too."

"*Ja*," Jan replied. "We must be careful, especially at night. Perhaps, though, one evening we will lay in wait for antelope to come?"

"Good, fresh meat!" Karl laughed. "That would be nice, eh?"

The slough was not the only thing they discovered that day. Søren called excitedly from beyond the slough. "*Pappa! Onkel!* Come quick!"

When the men trudged around the slough to other side of the mound, Søren was waiting for them, his face animated. "Look! This must be where *Herr* Gloeckner and his family lived!"

On the side of the hillock the faint outlines of a dugout's exterior wall could be seen. The wall was built from blocks of sod. Karl and Jan were as enthused as Søren. They fetched tools and, with a little effort, were able to clear and prize open the rough, weathered door.

Inside the air was cool. Neither Jan nor Karl could stand fully upright inside the room, but they immediately grasped the blessing of the place.

"Let us call the women to see this," Karl suggested.

Elli and Amalie hung back, outside the door, unsure about going in.

"It is safe," Jan assured them. "The door has been closed for more than a year—maybe two years. We have checked and found no bugs or snakes inside."

Amalie frowned, still unsure about a "dirt house." Elli screwed up her courage and followed Jan. Inside he lit a candle. In the yellow glow she found a modest room about eight feet by eight feet. She looked up. The ceiling had been hard packed and she was just able to stand upright.

"Karl and I think we could dig farther back," Jan said, "making it a little bigger. Until we have the barn built, this would be better than the tents."

"It is very small," Elli answered carefully, "and you know how Amalie is with bugs."

"I do not see any bugs," Jan looked about him. He held the candle up and examined the corners of the room and then down to search the "floor." "Do you see anything?"

"Nooo," Elli responded.

"Feel how cool it is in here? What a blessing it will be when the heat of summer is on us, *nei*? And it is dry, too."

His last remark got Elli thinking about the rain they had received the night before. Yes, they had sheltered under the wagons and under the tarps, but the ground had become wet. The edges of their blankets were still drying out.

"Amalie, come in," Elli called to her.

Reluctantly, Amalie ducked under the doorway. She stood up inside and gazed around in surprise. "Ach! I thought it would be wet. Moldy."

Elli took the candle from Jan. "Look. Look, no bugs, *Søster*."

Amalie huffed but took the candle and scrutinized the room, floor to ceiling. "Hmph. I do not know if I could stay in a dirt house."

"You will find more bugs on the ground under our wagons," Elli replied practically. "Perhaps snakes, too." Amalie huffed again, nervously, but said nothing more.

They stepped outside, and the men pushed the soddy door closed, making sure it was snug. Jan asked Karl, "What if we built out this soddy, *Bror*, and made it bigger? It would not take long, and I would feel better if we had a good roof over our families, even a dirt one, wouldn't you?"

Yesterday they had decided to build a small barn near the division of their properties. It would be large enough for their stock for a number of years and, initially, they had planned for the two families to set up housekeeping in the barn. Now, though, they were considering the advantages of expanding and moving into the soddy.

Karl nodded. "It is a good idea. Let us think on this more. Come," he said, putting their discussion on hold. "We need to get water. We should drive down to the creek and bring back drinking water."

The sun was crossing into the west when they loaded the water can, washtub, and cauldrons into the wagon. Jan and Søren finished yoking two oxen to the wagon and they set off toward the creek. As they approached, their neighbors saw them coming and came down to their side of the creek, waving.

"*Ja*, we saw you arrive yesterday," a young man hollered in Swedish. "*Välkomna!* Welcome! Come across and have some tea!"

Karl pointed the oxen into the rushing creek. The stream was running high from spring runoff, but the water looked clean and clear.

The young couple introduced themselves as Henrik and Abigael Anderson. Their toddler, a sober boy named Abel, clung to his mother's skirt and watched the strangers.

Abigael was obviously "expecting." She spread a quilt under the sparse shade of a young cottonwood tree and offered them cold tea from a jug cooling in the stream.

"We have been here two years," Henrik told them. "My family settled in Illinois fifteen years ago when I was a little boy, but of course Abigael and I wanted to have our own land. You are *Norsk, ja*? We are *Svenska*, but now Americans!"

"It is good to hear words we can understand," Karl declared after introducing their families. "We have two claims across the creek. So much to do! We hardly know where to start—because too many things clamor to be done first."

After drinking the tea, the men and Søren climbed to the top of the bluff to see Henrik's field. The women looked over Abigael's garden. "I planted it two weeks ago," she mentioned, "the day after Henrik put his corn in the ground."

Amalie surprised Elli by saying to Abigael, "We have found the Gloeckner's old dugout. Our men are talking about living in it for a time, but I am not so sure, *ja*? Would you mind showing us what yours is like inside?"

The women and children filed into the little room stepping over a high threshold. "It is not a big house, but is nice and warm in the winter and always cool in the summer. Even when the wind blows hard, we do not feel it much in here."

Amalie and Elli were both pleasantly surprised at how Abigael kept her house, a single room dug into the bluff but with a sod face. Abigael's small stove was piped through the sod wall. Neatly stacked boxes acted as cupboards. The dirt floor was packed and swept.

Three stools and a tiny table with a colorful cloth were pushed against one wall and a bed against the back wall. A closed trunk sat against the edge of the bed near its foot. Someone had hammered pegs into the walls of the soddy. Clothes hung from some pegs and baskets from others.

Light came from the open doorway and a small window near the stove with shutters on the outside. The window was not paned with glass but with thin muslin. Abigael could not see through the muslin but it did allow a little light through.

"Ach! What a clever idea," Elli praised.

"We have not much glass out here, for sure," Abigael agreed. "In the summer the muslin keeps the flies and gnats outside but lets a little air in. When the wind blows, we close and latch the shutters."

"Do snakes come in the soddy?" Amalie asked, more than a little impressed. "Ants? Bugs?"

"No more than one would find in a house out here," she answered. "You see our high threshold? That keeps out water when it rains hard. But be careful for snakes, *ja*? We have many here—not all venomous, but some. Of the venomous, we mostly see prairie rattlers and, where it is wet, what the Indians call *massasauga*."

She added seriously, "It is good to always check your shoes in the morning and never put your hand where you haven't checked first."

Elli and Amalie's eyes went wide; if Abigael noticed their chagrin, she did not let on. "One thing can easily tell you if a snake is dangerous or not," she told them. "The eyes of a venomous snake are like a cat's, *ja*? With the slit? But harmless snakes have round eyes."

"I do not wish to ever be close enough to check a snake's eyes," Amalie murmured.

"So? But you cannot avoid snakes out here. The prairies may look wide and empty, but you can be sure that they are not. They are home to many things. Everywhere is the tall prairie grass, and many things live and move in the grasses—prairie dogs, rabbits, and mice—all things snakes eat."

She added, "I keep my little boy where the grass is short. Please teach your children to take care in the tall grass?"

Elli noticed how white Amalie had grown by the time Abigael finished talking about snakes. Amalie called Sigrün to her and held the girl's hand until they left.

After the Thoresens had filled their vessels with water and returned to their camp, they spent an hour discussing the location of a green garden. The men would plow up the garden space on the morrow and the women would put the garden in while the men began to build the barn.

No one brought up adding on to the Gloeckner's dugout or moving into it again.

As it turned out, the weather decided the matter for them.

ༀ ❈ ༚

CHAPTER 8

"I think we will be fine camping out this way while we build the barn, *ja*?" Karl said to Jan as they surveyed the proposed outline of their barn. "Many settlers traveling west sleep under their wagons the entire journey. What do you think?"

The men had chosen the site for the barn and were determined to begin work on it as soon as they had plowed up the garden area. They planned to take the empty wagon down the creek to the river, a journey of several hours, and bring back a load of large river rock to begin the barn's foundation as soon as the garden was plowed.

"Sure. We might have some rain, eh?" Jan replied, focused on the plans for the barn. "But we had some rain as we were coming from the train. It was not bad."

Karl clapped Jan on his back. "So. We must work hard to build the barn *and* put in a crop. We don't have any extra time. It is summer, and we will be fine under the tent and wagons for now."

Jan and Søren unpacked the field tools and stood them upright against the lumber. "Søren," Jan said, "You will clean the tools when they are used and wipe them dry, *ja*? See this oilcloth and rope? After you clean the tools each day, you will cover them to keep the rain off them. When we have a barn, we will always hang the cleaned tools in a dry place."

"Yes, *Pappa*," Søren answered. "Just like at home!"

"This *is* our home now, eh?" Jan smiled. "It will just take some time and work to make it feel like home."

Karl yoked and hitched a pair of oxen to the sod cutter while Jan watched to see how the new tool would work. Karl shouted to the oxen to pull. After a few feet he frowned. He realized he could not get the cutter to "bite." He gestured to Jan.

"Stand on the cutter, will you?" he asked, pointing. "It is not heavy enough to dig into the sod."

The cutter was a flat, sled-like frame with a wide blade on the underside of the tool. Jan stepped atop the cutter in front of Karl. Karl called to the oxen and the beasts strained; the cutter dug down into the grass.

After Karl had cut a swath of about twelve feet, Jan dropped back to check the results. Søren was already lifting up a sod block.

"It is so heavy, *Pappa*!" Søren exclaimed. Jan agreed. They were both amazed at the weight of the sod blocks still damp from the rain.

Karl called to them. "So? What are you looking at?"

"Come see," Jan pointed.

Karl left the oxen standing in the garden and bent over to look. He lifted one of the blocks. "So thick, these grass roots! We should thank *Herr* Rehnquist for selling us a sod cutter," Karl muttered.

Jan nodded. "Heavy, too. Søren and I should hitch the wagon to carry them."

Progress was slow. By late morning Karl had cut the swathes of sod for the garden. Jan and Søren had removed about half of them, stacked them onto the wagon, hauled them away, and taken them off the wagon.

"I will clean and oil the cutter and then help you finish removing the sod," Karl told them. "After that I will plow the garden for the women." He wiped his face with a sleeve. "I see now why it is so hard to plant this ground the first time. It is good, rich soil, but a man must work hard to get to it!"

He looked up at the sky. "I think by the time we finish, it will be too late to go to the river for rock today. And I do not like the looks of the horizon.

Jan and Søren looked where Karl was gazing. Dark, heavy clouds were building to the west. Just then Amalie called them to their midday meal.

"We will have your garden plowed soon," Karl told the women as they ate. "But it is too late for us to go to the river today. We will go first thing in the morning."

"*Ja,* we had thought to be planting it by now," Amalie replied. "But we can see how hard it was to cut out the grass! We will plant it this afternoon when you are done."

Karl plowed the quarter-acre garden three times, first one way, then across, and again the first way. Jan and Søren walked behind the plow breaking up clods and tossing out rocks. Kristen and Sigrün piled the rocks on the edge of the garden.

Karl unhitched the oxen and Jan and Søren led the team away with the other oxen and the cow to the slough to drink. Karl lifted the plow onto his shoulder and carried it to where the other tools rested against the lumber. He wiped it clean, covered it with oilcloth, and tied the cloth with a piece of rope.

He glanced at the sky again and his brows drew together. "Amalie! I think it will rain soon. Let us make sure everything is covered up, *ja*?"

The women and girls retrieved drying laundry and made sure the families' food supplies in the wagons were safely under canvas and tied down. Karl checked the chicken coop and pigpen.

The pens for the chicks and pigs provided some shelter from the rain; it was the oxen and the cow he was concerned for now. He went to find Jan and Søren and hurry them along.

"Eh! There is a storm coming, I am sure. I think we should tie the oxen together," Karl told Jan as they brought the animals back from the slough. "We don't know how they will act if there is thunder."

"The cow, too," Jan agreed. "Molly we can tie to the empty wagon, but not the oxen. If they panic, they might tear it apart. I will drive some stakes into the ground and run a rope between them. We can tie the oxen to the rope. If they break free, they are still hobbled and tied together. Surely they will not go far."

"You know," Karl said slowly. "We could have built two walls of a sod pen today with the sod we cut. I think we should do that tomorrow. We must give our animals *some* protection from storms while we are building a barn."

The women were heating a stew for supper when the first rolls of thunder reached their ears. White arrows of lightning streaked the sky to the west, and the clouds were certainly closer, heading their way.

"We won't have time to bake biscuits," Elli noted, watching the storm march toward them. "I will get out a loaf of bread instead."

A gust of wind, a precursor to the storm, caught the tenting over their table and lifted it for a long moment. Amalie and Elli looked at each other.

"What if the wind tears away the canvas?" Amalie asked, her voice trembling.

"Then we will get wet," Elli replied shrugging.

Lightning sizzled not far away. The women felt the static in the air. Thunder answered immediately and the air freshened. Rain was near. They could see it sheeting from the clouds to the ground, still hundreds of feet away, but closing quickly on the Andersons—and then them.

At the thunder, the oxen began to panic, their bellows loud and frantic, their eyes huge and wild. Molly pulled at her rope then lowered herself to the ground and cowered there, partially under the wagon.

"Children! Come!" Amalie called. She grabbed up the pot of stew while Elli banked the fire. The children were already huddled at the table when the women ducked underneath the tent. The men were right behind.

Thunder split the air. Kristen and Sigrün screamed, and each climbed into her mother's lap. Søren gripped Elli's arm until she winced.

As the wind howled and screeched, thunder crashed over them—so loud they could not hear each other. The tent canvas jumped and fell. For several minutes they sat, still and waiting, yet the storm did not abate. Rather, it increased.

The wind grabbed the canvas, whipping it up and down, up and down. Jan and Karl reached for the outside edges of the tent and held on, but they could feel the canvas being ripped from their hands.

Jan shouted to Karl. "Get our families under the wagons! Let us take the canvas down and wrap ourselves in it before it is torn away!"

Karl, his booming baritone barely heard over the storm, commanded, "Amalie! Take Sigrün! Under the wagon! Hurry!"

Elli, not waiting to be told, grabbed up Kristen and rolled under their wagon. Søren scooted in, and Elli opened her arms to him. She could see Amalie under the opposite wagon, her mouth open, her face white with terror.

Jan ran to the outside of one of the wagons and untied the ropes holding one of the tarpaulins forming their tent. Karl untied his side, wrestled with the flapping canvas, and pulled it in, shoving it at Elli. "Grab this! Hold it tight!"

As Jan loosed the second canvas, Karl dragged it to the ground. The table and benches were now uncovered, the pot of stew left sitting alone. Karl crawled under their wagon, clutching the canvas, trying to spread it over Amalie and Sigrün.

Just before Jan dove for cover, he stared into the heart of the storm . . . at something he had never seen before. A narrow funnel dropped from the clouds to the ground. It skipped and jumped, backed and skittered sideways. And then the clouds sucked the funnel up and it was gone.

Jan stared. *What was that?* Another crash of thunder jolted him, and the funnel—wider, fully formed, and whirling—dropped from the sky not far from them.

Jan's mouth opened in astonishment and fear. Then he leapt for cover under their wagon.

Lightning burned their closed eyes and thunder cracked over their heads. And then it was raining. Water poured from an angry sky pounding the ground and the wagons, whipping sideways, streaming under them.

The rain pelting the wagons hardened and became even louder. Jan felt something heavy strike his head. He pulled back the canvas and found a rock made of ice—perhaps a quarter the size of his fist—lying near him!

Hail pounded the wagons, terrifying in its fury. Over the shrieks of the storm Elli and Jan heard something else—Amalie, screaming in terror: "*Nei! Nei!* Make it stop! Karl, make it stop!"

Jan held Elli as tightly as he could, Kristen and Søren sandwiched between them. He drew the canvas over all of them, pulled it in as tight as he could, and prayed for morning.

❧ ❈ ❦

CHAPTER 9

Jan climbed out from under the wagon. He was wet, stiff, and cold. A chilly breeze ruffled his damp hair. He shivered and looked around in the dripping morning light. Here and there patches of hail remained.

"Ach!" he moaned. The chicken coop and pigpen were destroyed. He ran to them. Dead chicks lay motionless in puddles. The little chicken hutch rested on its back; he looked inside. Nothing.

He strode to the demolished pigpen. The pig's shelter lay flat; the fencing had been taken by the wind. *No, there it is, across the garden spot against the empty wagon!*

Jan ran toward the wagon. Molly raised her head and bawled pathetically. She had not been milked last evening. He slowed as he drew near to her . . . and heard a wonderful noise—the muffled grunting of two piglets rooting for a warmer, dryer spot against Molly's back.

O thank you, Lord! Jan rejoiced. Of all the animals, he would hate most to lose his father's pigs. He scratched the piglet's backs. They would be safe with Molly for a bit.

Jan saw Karl emerge from behind the wagons, saw him run his hand through his wet hair. "The pigs?"

"They are here, Karl. With Molly."

"Thank you, God in heaven!" Karl replied. He saw the dead chicks and shook his head. An ox bellowed, begging their attention.

Jan and Karl strode toward the oxen together. One of the oxen bellowed again, and Jan heard pain in its call.

The oxen were lying on the ground, bunched together, something unnatural in their arrangement. Jan and Karl approached the oxen cautiously, careful of their horns and hooves, but trying to figure out what was wrong.

As the oxen saw them coming, they struggled to stand—and could not. With the struggle another bellow of pain erupted from one of them. The closer Jan and Karl came, the harder the oxen struggled and the louder the ox bawled.

The rope Jan had strung from the two stakes had come loose, and somehow the hobbled oxen had tangled themselves in it.

Jan reached the first ox and placed his hand on its head, speaking calming words. The other oxen still struggled in agitation. Jan could not loosen the wet knot that held the ox, so he pulled his knife and sawed through it.

A moment later he removed the ox's hobble and the beast struggled to standing. Jan and Karl, working as quickly as they could, loosed each ox in turn until they came to the last one.

It was the temperamental ox, the one that had given them some trouble. He bellowed piteously but lay still. He could not rise, and the reason was apparent. His near foreleg pointed in an unnatural direction.

The brothers looked at each other and shook their heads. They could do only one thing for this poor animal.

Søren, Kristen, and Sigrün picked up the dead chicks and placed them, one by one, in a hole Elli dug. Five dead chicks.

"Who knows what has become of the rest?" Elli sighed. She glanced at Amalie with concern. Her sister-in-law sat on one of the benches with her arms wrapped tightly about herself, haggard from lack of sleep.

Elli heard the report of a rifle and knew that Jan or Karl had dispatched the poor ox. Jan walked toward her, his face grim, and hung the gun on the side of the wagon.

"Søren, set the tools upright to dry in the sun, *ja*?" Jan asked. He saw Elli tip her head toward Amalie.

Ja, I see, Wife. He shook his head and set his mouth. *Lord, what are we to do?* Such a storm he had never experienced—and he did not intend for his family or his brother's family to suffer through another like it again, uncovered to the elements.

The tarps covering the packed wagons had held against the wind, rain, and hail; the food and other things were safe and dry. Karl and Jan quietly re-erected the tent while Elli and Amalie hung soaked and muddy bedding out to dry. Amalie's movements were stilted, mechanical. She had not spoken yet.

Elli wanted to warm the stew from the night before, but could not get a fire started. All their fuel was drenched. She crossed her arms in frustration.

"*Pappa! Pappa!*" Søren's cry for help roused them all. He was standing near the tools with a hoe raised above his head—and then he was striking the ground over and over.

As they rushed to his side they heard the frantic *cheep! cheep!* of baby chickens. Huddled together among the fallen tools were six very bedraggled and frantic chicks.

Near them was a snake, its head newly severed from its thick body. The tail of the snake twitched and Søren struck it with the hoe once more, separating the snake's rattles from its body.

No one spoke until Søren said in a tiny voice, "It was after our chicks, *Pappa*. I couldn't let it get our chicks."

Jan laid his hand gently on Søren's shoulder. "Well done, *Sønn*. Well done."

Elli swallowed, grateful for Søren's courage, thankful for his safety. Amalie, behind Elli's shoulder, moaned and her moan rose, turning to a keening wail.

"Karl! You will move us to the soddy! You must! You must! Today!" Amalie's words were shrieked; she was both hysterical and angry. "I-I cannot, we *cannot* stay outside under the sky! I-I, the sky is too big, Karl! You must move us to the soddy, Karl! Please, Karl! *Please!*"

The children—and the adults—were wide-eyed and Sigrün began to cry. Karl pulled Amalie into his arms and away from the dead snake. He wrapped his arms about her and pushed her face into his shoulder.

"There, there, my love! It is all right. You will see. It will be all right." Karl spoke as if to Sigrün, his words soft and patient.

"I don't want to be outside in the lightning and the rain, Karl! Please!" Amalie sobbed. "*Please!*"

"Yes, all right. I will do as you ask, Amalie," Karl reassured her. His face was stricken and unsure when he raised his eyes to Jan and Elli.

"We went into the Andersons' dugout," Elli said quietly. "She saw that it was safe. Please. It would be better for Amalie to live in one for now than under the wagons, *ja*?"

Karl nodded and pressed his lips onto Amalie's hair. "We will move into the dugout, Amalie."

Søren, Kristen, and Sigrün crowded Jan and Elli, seeking comfort. "*Pappa*," Søren whispered, "Is *Tante* Amalie all right?"

"She will be, *Sønn*," Jan answered quietly, hoping he was right.

CHAPTER 10

The morning was miserable for all of them. They could find no dry grass or chips to start a fire, so breakfast was cold bread and cheese with milk. No coffee. No tea. Nothing to warm them on this wet morning.

Karl unpacked a dry quilt and wrapped Amalie in it. He sat her at the table under the canvas tent. He placed Sigrün on the bench cuddled up to her *mor's* side. After a while Amalie laid her head on the table and slept. Karl, his face resolute, headed toward the dugout.

Jan was about to follow when he looked west at the faint sound of "hallo!" The Andersons were walking toward them, Abel on his father's shoulder.

"We came to see how you fared," Henrik said. He looked about with concern. "We saw the twister." Abigael was carrying a heavy basket. She nodded to Jan and went to talk with Elli.

"We did not think you would be able to start a fire this morning," she said quietly to Elli, "so we brought some hot food. Just simple things— coffee and hot cereal."

"*Mange takk!*" Elli exclaimed. "You cannot know how we thank you. It was terrible!" She looked cautiously toward the tent and lowered her voice. "Amalie is having a very bad time of it. I did not know she was terrified of thunder and lightning. She is . . . distraught."

Abigael nodded slowly. "I am so sorry. We will pray for all of you. What is your plan for shelter?"

Elli glanced toward the tent again. She took Abigael's arm and they walked out of Amalie's earshot. "Our husbands had planned to build the barn first and we would also live in it until we have a crop and can build houses. But it will take some time to put up the barn."

She shook her head. "We thought we could live under the tent this summer while they built the barn, but oh! Never have we seen a storm like last night! This morning Amalie . . . insisted we move into the Gloeckner's soddy." Elli looked at Abigael. "She was so frightened, not in her right mind."

"What do you think you will do?" Abigael's forehead creased in concern.

"Karl has promised he will move her into the dugout. It is very small, big enough only for them." Elli sighed. "It is a ways from here, but we will manage. I suppose we can move the wagons and the tent."

She thought for a moment. "Unless Jan wants us to live in there, too. I don't know how, but perhaps we could all sleep there for a time."

Elli looked toward the children. Søren was trying valiantly to put the coop back together. Kristen and Sigrün were "helping." "We lost some chicks. Half of them. We thought we had lost our weaners, but we found them. Thank you, God in heaven!"

Shuddering, she added, "Søren found the missing chicks just as a rattlesnake was about to get one of them. He chopped off its head!" She smiled a little. "I am very proud of my boy."

"Oh, that is good! I would be proud, too!"

"Eh. One of our oxen also broke his leg. We will have to slaughter him today. I am sure we will give you some of the meat."

Abigael's eyes shone. "That would be wonderful! Not that we are happy you will lose your ox, but still, to have as much fresh meat as one wants!"

While Søren finished putting the coop and pigpen to rights and putting their residents within them, Jan and Karl asked Henrik if he would butcher the ox in return for a share of the meat. He readily agreed. This freed Jan and Karl to work on the dugout.

The sun rose and the earth gradually warmed; the grasses all around them steamed in the sun. Abigael went home to fetch some dry fuel, and then Elli was at last able to get a fire started. The women, including Abigael, were roasting a great piece of the ox for dinner. Amalie seemed more like herself, chatting and working with a will.

No one spoke of Amalie's actions during or after the storm, but Jan suggested to Karl that perhaps it would be best to expand the dugout for both families. Karl was relieved.

"We must shelter our animals this way, too, eh?" Jan added, "and after that get our crops in before it is too late this season. Perhaps we planned wrong; perhaps we must build the barn last."

"*Ja*, I think you are right," Karl agreed.

Søren found the men, bent on getting their families under a solid, safe roof as quickly as possible, marking the outline for additional walls. The outline they had marked was about 16 feet by 10 feet. When finished, the old dugout would open into the new soddy.

"What will you do here, *Pappa*?" Søren asked, curious.

"This house is dug into this hillside. We are going to build on to it, *Sønn*, making a new room on the outside." Jan answered. "We will hang a curtain across the room so our family has a private place to sleep. The rest of the new room will be our kitchen and where we will eat.

"Onkel and his family will sleep in the dugout room. We will still build the barn where we decided, but we will live here until then."

The men dug down and cut out the sod where they had marked the outline of the floor and walls. The hillock would form a portion of the soddy's back wall, so they scraped the hillock's side flat. They used the sod they had removed and the sod cut from the garden spot to lay the first foot of the outside walls. They framed in a door about six inches off the ground to provide a high threshold.

The cut sod was very wet from the storm, but Henrik, who offered to lend a hand, told them, "It is good that it is still wet, *ja*? Sod that dries out before you use it does not grow together and make a strong wall. Then the walls do not last very long."

"I hope we will not need this house very long," Karl muttered, "but we do not know what the future will bring. Thank you for telling us this."

At the same time, Elli and Amalie began to make mattresses. They spread a piece of canvas upon the ground near the wagons. Together they hauled a bale of hay to it and cut the twine holding it together.

The women and their daughters spread the hay over the canvas so the sun would dry it. Amalie had the girls turn the hay to dry it evenly as the day wore on. Then she sent the girls to gather sticks and chips. They placed them in a box under one of the wagons. She and Elli would not be foolish and leave their fire fuel in the open again.

"Every day it is the same: We have to gather more sticks and chips," Kristen grumbled, digging in the dirt with her "snake" stick, the one she used to warn snakes of their approach.

"*Ja*, I know. And every day it is the same: You wish to eat, eh?" Elli answered.

Kristen sulked a little but quickly caught up with little Sigrün. She knew better than to let Sigrün wander into the grasses without her.

Elli dug in the wagons until she found the striped ticking they had bought from *Herr* Rehnquist. She and Amalie cut lengths of the ticking for mattresses and began to stitch them together.

Over the next days they would sew mattress covers for themselves and their husbands and smaller ones for the children. As the sweet-smelling hay dried, they would stuff the mattress covers with it and then stitch them closed. During these days the families ate all the fresh ox meat they wanted; some of it Elli and Amalie sliced thin and hung over the fire to dry.

Karl and Jan worked until dark that day cutting more sod and laying all the bricks they cut. The weather was calm that night; Amalie was calm, too, seemingly comforted by the progress the men were making.

Early in the morning Jan and Karl returned to cutting more sod. They chose a new spot for the garden, closer to the dugout, and cut the sod from it. Jan finished plowing the garden while Karl laid sod.

Then they chose their first field and began cutting sod from it. It was slow, backbreaking work, but they kept at it. By late evening, the outside walls of the soddy were four feet high.

The next day was the same. The men and Søren cut and laid sod; the women and girls worked in the new garden and kept turning and drying hay for the mattresses.

Jan and Karl spent an hour after lunch planting the "old" garden area in corn. "We will have one small crop of corn for sure before our other crops come in," Karl said this with a satisfied air, but Jan fretted.

He was anxious to finish the soddy so they could attack their first large field. Once their families and animals were safely under a roof, planting a good-sized crop was the next priority.

While they were planting the small cornfield, Jan planted his two apple saplings. He wanted the trees to grow on a softly sloping rise not far from where he intended to build their house.

This is a good spot, he told himself. *We will be able to see them in the spring when they are full of flowers. And someday we will add more fruit trees here.* He made two cages of chicken wire, placed them around the little trees, and staked the cages to the ground to keep them from blowing away.

As the walls of the soddy rose to six feet, they framed in a small window with shutters in the common room wall. Now they were ready to build a roof.

The roof did not have to be made of wood. Henrik had showed them they could save their precious lumber by placing poles across the walls, filling the spaces between the poles with thatch, and then laying long strips of sod crosswise over the poles and thatch.

Before quitting for the day, the men and Søren drove the wagon to the slough and cut bundles of rushes. The women would tie rushes together to make thatch for the roof, but they would need a great many rushes for the job, more than the slough had.

Pressing forward the next day, Karl and Jan hitched the wagon and loaded their ax, hatchets, and saw. With Søren in the back of the wagon, they drove far up the creek to a stand of saplings growing on the creek bank.

They cut three dozen saplings and set to work trimming the branches from them. Jan showed Søren how to use the hatchet to bump little branches from the trunks. When they had the poles ready, they loaded them in the wagon. Then they scoured the creek banks for more rushes. After they had filled the wagon they returned to the women.

Because the soddy backed against the hill, they dug holes for the poles in the hill just above the roof line. Jan and Karl hammered the poles into the holes until they were solidly anchored.

It would not be a flat roof; they hammered the poles into the mound about six inches higher than the outside walls and rested the poles on the front wall of the soddy, making a slope. Rain would run off the roof toward the front of the house. After the roof was done, they would fill the gaps on the sides left between the top of the wall and the rise in the roof.

Early in the morning, Jan and Karl began to lay the bundles of rushes between the poles. Elli and Amalie had worked tirelessly to tie enough bundles to fill all the spaces.

About noon they drove to their field and began to cut sod in long lengths they would lay across the poles. It was difficult to handle the long, heavy swathes of sod. They wrestled them into the wagon and drove back to the soddy. Then the men stood in the wagon bed to hoist the thick lengths onto the roof. Little by little, they covered the roof's frame with sod.

When they finished laying sod on the roof, the poles stuck out about a half a foot over the edge of the walls but the sod stuck out only a couple inches. Karl mixed mud in a bucket. He and Jan filled the gaps along the top of the wall where the thatch lay between the poles. Then they chopped sod bricks to fit into the gaps on the side between the roof and the wall.

"Tomorrow is Sunday," Karl reminded Jan. "We should rest and spend time with God."

"*Ja*, sure." Jan's response was half-hearted. He wouldn't admit it, but it irritated him to stop before the job was done.

Lord, I am enjoying this land you have given me! he thought. *I just want to work it and see a harvest.*

The harvest truly is plenteous, but the laborers are few . . . Unbidden, those words came to him. Jan felt conviction under the implications of those words.

Ja, Lord, you are right. I do need to spend time with you. Your harvest is more important than my harvest. Ja, I see this.

With the roof complete, the men and Søren set to leveling and packing the house's dirt floor. They scraped away uneven places and used mallets and rocks to pack the dirt. They then poured water on the dirt and created a mud slurry that they spread evenly across the floor and left to dry.

The house was done but the floor needed to cure for a few days, so the men worked on pens for the animals. For two days they cut and laid sod. Off one side of the soddy they built a chest-high wall that followed the curve of the hillock; Karl built a crude gate across the end of the pen.

That evening Søren spread newly cut prairie grass inside the pen. After he and Jan watered Molly and the oxen at the slough, they led the animals into the pen. Their five beasts had enough room to turn about and to lie down. The sod wall provided them good shelter from the wind.

The oxen could not break out of the pen and, if a wolf or coyote came near, Jan and Elli would be sleeping on the other side of the pen's wall. They would hear the oxen's distress.

For the pigs, the men laid a shorter wall, perhaps three feet high, off the other side of the soddy. They built a wall to divide the pen in half and gates for each pen. Next spring after they mated the boar and the sow, the dividing wall would keep the boar away from the sow and her piglets.

Jan reinforced the chickens' house and placed it at the end of the pigs' enclosure. He and Søren built a strong coop around the chickens and their house, one that would not so easily be blown down by a storm.

The six surviving chicks, at around eight weeks, were fully feathered and beginning to act and sound like grown chickens. Elli started teaching Kristen and Sigrün how to feed and water the chickens. Later, God willing, they would gather eggs, too.

After days of dedicated labor, the soddy was ready to move into. Jan and Karl hitched the two loaded wagons, put the table and benches on them, and drove the wagons to the soddy.

Jan unpacked Elli's cookstove and reassembled it. It was a lovely thing, a gift from her parents before Jan and Elli left for America. Elli ran her hands over it, admiring her pretty new stove with its colorful tiled doors and enameled handles.

They placed the stove outside the soddy's front door. The women would cook outside during the heat of the summer. When the weather cooled, they would bring the stove inside. It would easily heat the two rooms of the soddy/dugout.

Jan placed an empty crate against the soddy and hinged its lid. He placed oilcloth over the lid and tacked the cloth all around the lid so that the edges would drape down the sides. Here the fuel Kristen and Sigrün gathered daily would stay dry.

The men unloaded and opened trunks and crates. The men and the women selected items to keep out and those to be repacked. The women asked Jan and Karl to stack a few of the empty boxes in the kitchen to use as cupboards, as they had seen in Henrik and Abigael's home.

Karl and Jan unpacked and set up the two iron bedsteads and built simple frames from wooden packing crates for the children's beds. Elli and Amalie placed the new mattresses stuffed with hay upon the beds and covered them with linens they had brought from home.

Jan whittled pegs and hammered them into the walls wherever asked to. The women unpacked clothes and kitchenware, hanging them on the pegs. Jan hung the two guns from pegs high up on the soddy's wall next to the door.

Karl brought in a trunk packed with their clothes and placed it in the dugout room. Jan did the same, placing their trunk next to their bed. Then they moved the table and benches into the soddy's common area.

They had slept in the soddy three nights when another storm rolled through. It was nothing like the one they had survived huddling under the wagons. Still, as they ate a quiet dinner around their table, they felt blessed to be inside, protected from the winds and rain.

When lightning sizzled particularly close to them, Amalie sighed and looked around, comforted. "I didn't think I could live in a dirt house, but I must be honest. Until I had nowhere to run from a storm except under a wagon, I think I could not appreciate this. Today I am grateful to God for this dirt house."

CHAPTER 11

It was nearing the end of summer. Life for the Thoresens had settled into something of a routine. Jan and Karl had planted a few fields and harvested the early corn patch; a second field of corn was ripening quickly. Elli and Amalie were feeding their families from the green garden and canning or drying all they could from its bounty.

Søren milked Molly twice every day. She was a good producer; they drank all the milk they wanted and still shared some with the Andersons; the women made butter and cheese with what was left over.

Abigael had her baby, another boy, and Amalie grew rounder as her pregnancy progressed. A neighbor from farther west, Norvald Bruntrüllsen and his son, Ivan, drove over to make their acquaintance.

"I am sorry we did not come to meet you earlier," he apologized. "This spring I had decided to break sod on another field. I know you have found how long this takes."

The men talked crops for an hour. Søren, delighted to see another boy his age, showed Ivan everything the small beginnings of their farm had to offer. Ivan was impressed with their pigs.

The boar was coming into his size, and it was considerable. The sow was not far behind him in weight. In the spring when they were both a year old, the Thoresens would mate them.

"You brought them on the ship, eh? I'll bet they were a lot smaller then."

"Oh, *ja*. Just weaners," Søren replied. "I could hold them in my arms like big puppies when we left." They wandered back to listen the men talk.

"Some of the farmers around here have decided to take our corn and wheat to Omaha together," Norvald was saying. "We can sell our corn to the feedlots there and negotiate a better price for our wheat if we sell it to the eastern buyers at the same time."

Jan and Karl were keen to hear more.

"We heard you have four oxen and three wagons," Bruntrüllsen continued, "but perhaps not a big enough harvest this first year to fill all your wagons? If this is so, we were thinking to make you a proposition."

It was true that Jan and Karl would not have much to send to market this first year. In fact, of every crop they grew, they had to save back some for feed, some for seed, and enough to eat until the next harvest.

What remained over and above these needs could go to market. The Thoresens would have little corn and wheat to send this first year.

"*Ja*, we are listening," Karl answered.

"We propose that you load what you have into a wagon. We will send responsible men to fetch your teams and wagons. Two of our neighbors have offered to pair their mules to pull your third wagon. The men we send will load your wagons with crops others have grown and haul them to the siding where the train stops for water. We will take your crops to market for you and barter something in return for the use of your oxen and wagons."

Karl and Jan both became quiet. They would not allow their oxen out of their direct control to men they had just met.

Jan cleared his throat. "Perhaps one of us will come along." Karl was relieved; Jan had said just the right thing.

Bruntrüllsen nodded. "Good; I said as much to the others. What would you like in return? We thought a calf. A heifer."

Karl and Jan looked at each other. It was a generous offer. "*Ja*," Karl answered. "We agree!"

"Most families are also sending supply lists to Omaha with us," he told the Thoresens. "We will keep accounts of every man's crops, how much they sold for, and how much we spend at the grocers and hardware stores to fill his list."

Norvald showed Jan a small book of lined pages. "Here are last year's accounts. Only four of us farmers did this last year. They voted to send me to Omaha with the crops. You can see how I managed each man's account."

"It is a big job," Jan noted, appreciating the careful figures under each man's name. "How many farmers are sending crops this year?"

"Eleven, now that you and your brother have joined us," Norvald answered. "The farmers voted for me and Klaus Schöener to take the crops this year."

He smiled. "We may fill two cars this year! I will keep the accounts the same way so that every man may see what he has earned and what we spent for him."

"Will we not pay you and Klaus for your work for us?" Karl asked.

"*Ja*; We agreed that whoever takes the crops will split two percent of every man's earnings. See here," Norvald pointed to Klaus' earnings from the previous fall. "Klaus earned $75 last year. I kept $1.50 for taking it to market. Also, we split the cost of the cars and my ticket back."

Karl and Jan were impressed with the system the farmers were putting together. "This is a good way to do business, Norvald," they both told him.

Elli and Amalie set to work cutting burlap and stitching bags together for the corn and grain they would send to market. Elli taught Kristen how to seam the coarse, open-weave fabric using a whip stitch.

They decided that Karl would stay on the claims with their families and Jan would drive one of the wagons. Jan would carry a list of items they had carefully made for Norvald and Klaus Schöener to fill. Jan planned to be gone two days.

On the appointed day Karl and Jan had their teams hitched and their crop loaded. The four sacks of corn and six sacks of wheat did not fill even half of one wagon, but it was all they could spare. Norvald and a farmer they did not know, Gunnar Braun, arrived on horseback with a team of mules for the third wagon.

Jan returned two days later with Gunnar and two of the wagons. A week later, Norvald returned their third wagon and brought the supplies they had requested. Behind the wagon he led a late-born calf.

Jan and Karl were pleased with the bargain they had struck and more pleased with their neighbors and the system they had devised to send their crops to market.

"Will you come to church with us?" Norvald asked. "It is a German church and a little strict, but they accept us Swedes." He shrugged. "Sometimes we don't understand everything, *ja*? But it is a good church with good people.

"I will warn you in advance that there are many differences between this German church and what you are accustomed to back home. Still, it is good to sing the hymns and hear God's word and pray together. I have asked Henrik and Abigael also."

Jan glanced at Karl. "We should go. We will meet new people and perhaps find out more about the neighborhood. Søren needs to meet other boys. Perhaps we can ask about school."

Karl looked a little askance. "Is that why we go to church? Just to meet people?" He shook his head dismissively and turned to Norvald. "*Ja*, we will come."

Karl did not seem to notice Jan's clenched jaw and white face, but Norvald glanced between the two brothers. He made his goodbyes and the family drove away.

As soon as their friends were out of earshot, Jan turned on Karl. "Listen to me, brother. You do *not* correct me in front of our neighbors as if I were a child." His anger was simmering, rising quickly to the boiling point.

Karl stepped back, surprised that Jan was angry. "What? Are you angry for those few words?"

Perhaps if Karl had stopped there or had apologized, the situation would not have escalated. But he added, "Brother, I would not have spoken like that if you had not said a childish thing!"

Jan's fist shot out and clipped Karl's jaw. Karl staggered back, stunned.

"So? Why did you do this, *Bror*?" He touched his chin, still confounded.

Jan was already walking away, his strides long and angry. He strode past Amalie and Søren, not acknowledging them. They had both witnessed the short yet explosive argument. Søren ran crying to his *mor*, unable to understand what he'd seen and terrified by it.

"Jan, you must tell me what you are feeling," Elli pleaded. "Please." Jan had fled to the other side of the low rise on which he planned to build their house, where he had stood that first day surveying their land.

It was hard for Jan to speak of his feelings to Elli, to anyone for that matter. But he knew, instinctively, that the anger seething within him was dangerous. It may have been easy to forget about it while he and Karl labored through the summer, but it was clear that the anger was still there.

I know this anger is not pleasing to you, Lord. Jan's mind and heart were in a tumult of confusing emotions.

"Ach, my love, it seems I am always struggling so with my temper," he finally muttered.

"Ah." Elli was quiet for a minute. Then she asked, "Is it your temper that is the real problem?"

Jan rubbed his face. "What do you mean?"

"I know you, *ektemann*—my husband. You are not often angry, but when you are it is almost always with Karl, not so?"

Jan was silent but his anger shouted *yes!* within him.

"You and Karl are very different. He is more like your *far*, serious, maybe even a little cold at times. I think you rub him the wrong way sometimes and I know he rubs you the wrong way sometimes."

Jan expelled his pent-up breath. "You make it sound simple, but it *isn't*. Karl acts as though I live in *his* home and I am to obey him as we obeyed our *far*. This is not how it is, and I cannot let him continue acting so."

Elli nodded. "I know. I have seen it, too. But I think the real problem is that you have never told him how you feel and how it damages your relationship. You must have a good talk with him. Explain to him why you are angry. Explain how things need to change, that he must treat you as an equal, *ja*? But not while you are angry. The Bible says we are to speak the truth with love, so you must do it when you are calm."

Jan considered Elli's advice. "Perhaps you are right. I will pray on it."

❧ ✳ ☙

CHAPTER 12

The Thoresens' wagon rattled into the yard where the German church met, alongside others who were just arriving. The Thoresens watched families they did not yet know greet each other. They were being scrutinized, too. It was an uncomfortable feeling.

Soberly, the Thoresens climbed down from their wagon. Jan and Karl unhitched the oxen and walked them to an open stand of prairie grass. Together they hobbled the oxen and lifted the yoke from their necks.

Karl was much less comfortable with strangers than Jan. He looked around, sighed, and clamped his mouth shut. They rejoined their wives and children and entered the house.

The church members had added a large room to the house and filled it with narrow wooden benches. The Thoresens counted perhaps fifteen families, but the room was large enough.

Even though Norvald had warned them, the differences between this church meeting and their village church back in Norway were considerable. Elli was disappointed when she saw that the room was divided down the center with the women and children on one side and the men and older boys on the other.

Elli and Amalie and their daughters found seats next to Norvald's wife, Inge. The Thoresen women nodded pleasantly to the faces staring back at them. Elli felt that soon her face would crack from smiling so much.

The church's lay minister, Tomas Veicht, was an old man. He did not have much hair but he was possessed of impressive bushy white brows. When he spoke, his brows wiggled like fat tomato worms.

Søren stared, his mouth agape in amazement until Jan squeezed his leg a little. "It is not polite to stare, *Sønn*," he whispered, trying himself not to smile.

Søren wanted desperately to say something to his *pappa* about the old man's eyebrows but knew he should not talk in church. After a moment's struggle, he was able to keep quiet and look around. He nodded to Ivan and noticed one or two other boys who were looking at him with as much curiosity as he was looking at them.

The service began with the minister asking Norvald to introduce his guests. Norvald stood up and, in broken German, gave the people Karl and Jan's names. Several men reached over to shake Jan and Karl's hands.

Jan nodded to Gunnar Braun and Klaus Schöener and some of the other farmers who had sent crops to Omaha with Norvald. Henrik and Abigael arrived a little late, and Norvald introduced them also.

After a short prayer, the congregation stood and began to sing. Elli noticed that the families owned their own hymnals. The elderly woman standing in front of them wore an old-fashioned *kapp*. She turned and smiled, offering her hymn book to Elli.

When the woman smiled, Elli could see that her mouth was missing many teeth. Nevertheless, the old woman's eyes sparkled as she patted Kristen and Sigrün's hands, her smile growing even larger.

"Heidi," she whispered. "*Ich bin* Heidi Veicht." Her voice was soft and papery. Her chin wagged and quivered when she spoke. "*Willkommen.*"

"Elli Thoresen," Elli whispered back. "Amalie Thoresen," she pointed at her sister-in-law. She thanked the woman and took the book even though she would likely not be able to read or understand many of the words.

Heidi's kapp bobbed, her smile broadening further, if possible. The woman standing next to Heidi, perhaps her daughter, nudged her. Heidi smiled again and turned back to sing.

A lay elder led the singing. All the songs were slow and reverent, and the voices rose in well-known a cappella harmonies. Elli and Amalie recognized a few of the hymns, but the words were all in German, of course. Occasionally they hummed a little under their breath.

The small congregation sang for more than an hour. After a while, Elli closed her eyes and gave herself over to just listening to the beauty and reverence of the harmonies. When the last song began, slow and stately, Heidi turned around again.

She took her hymnal from Elli and turned to the right page, pointing to the words. Grateful, Elli and Amalie tried their best to sing the unfamiliar words to a most familiar song.

> *Ein' feste Burg ist unser Gott,*
> *Ein gute Wehr und Waffen;*
> *Er hilft uns frei aus aller Not,*
> *Die uns jetzt hat betroffen.*
> *Der alt' böse Feind,*
> *Mit Ernst er's jetzt meint,*
> *Groß' Macht und viel List*
> *Sein' grausam' Rüstung ist,*
> *Auf Erd' ist nicht seingleichen.*

A mighty fortress is our God,
a bulwark never failing;
our helper he amid the flood
of mortal ills prevailing.
For still our ancient foe
doth seek to work us woe;
his craft and power are great,
and armed with cruel hate,
on earth is not his equal.

Singing the familiar hymn, even with different words, strengthened Elli somehow. She drew a great breath when the song finished and clasped Amalie's hand. They were both encouraged.

Elli tapped Heidi on the shoulder and handed the book back to her. *"Tusen Takk!"* she whispered. Heidi, smiling and full of such good will, clasped Elli's hand, and Elli beamed in response.

But Heidi's companion offered no such welcome. Rather, she turned and stared at Elli. She said nothing, offered no smile, but examined Elli from head to toe. With a small sniff, she turned and sat down, her back straight and rigid. Elli's smile faded abruptly.

"Goodness," she breathed. Amalie looked at Elli and shrugged.

The minister, the old man with such amazing white brows, then stood before the people with his Bible opened. He read a Scripture and spoke calmly and directly on the passage. Elli and Amalie, again, understood only a few words. They listened as attentively as they could.

The message lasted an hour. Elli looked down. Kristen was slumped against her side, sleeping soundly. As the congregation rose for the final prayer, Elli smiled and gently woke Kristen, helping her to her feet.

Kristen involuntarily yawned and Elli smiled again. When she looked up, the woman in front of her was staring as before—but this time she was also frowning her disapproval. She gave another sniff and turned toward the front to pray.

Elli was disconcerted by the woman's cold reception. Fortunately, as soon as the prayer ended, Heidi reached for Elli and Amalie, giving them hearty hugs and taking time to touch each of the girls and say something in a kind voice.

As the service broke for the shared midday meal, the men took up the benches the congregation had been sitting on and carried them outside to where other men were setting up long tables in the yard. Jan and Norvald went to help. Elli saw Karl across the room having a conversation with one of the men.

Amalie and Elli had brought food to contribute to the meal, Elli a strudel and Amalie two pies. Inge showed them where to put their dishes and was called away.

The two women stood about, uncomfortable and wishing to help. Elli spied Jan carrying one end of a wooden table. The other men were taking to Jan immediately, Elli saw.

Lord, Jan is so cheerful and easy to talk to; no one stays a stranger long around my husband, she smiled happily to herself. Soon one or two of the men were joking with Jan and clapping him on the back.

Karl stepped out on the porch. The man Karl had been speaking to stood next to him. He was not a large man, but he had an air of authority. Unlike the other farmers, he wore a proper suit of clothes and shiny boots, both dark and somber. The man looked around as if to see that the business of setting up the meal was going properly.

He is very serious looking, Elli thought. The man noticed Jan's easy interaction with the German men and watched intently. His expression did not change but something about it concerned Elli.

She was relieved when Jan reclaimed her and took them to sit at one of the tables. Amalie trailed behind with Sigrün and soon Norvald and Inge claimed seats across from them. Søren and Ivan grinned and kicked each other under the table until their mothers intervened.

Karl slipped into the seat Amalie had saved for him. "Who is that man you were talking to?" Jan asked.

"Adolphe Veicht. His father is the minister, Tomas Veicht." Karl pointed to the women bringing food to the tables. "That is his wife, Rakel." Elli and Amalie looked to where Karl was pointing.

"Oh, dear," Elli hardly realized she had spoken aloud. Adolphe Veicht's wife, Rakel, was the woman who had reproved her with a glance and a sniff. She was dressed as plainly and somberly as her husband.

"Eh?" Karl asked.

"It is nothing," Elli murmured.

Rakel Veicht was clearly in charge of the women providing the food. Although she spoke few words and made few gestures, she watched with that same cool air of authority Elli had noticed in her husband. Elli shivered.

"So? Are you cold, wife?" Jan asked, surprised.

"*Nei*, husband," she muttered.

They ate and chatted as they could with those at the table with them. Elli did not eat much and wished for them to leave as soon as possible.

When cleanup after the meal began, Elli and Amalie watched the other women don aprons. The Thoresen women had packed aprons in their wagon and immediately followed suit. They stayed close to Inge Bruntrüllsen, helping wherever she was working.

Inge introduced them to many friendly and welcoming women. Soon Elli and Amalie were ferrying dishes to the kitchen with the others, feeling helpful and included.

Elli almost tripped over Heidi Veicht, who was sitting next to the minister on a bench near the house's kitchen door. "Elli! *Kommen sie, bitte,*" Heidi beckoned her.

Elli put what she was carrying down and dried her hands on her apron. Heidi took her hand and introduced her to the nearly bald minister.

So Heidi was the minister's wife! Elli was pleased and gave her name, gesturing to Jan as her husband and to Søren and Kristen as her children.

Tomas Veicht was as kind and gracious as his wife. Right then Elli determined that the minister's son and his odd, cold wife—both of them so different from Tomas and Heidi Veicht—would not influence her decision to be part of this church.

Still, as they pulled out of the Veicht's yard that afternoon, Elli felt as though a weight had dropped from them. Amalie expressed it. "It was hard meeting so many new people, *ja?* All their ways so different from what we are used to. Everything was a little confusing, but I liked their singing."

"I liked *Fru* Veicht," Elli murmured. "She was very welcoming."

"You met Adolphe Veicht's wife?" Karl asked.

"*Nei*; we met Tomas Veicht's wife," Elli replied. "Adolphe's wife was sitting next to *Fru* Veicht, but she did not introduce herself." *Or even indicate that she was interested in meeting us*, Elli thought.

"I met many of the men today," Jan commented. "I liked them. We will have good fellowship. They love their minister—that says a lot about a church, *ja?*"

"I am glad, Jan!" Elli responded. "We were meeting some of the women as we cleaned up. Inge was very helpful."

As though Jan and Elli had not even spoken, Karl turned to the women in the back of the wagon. "You must both make an effort to meet Rakel Veicht next time and be courteous to her," Karl said. "I had a good conversation with Adolphe. He is an important man in the church. I was glad that he can speak a little Swedish."

Jan closed his mouth on the words he wanted to say. *There goes Karl again, now ordering my wife around. I do not like it, Lord, but I will not say anything right now. Later, perhaps, when I am calm.*

Jan had determined to keep his temper in check. He had been able to restrain his tongue just now because he was praying for the Lord's guidance and timing to talk to Karl.

Man-to-man, Lord. I must have your wisdom and words to speak my heart clearly, he prayed.

With cold weather beginning to set in, Jan moved Elli's stove into the soddy. He cut a hole in the sod wall and piped the stove through the hole. It would not take much to keep the soddy warm in the winter.

Jan and Karl turned their energy to building a foundation for the barn. In the morning, as soon as they had light to do so, Jan and Karl hitched both teams of oxen to empty wagons and loaded up pick ax, crow bar, and shovel.

Frost rimed the fields, but it would burn away as the day warmed. Jan, Karl, and Søren were dressed warmly for the day's early start.

"Here." Elli handed Jan a heavy tin pail.

"*Takk*," he replied, grinning. Elli and Amalie would have packed them a hearty lunch, enough to feed them all day.

Karl pointed his oxen toward the river, some five miles away. Søren drove the second wagon, following Karl. Jan sat back, observing his *sønn's* driving and offering occasional suggestions.

When they returned at sunset, weary and sunburned, the wagons groaned under the weight of large stones for the foundation of the barn. Two days later the men repeated the process and again a few days after that.

For two weeks the men worked on the barn's foundation and floor. The weather was increasingly cold until the ground froze, but by then they had dug the footprint of the barn and laid the stones, cementing them and smoothing the floor with lime mortar. After planting crops in the spring, they would host a barn raising.

Now they hunkered down for the winter. In November Amalie gave birth to a boy. Elli and Abigael helped Amalie with the birth. Karl and Amalie named the baby Karl after his *pappa*. Almost immediately everyone called him Little Karl.

As the winter nights wore on, Jan held Elli in his arms. "Why haven't we had another baby, Jan? I don't understand." She kept her voice low but he could hear her tears.

"We will have more children, you'll see," he assured her. "We still have lots of time."

CHAPTER 13

1870

Another spring! Jan rejoiced. *Lord, this is our year!*

Karl and Jan had worked their land four years now and had added a few cattle, some goats, and several milk cows to their livestock. They had grown their herd of Landrace pigs and made good money from them. They had enlarged and improved the barn they built their second spring to include a milking shed and additional pens for pigs and goats.

And Elli and Amalie had picked apples from the two trees Jan had planted on the slope to the south of where Jan and Elli would build their house.

After four years, the Thoresens were still living in the soddy even though it was an inconvenient distance from the barn. As their livestock grew, it had made more sense to shelter the hay and grass to feed the animals each winter than to make room for the two Thoresen families; it had made no sense to spend precious money making over part of the barn for them to live in temporarily.

Instead both families had agreed to stay in the cramped soddy—even though Karl and Amalie had added another baby boy, Arnie, to their family. They were determined to save the money needed to build the first house.

The Thoresens and Henrik had built a bridge across the creek. Jan and Karl had plowed more fields on both of their properties to grow corn, wheat, hay, and oats.

In another month their fields would again be planted. Afterward Karl and Jan and the rest of the community would have a few weeks to spare for other tasks.

"We have but a year more to prove up our claims, Karl," Jan said, his excitement barely in check.

Karl answered slowly, "*Ja*, we have the soddy, but it is on my property."

Karl alluded to the government's requirement: For every 160 acres claimed under the Homestead Act, the claimant must build a dwelling, make improvements on the property, live on and farm the land—and prove they are doing so—by the end of five years.

"Just so, Karl. Now we must be building a house on my property. Thank you, God in heaven, we have money from our hogs to pay for the lumber!" Karl and Jan would soon be taking their wagons to pick up the lumber Robert Bailey would have off-loaded from the train for them.

A tiny town had grown up northwest of the railroad's water tower prompting the railroad to move its water tower and build a small siding at the town. The people had attached the name RiverBend to their village, because the town was near the river as it turned toward the Platte.

RiverBend—and the railroad—were closer to the Thoresen's homestead than where they had first arrived and left the train. Even better, the railroad had hired Mr. Bailey to manage RiverBend's little station.

For a minute Karl didn't say anything more and then, "We spoke of building a house close to the barn first. That makes sense, eh? Later we will build a second house and maybe even a second barn, but first we must prove up our claims."

"This is so," Jan replied. "We have talked about this many times. I have paid for the lumber. This month we will lay the foundation. It is time to build the house. We should set a date and, when we build the Gustav's barn in two weeks, ask our neighbors to come to the raising, *ja?*"

Karl dithered for another minute. "I have been thinking."

Jan turned toward Karl, something setting him on his guard. "Thinking of what?"

Karl looked away, a little uneasy in his manner. "I was thinking maybe you wouldn't mind if we . . . switched claims. Traded?"

Jan stared at his brother. "Trade land? Why do you say this?" For a moment he was puzzled. "Oh, I see. If we switch claims, then the first house we build will be yours, *ja?* Is that it?"

"It is only because Amalie . . . we already have three children and . . . she is pregnant again."

Jan said nothing. He did not trust himself to speak. Of course he was happy about another baby coming, but . . .

"No, Karl. This is my land." The words came out before Jan even had a chance to think of forming them. *Of course he would not trade. This was **his** land! Hadn't he stood on it that first day and thanked God for it?*

Jan added slowly, "If we could build on your land first, I would gladly agree to that, but we don't have a choice, *ja?* We must build on mine to prove up. This is what we agreed on when we decided to build out the soddy and live there, is it not?"

He was leery of Karl's suggestion. The conversation that Elli had suggested Jan have with his brother, now several years past, came back to him. The discussion had been tense and uncomfortable.

It had not been easy for Jan to talk of his feelings and do so calmly. It also hadn't been easy for Karl to listen. He had struggled to see Jan's perspective.

It had taken patient explanation on Jan's part for Karl to realize their relationship was being damaged. Jan had to point out where Karl unconsciously treated Jan not just as a younger brother but as a brother under Karl's authority—when in fact they were both grown and the heads of their own families.

In the end, Karl had responded well and changed toward him in many ways. In turn, Jan had let the anger go. Jan had worked hard to keep his heart free of offense and had learned to assert himself—*calmly*—when he felt it was necessary.

Jan swallowed. "You know, Elli and I wish to have more children, too. Who knows? We could have another *barn* by next spring!" Jan thought of Elli and the disappointment each month brought. *If I trade, Elli will believe I have given up hope for us to have another child.*

"I'm sorry, but I won't trade with you," he repeated quietly.

Karl just nodded. "*Ja,* all right. I thought I would ask."

Jan hastened to add, "We will build the house as we planned, Karl. The house will have enough bedrooms for you and Amalie and the children to live with us while we build your house *next* spring. Isn't that what we planned?"

He rushed on. "It is but a year. Next spring our neighbors will testify that we are building a new house for your family on *your* property to replace the soddy, eh?"

"Sure, sure. You are right, Jan." Karl wandered off to work in the barn, but for some reason Jan was still uneasy.

Elli stared at the incontrovertible evidence. She was not pregnant. Again. *O Lord!* she moaned. *I'm not too old! I still have regular cycles! Please!*

Only last evening Amalie had announced that yet another baby was on the way. Karl and Amalie already had Sigrün, Little Karl, and Arnie—and now another was coming!

Lord, I am only thirty-one, Elli begged. She had become pregnant the first time right after she and Jan had married. Søren was born when she was nineteen years old. She hadn't had any difficulties with her pregnancy or the birth.

After that, it had taken only a year before she became pregnant with Kristen. But then . . . nothing. Søren was now twelve, Kristen was almost ten, and Elli's arms ached to hold another baby.

Elli wanted to ask, *Lord, do you hear me? Do you not care?* But in her heart she knew that God heard her prayers, even her very thoughts. Nothing was hidden from him!

She cried herself to sleep in Jan's arms when each month ended in disappointment. He comforted her by talking of the home they would build, and they dreamed together of the day they would finally have their own roof over their heads.

With more children, please, Lord! Elli cried out to God.

Jan and Karl began work on the house's foundation as soon as their last field was planted. The two men and Søren again took both wagons to the river to gather rocks.

As he and Søren drove toward the river, Jan was sober, thinking of Elli's most recent disappointment. They still had no child on the way, and Elli was increasingly despondent.

Why, Lord? he asked. *Søren and Kristen are healthy! Elli is healthy! Certainly our love life is healthy, ja?* He chuckled aloud, drawing a curious look from Søren, seated beside him.

Lord, we would like more children. We are still young, so would you please bless us with a house full of them before I am too old to be a new pappa?

The Andersons, Bruntrüllsens, Kappels, and many other families from the German church came to help them raise the house. Jan could scarcely sleep the night before. By noon the full frame of the two-story home, raised upon the foundation he, Søren, and Karl had laid, was standing.

Elli, Amalie, and their neighbors' wives fed the men and their families a hearty midday meal. Jan could not eat—he was giddy with the realization of this dream, the happiest he'd been since the day he had first seen his claim. He spent much of his time during the meal thanking and shaking the hands of the men who came to help, often making small, encouraging comments.

The only irritation in the day was the appearance of Adolphe Veicht and his wife Rakel. "Tomas is not well, *Herr* Thoresen. He has sent us in his stead," Adolphe announced in his cool, aloof way.

The Thoresens had been attending the German church, usually twice a month, for the past four years. Although language was still a barrier, Jan and Elli had picked up enough German to understand the hymns and to make simple conversations.

The sermons were more difficult to follow, but Jan loved Tomas Veicht, as did the congregation. And in Heidi Veicht Elli felt that her children had been gifted with a *bestemor*—a grandmother of the heart.

"It is hard for children to grow up without their grandparents, Jan," Elli mused. "We are so blessed to have Tomas and Heidi in our lives."

The Thoresens knew that Tomas and Heidi had lived and farmed in this area for more than twenty years—far longer than most in the church. However, it was also clear that Tomas was not as strong a man on the outside as he had been at one time. Tomas still farmed some of his land, but his grandsons and others in the church did much of the work for him.

Yet as much as Jan and Elli loved Tomas and Heidi, their son Adolphe was another story. Adolphe knew the Bible well and sometimes taught the Sunday message, but he and his wife espoused a more severe approach to Christian living than did Tomas and Heidi. Adolphe, Rakel, and their two sons dressed plainly, with little color. They believed frivolity or much humor to be inappropriate.

Despite Jan and Elli's efforts to break the ice with the younger Veichts, the couple remained aloof, almost disapproving of them. To his puzzlement, Jan felt Adolphe's eyes continually watching him as though probing for faults.

And so Jan and Elli thought it strange that Karl and Adolphe Veicht got on well. In fact, Adolphe was probably Karl's closest friend, next to Jan. Amalie, on the other hand, was close-mouthed about the Veichts.

Elli wondered how Amalie fared in a one-on-one conversation with Rakel. The woman invariably had an opinion about everyone and everything—generally a critical one. With Karl so friendly with Adolphe, Amalie could not help but spend time with Rakel; nevertheless, she never spoke to Elli of Adolphe and Rakel.

Why is Adolphe Veicht always cool to me, Lord? Jan thought as the house raising began.

While Jan encouraged and cheered the workers, Adolphe watched him closely as if he wanted to catch him doing something wrong! When Jan told a good story—one that made his listeners laugh—Adolphe frowned.

And today Rakel stands apart from the other women as though offended that she is not supervising the meals! Why is that, Lord?

Jan saw Elli and Amalie make attempts to include Rakel and heard her sniff and reply, "I'm sure I would do things differently if I were in charge, but I'll leave you to manage it your way."

As if Elli and Amalie should not manage it their way? Why are Adolphe and Rakel so sour? Jan asked himself again. *And how is it that Tomas and Heidi, so full of God's graciousness, have a son like this?*

Jan shook his head, frustrated. He noticed Karl and Adolphe in deep conversation. *Adolphe seems to have no problem with Karl!* Adolphe and Karl's friendship—more than anything—confused and, Jan admitted, concerned him.

He looked over the workers and saw Adolphe's sons, Ernst and Frank, working hard—but apart from the other men.

I feel bad for these young men, Lord, Jan prayed. *They always look whipped and discouraged.*

Jan went out of his way to compliment Ernst and Frank. Although they were in their late teens or early twenties, Adolphe treated the two boys like youngsters rather than as men who were now doing men's work.

Jan knew exactly how they felt; he made sure to encourage the young men by bringing them into the circle of other men and their conversations. Ernst and Frank exchanged stolen glances with Jan, their eyes brimming with mute gratitude.

When the shadows began to fall that evening and the many friends and neighbors took their leave, each one looked with pride on the results of the community's labor: No rooms within the house were yet finished and no windows were set within their frames, but the house itself, tall and narrow, was sided and roofed. It had been a good day.

So much of what Jan and Elli had dreamed—built in just one day! That evening they wandered happily through the large living room, the kitchen, and the pantry. They stood in the doorway of the room just off the living room, the room that would be their bedroom.

They walked up the unfinished staircase and stared at the open space. On the second floor Jan would frame four bedrooms, one for Karl, Amalie, and the new baby; one for Søren; one for the "little boys;" and one Sigrün and Kristen would share.

Through the spring and into summer, Jan and Karl spent what time they could spare on the house. Jan focused first on making and installing sturdy doors and shutters. Most of the windows did not have glass; this year they could afford glass only in the kitchen, but someday all the windows would have glass. For now, they would make do with shutters and screens.

In July, Jan and Elli moved into the still incomplete house. It was easier for Jan to do the finish work while living there. Jan, Elli, and the children set up housekeeping in the living room while Jan framed in the upstairs rooms and then lathed and plastered the walls.

Karl and Amalie would stay in the soddy until the upstairs bedrooms were finished and winter closed in. For the few months until then, Jan and Elli would taste life as it would be when they and their children lived in their own home by themselves.

When the family awakened their first morning in the house, they ate breakfast in the living room. Jan had knocked together a small table for temporary use. After the meal Søren and Kristen waited expectantly for their father to read to them from the Bible.

Jan blinked in surprise. He had never led his family in daily Scripture reading and prayer. *Always it has been either my father or Karl!* he realized. Now, for the first time, he was to realize his role as head of their family.

"Elli," he whispered, "Karl has the Thoresen family Bible, and I do not have one of my own!"

Elli ran to her trunk and brought back a bundle tied up in a scarf. "My *pappa* and *mamma* gave this to us when we married, remember? I have been saving it for this day."

Jan untied the scarf and held the book reverently. The print on the front cover read, *Our Family Bible.* Jan was overcome at the import of those words. *Our Bible. Our family.*

He shook his head in wonderment. Inside, on the family page, Elli's father had lovingly written Jan and Elli's names and the date of their marriage.

Elli and the children still waited. Jan looked at each of them in turn, giving silent thanks for this day. "Matthew, Chapter 1," he choked.

It was a moment before he could continue.

Every part of the house was special to Jan, and he worked many more hours than Karl did on it. He did not mind. *Because it is our house, mine and Elli's!* he sang to himself.

Jan cleared a corner in the barn just for carpentry. He put all his wood craft to work, often toiling far into the night to shape pretty wainscotings, doors, and trim he knew would please Elli.

The kitchen was of particular importance to Jan. The ceiling was high and the room was open and airy. He and Elli designed the cupboards, drawers, and nooks together. Across an entire wall he built shelves for Elli to display the dishes she had packed in sawdust for their journey from home.

The highlight of the kitchen would be her stove with its beautiful tiled doors and enameled handles. *Someday we will order tiles with pretty designs to mount on the walls,* Jan planned.

But Elli's stove would not come over to the house until Karl and his family joined them, for they needed a cookstove, too. Until then, Elli made do, cooking in the living room on the large heating stove they had brought with them from Omaha. The stove did not have ovens as her cookstove did, but Elli managed somehow.

Jan lined the cupboard and pantry shelves with cured red cedar. He sought out the native trees himself, up and down the river, for their wood's aromatic and insect-repelling qualities.

He and Elli painted the kitchen walls and the shelves white. After the shelves dried, Elli—with slow, painstaking strokes—covered the shelf edges, sides, and backs with the intricate and colorful designs of Norwegian rosemaaling.

One day soon I must make a wedding chest for Kristen, Jan thought. *I will make one even grander than Elli's and line it with cedar. Elli will paint it with Kristen and teach her the art of rosemaaling.* He found that he did not like to think of Kristen growing into a woman who would eventually marry and move away.

Jan watched his wife work late one evening when they both should have been in bed sleeping. He thought he had never seen a sight so beautiful: His Elli, intent but peaceful in her labor, her wheat-colored braids pinned around her head in a glowing crown, tendrils of hair escaping from her braids to curl about the nape of her neck . . . Jan's favorite place to kiss.

He came up behind her and *did* kiss her . . . right there, on the back of her neck, pressing his lips against her skin and then breathing softly over it. She sighed and giggled. Jan placed kisses on the sides of her neck. He gently rubbed his chin along her jaw.

"Shall we make a new baby in our new house?" Jan whispered, nuzzling her ear.

Elli sighed again and leaned back into his arms. Jan slowly took the brush from her hand and put it in the jar with the others.

Summer passed in a blur of unrelenting work for them all. Jan, even as exhausted as he was, had never been happier. Elli and the children thrived, but Amalie struggled and was always weary.

Midway through her fourth pregnancy, Amalie had her husband and three children to cook for, constant laundry to wash—particularly with a toddler—the soddy to keep clean, and her part of the garden to maintain.

Now that the garden was producing, she and Elli were canning every day, putting up the food they would need for the winter. They had goat and cow milk to strain and butter and cheeses to make.

The work never abated.

The men worked from daylight to nightfall bringing in the harvest. The farmers of the area again made arrangements to cooperatively send their crops to Omaha.

This year four box cars sat waiting on RiverBend's little siding. This year Jan and Karl's three wagons were filled with their own bagged grain and corn and with crates of hogs for the feedlots. And this year their third wagon was pulled by a new team of fine bay Morgans bartered in the spring for a boar and several female hogs.

Their crops—and especially their fine hogs—would bring in the money to buy the lumber to build Karl and Amalie's house in the spring.

As soon as the crops were sent to market, the men would plow under all the fields in preparation for winter. Then butchering would commence. The Thoresens would kill three hogs and lay up hams, bacon, sausages, and lard.

Then, as the cold weather set in, Karl and his family would give up the soddy and move to Jan and Elli's house. The winter would pass more easily for them in the house, and Elli would be able to help Amalie. Until the ground froze, Jan and Karl would work on the foundation for Karl and Amalie's house.

In the spring after the planting was over, just as they had done this past spring, the Thoresens would host another house raising: Friends and neighbors for miles around would come to raise the walls and roof of Karl and Amalie's new house.

It would be as important for Karl to live close to his house while he worked on it as it had been for Jan to live close to his.

It will only be seven or eight months, just until Karl and his family have their own home, Jan told himself when he thought about Karl and his family moving in with them. *We have plenty of room; it will not be crowded like in the soddy.*

Of course, they would pass the most important landmark in June: Jan and Karl would complete and submit the proof paperwork for their claims. Henrik Anderson and Norvald Bruntrüllsen had already said they would testify to their proof.

Then this land will truly be mine—at last! Jan lifted his head in happy thanksgiving.

CHAPTER 14

After the harvest and after the slaughtering was over, the German church had a celebration of sorts at the Bruntrüllsens. It was to be a day of fellowship, food, games, and the sharing of bounty.

Norvald asked Jan to help him organize races for the young folk, and Jan threw himself into it wholeheartedly. Norvald could not have picked a better helper, for Jan brought humor and good-natured sportsmanship into the games.

The children and young adults had not had such fun in many months. They competed in running races, three-legged races, relays, and gunnysack races. Jan and Norvald recruited some of the young men to coach the smaller boys and then compete in team races. Four teams, with members of all ages, would race.

"You young men," Jan counseled them, "are role models for these little ones, *ja*? Help them along and give them good advice. Make this a fun time and see what a sparkle you put in their eyes!"

The teams went off to a great "Hurrah!" and cheers from the crowd of onlookers. The young men of one team threw their smallest teammates atop their shoulders and ran the circuit for all they were worth. The little boys riding on their shoulders bounced and laughed. Jan chuckled at their ingenuity and then laughed until he had to hold his sides.

This team was easily on its way to victory—until one of their leaders tripped. Both he and the teammate atop his shoulders tumbled to the ground, inadvertently tripping up two other runners, who caused a fourth to also stumble.

The runners got up laughing and clapping each other on the back. At the end of the race, every young man hoisted a little boy to his shoulders and carried him off the field to the shouts and cheers of the onlookers.

Tomas Veicht gave Jan his hearty approval. "These *kinder* were in sore need of a day of pleasure, *Herr* Thoresen," he told Jan through Norvald. "And so were all of us! We have worked hard this year. And do not the Scriptures say *a merry heart doeth good like a medicine*? This is a good day!"

At that moment they saw Adolphe speaking to his sons, Ernst and Frank. They had been two of the young men to carry their little teammates off the field.

Adolphe gestured toward the field where the games were held and shook his head, then pointed toward the barn. The boys wearily trudged off to perform some chore for Norvald.

Jan happened to glance at Tomas just then and saw sadness in the old minister's eyes. Norvald cleared his throat.

Jan looked back to Adolphe, wondering again what caused this man to have such a sour outlook on life. He was startled to see Adolphe staring back at him, his face set in grim lines of disapproval.

After the games the women set out a feast on long tables in the yard. Everyone was to eat their fill of fried chicken, glazed ham, and roasted beef, antelope, and duck; mountains of creamy mashed potatoes and turnips running with thick gravies; flakey homemade biscuits, jams, and jellies; and vegetables of every variety.

The congregation slaked their thirst with cool ciders, sweet teas, and a fruity punch provided by Inge Bruntrüllsen. Another whole table was set aside for apple, cherry, berry, and peach pies and strudels and cakes of many flavors.

When all the women and children were seated, the men remained standing by their chairs. Tomas and the elders led the congregation in prayer.

"Lord God, we thank you for your bounty. Today we celebrate your goodness to us in this harvest. We thank you for the health of our brothers and sisters and their families. We thank you for fun and laughter, for your word teaches us

To every thing there is a season,
and a time to every purpose under the heaven:
A time to be born, and a time to die;
a time to plant, and a time to pluck up that which is planted
A time to weep, and a time to laugh;
a time to mourn, and a time to dance . . .
And also that every man should eat and drink,
and enjoy the good of all his labour, it is the gift of God.

"Father, we have planted and harvested, and today, Lord, we laugh and eat and drink and enjoy the good of our labor, your gifts to us."

"Amen!" the men roared, and the people set to the food with a will.

Such a good day, Lord, Jan thought, patting Elli's hand and smiling at those sitting near him. The young men of the church in particular grinned across the tables at Jan.

After the feast, families brought out whatever bounty they wished to share. This was a time of bartering and selling and sometimes gifting extra foodstuffs to other families in the church.

Karl and Jan brought late weaners to barter or sell. Others brought chicks and calves or late produce from their gardens.

One farmer, a bachelor, kept bees. He traded his honey for ham, bacon, sausages, chickens, and canned fruits and vegetables. Amalie and Elli were excited to barter a ham for a precious half-dozen jars of honey.

Whoever was knowledgeable of a need within the community—such as a family experiencing a hard time—shared that knowledge with Tomas and the church elders. They quietly made known the need to the church. What was given to meet those needs was set aside. Before the end of the day, Tomas or one of the elders would ask a congregation member who lived near the family in need to deliver the gifts.

When the weather turned frosty, Karl and Amalie moved from the soddy. The move was accomplished one afternoon without too much effort. Elli peeked into the kitchen. Jan had almost finished reassembling her stove! Her beautiful kitchen would at last be complete.

Elli and Amalie prepared the evening meal companionably as Karl and Jan carried in the long table and benches from the soddy. After dinner Elli unpacked and ironed a pretty blue cloth and covered the table with it. She smiled. It was ready for breakfast in the morning.

Together Elli and Amalie got the children settled for the night. Sigrün was delighted to be sharing a room with Kristen, but Little Karl and Arnie were not so sure about sleeping in a room by themselves for the first time in their young lives!

The women both collapsed in the warm living room, content to sip a quiet cup of tea before climbing the stairs to bed. Their men were still rumbling about in the barn, but would soon seek their rest, too.

The next morning Elli busied herself getting breakfast; Amalie packed the lunch the men and Søren would need as they went to the river to gather rock for the foundation of Karl and Amalie's house. Jan and Karl were taking advantage of a two-day window before they planned to butcher the hogs.

After the men finished with the milking, the families gathered for breakfast. Karl placed his family Bible on the breakfast table and automatically bowed his head and prayed aloud.

Jan sat blinking during the prayer. When Karl finished, Jan glanced at Elli. She was serving Kristen's plate but Jan could tell that she was avoiding his eyes.

Lord, Jan prayed silently. *Isn't this my house? Help me to be gracious while Karl and Amalie are here. But also, help me to assert myself in a way that pleases you.*

When the meal was finished, Karl stretched his hand to his Bible. "Excuse me, Karl," Jan said quietly. "If you please, I will read aloud this morning. Would you lead us in prayer when we finish?" He opened his Bible. "We are in Romans, chapter 2."

He stared as mildly as he could muster at Karl. Karl's mouth was open and then he shut it and frowned. "I always read, Jan," he replied, somewhat testy.

Elli and Amalie did not look at either Karl or Jan. They knew how contentious things had been between the brothers in the not-too-distant past.

"*Ja*, I know, *Bror*," Jan answered, careful of his words and tone. "But as this is my home, I have been reading for my wife and children. I would like to continue doing so. Perhaps we can take turns." He cleared his throat. "So. Let us begin."

He finished the chapter and closed their Bible. "Karl, would you like to pray for us?"

Later that day Karl and Jan were loading rocks into a wagon. Søren was downstream from them some ways. Jan could sense that Karl was disturbed. He hoped Karl would say something so that the tension would be relieved, but Karl was not a man of many words. Jan wondered if he should say something.

"Jan, I have been thinking about what happened at breakfast this morning," Karl finally ventured.

"*Ja*, I have been, also," Jan admitted.

Karl faced him. "You were disrespectful of me in front of my wife and children." Now that he'd said it, his face reddened.

Jan carefully considered his response. "Brother, I said no disrespectful words. I used no disrespectful tone. I would ask you to look at the situation from where I am, please. You sat down to eat in my home this morning, *nei*? Did you consider that?"

Karl frowned more, and Jan hoped he was thinking on what he'd said. Instead, he repeated himself. "I still think you disrespected me in front of my family."

"*Nei*, brother, I did not mean to. But we spoke of this a few years ago, of you treating me as an equal, eh? Perhaps you can understand that, in my house, I might feel you disrespected me? Did you not *presume* to lead us without thinking? This is the very thing that has caused strife between us in the past."

"Truly," Jan said, placing his hand on his brother's shoulder, "I do not want strife between us ever again. So let us be clear with each other when we trespass, *ja*? Otherwise, the anger festers."

Karl considered what Jan asked for several minutes without speaking. "I am not sure I agree with you, Jan. I will pray on it."

Jan nodded. "Thank you, Karl."

CHAPTER 15

1871

In February, Amalie welcomed another son into the world. She and Karl named the baby Kjell after his great-grandfather on Amalie's side.

That same month Jan and Karl asked Henrik Anderson and Norvald Bruntrüllsen to write their letters of testimonial for Jan and Karl's homestead claims.

"We know you will not have time for this during planting season," The Thoresens told them. "If you have already written them, we will mail them to the land office in Fremont at the right time."

"We are glad for you," Norvald said the next Sunday as he handed his letters to Jan and Karl. "You have worked hard and have much to show for it!" He and Henrik shook Jan and Karl's hands, grinning with them.

Two days later, Henrik walked to their house through a bitter wind. Elli let him in the kitchen door, and he went directly to the stove to warm himself, greeting Amalie and Elli as he shivered in front of the stove's open door.

"Ach. I bring sad news," he told them. "Will you call Karl and Jan?" Elli immediately rang the bell to call them from the barn. Jan and Karl shook Henrik's hand and waited for what he had to tell them.

Henrik sighed. "I have heard from Norvald. Tomas passed away in his sleep last night." He choked a little as told them. "Norvald heard it from Rikkert. Adolphe sent for the elders of the church to come to Tomas' house to plan the burial."

Silence reigned in the kitchen as they digested his news. While Elli served coffee, the adults sat at the table and mourned Tomas' passing.

"Poor Heidi! She will be so grief-stricken." Elli's tears for Heidi filled her eyes and ran down her face. "They had an exemplary Christian marriage. I do not know what she will do now."

"Adolphe will take over Tomas' fields," Karl stated, matter-of-factly. "He and I have talked of this."

"That is good," Jan murmured. "Heidi will not be alone in her grief." But he and Elli exchanged concerned glances.

At the service Jan was surprised to see the three elders wearing new suits as dark and sober as Adolphe's. "In respect for Tomas," Jan decided.

To be sure, the mourning for the gentle lay minister was deep and heartfelt. Heidi was also dressed all in black, her head covered in a thick veil. Jan and Elli had never seen the sweet, gap-toothed old woman as solemn and quiet as she was that day.

The women of the church had baked and cooked for the Veichts and for the meal after the service. Unfortunately, the weather was too bitterly cold to eat out-of-doors and the number of funeral attendees greater than what the meeting room could accommodate.

The men of the church began setting up tables in the barn for the meal afterwards. Jan and Karl hurried to help so that the barn would be ready when the service ended.

As they were hauling tables, Jan noticed Ernst and Frank laboring under a tree in the far corner of the yard. One glance was all Jan needed to see that they were struggling to dig their grandfather's grave in the frozen earth.

Jan nudged Karl and tipped his head toward the young men. "They need our help, *Bror*. Let us find some picks or pry bars and help them, *ja*? This is too much for them."

Jan was surprised that digging the grave had been put off so long and that the two boys were doing it alone. *Where is Adolphe?* he wondered. *Why is he not helping to dig his father's grave?*

Jan found some additional tools hanging in Tomas' barn. He and Karl walked over to where Ernst and Frank were struggling.

"Let us help you," Jan said quietly. He noted the unshed tears in the boys' eyes and their gratitude. The two Thoresen men totaled at least five of Tomas' grandsons in height and weight.

Karl and Jan drove the picks into the frozen earth again and again, gradually loosening the icy soil. When they moved back, Ernst and Frank stepped in with shovels to dig out the hard clods of dirt.

Before long, several other men came to help, spelling Jan and Karl with the picks and Ernst and Frank with the shovels. It was past time for the service to start and the grave was not yet ready.

More men brought their fresh energy to the task. Jan and Karl, sweating in the bitter air, herded Ernst and Frank into the house. "We should not be outside in the freezing wind covered in sweat," Jan said. They climbed the steps to the house, hoping to get close to the fire and dry off quickly.

"What is this?" Adolphe Veicht frowned at his sons and at Jan. "*Herr* Thoresen. Have you been interfering between me and my sons?"

Jan did not know what Adolphe said, but he knew the man was angry with him. Not angry with *Karl*—who looked between Adolphe and Jan, puzzled—but angry with *him*.

Jan looked about for Søren and called him to his side. "*Sønn*, tell Minister Veicht in German that others stepped in to help dig the grave. We were sweating and needed to come inside out of the cold."

Søren, as carefully as his nervous thirteen-year-old voice could muster, passed the message. Veicht stared at Søren with the same disapproval he regularly leveled at Jan.

"Tell your father that I gave instructions to Ernst and Frank to dig the grave—not to him. Tell him that in the future, he should mind his own affairs."

Søren gaped. He was not about to pass such words to his father!

"Go on, boy. Tell him," Adolphe insisted.

With his eyes glued to the floor, Søren mumbled Adolphe's message. Jan had already figured out the gist of it, and had prepared himself.

"Thank you, Søren. You are a good boy," Jan said softly. "Do not let this bother you, eh? Please tell *Herr* Veicht that I apologize."

Søren reddened then took a deep breath and repeated, "My father apologizes, *Herr* Veicht."

Veicht sniffed and nodded. He turned to his sons. "Clean yourselves up and take your seats for the service." The two boys nodded mutely and turned away to do as told.

The service was a solemn, cold affair, not representative of Tomas or his ministry. The three elders—Rikkert, Klaus, and Gunnar—read Scripture passages as directed by Adolphe.

Adolphe preached the message and closed the service saying, "With my father's passing, the mantle of leadership of this congregation has fallen to me. We will mourn him, but not as the world does. Instead, we will carry on our duties as usual."

He motioned to the pallbearers to carry Tomas' casket out to the grave, but Jan could not move. Adolphe's words had dropped like a stone in Jan's heart.

He looked at the elders after Adolphe's announcement. Klaus and Gunnar nodded almost imperceptibly, but Rikkert stared at his feet, a small frown on his face.

How did this happen? Jan wondered. *Isn't the lay minister elected by the congregation?*

He looked around and saw others as stunned as he—but Tomas' burial was not the time or place to challenge this fait accompli. He glanced at Karl and was dismayed to see his brother nodding in approval.

The rest of the afternoon passed in a blur for Jan. He watched as some of the men of the church shook Adolphe's hand, publicly acknowledging his rise to the leadership of the church.

Others, like Norvald, sent troubled glances Jan's way but said nothing to disrupt the reverence of Tomas' memorial service and burial.

The wind howled about the house, but here in the kitchen after supper it was warm, even if the icy fingers of the wind did occasionally find their way through cracks around the doors or windows.

"Elli, put the boys to bed," Karl said, not looking up from the Norwegian language newspaper he was reading.

Jan looked up. Amalie was exhausted by a day of managing her work and now four children. So too, was Elli, who had taken on many of Amalie's responsibilities. She did not say that she minded, but Jan frowned.

He did not like Karl ordering Elli about. Sighing, he prayed for patience and kept his thoughts to himself.

In the Sundays following Tomas' funeral, Jan realized how deeply their church was changing under Adolphe's leadership. Rikkert, Klaus, and Gunnar now always wore their dark, somber suits to church. Their wives, too, assumed a plainer dress.

Elli commented on her friend Duna, Rikkert's wife. "She does not much like dressing for a funeral all the time," Elli mentioned on the way home. "She says Adolphe requires the elders and their wives and children to *set an example*."

"As they should, Elli," Karl said sharply. "And you should be careful with your tongue, *Søster*! It is disrespectful to call him Adolphe. He is Minister Veicht, and you should not be repeating idle gossip."

Elli's mouth fell open and her eyes reflected the hurt Karl's words inflicted. Jan pulled the team to a halt by the side of the road and jumped down. "Out," he shouted to Karl. "We will talk—right here and now."

Karl, his face flushed with anger, jumped from the wagon, too. Jan commanded, "Søren, take the reins. Drive on. We will walk from here."

Søren obeyed, but his eyes were scared. Amalie stared at her hands, saying nothing; Elli sent a silent plea to her husband to be calm.

Jan waited until the wagon passed beyond their sight, then he said to Karl, "*Bror*, this must stop. You are not to speak to my wife so."

"*You* do not correct your wife," Karl snarled, "so someone must do it! I will not have my children listen to gossip or criticism of our minister!"

"It is not *gossip* to wonder about the many changes happening in our church—happening without the consent of the people!" Jan shot back. "Who made Adolphe our minister? Eh?

"It is supposed to be decided by the church's vote! Instead, he assumed this role. And I do not like it, Karl. I do not like what our church is becoming."

Karl studied Jan, his face set in hard lines. "Do you wish me to convey your feelings to Minister Veicht?"

"I do not need you to voice my concerns to Minister Veicht," Jan snapped, his anger growing. "If I want him to know them, I will tell him myself! But know this, Karl: It is not your place to correct my wife or order her about. It must stop *now*. I will not speak to you of it again."

Jan clenched and unclenched his hands, willing himself to keep them at his side, because at this moment, they threatened to pummel his brother within an inch of his life.

Karl's eyes narrowed. "So. Elli is complaining about helping Amalie, is that it?"

"*Nei*, Karl. She has said not a word. She would not! She loves Amalie. *I am the one complaining*—not that she is helping with the *barn*, but that you are ordering her to do so as if she were a servant. This is the problem, Karl—that you treat her as an underling, *a servant*, in her own home!"

Karl looked across the fields and thought for a long moment. Jan could still see his jaw working.

"It will be good for us to get our house built," he finally ground out. "Then we can be out from under your feet."

"Do you hear yourself, Karl? It is not a good feeling, is it? To feel 'under someone's feet'?" Jan blew out his breath in exasperation. "I do not wish you to feel this way! Isn't it better to do as the Scripture says: *And be ye kind one to another, tenderhearted, forgiving one another, even as God for Christ's sake hath forgiven you?* Can't we live together in kindness and agree that you will take care of your family and I will take care of mine, eh?"

Karl looked down. "I don't think I've heard you quote a whole passage of *Skriften* before." When he looked up, his eyes were softer, less angry.

Jan's laugh was rueful. "I must study to keep ahead of my *barn*. They ask so many questions. Wait until your children are so old!"

The tension broken, Karl chuckled a little, too, and then said quietly, "It must be hard to see Kristen growing into a little woman. Sometimes she says such grownup, womanly things! And Sigrün is only two years behind her . . ."

"*Ja*. And Søren! He is already thirteen and doing a man's work. In a few years Little Karl and Arnie will be following you out to the fields. Time is flying by so quickly."

The two brothers looked at each other.

"I am sorry, Jan," Karl said quietly. "I will tell Elli I am sorry, too."

"Thank you, Karl. That would be good. Then it will be all right."

"Do you really feel that way about Adolphe?" Karl asked, his brow furrowed. "That you don't like what is happening in our church?"

Jan took a deep breath, hoping to answer Karl's question well. "I am worried, Karl. Tomas taught us from Jesus' messages, *ja*? He spoke the deeper meanings of the *Skriften*—he spoke to our hearts and caused us to grow in our love of God . . ."

Karl continued to frown. "And Adolphe?"

For a time Jan was quiet. *Lord, help me to say this right, eh?*

"I think Adolphe is too concerned with what Jesus already took care of, eh? We cannot make ourselves more holy by the way we dress, can we?" Jan answered carefully.

Jan thought a moment longer. "And Jesus said, *the tree is known by its fruit*. I confess I do not like the fruit I am seeing—how he treats his *sønns*? How he treats Heidi? Do you see how she no longer smiles? And *making* people change the way they dress? This is not good fruit."

He sighed. "I think that time will tell, Karl. Time will tell."

Karl nodded. "I confess I see a few . . . things I do not like. But Adolphe has always been so friendly to me. I . . . I am not sure."

"So we should search the *Skriften*, pray, and wait on the Lord, eh?" Jan suggested. "Pray about everything. You, me, our families, our church?"

Right there, in the ice-coated ruts of the dirt track leading to their farm, Jan and Karl prayed together. When they arrived home an hour later, chilled and famished, they were in good spirits. Amalie and Elli exchanged relieved glances.

Then Karl, with everyone gathered around said, "*Søster* Elli, I ask your forgiveness. It is not my part to speak correction to you. I should not have done so. I am sorry."

Elli cocked her head to the side a little, surprised and touched. "Brother Karl, I forgive you from my heart. Thank you."

Søren looked at the adults, relieved but a bit apprehensive. Jan hugged him around the shoulders and whispered, "Everyone makes mistakes, *Sønn*, including me. It is what we do with them that tells the world if we are Christian men, *ja*? Your *Onkel* Karl is a man of God, you can depend on it."

❧ ✳ ☙

CHAPTER 16

In April, the ground thawed and every farmer focused on plowing and planting his fields for the next harvest. Jan and Karl began the grueling task of breaking sod on Karl's land to the north.

"We need more feed corn now that we have our hogs, three steers and ten cows—and their calves too—to feed in the fall, eh?" Karl was exhilarated by the growth of their livestock, and this mild rejoicing was as exuberantly as ever Karl expressed himself.

Two months later Jan and Karl mailed their proof papers to the land office in Fremont. They laid their hands on the letters before they sent them, thanking God for his grace and favor.

Elli smiled for her husband's joy . . . and for a secret joy of her own.

Despite a drought that had begun the year before and had worsened over the winter, the Thoresens had done better than many of their neighbors, mainly because of their well-established herd of hogs. Even so, they had barely afforded the lumber and hardware to build Karl and Amalie's house. They needed a good harvest this year and prayed for rain, as did their neighbors.

On a crisp morning a few days after sending the proof papers, Karl and Jan hosted the raising of Karl and Amalie's house. Karl and Jan had laid the foundation even with Jan's house, not far across the property line, and about the same distance from the barn as Jan and Elli's house.

The Andersons brought along another family new to the neighborhood—Brian and Fiona McKennie and their little brood. Brian had claimed land to the west of the Andersons, a few miles closer to the growing town of RiverBend.

As if the ethnic mix of the community was not diverse enough, the McKennies were newly emigrated from Ireland. Fortunately, they knew some English; unfortunately, they spoke it with a heavily accented brogue. Of course they knew no German, Swedish, or Norwegian.

In spite of the language barrier, Brian and Fiona were a smiling, happy couple. Brian set to work with the men, whistling a quick, merry tune as he did. Fiona, pregnant with her third child, bustled about with the other women, easily making new acquaintances.

Brian was a ruddy redhead; his oldest child, Meg, at age six, took after him with a bright complexion and deep auburn braids that hung down her slender back. Meg's makeup could not have been more different from her mother's curling black hair and black eyes, but the McKennie's two-year-old son was the spit and image of Fiona.

The Thoresens, even reserved Karl, took to the McKennies and their cheerful ways. "I like them, Karl. These are Christian people," Jan said with appreciation. "It is good to have another Christian family in the neighborhood."

Karl nodded his agreement but pursed his lips. "Likely they are Catholic, Jan," he answered quietly.

"*Ja*, likely they are," Jan said, shrugging his shoulders. "But there is no Catholic church anywhere near. Maybe they would like to come to our church, eh?"

Karl shot his eyes to where Adolphe stood, carefully watching the work going on around him. "I would not mention it to Minister Veicht, Jan."

"So, Adolphe would not welcome the McKennies, is that it?" Jan muttered darkly. "Is that now how we treat our neighbors? Is that how we show the love of God?"

"Jan, keep your tongue," Karl shot back. "You are speaking of our minister!"

"*Ja*, and I will ask again—*how* did he get to be our minister? I would like to know! Was it ever put to a vote of the people?" Jan's voice had risen and several men had stopped working to listen.

"Shush, Jan!" Karl hissed. "People are listening!" Before he turned aside he muttered, "You should be more careful of your words lest someone hear you!"

"Maybe they should hear me, Karl! And I tell you—*Tomas* would not have stood around telling everyone what to do while never dirtying his hands."

Jan curbed his tongue after his last outburst even though his heart was still hot in his breast. He knew most of the men within earshot would not have understood *what* he'd said; nevertheless, they surely would have recognized his ire.

He glanced around. Norvald caught his eye. "*Ja*, Norvald knows what I said," Jan muttered.

His Swedish friend nodded once in his direction and then went back to work. Jan, however, as hard as he tried, could not find his peace again.

Lord, this man Adolphe has taken over our church and preaches only rules and regulations as 'holiness,' never encouragement or your love and grace, Jan fretted. *I am having a hard time accepting his leadership.*

He sighed as the Lord convicted him again regarding his temper. *All right, Lord. I put it in your hands again, ja? I will let you deal with it in your time.*

After the raising, Karl and Jan busied themselves framing the bedrooms and other interior rooms. Karl and Amalie's house was the mirror of Jan and Elli's—two stories, tall and narrow, with four small bedrooms upstairs and a bedroom, living room, kitchen, and pantry downstairs. Jan worked side-by-side with Karl to get the house to a place where Karl and his family could move in.

I am being selfish in this, I know, Lord, Jan confessed, *but still, it will be a good thing for both our families when we have our own houses, ja?*

Karl and Amalie had ordered Amalie her own cookstove and a larger stove for the living room. Money was tight, but by economizing elsewhere, Jan and Karl found what was needed. They set the stoves in place and plumbed their pipes.

Jan labored tirelessly, building the kitchen cabinets and doors in his carpentry shop out in the barn. Even with the house not quite complete, Karl was certain that they could move into the new house in another week or two.

The two Thoresen families went to bed one evening to the tumult of a much-needed spring rainstorm. Lightning flashed repeatedly and thunder shook the kitchen as they finished dinner.

"Ah, we thank you, God, for the rain!" Jan rejoiced. Thunder rumbled overhead and rain slapped the sides of the house. Then he added, speaking to Karl, "But I am glad we had your house raising three weeks ago!"

"I am glad we already did the milking, eh?" Karl chuckled. "And that all our livestock is under a good roof. I would rather sit in front of this warm fire than go out in such weather!"

Jan grinned. He was pleased to hear Karl joke about the storm. Since the raising, Jan had seen his brother happier and more relaxed.

I am glad to see my bror happy, Lord! Jan rejoiced.

Elli woke in the night, not understanding why, but she was immediately wide awake. Their bedroom, with its windows shuttered against the night's rain and cold, should have been quite dark.

She sat up and looked around, wondering if it was truly morning. Not that she saw daylight, but she could faintly make out their simple bedroom furnishings. Perhaps a full moon had risen?

Still confused, Elli climbed from their bed, went to the window, and slid it up. She loosened the shutters' latch and opened them out a crack.

Across the field a great fire blazed. Karl and Amalie's house, engulfed in flames, lit up the night sky.

Jan, Karl, and Søren battled the blaze into the morning hours. There never had been a chance of saving the house; it had been fully aflame when Elli's screams had wakened them. They battled the fire so hot cinders would not jump to any of the sheds attached to the barn.

Karl hoped they could recover the heating and cookstoves. The coals from the fire would take hours to cool, but Karl could make out the shapes of the stoves through the rubble.

"We cannot afford to buy more lumber this year, not enough anyway," Karl muttered. He hadn't needed to say it; he and Jan had worked the numbers together and had already scrimped on other necessities to buy the materials for Karl's house.

Jan put his hand on Karl's shoulder. "I am sorry, Karl."

They both were. It meant another year, at least, of Karl's family sharing Jan and Elli's house with them.

"To tell you the truth," Karl said softly, "I didn't know how Amalie would cope with the three little ones without Elli and Kristen. Sigrün is a big help. But still . . ."

Jan nodded. It was time to readjust expectations and attitudes, beginning with his own. *It is all right, Lord. It is all right*, he prayed over and over. *I trust you.*

"Lightning likely struck your house . . ." he speculated softly. Then the import of what he said dawned on him. As it did, he gasped and prayed aloud, "Lord! We are grateful! So grateful that Karl and Amalie and their *barn* were not in their house last night!"

Karl stared at Jan, struck dumb by the revelation. "My God!" He staggered and Jan caught him, lowered him to his knees.

Karl choked on his sobs, hiding his eyes behind his hands. "Thank you, my God! Ach! I thank you for your mercy!"

The two men knelt in the soot and ash together, praying and thanking God.

That evening when the children were abed, the adults gathered around the table. They were still sober—shocked and stunned from the loss of the house, but grateful for God's mercy.

"I wish to say something to us all, something important," Jan said softly. Elli, Amalie, and Karl turned their attention to him.

"I have been . . ." Jan's throat closed up on him and he had to swallow before more words would come out. "I have been . . . too mindful of what is mine and Elli's and what is yours, Karl and Amalie. I have been . . . too concerned about my own needs and wants. I—"

Again Jan's tongue seemed to stick in his mouth, and tears were close to the surface. "I want you to know, Karl and Amalie, that I am sorry I have insisted on my own way, my 'rights'. If I have made you feel unwelcome in this house, I ask your forgiveness."

Karl and Amalie were silent but their eyes were bright with moisture. Jan continued, "I ask you to consider this house as much yours as it is ours—in every way. I—"

Karl's hand touched Jan's arm. "*Bror*, we thank you. From our hearts, we thank you. But it is not necessary. The things you and I quarreled over in the past needed to be fixed, *ja*? And haven't we been better friends, better brothers for it?"

Karl swallowed, moved by emotion. "Our great God knows our needs. If it takes another year to build another house, we will patiently wait for it. While we wait . . . we are thankful for you sharing your home with us."

Elli wiped her eyes with her apron and Amalie sniffled. Jan and Karl studied each other, a new understanding blooming between them.

CHAPTER 17

At church services Sunday, word of the fire spread. All of Karl and Jan's money and all of the community's work that went into the house—gone. Every woman commiserated with Amalie; every man expressed his condolences to Karl.

Heidi Veicht had led the way with the women of the church to hug Amalie and pray with her. Then she had turned her attention to Jan and Elli. She brought Norvald with her to translate.

"Everyone is sorry for Karl and Amalie," she said softly to Jan. "But no one considers that you worked on that house as much as Karl." She put her hand on both of theirs. "The Lord will repay you for your work and love."

She smiled at Elli, that incredibly happy, gap-toothed smile, and hugged her wordlessly. Elli melted into Heidi's embrace, even letting a few needed tears fall. Just knowing someone cared meant so much.

Heidi held Elli until someone near Elli's elbow spoke. "*Großmutter.* We have the meal to prepare now. Come along."

Elli felt Heidi's arm tighten convulsively. Although Elli did not know what was said, she saw Heidi's face as she looked up into Rakel's cool gaze. Elli saw a flash, just an instant, of anger.

"I have asked you not to call me *Großmutter*, Rakel," Heidi said quietly, her eyes not leaving her daughter-in-law's face. "It is for my grandchildren to call me that."

Rakel's eyes narrowed. "Shall I repeat this conversation to your son?"

Again, Elli did not know what Rakel said, but she saw Heidi's eyes shutter, saw her become compliant. Without a word of goodbye, Heidi, her head held high, followed Rakel into the kitchen.

Elli and Jan stared at each other and Elli clasped Jan's hand. Jan shook his head.

Just then Jan saw Adolphe gesture Søren's friend, Ivan Bruntrüllsen, to his side. Ivan actually spoke better German than his father, Norvald, did—just as Jan and Karl had seen how quickly their children had picked up German.

Karl stood next to Adolphe. Adolphe talked with Karl for quite a while with Ivan translating. Jan wasn't worried. He knew Karl would not whine or complain about the loss of his house or the difficult year ahead; that was not what Thoresen men did.

Jan was utterly at peace with his brother, perhaps more than at any time in their lives. He was curious, though, about the many questions Ivan put to Karl at Adolphe's request. He was curious—and a bit uneasy.

His uneasiness did not abate until they were on their way home. "What did Minister Veicht wish of you, Karl?" he asked as nonchalantly as possible.

Karl frowned. "I have to say, he asked many questions of me. I am wondering what he is thinking." He shrugged as if to say, "Who knows?"

Jan said nothing more, but he continued to sense something in his spirit during the week. He prayed about it, giving it to God to carry until he was peaceful again.

Whatever it is, Lord, you already know about it, eh? I can trust you with it.

His uneasiness resurfaced two Sundays later after service as he was conversing with Norvald. Rikkert approached them, nodding at Norvald before saying, "Jan, Adolphe and the elders would have words with you."

Adolphe had again appropriated Ivan to translate for him. After Jan went to tell Elli, Karl, and Amalie that he would be delayed, he was gratified to see Norvald waiting for him. Jan shot him a questioning look.

"I do not like this," Norvald said under his breath. "If he wishes my son to translate for him, he will have my presence also."

"I am glad of it, friend," Jan replied, and he meant it. He felt on his guard, but could not think why.

Jan followed Minister Veicht, the three elders, and Ivan into the family's kitchen. Norvald entered right behind him.

"*Herr* Bruntrüllsen, this is a private matter with *Herr* Thoresen, if you please," Adolphe Veicht said, surprised to see Norvald following Jan.

"*Ja*, I understand; however, if my son is to be privy to this matter, I will be also." He frowned. "I will also say that I am not comfortable with you asking my son to be involved in *Herr* Thoresen's private matter without first consulting me." Norvald sent Adolphe a look that did not invite argument.

"I see," Adolphe said, considering Norvald.

Gunnar spoke up. "Norvald, we do not know what this matter is either; I apologize—I did not know Minister Veicht had not your consent for Ivan's assistance."

Adolphe glared at Gunnar who shrugged as if to say, "I am just speaking the truth."

Adolphe turned back to Norvald. "Very well. You may stay, if *Herr* Thoresen agrees." He indicated that Ivan should translate his words for Jan.

"Norvald Bruntrüllsen is a good friend of mine," Jan answered. "However, I am as unaware of this matter as he is. What is it you wish to discuss with me?"

"Why don't we all sit down?" Adolphe seated himself and indicated the other chairs in Tomas and Heidi Veicht's kitchen. When everyone had been seated, he leaned forward, steepling his fingers.

"We are most saddened to hear of the loss of your brother Karl's house, *Herr* Thoresen. A terrible thing to happen after all the time and effort put into it."

Jan nodded. "*Ja*, we thank you for your concern." Ivan diligently translated for both of them.

Adolphe, looking over his fingers, asked, "*Herr* Thoresen, you are the younger son, are you not?"

Jan was surprised. "Younger son? You mean of Karl's and my parents?"

"Yes; that is what I mean, of course," Adolphe replied, as though Jan were thick-headed.

"*Ja*, I am the younger son," Jan answered.

"Do you know that the Bible teaches that the elder son has preference over the younger?"

Jan's jaw tightened. "I was not aware this was to be a Bible lesson, *Herr* Veicht. I would prefer that you say what you wish to say to me plainly."

"Very well. It is truly sad that your brother's—your *elder* brother's— house burned. He was telling me last week that he will not be able to rebuild his house this year. That is, he happened to mention, unless he builds *a much smaller house*." Veicht placed emphasis on the words *a much smaller house*.

"Of course," Adolphe said casually, "Karl has a *growing* family and a smaller house would be a hardship. You, on the other hand, do not need the large house you have at present as much as your brother surely does."

Jan's mouth fell open and he was not the only one looking at Adolphe with open-mouthed astonishment. But Adolphe was not finished.

He smiled and spread his hands as if to be gracious. "I believe, after spending a week thinking and *praying* on this, that God has told me it would be your Christian duty to give your elder brother and his family your house. After all, you have a *small* family, not likely to grow any further—"

"Stop!"

Ivan had been studiously translating what Adolphe said from German to Swedish. Jan cut him off. He stared at Adolphe for several moments. For some reason, he no longer felt uneasy. No, he knew he was standing on firm ground.

Jan deliberately turned to Norvald, who was shaking his head. "What do you think of Adolphe's proposal, Norvald?" Jan asked. He raised his eyebrows at his friend.

Norvald looked at the other men in the room. "Did any of you know this was what Adolphe was going to say?"

The three elders slowly shook their heads.

"That is all right," Adolphe said smoothly. "My elders trust my spiritual leadership. I have prayed on this and God has spoken to me. And Biblically, because Karl is the elder son, you should give the larger house to him, and you should build a smaller, less expensive home."

Jan couldn't help it. He chuckled and followed the chuckle with a booming belly laugh. He held up his hand apologetically, but kept laughing. When Norvald slanted his eyes toward Jan, he laughed harder.

Adolphe reddened and stood up. "Your behavior is extremely disrespectful, *Herr* Thoresen," he snapped.

Jan made an effort to control himself. He looked around at the adults at the table, wiped his eyes, and then addressed himself to Adolphe.

"So, to be clear on this, Minister Veicht, you believe God has told you that because Karl is my older brother, I should give him my house, *ja*?" Ivan quickly translated Jan's words to German.

"Yes. That is what—"

Jan interrupted him. "And you believe that because my wife and I have only two children, we won't have any more? Is that also it?" Jan's tone became cold. Ivan looked uneasily from Jan to Adolphe as he translated.

"As I said, I have prayed on this—"

Jan interrupted him again. "So—just to be clear—God did not tell you that my *fru* is expecting? That our family will soon be growing larger? That is surprising, *nei*?"

Adolphe reddened further, but Jan continued speaking.

"Let me tell you what I believe, *Herr* Veicht. I believe my brother's house and my house are not your business. I believe how many children I have or my brother has is also not your concern. And, finally, I believe you have *not* heard from God on this matter. Shall I prove it to you?"

As Ivan translated, Jan stood up, went to the door, and bellowed for Karl. A few moments later, a puzzled Karl stepped into the room.

Adolphe had jumped to his feet again. "This is outrageous! You do not presume to speak to me, your minister, in such a way—"

Jan ignored him. "Karl, Minister Veicht had some interesting things to say to me just now. I will tell you, in front of Norvald Bruntrüllsen and our elders so that they may be witnesses to it."

Jan faced Adolphe. "Minister Veicht tells me *God has told him* that, because you are the older brother and I am the younger brother, because you have more children than I do and have need of a larger house, I am to give you my house and build myself a smaller one on your property."

He turned to Karl. "*Bror*, did you ask Minister Veicht to tell me this? Did you know he would ask such a thing?"

Karl's jaw hung open. He swiveled from Jan to Adolphe and back. "What? What foolishness is this? You and I have already talked this over, *ja*? We will stay in your home another year until we can rebuild our house. It is not a problem."

He growled and glared at Adolphe. "I have asked no such thing of Minister Veicht—nor would I!"

Jan slowly leaned toward Adolphe. "*Herr* Veicht, out of respect for your office, I will not take you outside and teach you not to use the Lord's name in vain.

"But listen to me and listen well: Never again interfere in affairs over which God has not given you authority. The Bible teaches that *the husband* is the head of his home, sir, not the minister.

"And as a husband and father, I am no longer the younger brother you spoke of, *Herr* Veicht. You should know this, because the Bible also teaches, *For this cause shall a man leave his father and mother, and cleave to his wife.* While I lived under my father's roof I was the younger brother, but no more.

"I am the head of my *own* family. Never again interfere with that for which God has given *me* responsibility." Jan's gaze swept over each of the elders, one at a time, scorching the men with its intensity.

Rikkert spoke up hurriedly, "Brother Thoresen, we did not know. I am sorry."

Jan nodded and then, giving Adolphe one last glare, turned on his heel and strode out the door. Karl, shaking his head, hurried after him.

"Brother, I had no idea," Karl reassured him the fourth time. "I would not air our business before others! Surely you know this?"

"*Ja*, I know, Karl," Jan answered for the fourth time. "But this explains *Herr* Veicht's questions two weeks past, eh?"

The ride home had been completely silent with the exception of Karl and Jan repeating the same things to each other. Jan and Karl rode side-by-side on the wagon bench; the women and children rode in the back.

Jan glanced behind him and, seeing the children dozing, added quietly, "We have spoken of *Herr* Veicht before, Karl. I am troubled by where his leadership is taking our church, *ja*? Is this not a good example of what troubles me? Tomas would never have presumed such a thing."

"But what would you have us do?" Karl asked, his lips pursed. They both knew their wives were listening to their conversation.

"*Nei*, I ask nothing. I am praying, especially for our elders. *Herr* Veicht could not have taken the leadership without a vote if the elders had held him to the congregation's rules, *ja*? Now we must wait for God to show us the way, because I will have no part in strife or division."

Jan realized then that Karl had not defended Adolphe as he had in the past. "You see now, do you not?"

"*Ja*," Karl answered. "*Ja*, I do."

He was silent a while. "Jan, I miss Tomas. My heart struggles to remember that *to love the Lord* is the most important thing. Instead I find myself asking *what would Adolphe think of me* or *would this displease Adolphe?* That is not right; I see that now."

Karl was startled to feel Amalie's hand on his elbow. He looked back at her and found tears in her eyes. "*Tusen takk*, my husband. I thank you for saying this so I could hear it! My heart has been starving for months."

Jan and Karl looked to Elli. She was nodding in agreement. "*Ja*. Where is the joy we used to feel in our church? Look at Heidi!" Elli glanced down guiltily. "I do not wish to gossip, Karl. I only wish to say that Heidi is . . . is not allowed to, to express joy any longer."

The four of them were silent the rest of the drive home.

CHAPTER 18

Elli knelt by the side of her and Jan's bed and thanked God for the babe growing inside her. *O Lord, you have heard my prayers and I am so grateful!*

She rose and started to dress, thinking of her day and planning her tasks. She and Jan had decided not to tell anyone of the baby until Elli's pregnancy was farther along, but Jan had told Minister Veicht and the elders—and Karl, Norvald, and Ivan had been present.

Elli smiled. *Well, so the cat is out of the bag!* She did not mind. She laid a gentle hand on her belly. *Soon you will let the world know you are coming, eh? You are not yet five months old, but soon you will grow bigger and my belly will proudly announce you are coming.*

That night Elli woke to a vague discomfort. She turned, trying to get comfortable. Instead, her back ached and would not allow her to return to sleep. She got up and walked around the room, rubbing at the ache. A moment later she gasped in pain. The cramping took her by surprise, but she recognized it for what it was.

"*Nei*, O Lord! Please keep this baby safe inside me!" she whispered. Despite her discomfort, she lay down, pulled her knees up, and remained still, hoping the cramps would ease.

Instead, she felt a warmth trickle between her legs. She shuddered and sobbed, wadding her nightgown and pressing it between her legs from where the warm flow came.

Jan woke to Elli's sobs. "What is it?"

Elli's whole body now shook, causing her teeth to chatter as she tried to answer. "The, the baby . . . the baby is coming! Too soon, too soon!"

Jan pulled on his trousers and ran upstairs to pound on Karl and Amalie's door.

Hours later, Amalie uncovered the tiny remains and showed them to Elli and Jan. Jan stared at the tiny boy baby . . . no bigger than a tea cup but perfectly formed. He lifted the tiny fingers—so perfect—and stroked them. Then he gripped Elli's hand and they wept together.

"Where is my *mamma*?" Kristen demanded. "What has happened? Everyone is sad!"

Jan looked at his two *barn*, his treasures. "Your *mamma* has lost the baby," he said softly.

"What does that mean?" Kristen insisted, her voice rising. "Where is the baby? Where has it gone?"

Jan took Kristen's hand and held it between both of his. "It means the baby was born too soon, *datter*. He was too little to live, so his little spirit has gone to Jesus."

Søren stared at the floor, but Jan could see him struggling with tears. Jan pulled Kristen onto his lap and reached out an arm to Søren. As he had wept with Elli, he now wept with his children.

Late that day Jan and Elli buried the baby on the gentle, east-facing slope near their apple trees. "Tomorrow the sun will rise and warm this ground," Jan murmured. "It is such a pretty place! I will place a marker here for this little *sønn* of ours and we will see him again in heaven."

Through the late summer months Elli cried her broken heart in Jan's arms. During the day she did her duties and cared for Søren and Kristen.

But at night, she wept.

For weeks this had gone on. Until last night. Last night as she had cried in Jan's arms, he had spoken words to her, words she did not like to hear but . . .

Elli's tears stained the quilt that was spread across their bed. *Lord, you have given us two beautiful children, children any mother or father would be proud to have.*

She wiped her eyes and struggled on. *I thank you for them, Lord. I have desired more children and I have asked you these eleven years to give us more babies, but they have not come, ja? Now I must surrender my desire to you, once and for all.*

I know Jan and I are not too old, but Jan has said it best. I am wasting my life and joy pining over what I do not have, when I have so much! Now, for good, I must lay this desire of mine on your altar. If it dies, I will be content in your love. If, someday, you surprise us with another child, I will be just as content in your love.

She rested her forehead on the bed and waited, just waited. *Do you have something to say to me, Lord?*

Her heart picked up as she lingered, hoping to hear God speaking to her. Instead, a Scripture passage came to her.

For I was an hungred, and ye gave me meat:
I was thirsty, and ye gave me drink:
I was a stranger, and ye took me in:
Naked, and ye clothed me:
I was sick, and ye visited me:
I was in prison, and ye came unto me.

She covered her eyes with her hands, shutting out the light. *O Lord,* she breathed, *I am waiting for you to speak to me!* Another verse intruded on her thoughts.

Verily I say unto you, Inasmuch as ye have done it
unto one of the least of these my brethren,
ye have done it unto me.

Elli groaned. *Yes, Lord. I know this. But I am waiting for you to speak to me!*

When nothing but silence greeted her, she finally rubbed her face and stood up. "Oh, *Fader*," she prayed aloud. "I give my babies to you. The babies I have longed to hold. The little *sønn* who is with you already. I trust you, Lord. I am ready to move on now."

The Scriptures she had remembered earlier again resounded in her mind.

For I was an hungred, and ye gave me meat:
I was thirsty, and ye gave me drink!

Elli stopped short. Was *this* God speaking to her?

She thought for a long while; she pondered the number of families she knew who had struggled in the past year in some way. Could she do more to help them?

All right, Lord, she breathed. *I am listening . . .*

CHAPTER 19

1872

A year had passed since she lost the baby. Elli marked the anniversary in her heart, but she turned steadfastly from self-pity. She no longer allowed it a place in her life. It had been hard to do so at first, but she had persevered.

How she had grown in her walk with the Lord since that day, the day God had spoken so clearly to her!

Even with Amalie pregnant again, Elli no longer felt the sting of her own empty womb. Over the past year she had made it her undertaking to give herself to those in need, often nursing sick families or providing hot meals for them. *I have found comfort in comforting others*, she acknowledged.

Their whole farming community, indeed their state and bordering states, were struggling with drought. Two growing seasons without enough rain had left them with meager crops. Many families were barely getting by.

Tomorrow I must do something for the Beckers, Elli planned on the way home from the church meeting. *Talbert and Maria must be struggling to care for their family right now!*

The Beckers, another German family in the church, lived a few miles north and east of them. According to a nearer neighbor, all the Beckers except Talbert—*Herr* Becker—were sick.

"Maria had a baby only a few months back and now she is down with fever. Talbert is caring for her, the baby, and their other children," the neighbor said, clearly concerned. "I did his chores yesterday and the day before and my wife has brought them several meals."

Talbert must be pulling his hair out by the roots. Elli shook her head. When a wife was ill in bed, many a husband was at his wit's end to feed and care for the sick wife and children. He must still manage his own chores, many which could not be neglected or put off.

The next morning, thinking to provide the sick family with a few nourishing meals, Elli doubled her bread making. While the loaves were rising, she cut onions and the butt of a leftover roast into small pieces and set them to braise in hot, melted fat.

While the onions and chunks of roast were sizzling, she scrubbed and cut up carrots, potatoes, cabbage, and turnips. She slowly added flour, water, and the drippings from the leftover roast to the meat and onions, stirring until the bubbling mess thickened.

Elli set a large pot on the stove and poured the meat, onions, and gravy into it. Then she added the chopped vegetables, and a jar of canned mixed vegetables—corn, lima beans, and chopped winter squash. She seasoned the stew with pepper, fresh sage, and rosemary and set it to simmer on a back burner.

In another pot she boiled a chicken for broth. *You're a tough old bird,* she laughed to herself. *But your meat will make a small chicken pie for us and your broth will feel good on sore throats, eh?*

She took inventory of her preparations: *Nourishing broth, my good stew, several loaves of fresh bread, a dish of butter, some cheese, and dried herbs for tea. That should keep them a day or so,* she deliberated. Then, considering the number of Becker children, she began rolling out crust for pies.

Elli tripped down the cellar steps and hauled up a basket of apples. *Two pies for them, two for us,* she hummed.

Later, as she pulled the browned and bubbling pies from the oven, Elli saw Søren striding past the house on his way to the barn. She leaned out the back door and called to him. When he came near she asked, "Will you harness the bays for me in an hour? I want to take a hot meal to the Becker family."

It will be an hour's drive to take the food to them, she figured as she began packing the items she would take. *I will stay only an hour so that I am back in plenty of time for supper.*

The faint track to the Beckers' farm was dry and Elli had no difficulty finding her way. The wagon sped along at a good clip until she pulled into the yard fronting the family's small house.

Elli looked around and, frowning, recognized that the Beckers were in a worse way than she had thought. The rundown appearance of their house and barn bore stark testimony that they were struggling just to survive during these years of drought.

Elli knocked and, after several minutes, Talbert opened the door to her.

"Ach, you poor dears," she commiserated as she stepped inside.

The few windows of the house were cloaked. The house was unbearably stuffy and Elli could scarcely see in the dim light.

"Please don't open the curtains, Elli," Talbert begged in German. He gestured to the windows and Elli understood. "Maria has a bad headache and the light pains her so."

Although she did not grasp the meaning of all his words Elli nodded. "I brought some hot food," she answered him.

Coughing into his hand, he nodded his thanks and then disappeared into the back of the house. Elli had observed how poorly he looked himself.

It took Elli two trips from the wagon to the house to bring in the meals she had brought with her. She made her way to the little kitchen on her first trip and paused in shock.

Every dish in the house must be dirty, she realized in dismay. Before she could unpack the food and serve a meal, she would need to clean the kitchen.

She opened the back door for light, built up the fire, put the broth and clean water on to heat, and spent half an hour washing and tidying up. As she worked she heard children coughing and fussing weakly from a nearby bedroom.

When she finished cleaning the kitchen, Elli poured warm broth into mugs, set them and a lighted candle on a tray, and made her way toward the crying. She found four of the Becker children in a single bedroom.

The stench of urine and feces struck her.

Dear Lord! The children are not making it out of the room, let alone out of the house to use the necessary! She struggled to swallow the gorge that rose in her throat.

When she had mastered her reaction and set her mind to ignore the filth for the time being, Elli spooned broth into the children's mouths. They cried piteously as the broth crossed their raw throats and she had to cajole them to take more.

The children coughed and complained of sore throats; they were also feverish and listless. Elli returned to the kitchen and filled the mugs with tepid water. It took her a long while to get the water down their raw and swollen little throats.

Elli realized she had already been at the Beckers' far longer than an hour. *I will be late getting home,* she conceded, *and it cannot be helped. I haven't even seen Maria yet. And, dear God, the children's room!*

She would have to do something about the children before she left but, with increasing concern, she pushed that thought aside. She finally made it to the other bedroom and found Maria lying in the bed, her youngest beside her clutched in the crook of her arm.

Talbert sat in a straight-backed chair next to the bed, head bowed. Elli realized Talbert was sleeping sitting up, holding Maria's hand.

"Maria," Elli called softly. "Maria!"

The woman slowly opened her eyes. "Elli?" Her eyes were unfocused, glazed in fever.

"*Ja*, Elli," she answered keeping her voice low. But Maria's eyes had closed in sleep again.

Elli reached to take the baby from Maria, thinking, *This one will likely need a clean diaper!*

She lifted the tiny bundle from Maria's arm and took it into the kitchen. Once in the light, she peeled back the baby's blanket.

The chubby little face was gray and still.

"No," Elli moaned, her knees buckling. "Oh, no, no, no!" She held her hand to her mouth but could not stifle her sobs. "Oh, dear Lord! What am I going to do?"

She covered the baby again and laid him on a chair in the living room. She sat trembling near the still little bundle. *O Father God! How am I going to tell Talbert and Maria!* Even as she quelled her grief, the possibility began to dawn on Elli that the Beckers were suffering from something much worse than a cold or flu.

At a faint groan from Maria, Elli jumped up. She twisted her hands in her apron for a moment. She heard Maria's voice again, this time weakly calling, "*Wasser! Bitte*, Elli!"

Elli steeled herself and placed a mug of broth and one of water on the tray. She carried it into the bedroom and found Talbert flung across the other side of the bed, sleeping soundly. Elli took the chair he'd been sitting in and sat down.

"Here," she murmured, spooning water into Maria's mouth. "All of it, please. *Alles, ja?* After the water, she fed Maria the broth. Talbert did not stir.

"*Meine kinder?*" Maria begged. Elli could tell the woman's mind was fogged with fever and pain, but still she was concerned for her children.

"*Ja, gut*," Elli answered, not looking at her. She returned to the kitchen and put a large pot of water on the stove to brew the herb tea. The fire was nearly out, so she built it up again, using the last lump of coal in the box—and a small one at that.

I lied to Maria, Elli groaned. *How will I ever be able to tell her the truth?*

She pushed down her mounting anxiety and made the rounds again with honeyed tea for the children and Maria. Talbert had not moved.

Long after dark she heard an ox-drawn wagon pull into the Beckers' yard. She knew it had to be Jan. When she had not returned by dusk he would have become worried and come looking for her.

She stood in the doorway and spoke across the yard. "Please come no closer, Jan! Do not come closer."

He jumped from the wagon and faced her from several yards. "What is it, Elli?" She could see the worry on his face.

"I don't know . . . but it is bad. All of them are sick, even Talbert." A sob escaped from her throat. "Oh, Jan! Their baby died."

"Father in heaven!" Jan ran both of his hands through his hair, a gesture of frustration so familiar to Elli.

"Jan." Elli swallowed hard. "I can't take care of all of them by myself."

"What should I do? Tell me, Elli. I will do it."

"Fetch Fraulein Engel, I think," Elli replied.

Fraulein Engel was the spinster sister of the farmer who raised bees, both members of the German church. As the neighborhood had no resident doctor, Adeline Engel was often called upon to nurse the sick—and she readily came. The near-fifty-year-old woman had no children of her own to care for, only her unmarried brother.

Jan looked away a moment. "*Ja*, I will go for her." He glanced back and fixed her with a fierce look. "Then you must come home!"

Elli knew her husband was terrified for her.

Jan took the team of bays; still it was midnight before he arrived back with Fraulein Engel. She had packed a sparse bag for herself and stuffed another with remedies and notions based on what Jan had been able to tell her.

Elli was relieved to see her and, even more so, that Fraulein Engel immediately took charge. The spinster allowed Jan to help her down and carry her bags partway to the house. As they approached the door she stopped. "*Danke, Herr* Thoresen," she said kindly.

She pointed Jan back to the wagon with a firmness that broached no question. Casting a look over his shoulder at Elli, Jan retreated to his wagon.

Fraulein Engel stepped inside. Elli showed her the baby first. The woman clucked her tongue sadly and then, as she unwrapped the still infant, became quiet. She pointed to the thick rash on the baby's chest. Elli wasn't sure what to make of it.

Fraulein Engel lit a lamp and carried it into the first bedroom to examine the other children. At the light the children fussed and one of them cried piteously for them to turn it off. Fraulein Engel handed Elli the lamp and gestured for her to keep the light over the children.

The woman wrinkled her nose at the smells in the room and then checked each child, feeling their foreheads, looking at their chests, examining their arms and legs.

While Elli held the lamp, Fraulein Engel pointed to a number of scratched and reddened bites. She lifted one of the children to sitting and scrutinized the bedding. She found and squished between her fingers several tiny black fleas.

The children showed unmistakable signs of flea bites, and their bedding and clothing were more than likely infested with them.

I should have seen! Elli chided herself, *But I was more concerned with the children's coughs and fevers.*

When Fraulein Engel finished with the children she examined Maria and Talbert. Maria moaned and asked for water. Talbert remained asleep. Fraulein Engel was quiet when she and Elli returned to the kitchen.

"*Was ist?*" What is it? Elli demanded.

Fraulein Engel shook her head, clearly puzzled and unsure. Finally, she muttered, "*Typhus?*"

Elli froze. Typhus! Here in Nebraska?

CHAPTER 20

Jan could not bear waiting in the dark and doing nothing. He lit a lantern, circled the house, and found Talbert's axe lying in the dirt next to a pitifully small pile of wood for kindling. He frowned as he picked up the axe.

Within a few minutes he had chopped an armful of kindling and laid it next to the back door. Then he went in search of the Beckers' coal bin. It was nearly empty.

It is still cold at night and this family is in real need, Jan realized. He filled a bucket with what was left of the coal and set it on the back stoop next to the kindling. Later he would make a trip home to bring back more wood and coal.

He let himself into Talbert's barn to check on their animals. In the lamplight their lone cow lowed mournfully, begging to be milked; their mule stamped in agitation.

Likely these animals have not been cared for this day, Jan surmised. He filled a pail with water for the mule and looked for grain to feed him. As he neared the grain bin, holding the lamp before himself, the scurrying of mice caught his attention.

They do not have a mouser? Jan wondered. *Ach! Not good for the grain or for healthy living.*

Jan held the lantern aloft, opened the grain bin, and saw droppings. Mice had indeed been in the grain. He searched for and spied nesting material behind the bin. Had the Beckers been eating from this bin as well as feeding their animals? Jan began to get a very bad feeling.

Inside, the two women retreated to the kitchen. There they scrubbed their hands and forearms with strong soap and hot water. Since they had both been handling the children, Fraulein Engel inspected Elli carefully for fleas and then Elli did the same for Fraulein Engel.

They bound clean kerchiefs about their heads, taking care to tuck in all of their hair. Then they placed kerchiefs over their noses and mouths, tying them behind their heads.

Elli found the kindling and bucket of coal on the back step and built up a good fire to heat more water. When the water was boiling, they set to work cleaning the children and their bedroom.

To say it was difficult work would be an understatement.

Elli and Fraulein Engel stripped the children and their beds. In a few minutes the women had the four sick, naked children huddled under a thin cover in the corner of the kitchen next to the stove. Then they scrubbed the bedroom's bed, floor, and walls. Elli helped Fraulein Engel to remake the bed with the few clean bed linens they could find.

"Be careful," Fraulein Engel admonished in German. She pantomimed to Elli her concern over the soiled clothing and linens. Through Fraulein Engel's gestures, Elli understood that all the clothing and bedding were to be boiled.

"*Ja*," was Elli's sober answer. She bundled the filthy things in a soiled sheet and took them out the back door, making a pile several yards from the house. Jan watched her from the barn. He noted Elli's covered head, mouth, and nose with concern.

"What does she say?" Jan asked.

Elli hesitated. It was now the middle of the night. She was exhausted and needed to re-wash her hands and arms in strong soap as soon as possible. There was still much to be done in the house. She did not have the energy to deal with Jan's reaction.

Elli pulled down the kerchief covering her mouth. "She . . . *thinks* it could be some form of typhus, but I do not think she is certain because of how uncommon it is in these parts," she answered softly. "But, in fact, the children are covered in flea bites."

Jan stared across the distance between them. When he did not say anything, Elli turned toward the house.

"*Elli.*" Jan spoke her name roughly. She turned back. They stared at each other across the yard until Elli, shaking her head, walked back to the house.

She removed a large tin tub from a nail outside the door on her way in. She placed the tub on the kitchen floor near the stove and began to pour hot water into it. When the bath was ready, she and Fraulein Engel bathed the children, one by one, drying them and dressing them in clean nightclothes.

The children moaned and cried as they bathed them. Elli and Fraulein Engel scrubbed every inch of the sick little bodies with hot water and lye soap and afterward doused them with flea powder. Once they had cleaned a child, doused him with powder, and put him into fresh night clothes, Elli placed him on the other side of the stove where he would still remain warm.

When all four children were bathed, they tucked them into the clean bed.

The night flew by in a blur of work and patient care for Elli and Fraulein Engel. Elli had built a fire in the yard and boiled all the soiled clothing and bedding. For hours she had toiled, scrubbing, rinsing, and hanging sodden quilts and clothes on a fence to slowly dry, while Fraulein Engel tended Talbert and Maria.

Fraulein Engel lectured Elli on eradicating the fleas and "flea dirt" (flea droppings). She emphasized taking care not to inadvertently breathe the droppings in—hence the kerchiefs over their mouths and noses.

It was the *flea droppings* that carried the sickness, the older woman pointed out. The scarcely visible droppings could carry the infection inside when breathed in or carry the infection into the bloodstream when flea bites were scratched raw.

Elli understood the gist of Fraulein Engel's warnings from her gestures—and from the fear lurking in the woman's eyes. They took care to clean themselves every time they touched a patient.

Jan went home and returned in the morning with coal, kindling, clean bedding, strong soap, and hot food prepared by Amalie. He also brought a burlap sack that struggled and yowled in the wagon bed.

Elli stepped out the front door. She hugged herself in the chill morning air and spoke to him across the yard. "Talbert is very sick now. Maria may be improving a little." She looked down. "Fraulein Engel is unsure about the children. The oldest seems a little better but the other three . . ."

Jan licked his lips. "I sent Søren to the Andersons and Bruntrüllsens. They will pass the word to the church to pray. We are all praying."

What he yearned to say—to shout and insist—was, *Elli! Just come home before you become ill! Please!* Yet he knew he could not ask it of her.

Elli stared at the ground. "Will you bury the baby?"

The horror of the request was not lost on Jan. "*Ja*, I will. Give me an hour." He sighed, grabbed the burlap bag, and went inside the Beckers' barn.

He untied the neck of the sack and released a scrappy orange tom cat Kristen had named Ginger. The cat shot across the barn, his tail standing straight up.

"*Ja*, you'll have all you want here," Jan murmured. He knew that to eradicate the fleas, one must eradicate the mice.

He milked the cow and left the pail on the back step, knocking to alert Elli of its presence. He pumped water into the trough and turned the cow and the mule out into the small pasture.

Then he sought out Talbert's shovel and pick and trudged toward a lone tree to dig a tiny grave beneath its branches.

Elli and Fraulein Engel cared for the Beckers for three weeks. Fraulein Engel's brother brought more flea powder and other remedies his sister requested. Jan came daily, as did other neighbors, to do Talbert's chores and bring food and clean clothing.

No one in the community could believe it was typhus and Fraulein Engel herself was uncertain. Jan attested to the mice in the grain bin and the fleas Fraulein Engel had uncovered in the house. It just didn't make sense this far north, but the evidence was there, and the community took precautions accordingly.

Then in the last week, as though to prove Fraulein Engel's diagnosis, Jan and Henrik buried the Beckers' three younger children . . . followed by Talbert. Only Maria and her oldest child, a boy of about eight years, seemed to be on the mend.

Elli called to Jan from the Beckers' front door. "Fraulein Engel says I am to go home tomorrow. She can manage without me now."

She saw the hunger kindle in Jan's eyes and knew her own eyes radiated her need for him. *Oh, Jan! How I long to feel your arms around me!* her heart cried.

"Before I can leave, I must bathe and wash my hair. Fraulein Engel will check me to be certain. It will have to be back there in the yard." Elli waved in the direction of the fire pit on the other side of the house where the infested bedding and clothing had been boiled. "Then I must put on all clean things."

Jan nodded. "I will bring everything you need. Amalie will help me. I will bring our tub, too, and build a fire to heat the water and keep you warm."

He paused and chewed his lower lip. "Are you truly coming home, Elli?" Elli saw his pain and longing even as he desperately tried to mask it. "It has felt like . . . such a long time without you."

"*Ja,* my husband. I am truly coming home." It was all she could muster without breaking apart.

Karl came with Jan in the morning. Together they built up a large fire and set the Thoresens' hip bath near it. Karl set a grill over the fire and began to heat water. Jan spread a folded sheet on the ground. On it he laid towels, a washcloth, soap, and the clean clothes Amalie had selected for Elli.

When Elli's bath was ready, Karl retired to the other side of the house. Jan intended to stay and help Elli, but Fraulein Engel would not allow him. With gestures and many stern, unintelligible words, she indicated that Jan should still stay clear.

For Elli, the bath and precautionary flea powder were rites almost spiritual in nature. Fraulein Engel scrubbed every square inch of her body and, while Elli huddled in the tub, carefully combed through her clean hair. If Fraulein Engel had found any evidence of fleas at all, she would not have permitted Elli to leave.

Elli emerged from the now cool water and was pronounced clean.

As Elli dressed, Fraulein Engel dumped Elli's soiled clothing into the large cauldron over the fire, grated soap into the pot, and stirred the bubbling mass with a wooden paddle.

Elli was ready to leave; she knew Jan and Karl were waiting for her on the other side of the house. She and Fraulein Engel stared at each other across the sheet—across a divide they now dared not to cross.

They had battled death together and had prayed side-by-side on their knees over dying children, yet they now could not embrace. Tears sprang to Elli's eyes and then to Fraulein Engel's.

"*Tusen Takk*," Elli choked out, her face awash in tears. *A thousand thanks.*

Fraulein Engel nodded and murmured, "*Geh mit Gott, meine Tochter.*" *Go with God, my daughter.*

Elli covered a sob with her hand and hurried away.

Fraulein Engel peeled off her kerchief, allowing her head and hair to breathe. She stood motionless for a moment before swiping away the unshed tears. The strain of the past three weeks had exhausted her—but she had grown to love Elli, and to have her safely returned to her family was a great relief.

She unbraided her own hair, picked up the comb she had used on Elli, and began to pull it through, from scalp to end, looking closely at it after each pass.

CHAPTER 21

Near dusk a week later, Kristen gathered up the tablecloth from dinner and carried it out onto the kitchen porch to shake out the crumbs.

A demanding *meow* greeted her.

"Ginger! You naughty boy. You were supposed to stay at the Beckers' and kill all those nasty mice," Kristen scolded.

Ginger wound his way between her legs, begging and purring. The Thoresen barn cats, like most farm cats, were hardly domesticated. They lived in or near the barn and its sheds and were accustomed to having people about, but they generally did not allow themselves to be picked up.

The cats haunted the milking shed during the morning and evening milkings. They would open their mouths, and the men would squirt milk into them, making a game of it. Kristen, who loved all animals, often set out dishes of cream for the cats. Only then would they allow her to pet them.

Her braids swinging loose about her shoulders, Kristen bent down to rub the top of Ginger's head. Ginger meowed and swatted her hand.

"Oh, all right. I'll get you some cream. I'll bet that's why you came home, eh?"

Kristen went inside, spread the cloth on the table, and returned with a saucer filled with cream. As Ginger lapped the thick cream, Kristen squatted next to him and gave him a good scratching around his ears and along his spine.

The cat arched his back and stretched, purring and pushing against her fingers, and he leaned, replete, on her legs, to enjoy her affectionate rubbing.

Then, with another swish of his tail against her legs, he leapt away and set off toward the barn.

"Amalie," Karl's voice carried concern. "I have found a flea in our bed." He had just cleaned up after morning chores and come downstairs for breakfast. The family was gathered at the table for the meal. He held the offending insect between his fingers.

Amalie paled. "No! Let me see." She examined the squished bug and breathed, "*Ja*, it is a flea."

Elli and Jan looked at each other. "I know I didn't bring any home with me. Fraulein Engel scrubbed me raw out in the yard before I left." Nevertheless, Elli's heart began to race.

After a hasty meal no one could enjoy, Elli took Kristen into her and Jan's bedroom while Amalie kept Sigrün and her little boys in the kitchen. One-by-one, Amalie and Sigrün stripped and examined the boys for flea bites. Jan, Karl, and Søren were in the living room checking themselves.

Elli found five small red bites on Kristen's legs. She stared at her daughter. "You did not feel them? They didn't itch?"

"I did not notice them, Mamma," Kristen replied. Her eyes were wide. Yet clearly she *had* scratched them. The red streaks across the bites attested to it.

Elli reported her findings to Amalie. Amalie swallowed and stared at her daughter: Sigrün and Kristen shared a bed.

She and Elli sent the boys into the living room and had Sigrün take off her clothes. The women did not find any telling bites. Until. Until Sigrün absent-mindedly scratched her neck, near her hairline.

Elli saw her scratching and pulled her fingers away. "Amalie, look here." They stared at two red spots, one starting to form a welt from the scratching.

"Don't scratch it, Sigrün," Elli breathed. Her heart was pounding. *Scratching spreads the sickness!*

The rest of the day was spent in a furor of cleaning. They found evidence of fleas only in the girls' and Karl and Amalie's room, which was next to the girls' room. Nevertheless, the women and girls stripped every bed in the house and washed all the bedding in boiling water. They swept and dusted every room and shook out and inspected all their clothing.

Jan and Karl, armed with strong soap and flea powder, took the boys to the barn to bathe them and wash their hair. Jan and Karl, the sights and smells of death by typhus too recently in their nostrils, scrubbed the scalps of the young ones until they howled.

The women and girls bathed in the kitchen. Elli showed Amalie how Fraulein Engel washed her hair and then combed it and checked for fleas or their larvae. Every piece of clean clothing donned after bathing was scrupulously examined first.

Now that she had seen the bites on her legs, Kristen was overwhelmed with the urge to scratch them. Elli stuck small plasters over Kristen and Sigrün's bites to discourage them from scratching.

After the day's regular chores were done, the family came together, exhausted, for a late supper. When the meal was over, the adults left Kristen and Sigrün to clean up and sent Søren and the younger boys upstairs while they adjourned to the living room to talk privately.

"I found bites on my legs," Karl confessed to an already anxious Amalie.

As Elli's eyes asked the question of her husband, Jan shook his head. "*Nei*. I found no bites on myself nor did we find any on Søren or the little boys."

Three of them had bites: Karl, Kristen, and Sigrün.

Jan paused and then added quietly. "Today we also found Ginger in the barn."

"*Ginger!*" Amalie's voice was alarmed.

"He must have found his way home from the Beckers'. When we saw him today he was sick and could hardly move. We put him down and buried him quickly. I am afraid we must do the same with all the cats." Jan's voice was grim.

"I don't understand!" Amalie cried. "Ach! Perhaps the fleas we found are just normal fleas, eh? And why should we think all the cats are sick? Perhaps Ginger just ate something that made him sick?"

Elli shook her head, worry creasing her brow. "Maybe so, maybe so, eh? But Maria Becker told Fraulein Engel that a traveler came by about six weeks ago asking for shelter. They fed him and he slept three nights in the barn before moving on."

Elli's voice shook. "Fraulein Engel questioned Maria about the man. She said the man had a dog with him—a sick dog. Maria remembered that the stranger said he and his dog had traveled the world together. He spent six months working on a steamer before landing in Houston and making his way north on the trains to see the plains and the mountains of America.

"The man loved his dog very much. But before the man went on his way, his dog died," she finished.

They were still as they mulled Elli's information. Then Amalie whispered, "The dog. The dog had fleas. And the fleas carried the sickness?"

Jan looked at each of them in turn. "Some of the dog's infected fleas may have gotten on the mice in the Beckers' barn," he muttered. "I found evidence of mice in the Beckers' grain bin. That is why I took Ginger to the Beckers'—to rid the barn of the mice."

"And—and then she came home last week . . . sick . . . and with fleas?"

Jan nodded, his face grave. "You know Kristen has a way with our barn cats."

Elli trembled and Jan wrapped his arms around her.

Sigrün knocked on her parents' door in the middle of the night. Amalie groaned and rolled from the bed. She was five months gone in another pregnancy, already heavy and unwieldy, but used to being wakened in the night by one child or another.

She struggled to her feet and opened the door. "*Ja*, Sigrün? What is it?"

"*Mamma*, Kristen is crying. Should I wake *Tante* Elli?"

"*Nei, nei.* I will be right there." Amalie threw on a wrapper and padded to the girls' room. She bent over Kristen's bed and felt her forehead.

"Burning up!" Amalie exclaimed, backing away.

Kristen stirred. "My head hurts," she moaned.

"Go. Fetch your *Tante* Elli," Amalie commanded Sigrün. "And bring a bowl of cold water and a clean cloth." Sigrün left the room immediately.

A few moments later, Elli rushed up the stairs. Jan was not far behind her. By then Amalie had lit a candle but stood a few feet from Kristen's bed. Elli could feel the heat radiating from Kristen's body before she touched her forehead.

"Oh, dear Lord! *Nei!*"

Jan turned to Søren who was standing in the doorway behind him. "Søren, hitch the bays and fetch Fraulein Engel. Bring her as quickly as you can, *Sønn.*"

Søren looked into his father's eyes. Jan saw his fear and gripped his shoulders tightly. "We will trust God, eh? We will not give into fear."

Søren nodded and turned away.

Søren returned with Fraulein Engel two hours later.

Being age fourteen and having grown up in such a diverse community, Søren was now as comfortable in German, Swedish, and English as he was in his native tongue. So, during their drive to the Thoresen farm, Fraulein Engel had asked Søren many questions and, by the time they arrived, she was well acquainted with the situation.

When the good woman stepped into the kitchen, she found Little Karl, Arnie, and Kjell at the table eating bread and milk. Excited to see a stranger, Kjell banged his cup on the table, dashing milk on himself, the table, and the floor. Little Karl and Arnie stared at Fraulein Engel with solemn eyes.

"Sigrün's sick," Arnie pronounced, pointing. Their sister was huddled, shivering, in a chair near the stove.

Fraulein Engel placed her hand on Sigrün's cheek and then forehead.

"Søren," she directed, "I must get this one to bed also. Please have your father and uncle come downstairs."

She was unpacking her medicines when Jan and Karl tromped down the stairs into the kitchen. Karl reached for Sigrün but Fraulein Engel waylaid him.

"You have flea bites, *ja*?"

Karl understood her. "*Ja*," he replied slowly.

"How do you feel?" She touched his forehead.

"I feel fine," Karl replied. He pulled back from Fraulein Engel's hand, his manner a trifle testy.

"*Gut*," she answered, but her eyes were worried. Then she began issuing orders that Søren translated.

"The girls' room is now a sick room. Only *Frau* Elli and I will enter the room." Karl and Jan looked at each other uneasily.

She demonstrated to Karl how to place a kerchief over his face, covering his nose and mouth, which he did. "*Herr* Thoresen," pointing at Karl, "You will please to take your daughter upstairs and let *Frau* Elli put her to bed, *ja*? But then you and your good wife will come down to see me."

Karl did not answer but he carefully scooped Sigrün into his arms.

"*Pappa!*" Sigrün whimpered. "You look funny!" Her head lolled against his chest. "My head hurts, *Pappa*."

A few minutes later a worried Amalie returned with Karl and greeted Fraulein Engel. Fraulein Engel took Amalie's hand in her own.

"Dear sister, I am sorry your child is ill. I am going upstairs to look at her, *ja*? You will stay here in the kitchen with the *kinder*. I will come back soon." She pointed to the sink. "All of you please wash your hands with hot water and plenty of soap while I am gone."

Amalie tried to protest, but Fraulein Engel shook her head and put a gentle hand on Amalie's swollen belly. "*Nein*. Wash your hands and stay here. I will be back shortly."

Amalie, Karl, Jan, and Søren looked at each other but no one spoke. Amalie washed her hands and arms and turned to clean up the table and her little boys. The men and Søren followed her example and washed up.

Søren shifted from foot to foot. "I should start the milking, *ja*, *Pappa*?"

Jan shook his head. "We will need you when Fraulein Engel comes down."

Fraulein Engel kept her word and returned in a few minutes. "Please, shall we sit down?"

The adults found places at the table. Karl started to pull Kjell onto his lap, but Fraulein Engel put a restraining hand on his arm.

"Kristen and Sigrün have the fever the Beckers had." Her words were uttered softly. "They were bitten by fleas as you were, *Herr* Thoresen. Please do not touch the little ones, eh?"

Amalie made a strangled noise. "Karl is sick?"

"Not yet," Fraulein Engel responded. "But he may be soon." She leveled an earnest look at Amalie and Karl. "We do not want these little ones to sicken, do we? Or you, *Frau* Amalie. You have little ones to care for and a baby coming."

She folded her hands on the table and spoke calmly. "*Frau* Amalie, I wish you to remove yourself from this house and take your *kinder* with you."

Amalie was already shaking her head in protest. "*Nei, nei.* I will not leave my daughter or husband!"

Fraulein Engel looked at Jan. "You and Søren must go too. It is not too cold at night yet. Can you make a place in the barn for all of you?"

Jan ignored her question. "What about Elli? What about Kristen?"

"*Frau* Elli and I nursed all the Beckers. You know what we will need. You can help us as you did then. Karl can as well. But we cannot allow anyone else to become sick, can we?"

"But Kristen and Sigrün? Will they be all right?"

Fraulein Engel studied her folded hands. "God willing."

Jan and Karl stared at each other. Finally, Jan spoke. "We should send Amalie and the children to the soddy. It will be warmer. Karl, we can take the kitchen stove we rescued when your house burned and put it in there."

Amalie glared at her brother-in-law with a rage he had rarely seen in her. Karl pulled her to him. "Please do not be angry with Jan, my love. Please do as we say, *ja*? I do not want you . . . or our sons to become ill."

He did not need to say more. The death of four of the Beckers' *barn* was all too real to Amalie. She crumpled against Karl sobbing.

Karl returned that afternoon from taking Amalie, the children, and a wagonload of bedding and supplies to the soddy. Jan and Søren cleared out Jan's carpentry shop and made up beds for themselves. Karl, Fraulein Engel decided, could continue sleeping in his and Amalie's bed. But he was no longer to have direct contact with those outside the house.

The three men said little as they went about their chores as usual. Karl walked to the soddy each day to bring fresh milk and speak to Amalie.

"*Pappa!*" Little Karl, Arnie, and Kjell rushed toward him when they saw him coming, but Amalie held them back, as instructed.

Three days later Karl complained of an unrelenting headache and began coughing. Fraulein Engel sent him to bed. The next morning she called Jan and Søren.

"Your brother is very ill, *Herr* Thoresen."

Jan stared at this kindhearted woman, trying to understand what her eyes were telling him. "We will pray," he replied with firmness.

"*Ja,*" was her answer.

She reported that Sigrün and Kristen were holding their own. She did not answer Jan when he asked if they were improving.

That morning it was Jan who walked to the soddy with the fresh milk. Amalie stared at Jan when she saw that he, not Karl had come.

"He is sick then?" Amalie whispered.

Jan turned his face away but nodded.

"And Sigrün? Kristen? Are they any better?"

"They are no worse," was all Jan could tell her.

CHAPTER 22

The Thoresen's neighbors received word of the sickness through Fraulein Engel's brother, who spread the news to the German church. Many in their church had been the recipient of Elli's care and compassion in the past year. Yet, as much as their friends wished to help them, they kept a strict distance from the Thoresen house and barn. The way in which the sickness—whatever it was—had decimated the Becker family was much too fresh in their minds.

Henrik and Abigael coordinated an influx of meals, leaving them near the pump each day where Jan or Søren would retrieve and distribute them. Amalie, too, cooked for them, but Jan would not allow her to bring food to them or to the house. Instead either he or Søren would fetch what she prepared.

Elli scarcely left the girls' sickroom except to go to the kitchen when she needed something. Perhaps once a day she spoke to Jan from behind the screened and latched kitchen door.

Three days after Karl took to his bed, Jan saw Elli's pronounced exhaustion . . . and her fear. "Jan, Sigrün may be slowly getting better, but . . . our *datter* is still the same."

"And Jan," Elli said carefully. "Jan, my love, I am not well."

Ice swept down Jan's back, numbing his fingers and his feet as he realized Elli's eyes were glazed with fever. He stared through the door, Fraulein Engel's prescribed barrier between them.

"How? I don't understand! You had no flea bites!" Jan protested.

Elli shook her head once but the effort pained her. "I do not know."

He could see how Elli longed for him to hold her, and Jan wanted nothing more than to wrap his arms about her and shut out the world. Jan slowly raised his hand and placed it on the screen. Elli lifted hers and placed it against his.

"I love you," he whispered. "I will do anything to protect you and our family."

Elli swayed on her feet and Fraulein Engel appeared behind her, steadying her. "You must go to bed now, *Liebling*." Fraulein Engel shot Jan a look of compassion, and he stared, dumbfounded, as she ushered Elli away from the door.

But Jan could not bear it. He shook the door and, when the latch would not give, he wrenched it from the frame and threw it aside. He had made up his mind.

Elli and Fraulein Engel were not quite to the top of the stairs. He stood at the bottom and called after them, "I will help nurse Karl and the girls," he shouted. "I will help nurse Elli."

The two women turned. "*Nei!* Oh, *nei*, Jan!" Elli cried. "What if we both sicken? Our children would be left orphans! Think of our children, Jan, my love!"

Elli's panic was as real as Fraulein Engel's anger. The German woman sat Elli on the top step and strode down the stairs, her expression ferocious. She shoved Jan into the kitchen and toward the door, all the while shouting at him in German.

Jan did not understand her words but would never lift a hand to her, so he folded his arms and resolutely stood still. She could not move him.

"*Pappa!*"

Jan turned. Søren was standing in the doorway, his face a mask of fear. "Is *Mamma* sick? Is she? Fraulein Engel is saying you and *Mamma* could both die! *Pappa!*"

Fraulein Engel continued to shout and push him toward the door. Jan looked at Søren's face once more then held up his hands.

"Søren, tell Fraulein Engel I wish to say something to her," Jan said quietly. Søren did as he asked and Fraulein Engel stopped shouting.

Jan faced the woman and studied her tired, worn face—this fine, godly woman, who had given so much of herself for so many. "Søren," Jan said again. "Please tell Fraulein Engel that I have made up my mind. She must accept my decision. I will help her with the sick ones."

He turned to Søren as he spoke those words. "And I am sorry, my *sønn*, but your *mamma* and your *søster* need me. You, too, must accept this."

He gestured. "Stay out of the house. Go tell Henrik what is happening; he will help you with the chores. And tell your *tante* Amalie."

A resigned Fraulein Engel had Jan place a kerchief over his nose and mouth and wash with soap and water. Together they put Elli to bed. Then Fraulein Engel took Jan to see Karl, Kristen, and Sigrün.

That was when he saw how dire the situation was.

O God! his heart cried. *Be my strength, Lord! We need you desperately.*

Karl passed away two evenings later. Jan prayed over him in the morning and then had seen Karl watching him with pain-racked eyes, eyes that pleaded with him.

Jan pulled the kerchief down and gripped Karl's hand. "I will take care of your family, *Bror*. I promise you." Jan choked on the words, choked back his tears. "I promise you I will."

Karl could not speak, but his eyes were fixed on Jan and his face grew peaceful. When his eyelids slid shut in sleep he did not wake again. Jan stayed until the sun set when Karl breathed his last.

Jan shuddered as he thought of telling Amalie and her children, and his breast ached with every breath. He had no further time to mourn just then, for he heard shrieking from the girls' bedroom. He ran and found Fraulein Engel struggling with Sigrün.

She was trying to carry Sigrün from the room but his ten-year-old niece, even weakened by the sickness, fought Fraulein Engel, screaming and kicking. Concerned the girl would do herself harm, Fraulein Engel returned her to her bed.

"What is it?" Jan cried. "What are you doing?"

The woman ignored Jan and busied herself tucking Sigrün back under the covers, speaking soothing words to her. Soon Sigrün calmed and her head fell onto her pillow.

Fraulein Engel gestured Jan to the door and they stepped into the hallway together. She took a breath and finally looked Jan in the face.

"Kristen," she said softly. "Kristen is dying." She searched for a word Jan would understand. "Kristen *døende*," she said using a Riksmaal word. "*Verstehst du?*" Do you understand?

Jan reeled against the wall. He understood. *Fraulein Engel had been trying to remove Sigrün from the room so that she would not witness Kristen's passing.*

His little datter dying? How could it be? Jan knelt by Kristen's bedside.

The sickness had ravished her young body. Now at the end, the form under the blankets was small, her face thin, the skin waxy and transparent. Jan found her little hand and covered it in both of his. Then Sigrün was beside him, huddled against his side, keeping vigil with him.

Kristen did not wake but slipped away quietly while Jan prayed for her and prayed for his family. When he knew she was gone, he wept— long, racking sobs to which he could scarcely give voice, for he could not breathe.

Sigrün flung her hands about Jan's neck and pressed against him until he opened his arms to her. She buried her face in his shoulder and clung to him as he grieved. Jan felt her hot tears trickle down his neck, but she uttered not a sound.

Night had fully fallen when Jan awoke with a start, lifting his head from Kristen's bed. He still held Sigrün against his chest and he could tell by her even breathing that she, too, was sleeping.

Fraulein Engel had covered Kristen's face while Jan and Sigrün slept in exhausted anguish. Jan hugged Sigrün to him as he stood up, but she awoke.

She would not allow Jan to put her to bed; she clung even tighter. Jan, giving in, wrapped her in a blanket, held her near, and went downstairs to the kitchen where he found Fraulein Engel.

She gave Sigrün a cursory examination. "*Gut!*" She turned to go upstairs, then stopped. She pointed to the kitchen door and Jan understood. He opened the door and found Søren seated on the steps, weeping alone in the dark.

"Fraulein Engel has told you?" Jan asked.

"*Ja, Pappa,*" he sniffed. "Is that Sigrün? Is she better?"

"She is getting better, I think. See?" Jan stepped back from the open doorway as Søren drew near. "I'm sorry I broke the screen door, *Sønn,* but I still want you to stay back and safe, *ja?*"

Søren gave a little wave to Sigrün who held tight to Jan's neck. She lifted a hand in return.

"What of *Mamma?*" he asked anxiously.

"I will check on her soon." Jan's throat tightened, the sadness overtaking him again. Sigrün reached up and pressed a hand to his cheek. "*Takk,* little one," he whispered.

He looked at Søren. "I am sorry you are alone this night, *Sønn.* It is a heavy burden to bear." Søren bowed his head, and Jan longed to comfort him, but he could not.

"Will you go to Henrik tomorrow and tell him we need him? Amalie will need Abigael, too."

When Fraulein Engel came downstairs an hour later, Jan could see her weariness. Nevertheless, she took Sigrün when Jan placed her on her lap. "I must go see your *Tante* Elli, Sigrün," Jan whispered. "I promise to come back."

Sigrün released her hold and clung to Fraulein Engel.

Jan went first to Kristen's room, almost to assure himself that the nightmare was true and not something the dark of night had conjured. Jan stood stock still and his heart pounded, for Kristen's bed had been stripped bare and her body was gone.

Jan ran to Karl and Amalie's room. There he found Karl and Kristen's bodies, side by side, washed, and reverently wrapped in clean sheets.

Ah, Lord God, Fraulein Engel has done more for us than we can ever repay. Jan knelt by the bed and prayed for his brother's wife and children. He prayed for his own family. He prayed that God would give him strength for the dark days ahead. And he prayed for Elli.

Morning dawned. Strengthened in his spirit, he stood and went to see his wife.

Jan and Fraulein Engel had put Elli to bed in Søren's room. Jan placed the kerchief over his mouth and nose and cracked the door to see if Elli was awake. She moaned and called for him. "*Jan! Jan!*" Her voice was rough from coughing.

"I am here, Elli. Let me give you water to drink." He sat beside her, lifted her head, and helped her to sip.

"It hurts too much," she whimpered.

"Then I will fetch warm tea with honey." Jan moved to go but Elli stopped him.

"*Nei!* Jan! Please . . . I heard so many things in the night. I . . . Jan, I heard Sigrün screaming and . . . Please tell me what has happened?"

Jan had not intended to tell Elli about Karl . . . about Kristen . . . while she was so ill. He bowed his head now and prayed again, *Lord, I need you right now. Elli needs you. I do not know how to tell her! We are hopeless without you!*

But Elli gave him the words. "Jan . . . is our *datter* gone to heaven?"

Jan covered his eyes with his hand and choked on a sob. "*Ja*, my love. She is gone to heaven."

"O Jesus!" Elli cried. "O Jesus! Help me!"

Jan would not let her grieve alone. He removed the kerchief and gathered her into his arms.

CHAPTER 23

Hours later, Fraulein Engel knocked. "*Herr* Thoresen, *kommen sie, bitte.*" She took over Elli's care and sent Jan down to the kitchen. He opened the door and saw Norvald and Inge, Henrik and Abigael, Rikkert and Duna, and Brian and Fiona waiting a safe distance from the house for him. Henrik had his arm about Søren's shoulders. Søren's friend Ivan stood at his side.

"We are truly sorry, Jan," Henrik murmured, sorrow written across his brow. "You cannot leave the house, *ja*? Who do you wish to tell Amalie? "

Jan saw the love and kindness on his friends' faces. "Will you and Abigael go, Henrik?"

Henrik nodded. "*Ja*, we will go." He shuffled his feet and glanced at Norvald who nodded. "Please tell us where to dig the graves, eh? We would do this for your family. Søren will help us."

Graves! Jan was crushed again. *I must put my bror and my datter in the ground!* He gazed across the yard to where the ground sloped up to the apple trees.

He pointed with his chin. "Elli and I buried our little baby *sønn* just there, below the apple trees."

His thoughts wandered away for a moment. Norvald coughed softly, calling him back.

"Will you mark off a place for Karl and Amalie and their family? And on the other side of the baby's grave, for us? . . . For Kristen?"

We hadn't planned a cemetery, Karl and I, his thoughts rambled. *Someday Karl and Amalie will lie there together. And Elli and I will lie, side-by-side, near Kristen.*

"We will take care of it, Jan," Norvald answered. He understood what Jan was asking.

Amalie was able to grieve openly. Their neighbors and the women of the church, particularly Heidi, gathered around her and took care of the children and the cooking.

The men set up an outdoor kitchen; Norvald and Ivan brought the tables and benches from the German church. And all kept their distance from the house and the sickness inside.

While Amalie wept and mourned, her sons, not understanding the magnitude of their loss, alternately cried for their pappa or played quietly. They endured the women of the church doting on them only because watching their mother weep was too much to understand.

Jan watched silently from the kitchen doorway. His friends, standing safely away from the porch, spoke their condolences. Sigrün, wrapped warmly, stayed glued to Jan's side and made no sound.

Other friends arrived as the morning wore on. Jan heard the sounds of sawn lumber and hammered nails. In the background he glimpsed Adolphe and Rakel Veicht. Adolphe stared at Jan but made no gesture.

When the men finished the caskets, they set them just at the bottom of the steps. While Fraulein Engel put Sigrün to bed, Jan, by himself, carried Karl's wrapped body downstairs and outside. Mothers called their children to their sides, and his friends moved their families farther back.

With every muscle of his back and arms groaning, Jan lowered his brother slowly and carefully into the larger of the two caskets.

"Please, Jan!" Amalie begged, straining against Henrik and Abigael. "Please let me only *see* my husband once more!"

"I am sorry, Amalie," was Jan's weary reply.

He returned a few minutes later with Kristen. His friends and neighbors had restrained their grief as Jan laid Karl in his coffin, but at the sight of Kristen's tiny body they no longer could. Their open weeping nearly undid Jan. He could not see through the mist covering his eyes as he placed Kristen in the casket.

Hammer, nails, and lids lay nearby. But he could not place the lid on Kristen's coffin. His arms lost their strength and he could not move.

"*Herr* Thoresen, let me help you," a gentle voice spoke by his side. Jan did not understand. Fraulein Engel took Jan's hand and they stood close to Kristen's body. Fraulein Engel lifted the cloth from Kristen's face so Jan could see.

Jan blinked. It was Kristen . . . *but it wasn't Kristen*. He stared longer, sure of what he saw. He inhaled, feeling life-giving air fill his lungs. *Ah, Lord. She is no longer here. She is with you.* He breathed again.

Fraulein Engel led him to the lid. Jan offered a half smile to her, this woman who had faithfully followed her calling. She smiled back and nodded.

Jan placed the lid on Kristen's coffin. Nail after nail he drove into the fresh wood until it was fastened securely. He moved to Karl's casket and looked a question at Fraulein Engel.

"*Ja,*" she answered, and lifted the cloth from Karl's face.

"Amalie," Jan called. "Come. Just you, please."

Amalie stumbled toward them, her grief and pregnancy making her clumsy.

"Stand just there," Jan instructed, pointing to a spot a foot from the coffin. "Do not touch him, *Søster*, I beg you." He and Fraulein Engel stood on the other side of the coffin, from Amalie.

Grateful, Amalie nodded. "I thank you, *Bror*."

She gazed down on Karl's face, so changed by the sickness, and sobbed once, covering her mouth with her hands.

"Do you see?" Jan asked. Wonder hung in his voice. "I looked at Kristen, Amalie. She was not there! Do you see?"

"But I want him, Jan! *I want my husband!*" Amalie wailed.

"I know. My heart is breaking with you," Jan whispered. "But you are not putting Karl in the grave, do you see? He is not here. He is already with Jesus!"

Amalie stared and sobbed again. But her brow furrowed. "I-I think I see." She gulped. "It is very like Karl but, no, it is *not* him!"

"Can you be comforted, Amalie?" Jan asked. "Now you know it is not truly him we place in the ground this day?"

Amalie still stared at Karl's face. Then, resolute, she straightened her spine. "*Ja.* I know my *ektemann*, my husband, is with the Lord, as the *Skriften* promises us."

She turned to the other mourners and raised her voice. "I know he will rise again, when our Savior returns."

A chorus of amens affirmed her declaration. Amalie backed away and Jan placed the lid on Karl's coffin.

While Jan secured the lid to Karl's coffin, he noticed Fraulein Engel call Norvald's wife Inge to her. Fraulein Engel, from a safe distance, spoke a request. Inge nodded her agreement.

Then Jan and Fraulein Engel retreated to the kitchen. Six men from the church carried Karl, and four men, including Søren, carried Kristen. Jan and Fraulein Engel watched them climb the slope, but they would not go with them.

Norvald paused a safe distance from Jan. "Inge and I would take Amalie and her boys home with us," he told Jan. "Until the house is safe again."

"*Tusen takk*," Jan answered. He went slowly up the stairs to comfort his wife.

Elli's fever increased during the day, and she thrashed and writhed under her covers, deep in delirium. Fraulein Engel directed Jan to bathe Elli in cool water to bring her fever down and she brought fresh, cold water to Jan from the outside pump.

Jan did all Fraulein Engel asked; he did not leave Elli's side, even to sleep. The day ended, and when night fell, Elli remained unresponsive.

Jan awoke in the dark but did not know why. The candle by Elli's bed had guttered and gone out. He fumbled until he found and lit a fresh one.

Elli was staring at him with bright, glittering eyes.

"Elli!" Jan caught up her hand. "My love! How do you feel?"

Her eyes closed for a moment, and Jan feared she had sunk back into sleep. Then they opened again and fixed on Jan's face. Jan felt the smallest of pressure from her fingers in his hand.

"Jan," she mouthed. Jan was quick to bring a cup to her lips and bid her drink. "Jan," she rasped, after she had taken a sip.

"I am here," Jan answered. Even in the candlelight, he did not like what he saw—the same waxy transparency he had noticed on Kristen's skin, the sense that Elli's body was emptying itself of all that was her— leaving only a mere husk in her place.

A wave of panic rushed toward him. *Don't leave me, Elli!*

"Jan," she mouthed again.

"*Ja*, Elli! I am here!"

"I . . . *see* . . ."

Something so holy, so pure, and so sweet descended with those words that Jan stared, eyes wide, about the room.

"See . . . *him* . . ." Elli breathed.

Her gaze shifted beyond Jan, toward the ceiling, and Jan *saw* as her eyes cleared, the fever and pain gone. The hair on Jan's arms rose as Elli's visage filled with awe.

"*Oh!*" A smile touched Elli's mouth and remained, even as her spirit lifted away.

Jan knelt by her bed, praying and weeping, until the earliest morning light lit the window of the room. He had determined that he alone would prepare Elli's body for burial. By the time an exhausted Fraulein Engel woke for the day, he was finished.

It was she who fell to her knees in open grief when she stepped into the room and realized Elli was gone. "*Meine Tochter! Meine Tochter!*" *My daughter! My daughter!* Fraulein Engel wept.

Jan went down to the kitchen and stripped off his clothes, tossing them into a heap in the corner. With soap and the hottest water he could bear, he bathed his head, arms, and chest and dressed in clean clothes.

He stepped outside and strode to the barn. Søren and Henrik were mucking out the milking stations. Henrik noticed Jan first. He paused, and a look of sad resignation crossed his face. He inclined his head toward Søren.

Jan nodded. Henrik, tears already washing his cheeks, left the barn.

"Søren," Jan spoke quietly.

Søren turned. Jan held out his arms—he saw the exact moment when his *sønn* realized what his father had come to tell him. With an anguished cry, Søren ran to his father.

Jan sent Henrik to spread the news. "We will bury Elli tomorrow," he stated, staring into the distance. Later Jan set about building a casket for Elli.

"Come, *Sønn*. We will build her a fine coffin together, eh?" He and Søren sanded and oiled the wood until it gleamed. They took the coffin into the living room and set it upon two chairs.

Jan brought Elli's body downstairs and placed it inside the coffin. "Stay on the other side, *Sønn*, and come no closer," Jan instructed.

Then, as Fraulein Engel had done with Kristen and Karl, Jan lifted the corner of the sheet from Elli's face. The hint of a smile remained on her lips.

Ah, Lord! I can still feel your presence!

"My *Mamma* is so beautiful," Søren murmured.

"*Ja*, she is," Jan agreed.

He sent Søren from the house and fastened the coffin closed. Then he took another bath and changed clothes yet again. Fraulein Engel gathered his clothes and tied them in a clean sheet.

Early in the morning Jan arose and helped Søren with the chores. The smell of a fire drew both of them into the yard. They found Fraulein Engel burning every mattress in the house in the fire pit used for laundry. On the ground beside the fire were bundles of soiled clothing, sheets, and blankets.

Jan fetched the two heavy cauldrons for her and placed them over the fire. Fraulein Engel began filling them with water. "She is much better today." Fraulein Engel motioned toward the house.

Jan saw Sigrün curled in a chair, wrapped in a clean blanket. Fraulein Engel had placed the chair under a window where Sigrün could watch her work.

Families began arriving midmorning, and Jan realized what Fraulein Engel was about when several of the women, directed by Inge, draped new, clean mattresses on a length of fence near the house.

Even as more people arrived, Fraulein Engel busied herself cleaning every bedroom, washing the walls, floors, and bare bedsteads with harsh soap and scalding water.

Sigrün would live and was no longer contagious. *Fraulein Engel was expunging the sickness from the house.*

Jan and Søren brought Elli's casket outside.

Brian and Fiona's little daughter handed Søren a single faded rose, the last of the year. "For your mother," she whispered. Søren accepted it, choking on his thanks, but Meg's kindness would remain with him. Then Søren ran from the house and hid, and Jan understood.

He was too old to be mothered as the women of the church had mothered his small cousins, and too stricken to face the men of the church. His *sønn* needed to be alone to grieve the loss of his mother and sister.

Jan wanted to run and hide, too, but he knew he could not. He could not run and he could not grieve. Not yet.

Fear of the sickness still caused his friends to keep their distance. Jan held himself rigidly, turning his insides to stone and his face to a mask as they spoke their condolences from a few yards away.

Adolphe Veicht approached. Norvald edged up to the German minister's side.

"I would ask what Scripture you wish read over *Frau* Thoresen's grave," Adolphe asked. He made no gesture of sympathy and offered no condolences. Norvald repeated his words in Swedish.

"*Nei*, but I thank you," Jan replied, staring over Adolphe's shoulder at Norvald. "I would have no unfamiliar words spoken over Elli this day. My *sønn* and I will read the *Skriften* in our own language and pray over her in words she would understand."

Behind Adolphe's shoulder, Norvald nodded, but Adolphe's expression tightened. "As you wish, *Herr* Thoresen."

Jan strode up the slope toward the apple trees and his brother and daughter's graves. Henrik, Brian, and Norvald followed close behind carrying shovels and picks.

"Our baby is here," Jan pointed. "I wish Elli to be placed with him." Kristen's grave was to the right; an obvious space remained between Kristen's and the baby's graves.

For me someday, Jan mused. He saw Søren, red-faced from weeping, striding up the hill.

"I want to help."

"*Ja, Sønn.* You and I will dig. Our friends will help us."

❧ ✤ ❧

CHAPTER 24

Fraulein Engel spent three more days restoring the house to order and caring for Sigrün. Four days after they buried Elli, Fraulein Engel took her departure. The dear woman had aged and weariness etched her face permanently; her brother, concerned for her, came to fetch her home.

"We can never thank you enough." Jan had held her hand and spoken from his heart.

After another week when neither Jan nor Søren sickened and as Sigrün strengthened, Amalie and the boys returned to the house. Jan spent hours holding first one child then another as they searched for and could not find their *pappa*.

That night Jan stared at the sheets of paper before him. He picked up a quill but did not dip it into the ink bottle. He was still numb and could feel nothing inside except the voice of habit—do this, do that; go here, go there.

Amalie had seated him before this table to write. "You must do this, Jan," she'd said gently, her voice catching. "They must know."

Jan thought these past days—weeks!—would remain the worst of his life. Now he wasn't so sure. How would he find words to tell Elli's *foreldre*—her parents—that their *datter* and *barnebarn*—granddaughter—were dead? How could he commit those words to paper? And how would he tell his and Karl's *foreldre* that their eldest *sønn* was dead?

He looked at the paper and dipped his quill in the ink.

Dear Herr and Fru Mostrom,

His hand hovered above the paper. Nothing came to him.

He had never understood why Elli's *pappa* had given his blessing to their marriage. As the younger son of only a moderately successful farmer, Jan had no prospects of ever owning his own land or giving Elli a prosperous life.

Elli's father, Lars, had no sons of his own. In his heart, Jan had cherished the thought that Lars Mostrom had looked on him as a son, had seen something in his future son-in-law, something that he approved of and valued, as Jan's own father had not. When Jan and Elli told the Mostroms that they were going to America, a light had flared in Lars' eyes.

"I would go with you, Jan, if I were younger!" he had said with wistful enthusiasm, "But . . . Elli's *mamma* could not stand the strain—and I would not place my own dreams above her health."

Jan choked on a laugh that turned into a sob halfway out of his mouth. *O God, did I place my dreams above Elli's wellbeing? Above Kristen's life?*

Amalie moved quietly to stand behind him. She clasped her hands together under her growing belly. Jan still did not move.

She sighed and wiped her eyes with the corner of her apron. "Write this, *Bror*," she whispered: "*I send you sad news. A bad sickness arrived in our home three weeks past. Elli and Kristen have gone home to the Savior. So also has my bror—*"

Amalie's voice broke. She pressed her face into her apron, but Jan could still hear the keening of her grief.

Mindlessly he wrote the words she had spoken. He looked down at the paper and read what he had written.

Dear Herr and Fru Mostrom,

I send you sad news. A bad sickness arrived in our home three weeks past. Elli and Kristen have gone home to the Savior. So also has my brother Karl. Sigrün survived the fever, thanks be to God.

Please pray for us. My sønn misses his mamma and søster, as do I. I hope you can forgive me for taking them so far from you.

He could finish it now. He dipped the quill, wrote the final words, and signed it.

With great respect,

Jan Thoresen

The letter to his parents was as difficult, so he used the first letter to begin.

Dear Pappa and Mamma,

I send you sad news. A bad sickness arrived in our home three weeks past. Karl, Elli, and Kristen have gone home to the Savior. Sigrün survived the fever, thanks be to God.

Amalie and the rest of the children are fine.

He wanted to scrawl, *I don't know what to do! Help me! Please tell me what to do!* Instead he ended the letter quickly.

Please pray for us.

Your sønn, Jan

The days somehow passed in a blur of chores and duties performed by rote. He ate what Amalie set before him. He answered when spoken to. But nothing Jan saw or heard penetrated the ache in his chest, the fog in his mind.

One morning Søren bowed his head dejectedly over one of their milk cows. "Nothing will ever be the same again, *Pappa*, will it? I love *Tante* Amalie, but it, it hurts my heart that, that she has made *Mamma's* kitchen her own. I know it is not her fault, but I am, am, am *angry*!"

"Shush, my *sønn*. I know how you feel, but I don't think you are angry with *Tante* Amalie, eh? Is it not that you are really angry that your *mamma* is not here anymore?"

Large tears glimmered in Søren's eyes. "I think maybe so, *Pappa*." He choked a little. "Is it a sin to be angry, *Pappa*?"

"Only if we hang on to it, *Sønn*. Only if we do not give it to the Savior each hour."

Søren nodded. "And what is wrong with Sigrün, *Pappa*? She will not speak to me. Haven't you noticed?"

Jan hadn't noticed. His niece, again a healthy ten-year-old, would still crawl up into his lap after dinner and they would hold each other, neither of them speaking.

How she must miss her pappa, Jan thought. *How she must miss her cousin Kristen!*

Now that Søren had drawn Jan's attention to it, he realized he had not heard Sigrün speak since . . . since when?

Since the night Karl and Kristen died.

Somehow life continued. Norvald decided he needed to learn English to better serve the community when he took crops and livestock to Omaha to sell. He enlisted Henrik and Brian to study with him. Of course, the three of them tried to convince Jan to join their group.

Jan saw it for what it was: a well-meant and transparent ploy to draw Jan out of his sorrows. He refused.

I will not learn the English, he vowed, stubborn in his grief.

I do not need to learn; I have Søren.

☙ ❈ ❧

CHAPTER 25

All day the ache in his chest had grown. Now the throbbing pain threatened to erupt, and he did not know what it would do to Søren to see his father lose control. He could not remain in the barn another moment.

With no word to his *sønn*, Jan left off milking and walked away from the barn. And then ran. He ran until he was far enough away and knew Søren would not be able to hear the sobs burst from his mouth.

O Lord! I am undone. I am breaking. How can I give up my wife and datter? How can I take up Karl's family for him, O God? I have not the strength or the heart.

Sorrow racked his body; he could not breathe. *Lord, would it not have been better for me to come to you than Karl? Did you make a mistake, Lord?*

It was early November; winter cold had not yet set in. He stumbled, weeping, up the slope to where Kristen, Karl, and Elli, with their baby *sønn*, were buried. After only a few weeks, wild grasses were greening the mounds that marked where they lay.

Kneeling between Elli and Kristen's graves, Jan pounded his thighs and cried aloud, unable to control the flood of grief: *It had a life of its own and it possessed him.*

His chest constricted, and long, aching minutes crept by before his breath returned to him. He gazed into the distance . . . stared at the prairie that stretched before him, timeless, endless, masterless.

Unbidden, an idea came to him. *I will build a wall here. To surround them*, he thought, wiping his face on his shirt sleeve.

He glanced around. *No, not a wall—a fence of wrought iron. Yes, that would be nicer. More open.*

He managed to stand. *A fence with roses climbing over the gate. Sunset roses! And I will plant another tree just there, one that will bloom over the fence and cover them with its flowers and sweet scent.*

Still weak from his weeping, Jan stepped out the corners and perimeter he imagined, finding a comfort in doing so—as though he was doing something for Elli. For Kristen. For Karl.

Søren appeared behind him, quiet, watchful. Like his father had, he would get his growth late. He was thin, lanky, and awkward with the promise of the man to come.

My sønn! Jan saw the anguish in the boy's eyes. *Lord, I was wrong. I would not have my sønn left alone in the world. I must be strong for him . . . no matter how hard it is.*

Jan reached for Søren and pulled him close.

"I was just thinking," Jan confided, his words low and rough with emotion. "I was thinking to build an iron fence around them, a pretty one, with twists and curls." He walked Søren around the graves, pointing. "Just so. With roses climbing on the gate? I think *Mamma* would like that. And a nice tree right here. What do you think?"

Søren looked up into his eyes. "Yes, *Pappa*. Will you let me help?"

"*Ja, Sønn.* We will do it together, eh?"

"What about . . ." Søren was sniffling, but this, whatever was happening, was somehow good, even healing. "What about the stones? With their names?"

"Ach! Of course. Perhaps we will go to town and ask where to quarry the best stone for engraving. Just you and I, *ja*? Just you and I."

Søren nodded and wiped his eyes. He held tightly to Jan's waist and Jan squeezed his thin shoulders.

"We will make it beautiful for them, eh?"

Søren nodded again and swallowed.

Far down the road, still on the other side of the creek, Jan saw a buggy and two riders approaching. "We are to have company. Please tell your *Tante* Amalie?"

Søren reluctantly obeyed. Jan heard him running up the path to the house, heard the scrape of the repaired screen door opening and slapping closed.

Jan went out to meet the men, four of them, two riding in the buggy, two on horseback. He recognized Gunnar Braun's little sorrel mare first. Then he recognized Rikkert Kapel astride his bay. Klaus Schöener and Adolphe Veicht rode in the wagon.

The minister and elders. All dressed in somber black.

So. A formal visit, Jan mused.

He did not offer a welcome when they drove into the yard but he watched them carefully. No hand raised in greeting. No one dismounted. Rikkert studiously avoided eye contact with Jan.

When Jan still said nothing, Minister Veicht cleared his throat. "Good evening, *Herr* Thoresen."

Jan nodded. He could feel his anger growing, so he said nothing.

Veicht cleared his throat again and inclined his head. "May we come in? We," he gestured to the others, "the elders and I, would like to talk."

Amalie served coffee and cake in the living room and then closed the door behind her. Still no one spoke.

Jan sugared his cup of coffee and stirred it. He took a sip. He waited. *Lord, I am trying. Help me to master my aching heart.*

"*Herr* Thoresen, we know you are grieving," Veicht said. "And your sister-in-law also. We have been praying for both of you. And the children."

Rikkert awkwardly translated Minister Veicht's words. Jan nodded his thanks. He studied his friend curiously, for the man was clearly uncomfortable. Klaus and Gunnar watched Veicht, attentive, but saying nothing.

"You do not answer me, *Herr* Thoresen?" Veicht was becoming a bit put out with Jan's silence.

"Thank you for your prayers," Jan answered. "You wished to talk? I am waiting."

"You are not much hospitable, *Herr* Thoresen." Veicht huffed. "Well, all right. What we came for must be said. You are a member in good standing of our church, *ja*? So we are here and must bring this to your attention."

Jan remained silent, but he locked eyes with Veicht, daring him to look away. He had guessed why they had come.

"It is that you are now a single man, *Herr* Thoresen, and your sister-in-law a single woman, both living in the same house," Veicht finally managed. "It is a difficult situation."

Jan's eyes never left Veicht's face. *O God, let me not sin with my heart or my mouth*, he prayed. He remained silent.

"We have discussed this, the elders and I. The appearance of it will be wrong. It would lead to temptations and, and likely to s—"

Rikkert made a sound low in his throat like a soft growl. Veicht turned his head in surprise and then moderated his thought. "Well, as I said, the *appearance* of it will be wrong, that is, the *appearance* of sin."

At the word "sin" Jan's eyes narrowed and his hand, lying on the arm of his chair, fisted. Veicht paused, his eyes on Jan's fist.

Lord, I am calling on you . . . Jan prayed. *I need your help.*

"We, we, that is, we have come with counsel. A good answer, one that would be right for all, *ja*? Even as soon after as it is, even while grieving, it would be right for you and your sister-in-law to—"

The look of loathing Jan turned on Veicht would have curdled milk— but he did not respond and did not need to, for the door to the room sprang open at that moment.

Amalie, breathing raggedly and heavy with her child, stood in the doorway. His brother's wife, gravely offended, spoke.

"I have been listening at the door, Minister, and am glad of it, for you are talking of me behind my back, *nei*? You do not have the courage to talk to my face?" Her hands were fisted on her hips.

"What? I am such a great temptation?" she demanded. Now she was cradling her distended belly. "*Such* a tempting morsel right now that my *bror* would not be able to control himself? Is it so?"

She laughed and the men cringed at its harshness. "Those are evil thoughts, Minister Veicht, if you think brother and sister would do such a thing!"

"M-m-my dear lady," Veicht stuttered, but Amalie was not finished.

She wagged her finger at him. "Hear me well, sir! I am grieving. I love my husband and *only* him. I would not marry—I *will not* marry—until and unless my grief has passed. But under no circumstances will it ever be right to marry my husband's brother. Hear me! I will never do so. *Never*."

She slammed the door behind her.

Silence reigned in the room. Jan took a large swallow of his coffee, marveling at what he had witnessed and proud of Amalie's spirit. He glanced at Rikkert. Even though the man was staring at the floor, Jan could still see a smile curve his friend's face.

Jan was *almost* able to stifle his chuckle. When Veicht's chin jerked up his face was livid.

"You think this funny?" he hissed.

"*Nei*. But you can see she is too much woman for me, *ja*?"

Jan regretted his flippant remark the moment it left his mouth. *O Lord! My mouth!* He cringed inwardly.

Veicht jumped to his feet. "So you treat this lightly? You reject our counsel?" he thundered.

Jan too stood up, all humor gone, but still he restrained his temper and his tongue. "Minister Veicht, you are in *my* home. You do not raise your voice to me here. My sister-in-law has heard your counsel; I have heard your counsel. We thank you for it, but we are more concerned to hear *the Lord's* counsel than we are to hear yours or any man's."

He finished in a flat tone. "You have heard my *søster*. We do not agree that marriage is the Lord's will for us." He caught a gleam of approval from Rikkert's eyes but the other two elders looked anywhere but at him.

Veicht, his jaw clenched, studied Jan. "We give you more time to think on it, *Herr* Thoresen. Your sister-in-law is correct. While she is with child, the situation is less onerous. But after she is delivered, we will speak on this again. If you will not hear us then, we will bring it to the church."

Jan nodded. His expression did not change and he said nothing more. Finally, the four men filed out of the room.

Rikkert was last to go out the front door. He turned for an instant and nodded to Jan.

Later, after the children were abed, Jan found Amalie in the kitchen trying, as usual, to work until her body demanded sleep.

"Amalie, let us talk," Jan said. "Sit. Sit down and have a glass of milk. You will sleep better tonight for it."

She laughed, that choked, brittle sound that had so startled the minister and the elders. "Ach! I cannot sleep, Jan. When I do, I wake up and find that all my nightmares are true. And then I cannot sleep anymore." She stared at the table.

"I know, *Søster*, I know. But we must talk of this because . . . because they were right."

Amalie's head jerked up.

"*Nei*, not about us marrying. Not that. That was wrong. But . . . after your baby comes, they are right. It would give the appearance of wrong."

Suddenly she looked frightened and the dark circles hanging under her eyes deepened. "You would not leave us, Jan? Abandon us or send us away?" Her voice was shaking.

Jan shook his head. "Why would you think such a thing? I could not abandon my brother's wife and his children! Never ask that again, Amalie."

"Then what? What will we do?"

"First we will pray, *ja*? That is the most important thing. The Lord's counsel is what we need."

"*Ja*. All right." Amalie dropped her eyes to the table again.

Jan knew what she was feeling. *Lord, have you forgotten me? Do you hear me?* But still he would pray, because whatever his heart *felt*, God was bigger!

And so he prayed aloud, "Lord, everything we have we lay at your feet. Our lives . . . we lay before you. Our futures, we offer you. Give us strength, Father God, and wisdom. We look to you for an answer to this . . . question."

Jan opened himself for the Lord to speak to him and waited. Three days later he felt he had an answer or, at least, a first step.

"Come, Søren." Father and son went out the kitchen door and headed for the barn. Inside, Jan pointed to an empty corner stall.

"I am going to build a bedroom for myself here, *Sønn*. Will you help me?"

Søren stared at him. "It is because of Minister Veicht and the elders? They said something to you." Søren was growing red with indignation; Jan well recognized the symptoms.

"Let's sit and talk a little, *ja*? Come here." Jan sat on the bench where they cleaned and repaired their tools. He pulled the young man down next to him, laid his hand on Søren's knee.

"I will admit that I do not like that they came as they did. I would rather they came as brethren as the Bible says: *Rebuke not an elder, but intreat him as a father; and the younger men as brethren.* However, some of what they said is true. Amalie is no longer a married woman and I am no longer a married man." Jan's voice grew rough as he said those last words.

"You know that she is like my *søster*, and I am like her *bror*, eh? But since we are unmarried and living together under the same roof, your *tante* and I, those who do not know us could interpret it wrongly. I would not have our testimony as Christians touched by even the appearance of evil, Søren. Do you see?"

Søren nodded, but his mouth was still set in a scowl.

"You are almost a man now, *Sønn*, and can understand these things. So I do not talk to you as a child; instead, I talk to you as a Christian man and ask you to pray with *Tante* Amalie and me, *ja*? Pray that God himself will give us wisdom and guidance in this situation?"

Søren mumbled a barely audible, "*Ja.*"

"Good. Let us pray right now. Then you will help me build a room."

Each Sunday Jan made a point of greeting Adolphe and Rakel, showing respect and deference to the office in which Adolphe stood. This Sunday was no different.

With Søren beside him, Jan extended his hand. "Good morning, *Herr* Veicht, *Frau* Veicht. Good Sabbath to you." Søren obediently offered his hand also.

"*Guten morgen, Herr* Thoresen. *Guten morgen*, Søren," *Herr* Veicht responded evenly. He always said the same thing and never anything more. His wife only nodded, her eyes coolly appraising.

Jan nodded back, glad to have the ritual over. He and Søren moved quickly away.

That morning Jan managed to corner Gunnar Braun, Klaus Schöener, and Rikkert Kappel individually before service. "I have built a bedroom for myself in my barn," he said to each man, with Søren interpreting. "I no longer sleep in the house. Søren will remain in the house to help Amalie with heavy chores, especially until the baby comes. From now on, I will be in the house only for meals."

Just like a hired man, Jan could not help thinking. *In my own house, like a hired man.*

"You will please inform Minister Veicht," Jan concluded. He had decided not tell Minister Veicht directly. Jan would not provide an opportunity to aggravate the man's obvious dislike of him, especially in a public setting.

Rikkert looked around and then clasped Jan on the arm. "I think this is a good solution for now, Jan."

Gunnar was not as positive. "I am glad to hear this, Jan. However, I am not sure Minister Veicht will think it is enough." He sighed. "Be on your guard, Jan, *ja*?"

"Why should I be on my guard, Gunnar? If I am in the wrong, then let the church show me where in the Scriptures. I am not afraid of the discipline of the Lord. *Whom God loves, he chastens*, eh? I am at peace in God's love for me."

Gunnar had no answer. He, too, clasped Jan's shoulder.

It was the same with Klaus. "I will tell you this, Jan, a bedroom in the barn will not be enough to satisfy Minister Veicht. He will bring you before the people soon." Klaus looked at Jan, a shamed expression on his face.

"How did we get to this place?" Jan demanded, his anger flaring. "This is not how Tomas served our church and our people!"

He saw Heidi Veicht hugging Amalie and whispering encouragement to her. The old woman was still loving and sweet.

However, Heidi had changed since Adolphe and Rakel had moved into her and Tomas' home. Now Heidi dressed in clothing as dark and plain as Rakel's. And she had adopted a set and serene expression, Jan noticed—one devoid of laughter or smiles.

Lord, I don't know what else to do, Jan cried silently. *Amalie and I will not marry, but what else can I do?*

Jan could barely tolerate taking Søren and Amalie and her children to church. When he did, he and Amalie assiduously avoided appearing like a couple. He would help her down from the wagon, but immediately find other men to converse with before and after church.

Likewise, Amalie never stood near him. She and Sigrün would herd the little boys into the women's seats as she felt they were too young yet to sit with the men.

If Little Karl, Arnie, or Kjell needed their uncle's oversight or correction, Jan was quick to provide it, but he and Amalie carefully kept their relationship distinct and separate.

Church was no longer the joyous place it had been. What had been a happy, gracious congregation was increasingly severe and morose. With his preaching and rules, Adolphe Veicht had altered the character of the church.

Jan wondered what Tomas would have thought of the changes.

Jan knew that many of the men were as unhappy as he. Rikkert shifted uncomfortably in the stiff, black suit he was required to wear every Sunday. The singing droned on unenthusiastically.

Why does no one protest this tyranny? Jan raged inwardly. *Are there no men of God to stand up to this? If I could speak their language well, Lord, I would say something!*

But Jan was convicted. Would he speak up if he could articulate his thoughts in German?

He looked at Heidi Veicht sitting demurely beside her daughter-in-law on the front row and shook his head. He saw Heidi's shoulders rise and fall in a sigh. Then, for just a moment, Rakel turned her face away and Heidi quickly looked back, smiling her toothless smile and nodding at other women and children. This was the Heidi they all knew and loved!

Rakel turned back and nudged Heidi. Jan could tell from Rakel's reproving frown that she was saying something sharp to Heidi. The old woman calmly nodded her head, faced forward, and remained still.

Jan's anger kindled against Rakel Veicht. *O God, what they are doing to this woman of God is not right!* he seethed within. But he could say or do nothing. Jan stared at the toes of his boots.

Lord . . .

ℭHAPTER 26

1873

"*Pappa!*" Søren cracked opened the door to Jan's room in the barn and leaned over the bed. "*Pappa,*" he said quietly, shaking Jan.

Jan was in a deep sleep when he heard Søren's voice calling to him. "What is it?" Groggy, Jan sat up and wiped his eyes.

"*Tante* Amalie says she is ready to have the baby," Søren answered. He sounded nervous.

The coming of a baby had always been kept within the conversation and domain of women, not talked of much among the men or to the children. After a baby was born, he or she was proudly shown to the men and other children, as though birthing the child had been nothing more than going into a room and bringing a baby back out.

Søren was learning it was *not* so. His aunt had called to him in the night, and he had heard her groaning in pain on the other side of her bedroom door.

"Ah! I will go for Abigael," Jan answered, already pulling on his boots. "When I bring her back, you will stay downstairs with me. Right now, pump water for her and build up the fire in the stove, *ja?*"

"*Ja, Pappa.*" Søren agreed readily. He frowned. "How much water, *Pappa?*"

Jan chuckled. "Fill the kettle and the big pot, eh? Put them both on the stove to heat."

Jan hitched the bays to one of the wagons. Within minutes they were trotting down their icy dirt road toward the bridge over the creek. Jan shivered and rubbed his eyes again. He was dressed in thick layers, but the January night was bitterly cold.

He turned off the bridge and directed the team up the rise and then down the rutted track to the Andersons' house below. A few minutes later he knocked on their door. Henrik, barefoot and dressed in a night shirt, opened it.

"So? Is it Amalie's time?" he asked, yawning.

"*Ja,* she sent Søren to me to fetch Abigael."

"I will get her. It will be a few minutes."

After Jan returned with Abigael and she went upstairs to help Amalie, Jan and Søren built up the fire in the living room and sank into the deep, overstuffed chairs. Both of them were sleeping soundly when Abigael woke them.

"It is a girl," she said happily. "It did not take long, and Amalie is doing fine."

"*A girl!*" Søren was flummoxed. After three boys in a row, a girl was not what he had expected from his aunt.

Jan laughed. "It is good we have another girl, eh? Sigrün and Amalie will like that." He chuckled again. "What name has Amalie given the baby?"

"A good one, I think! She calls her Uli."

"*Ja*, that is pretty. Uli. What do you think, Søren?"

The boy shrugged. "I do not know, *Pappa*. What do I know of baby girls?"

Jan clapped him on the shoulder. "A baby girl is a blessing. You will see." He looked at Søren and Abigael and said softly, "Karl would be glad to see this new child of his. We must be glad for him."

Abigael nodded, understanding. "Yes. I will fix Amalie something to eat now."

For weeks following the birth of Amalie's daughter, Jan felt the unrest of a looming confrontation. He dutifully took Sigrün, Søren, and the little boys to church while Amalie and the baby rested at home.

He knew in his heart that Minister Veicht was waiting and watching and that he would call them before the congregation soon after Amalie resumed coming to church with him. Yet the more Jan prayed, the more sure he was that the Lord had no further direction for him.

Fader, I have asked you what else I should do, but you have said nothing, Jan prayed. *If we are brought before the church, I can only answer what the Holy Spirit speaks to me. Your will be done, Lord.*

The first time Jan held Amalie's baby, he stared into her blue eyes, humbled by the awesome power of new life. "Little girl, I am your *Onkel* Jan. I will take good care of you, *ja?*"

Often as he held her, he thought of Elli and Kristen. How could he not? He held the infant close and drew comfort from her.

When Uli was six weeks old, Amalie felt ready to take the babe to church. Jan agreed, but he steeled himself for what he sensed was coming. *Lord . . . I am trusting in you.*

As soon as Amalie stepped down from the wagon that Sunday, the women of the church gathered around to see her new baby. Jan corralled her three little boys and took them off to give Amalie a few minutes of peace. He decided he would keep them with him during the service, too.

He had Søren sit on one end of the bench and placed Little Karl, Arnie, and Kjell between them. Jan took the seat next to Kjell. Amalie might have difficulties with the energetic two-year-old, but he would be still for his *onkel*.

Norvald Bruntrüllsen sat behind him. As Jan turned to shake his hand their eyes met. "If you have anything to say today, my friend, I will translate it for you." Norvald's eyes were sad but determined.

"So! You know we will be brought before the church today?" Jan asked quietly. Norvald glanced behind Jan and Jan knew Adolphe Veicht was watching.

Always! Always he is watching me! Jan fumed.

Norvald dropped Jan's hand and his eyes cut away, but under his breath Jan heard, "*Ja.*"

"Thank you. I will ask you to help me then," Jan replied before he sat down.

At the end of his message, Adolphe held up his hand. "Before we are dismissed to break bread, we have a matter of church discipline. As much as it pains me, I must bring a matter before you concerning Jan Thoresen and Amalie Thoresen."

A dread hush descended on the congregation.

Adolphe made sure every eye was on him before he spoke again. Jan looked across to the women and saw Amalie. Her broad, honest face was composed. Jan knew she would not easily break down.

My brother chose a good woman, he thought with pride.

Adolphe, sure of everyone's attention, continued. "The elders and I have already visited and given our counsel to Jan and Amalie Thoresen. We counseled them to be married and gave them four months to hear our godly wisdom and respond. They have not heard us. They have not stopped living in sin." Adolphe looked directly at Jan as he spoke.

A collective gasp sounded across the room. In Jan's ear, Norvald whispered what Adolphe was saying. Søren stared aghast at his father. Jan handed a sleeping Kjell to Søren and rose to his feet. He would not dishonor his family; he, like Amalie would remain composed.

He gestured to Norvald. "This man will translate for me so that I may answer this accusation." Norvald stood behind Jan and repeated what Jan said in German. Loud enough to be heard by all, he asked in Riksmaal, "Of what sin are we accused?"

Adolphe's face darkened but he kept his composure. "You and your brother's wife are living together without marriage."

"*Nei*, we are not," Jan answered in a clear voice.

"You add lies to your sins?" Adolphe thundered. "This will not be tolerated."

When Norvald repeated the word "lies," Jan's eyes hardened and his hands gripped the sides of his trousers.

"I call the elders of the church to stand!" Jan roared. No one had expected this—not even Jan.

Slowly, Rikkert, Klaus, and Gunnar stood to their feet. Adolphe had momentarily frozen, but soon enough he motioned to them to sit and started to say something. Jan cut him off.

"I will speak, Minister Veicht. You will not interrupt my response to this charge." He pointed his finger at Adolphe and, even though Norvald had not yet interpreted, Jan's meaning was clear.

Jan pointed at each elder. "Did I not speak to each of you saying I had built a room for myself in the barn? Did I not say that I would only be in the house for meals?"

Jan turned to Adolphe. "In December I requested them to convey this information to you. Did you not receive it?"

Norvald repeated everything Jan said. The elders nodded in affirmation, and the men of the congregation eyed Jan speculatively.

Adolphe waved Jan's words away. "So you say you live *in the barn*, but can anyone testify to this?"

Jan pointed at Rikkert, "Did you seek to verify what I told you? Have you seen this room?"

Rikkert cleared his throat. "I have."

Jan addressed the elders but also the entire congregation. "You have known me for nearly seven years. This man," he jerked his chin toward Adolphe, "calls me a liar. Am I a liar? Has my word or conduct ever been in question?"

As Norvald translated, loud calls and shouts of "*nein!*" answered Jan.

Jan again pointed at Adolphe. "If you doubted your elders' testimony, Minister, why did you not seek to verify it for yourself?"

Adolphe, his face a dark red, spat back, "No one can be there in the middle of the night, can they? When you sneak into the house and into this woman's bed? To prove the innocence of this arrangement would require a live-in chaperone, would it not?"

He had gone too far.

A murmur of outrage rippled over the congregation.

Sigrün pushed her face into Amalie's shoulder, sobbing silently. Amalie sat still and erect, but Jan could see her struggling to keep her composure.

Then Jan saw Søren staring at Adolphe with open hatred, and the little boys, scared and not understanding what was happening, were wailing and climbing on Jan's legs.

I must end this, Jan realized sadly. *This is injuring my sønn and my brother's family.*

He held up his hand to prevent Adolphe from saying more. "Minister Veicht. You need not continue. We wish no strife. We will leave the church in peace."

"*Nein!*" someone said loudly and others took it up. Jan spoke even louder to be heard over the growing unrest.

"God is our witness that there never has and never shall be wrong behavior between myself and my brother's wife. Amalie and I have prayed. We do not feel the Lord calling us to marry, but I must still provide for my brother's wife and children, mustn't I? That I will do, even though we do not marry."

Jan looked around the room. "And now we will go. We will leave this church rather than cause division and strife."

"Stop!" The tiny voice, raised to its loudest, came from Heidi Veicht. The congregation lapsed into silence.

"I will be their live-in chaperone," she said clearly into the silence. "I will testify to their behavior." Norvald quickly repeated her words to Jan.

"Sit down, old woman," Adolphe shouted. He pointed his finger at her and shook it. "A woman is not permitted to speak!"

"I *will* speak! You have made me a prisoner in my own home. I will no longer live with you."

Adolphe strode to the front row and grabbed her by the arm. With his other hand he threatened to strike her.

Jan had seen enough. "*Thou shalt honor thy father and mother,*" Jan thundered. "Do you speak to your mother with such disrespect? Do you dare raise your hand to her? A man who strikes his mother is not fit to be a minister of God!"

Norvald stumbled at this, but duly repeated it. The congregation had already erupted, some shouting in Jan's favor, some in Adolphe's.

Heidi Veicht wrenched her arm from Adolphe's grip and ran to Jan's side. "*Herr* Thoresen, will you take me into your home?" She was trembling and reached out her hand to him. Jan grasped the elderly woman's hand and pulled her to his side, understanding perfectly how frightened she was. Norvald looked from Heidi to Jan and then translated.

"*Ja*," Jan answered. "You are welcome in our home, dear sister. Come with us."

He lifted Kjell to his shoulder and led Heidi toward the door. Søren followed behind holding Little Karl and a sobbing Arnie by their hands; Amalie and Sigrün joined them.

"Where are you going with my mother?" Adolphe roared. "She is under my care and protection—she must obey me!"

Jan kept walking. Heidi clutched his hand and watched Adolphe, fear on her face. Jan handed her up into their wagon. Amalie appeared at his side and he handed her up also. All the children clambered into the wagon, even though the horses had not yet been hitched to it.

Adolphe called to his elders. "This man is taking my mother unlawfully!" He strode toward Jan's wagon with a reluctant posse behind him.

Jan stood between Adolphe and Heidi. Søren stood by him.

"You have no right to take this woman!" Adolphe shouted. "She is under my authority!"

"*Nei*," Jan answered. "This woman is free. She may do as she chooses," he declared.

Jan raised his voice to the congregation gathered around the wagon, "She has asked in front of all of you to be the live-in chaperone that Minister Veicht requires of us."

He turned to Heidi, who was trembling on the wagon's bench under Amalie's arm. "*Fru Veicht*, do you consent to live with us and bear testimony to our behavior?" Norvald, from the crowd, called up to Heidi, translating for Jan.

"*Ja*, I do!" she stated clearly.

Then Norvald was beside Jan and Søren, between Adolphe and the wagon. Ivan and Henrik joined him. Another man from the congregation came alongside them.

Adolphe, his face burning with fury, spoke again, his voice less strident but loud enough for the people to hear. "Listen, then, all of you! This woman has chosen. She is no longer my mother and will no longer be received in my home or this church."

He pointed at Jan. "Jan Thoresen, you are banned from fellowship with this church. Go! Do not show yourself here again."

Without a word in reply, Jan and Søren strode to the bays and unhobbled them. They led the team to the wagon.

The row of men between Adolphe and Heidi had grown. Several of them came forward to help Jan hitch the horses to the wagon. As Jan mounted the wagon and took the reins, Norvald shook his hand.

"Our fellowship is unbroken. The Lord bless you," he said loudly, first in Swedish, then in German. Norvald called to his family and began to hitch his team to his wagon.

He was followed by a phalanx of men, each shaking Jan's hand and repeating Norvald's words. "Our fellowship is unbroken. The Lord bless you."

"Norvald Bruntrüllsen!" Adolphe called loudly, a threat in his voice. "If you leave, you may not come back!"

Norvald nodded. "I understand." He stood up in his wagon and addressed the people.

"I have erred. I confess, here and now, that I have not been obedient to the Lord. He spoke to me many months ago to say to this congregation—*where is the grace and love that Tomas taught of from the Scriptures?* This church was founded on the *whole counsel* of God's word.

"The word brought by Adolphe is unbalanced. The Bible says, *For the law was given by Moses, but grace and truth came by Jesus Christ.* Adolphe has taught only law—and my soul is starving for the truth and grace of Jesus!

"I am leaving to seek the Lord for another minister. Until he provides, I will hold services in my barn every Sunday. If you wish to join me, you are welcome."

In the silence following Norvald's speech, a few men began harnessing their wagons while others followed Adolphe back into the meeting house.

Jan called to the team and they trotted out of the yard onto the dirt road. His and Adolphe's heated words rang in Jan's head during the drive home.

O Lord, my heart is breaking! Such strife and division is not of your Holy Spirit! he grieved. *What of the little ones? They will be tainted with our discord, discouraged from following you. O Father, I would not be part of harming your little ones!* He was sobbing and could not stop himself. Heidi and Amalie wept with him.

In the back of the wagon Sigrün buried her face in Søren's shirt and the three little boys huddled in his lap, seeking comfort from the storm of emotions. Søren, his young face set in hard lines, wiped his face, tears of rage and humiliation running down his cheeks.

Jan and Søren unhitched the team, rubbed them down, and released them into the paddock in silence. Jan could not miss the anger on Søren's face—it was written in a red, seething frown.

"*Sønn*, let us talk," Jan was weary beyond measure as he sat on the barn's bench. Søren reluctantly took a seat next to him, keeping his face turned away.

"I would not have you subjected to what happened at church today," Jan said softly. "It was an evil thing."

"*Ja*," Søren spat back. "Minister Veicht is an evil man!"

Jan shook his head, the conviction in his spirit growing. *The Holy Spirit has been warning me for weeks of this coming confrontation, yet instead of resolving it in private, my heart desired to vindicate itself in public. How much harm has my wicked, pride-filled heart caused?*

"*Nei*; that is not what I meant, *Sønn*," Jan replied, choosing his words with care. "What happened—the public strife and quarreling—that is the evil of which I am speaking. I should have resolved this issue in private with just the elders and Minister Veicht."

Puzzlement joined anger on Søren's furrowed brow. Jan looked away and tried to explain.

"Jesus said the church is his body on earth—and that the world would know we are his disciples by the love we have for one another. What do you think our Savior would think of what happened today within our church?"

"He would not like what Minister Veicht said!" Søren answered quickly.

"I agree. What he said was not true. But how I respond to such an accusation is just as important—"

"You said nothing wrong!" Søren retorted. "Even when he called you a liar!"

"Søren, listen to me. Do not interrupt me again, *ja*?" Jan stared at Søren until the boy reluctantly nodded.

"The Bible tells us that, wherever possible, disagreements are to be handled peacefully. It says that *mature* Christians will work hard to keep the unity of the Holy Spirit in the bond of peace. In another place *Scriften* tells us that man's anger does not produce God's righteousness.

"Yes, Minister Veicht is wrong, but some of my words to him were spoken in anger *and pride*. What happened because of my words? Because I spoke in anger, some of our friends have decided to leave and start a new church. The Bible calls this division. Is Jesus' body divided? Is this the love he spoke of?"

Jan stopped for a moment, wondering what the Lord would have him do to fix the damage his rashness had caused.

Out of the silence, Søren's quiet voice spoke. "Maybe there needs to be a new church, *Pappa*."

With a start, Jan realized he agreed with Søren. "*Ja,* perhaps you are right. But the manner of our leaving is wrong, *Sønn.* It will create unforgiveness and bitterness on both sides.

"The Lord is grieved when our hearts are bitter. I will repent and ask him to show me what to do next."

Jan slid to his knees and turned toward the bench. Søren knelt next to him. "Ah, Father," Jan prayed aloud. "I have allowed my tongue to speak in anger—and what a fire has been kindled by my angry words! O Lord, I repent. I ask your forgiveness for my pride and brash deeds. Please speak to me and guide me! Show me how to make amends for the damage I have done to many hearts and to our church."

He prayed quietly for a long while and Søren prayed beside him.

They walked back to the house together, Jan's arm about Søren's shoulder. Jan's heart was lighter, but he knew with certainty that the Lord would require him to go to Adolphe and others and ask their forgiveness.

He shook his head. Whether or not his apology was accepted, he would humble himself and do as God directed.

CHAPTER 27

Jan and Søren found Amalie and Heidi seated at the kitchen table. Amalie was nursing the baby. "Heidi and I fed the boys and put them down for a nap," Amalie said softly. "I know Little Karl is too old for naps, but Heidi wanted to talk to us alone. Even so, we will need Søren for Heidi to speak to us." She gestured at her nephew. "But first, eat your dinner, eh?"

As Jan and Søren ate, Amalie told them she had settled Heidi in the downstairs bedroom—Jan and Elli's room. It was the only logical place, Jan realized. Heidi was too old to be burdened with the climb upstairs and down.

Heidi watched Jan and Søren eat, her eyes clear and peaceful. Jan finished his meal, placed his arm on the table, and took Heidi's hand in his.

"You are most welcome in our home, *Søster* Veicht," he told her. "But I am sorry for the proud and angry words I spoke in church today. I am sorry for the strife they caused . . . and for the pain you must feel right now. I have asked God to forgive me—will you do the same?"

Heidi spoke for a minute, pressing Jan's hand as she did. Søren nodded and repeated in Riksmaal.

"*Frau* Veicht says she thanks you for taking her into our home. She says she is only sorrowful that Adolphe may not allow her to see her grandsons as often as she would like. She says she has known all along that such a, a—" Søren struggled to find the right word.

"Confrontation?" Jan asked.

"*Ja*, confrontation." Søren nodded his thanks. "She knew that such a confrontation was coming because she has often heard *Herr* Veicht talking about you . . . and Aunt Amalie."

Søren gulped and frowned, trying hard to again master the anger he had just released to the Lord. "And she says that God had already told her to ask you if she could come and be a—"

He looked at his father. "What is the word you used in church, *Pappa*? A live-in something."

"Ah!" Jan nodded. "A live-in chaperone. A trusted witness to attest that nothing wrong is happening."

Søren was old enough to understand, but still he asked, "Someone to say you sleep in the barn? Because you and Aunt Amalie are not married?"

Jan nodded again. "We do not believe the Lord wants us to marry, *Sønn*, but your *Tante* Amalie was my brother's wife, so I will take care of her and your cousins."

Jan mused for a moment. *So Heidi had already felt the Lord leading her to come live with them?* He turned the situation around in his mind, looking at it from all directions.

"Søren, please tell *Frau* Veicht that we are honored she would come to live with us, but . . . I am still grieved that my words have created a rift between her and her *sønn*." Jan sighed and started to say something else when Heidi shook her head vigorously and spoke again.

"*Frau* Veicht, she says that you did not create the rift between her and her son. It was already there." Heidi was nodding as Søren spoke.

Jan peered into Heidi's honest face. "Is it so? What I am hoping you can tell us, dear lady, is *why* Adolphe hates me so. He has disliked me from the moment he met me—and I cannot understand why."

"I can tell you," she answered quietly. "It is because of whom you remind him."

She shifted in her chair and sighed. "Tomas and I had been married for several years but we could not—I could not—have a baby. Many little ones I lost before they were ready to be born."

"Ach!" Amalie said. She touched Heidi's shoulder in sympathy.

"*Danke*, Amalie. We had a farm in Ohio then. A Czech family lived near us. They were nice people, good people. Just different than us, *ja*? But still good neighbors even though life had not been good to them. The father was often ill, the mother worn down with caring for him, their little son, and a new baby.

"Then the father died. Tomas and some other neighbors plowed and planted their fields that year. We all hoped to make a crop for the woman so that she would have money to return to her brother's house back in their homeland. But it was not to be.

"Ah, dear *Gott*! First her husband died, then her baby, and then she, too, passed away, leaving their little boy an orphan. Tomas and I took him in. He was only three years old, and we had no way to return him to his uncle—we had not even a name or address."

Heidi smiled when she remembered. "We called him Adolphe. Oh, he did not look like either of us with his dark hair and eyes, but we loved him so very much! Such a serious little boy he was. He followed Tomas everywhere he went, a quiet, sober little man, running after his new father, eager to help. Eager to be loved.

"We doted on him as if he were our flesh and blood. Nothing could ever change that! And yet . . ."

A long sigh escaped her. "When Adolphe was six, a miracle happened! I had a baby. A baby boy."

Søren stopped, amazed, when he translated Heidi's words. Jan and Amalie looked at each other.

"We did not know," Amalie murmured.

"*Ja,* I know you did not," Heidi answered quietly. "Not many of our friends remember. It was long ago now." She seemed lost in her memories until Jan spoke.

"What happened?" he asked softly.

Heidi looked at Jan and smiled. "Such a sunny disposition and merry blue eyes our little Dieter had! Everyone loved him simply because he was so easy to love.

"But Adolphe . . . Adolphe was not as easy to love, you see. Many people mistook his quiet watchfulness as sullenness. And, not knowing the harm they were doing, people made comparisons between Adolphe and Dieter.

"*Dieter is such a happy baby!* they would remark. *Dieter is so handsome, what with his blonde hair and blue eyes. It is too bad Adolphe is so dark, don't you think?* they would say. And later, when Dieter was older, they said, *I do wish Adolphe had a more pleasing manner, don't you? Like Dieter.*"

Heidi looked at Amalie and Jan and tears stood in her eyes. "They had no idea how Adolphe was receiving their words. We did not know either, at first. But later . . . as Adolphe grew toward manhood and Dieter was still a boy . . . In his eagerness to be loved, Adolphe compared everything he did—and everything he was—only with Dieter.

"He just could not believe we loved him for himself. And so he would pounce on any perceived preference we showed for Dieter. I say 'perceived,' because Adolphe's perceptions became skewed, twisted.

"I remember the first day Adolphe said to Tomas, *I am the elder son. Just as in the Bible, I am to receive your blessing and the larger part of the inheritance.* Well, that told us so much! He was a young man, but he was still trying to earn his father's love and approval.

"Tomas had a long talk with Adolphe then. Afterwards we were sure that Adolphe understood. He married Rakel and, when we left Ohio and moved here, he began to farm his own land."

Heidi tapped the table with a finger, remembering. "You know, I think that was the happiest I have ever seen Adolphe. He and Rakel worked hard and were well accepted by our tiny church when it began.

"For several years all was fine. Then Dieter married a lovely girl, Gretchen. They lived with us and Dieter farmed with his father. You see, by our customs the *youngest* son stays and inherits the father's farm, not the eldest son.

"A year later Dieter and Gretchen had a baby boy. Another year after that they were blessed with another son.

"How we doted on our little grandsons! They were so precious to us. But Adolphe and Rakel had no children. After a while we could tell Adolphe began to be bothered by his old thoughts again. He felt that he and Rakel were on the outside looking in, that Dieter and his little ones had everything including all of our love."

Heidi lifted her hand to Jan's face and peered into his eyes. "You see, *Herr* Thoresen, you are so very like Dieter! You even look like him," she said sadly. "I believe that is why Adolphe dislikes you so deeply. It is as though Dieter has come back—the people of our church so easily loving and respecting you. I believe that is why the bad thoughts Adolphe hid away have returned."

She sighed. "Just as he was with Dieter, Adolphe wants to be more loved and respected than you, Jan. And the only way he knows to do that is to try to tear you down."

Jan stared at Heidi. "What happened to Dieter, Heidi? Where are his sons?"

Heidi looked steadily at Jan, not speaking for several moments. "Dieter and our lovely daughter-in-law went for a drive one beautiful summer day. They left the little boys with us so they could enjoy the drive and the sunshine, just the two of them. When they had been gone many hours, we grew concerned. Tomas went to look for them."

Jan could tell the memory was difficult for Heidi to speak of, but she did not flinch from it. "Something must have startled the horses because they ran off the edge of the bluff that runs along the river. It is perhaps a thirty-foot fall. Tomas could see the wagon, all broken in pieces, on the bank below."

Heidi clung to Jan's hands, and Søren's voice dropped to a whisper as she finished. "He could see the horses and . . . Dieter and Gretchen still lying where they had fallen."

The clock on the shelf ticked on in the quiet after Søren translated Heidi's last words. No one spoke.

Jan pondered Heidi's tale, understanding—at last—the origins of Adolphe's animus toward him. And he thought he understood something else as well.

"Ernst and Frank," Jan said quietly. "They are Dieter's *sønns*, not Adolphe's."

Heidi nodded. "*Ja*, they are. When we buried Dieter and his wife, Adolphe and Rakel helped us through our grief. They took care of the boys, the farm, everything while we grieved."

Her shoulders moved in another heavy sigh. "They took the boys home with them *just for a few days*, Adolphe told us. But after a week or so they announced, *We will adopt them. It is God's provision, both for us and for them*. We did not want to give up our grandbabies, but Adolphe said we must think of their needs rather than ourselves."

And yet . . . Jan mulled over how Adolphe treated the young men. He realized Heidi's story was not finished.

"We prayed! Oh, we prayed! And we believed they were right. The boys would give Adolphe and Rakel the family they wanted and needed. That was almost nineteen years ago, and for a long time this was so."

She looked again into Jan's eyes. "Do you see how sweet a disposition Ernst has? How tender Frank is? As they became young men, the boys looked and acted more and more like their father—not like Adolphe, but like Dieter!

"We saw Adolphe change toward the boys. He has tried so much to keep them from becoming what they are—Dieter's sons. But nothing can prevent that, can it? And then *you* came, *Herr* Thoresen, so much like Dieter in your personality: A good man, a natural leader, and everyone liking you. Ach! I think our Adolphe hated you on sight.

"The worst part for Adolphe is . . . how Ernst and Frank look at you. They will never look at Adolphe like that, and it has driven him . . . mad."

Jan stood up abruptly and strode over to the stove, ostensibly to pour another cup of coffee. He stood at the stove, his heart breaking for Heidi and her grandsons, for his family and the church.

So much damage because of Adolphe's twisted mind and heart! And he, Jan, had unwittingly played a part in that damage. How could he undo the harm his own "righteous" anger had done—now that he understood how wounded Adolphe was at his core?

Lord, can you heal the harm I have done?

"I must go to the German church and ask forgiveness," Jan murmured. "I will pray first for the right timing, but it must be soon."

It was a few days after Heidi's revelations; Jan and Søren were at work with the cutter. Between the two homesteads, Jan and Søren still had sod to bust—more backbreaking labor so that they could plant all their fields.

It is our eighth spring here, Jan reflected. *And never did I dream Elli would not be here with me this spring.*

They were working the farthest fields north along the creek when they heard the echoing clang of the dinner bell. It was only midmorning. Amalie was calling them home for some other reason.

When they arrived at the house, a horse and wagon were tied near the kitchen door. Ernst and his younger brother Frank greeted Jan and Søren with silent nods. Heidi stood on the porch, her expression uncharacteristically sad.

"Father and Mother packed up *Großmutti's* belongings," Ernst muttered. "Father sent us to deliver them to her." It was not difficult for Jan to recognize the resentment simmering behind Ernst's hard face and clipped words.

"Come in, Ernst. Come in, Frank," Jan invited. "Have some coffee and visit your grandmother, eh? Let's talk together for a few minutes."

"We are not to stay," Ernst's words grated. He cut his eyes toward Jan. "We are not to step into your home."

So much anger roiled just beneath the surface of Ernst's words! But not toward *him*, Jan sensed. Frank studied his feet and added nothing.

"I see," Jan replied quietly. He glanced at Heidi who shook her head. "I am sorry for this. I have only good will toward both of you, *ja*? I hope you will still consider me a friend even if we cannot visit as such."

Frank looked up at him with what Jan felt was hope but quickly tore his eyes away. Ernst answered, his voice flat, "We are to unload her things and return immediately."

"*Ja*, let us help you do that," Jan answered.

The two young men, brushing off Jan's offer, lifted a few boxes and a heavy trunk from the wagon and placed them on the ground. "This is everything," Ernst growled. "We have to leave now so that we are home on time."

Jan nodded and the boys clambered up onto the wagon's bench. Ernst kept his eyes facing forward, but Jan saw his jaw working.

Ach, Lord! These poor young men! Jan lamented.

He and Søren made short work of bringing Heidi's things into the house; they set them on her bedroom floor. After they left, Heidi went into her room and closed the door.

That night after dinner, Heidi requested to speak to Jan and Amalie privately again, but of course their conversation required Søren.

She cradled an old Bible on her lap. "*Herr* Thoresen, I am thanking God that my grandsons brought Tomas' Bible—our family Bible—to me today. I was afraid Adolphe would not send it!"

Jan nodded. "It must be precious to you."

"*Ja*, but what is inside is more precious!"

"What can be more precious than God's word, eh?" Jan smiled.

Heidi opened the large Bible and offered Jan a shrewd grimace. "Of course nothing is more precious than God's word, but perhaps my grandsons' future is also important?"

On the table in front of her was a small, sharp knife. She placed the heavy Bible on the table, picked up the knife and, with care, began to slice between the back cover and the stiff paper glued to it. Amalie and Søren leaned forward, intrigued.

From between the outside and inside covers Heidi withdrew a thin sheet of paper. She handed it to Søren. "Read, please?"

Søren struggled with the fine script and formal German words. "*Letzter Wille und Testament?*"

"*Ja*," Heidi whispered. "Tomas' will."

Søren pored over the paper. "This says that Tomas leaves the sum of one hundred dollars to Adolphe but gives his homestead to his son Dieter. And that you may live there the rest of your life."

"Read on, Søren," Heidi urged.

"But if Dieter dies . . . before this will is in effect, then the homestead goes to his sons, Ernst and Frank Veicht?"

"That is right," Heidi affirmed. "Ernst and Frank are Dieter's sons. The homestead now belongs to them."

She turned to Jan. "You saw how beaten down my grandsons are, *ja*? Do you think if I had revealed this paper to Adolphe after Tomas died it would have survived?"

Jan slowly shook his head and Heidi leaned toward him. "*Herr* Thoresen, I need your help. Ernst is now twenty-one years old. He can inherit. When you go to ask forgiveness, will you read this before the church? It must be read before all—or I fear Adolphe will find a way to destroy it."

Ah, Lord! Jan groaned inside.

ℭHAPTER 28

Jan relinquished precious plowing time the next morning to visit Henrik, Norvald, and Rikkert. He took with him Heidi and Tomas' family Bible and Tomas' will.

When Henrik understood what Jan proposed to do, he joined him and rode with him to Norvald's farm. The three of them then drove to Rikkert and Duna's farm.

Rikkert's face paled when Jan told him what he would do on Sunday. "Ah, Jan! It will go badly, don't you think?" He licked his lips and frowned.

Jan studied his friend. "Rikkert, I say this to you as a brother, with these men as witnesses. You were ordained as an elder in the church— but you have neglected your duty to God and our congregation. Your silence has allowed many wrong things to happen."

Rikkert winced and his expression saddened. "I know," he whispered. "I know."

Norvald placed his hand on Rikkert's shoulder. "It is never too late to do the right thing, my brother. And we will pray the Lord to give you the courage to do the right thing when the time comes, *ja*?"

"Norvald will interpret for me, but I wish you to come with me Sunday," Jan murmured later to Søren. "I wish you to witness my repentance, but I leave the decision to you. I tell you now that it will be difficult for you to watch. I have promised the Lord that I will be humble and gentle. I will not speak in anger to Minister Veicht, no matter what is said."

Søren looked away and considered Jan's request. "I will come."

Jan clapped him on the back. "*Gut*, my *sønn*. Then shall we pray together about it?"

Søren nodded.

Service was almost over; Adolphe was concluding his teaching when Rikkert, who was sitting near the back of the men's side, stood and walked across the room to the door. When he opened it, Jan, Søren, Norvald, and Henrik quietly entered.

Adolphe paused mid-sentence. "You! You are not welcome here!"

The congregation began murmuring, and some repeated Adolphe's words.

"I have come to ask forgiveness," Jan said just loud enough for all to hear him. Norvald immediately repeated his words in German.

"So! You have come to repent, have you?" Adolphe's face was red, but he seemed to embrace the idea of Jan humbling himself.

"May I speak to the church?" Jan asked.

Adolphe studied Jan for several seconds.

"Let him speak!" one of the men called. A murmur of assent went around the room.

Adolphe thought for a moment more. "I wish the elders to come forward," he directed. "*Herr* Thoresen, you will come and kneel in front of us to make your confession."

Søren gasped, but Jan gripped his arm. "Be quiet, *Sønn*," was his stern instruction.

Jan, followed by Norvald, walked to the front. Jan knelt, facing the people; Norvald stood to the side.

"I ask forgiveness of you all," he said quietly. "When I was last here, I allowed my temper to speak. My temper brought strife and division to this church. Some who left and some of you here are still angry. The Bible says strife, discord, and division are works of the flesh."

Behind him, Adolphe was nodding his head.

Jan continued. "I ask your forgiveness for the words I spoke in anger. I ask your forgiveness for not handling the situation regarding me and my brother's wife better. If I had spoken privately with the elders and *Herr* Veicht, there would have been no public strife.

"I have asked forgiveness of my family and my brother's wife. I will ask forgiveness of those who have left the church. I will ask them to put away their anger and bitterness so that it will not lead to sin.

"I now ask your forgiveness for the strife my angry words caused. Will you forgive me? Will you also put away your anger?" Jan's words were spoken earnestly; he looked most of the men in the eye as he spoke. Many of them nodded in response.

Jan got to his feet. "I would also request the opportunity to speak to *Herr* Veicht and the elders on another issue. I would not speak of it openly, but in private."

"What! You are done? You do not ask forgiveness of me?" Adolphe asked, his voice rising. "You disrespected my office and stole my mother's affections! These are great offenses!"

"I am sorry for the discord between you and your mother. Perhaps we can speak of that privately?" Jan answered, his voice still quiet.

"*Nein!*" Adolphe roared. "Anything you wish to say will be said in the open. And you will not receive this congregation's forgiveness until your repentance is complete! You have disrespected my office. You have broken family ties. These things are great sins!"

Jan sighed. "If I had done those things, I would ask forgiveness. Perhaps you and I can speak of our trespasses to each other privately?"

"You can speak of nothing to me privately!" Adolphe scoffed. "I am the minister here. I have not transgressed against you; it is you who has transgressed against me and my office."

Jan looked at the floor for several moments. "Then, respectfully, I must also repent of something else. I repent of not speaking up earlier, when Tomas died and you took on the office of minister."

He sighed. "I now bring to the congregation's attention that the charter of this church was broken after Tomas passed." Norvald translated Jan's words as quickly as he spoke them.

"According to the charter, a new lay minister must be brought before the congregation by the elders and approved by a vote. This was not done. In assuming the leadership of the church without following the charter, I am obliged to say that you erred, *Herr* Veicht."

Jan's tone was gentle and even, but Adolphe blustered at his words. "More disrespect! You have not come to ask forgiveness but to stir up more discord!"

Jan, as though Adolphe had not spoken, now turned to the elders. "I call upon the elders to affirm if Adolphe was correctly installed as the lay minister of this church."

He looked first to Rikkert. "Rikkert Kappel. Was Adolphe Veicht selected by the elders, approved by vote of the congregation, and publicly ordained?"

Rikkert, his eyes glued to the back wall, spoke clearly. "He was not selected by the elders, approved by the congregation, nor ordained. I, too, must repent for allowing the charter to be broken. I ask forgiveness of the church for shirking my duties as an elder of this church."

Jan nodded. Klaus and Gunnar stared at Rikkert, their mouths agape.

"And you, Gunnar Braun and Klaus Schöener," Jan continued, still in a gentle voice, "Did you also shirk your duties by not following the charter of this church? Did you allow *Herr* Veicht to assume the leadership of the church without following the regulations of the charter?"

A confusion of congregational murmuring and shouting by Adolphe made it impossible to hear what Klaus and Gunnar said. It was Norvald who thundered the words, "Silence! There must be *order* in the church of God!"

He faced Klaus and Gunnar and repeated Jan's question. "Answer before the church, please," he insisted.

To his credit, Gunnar answered. "I wish to speak—" he said clearly.

The congregation quieted, but Adolphe shouted, "You will *not* speak! This is outrageous! Under a cloak of false repentance this, this *man*," he pointed a shaking finger at Jan, "has again brought strife into the house of God! He must be removed, immediately!"

"Twice I asked to speak privately of these things, *nei*?" Jan answered. "Twice you refused, even insisting that I speak of them openly."

Adolphe pointed to several large men in the congregation. "Remove this evildoer from us!"

"*Nein!*" Gunnar shouted into the din. "*Nein!* I am an elder in this church, and I *will* speak!" He faced Adolphe. "You do not have authority to silence an elder. You will listen, *Herr* Veicht."

It was Adolphe's turn to stare with his mouth open. Before Adolphe could recover, Gunnar continued. "What *Herr* Thoresen and *Herr* Kappel say is true. We did not follow the charter—but is that oversight not easily remedied? Can we not now vote on and ordain *Herr* Veicht as our minister?"

"Would you not first need to bring back those who have left over this issue and have them vote also?" Norvald asked.

"More importantly," Jan inserted, "Should not the will of *Herr* Tomas Veicht be read first?"

Red-faced, Adolphe sputtered and started to protest.

"Hold. You are not the minister here yet," Norvald interrupted. "*Herr* Thoresen is right. The error began at Tomas' funeral when we were all grieving. His will was never read, and the charter was not followed in filling his position."

"Will?" Adolphe shouted. "What will? There is no will! As his son, I inherited his property! There is no will that says otherwise!"

"*Ja*, there is," Jan answered quietly.

Norvald motioned again for the congregation to quiet. "*Frau* Heidi Veicht has provided Tomas' will. Do you wish to see it? To hear it read?"

"This is a lie!" Adolphe protested. "There is no will! I would know. I have searched and found nothing!"

"Because you did not know where Tomas placed it for safekeeping," Norvald replied. He held up Tomas' family Bible. "Do you recognize this?"

He showed it first to the three elders who all nodded their recognition. Then he showed it to Adolphe who attempted to grab it out of Norvald's hands.

"This is not yours!" Adolphe roared. "How dare you steal what is mine!"

"*Nein*," Norvald answered, still in a calm, authoritative voice. "This Bible belongs to *Frau* Heidi Veicht. You yourself packed it and sent it to her by the hand of her grandsons, Ernst and Frank Veicht.

"It is not *your* property but hers," Norvald insisted. "She asked *Herr* Thoresen and his son, Søren, to witness what we are about to show you."

He opened the book and gestured the three elders to gather around. Holding it toward the congregation, Norvald separated the back cover. "See this? Tomas glued the covers together. But first, Tomas placed his will between them."

A hush descended as Norvald pulled the single sheet from between the pages. He showed it to the elders. "Is this the writing of Tomas Veicht?"

"*Ja*," answered Klaus. "I know it well."

The other elders concurred. "It is Tomas' writing."

Adolphe attempted to wrest the sheet from Norvald, but Klaus held up his hand. "Let all things be done decently and in order, *Herr* Veicht. If this is Tomas' will, then we will read it aloud to the congregation. You will hear it as we hear it, *ja*?"

He pointed to the front row bench. "Please sit down."

"You do not tell me what to do!" Adolphe thundered.

But the three elders, in unison, pointed to the bench.

Rikkert added, "Until you are properly voted upon and ordained by the congregation, it is only right that you take your seat and allow us to perform our duties."

Adolphe's face paled. He turned to the congregation for help, but the men were nodding their agreement with Rikkert. Slowly Adolphe sank onto the bench.

By then, the elders had each scanned the short document. "I did not know that!" Gunnar was astounded. "Did you know?" he asked Rikkert and Klaus. They both shook their heads.

"Read the will!" a man in the congregation shouted. Others agreed and said so.

Gunnar slowly read from the sheet. "*I, Tomas Veicht, do bequeath the sum of one hundred dollars to my son Adolphe and, as is our custom, bequeath the remainder of my property to my younger son Dieter Veicht.*"

"Dieter? He has a son named Dieter?" the words flew through the congregation.

Adolphe jumped to his feet. "My brother Dieter died many years ago! Almost twenty years ago! As the surviving son, the property is mine!"

"I am not finished!" Rikkert's stern voice quieted the church again. "No one will speak until I have finished reading, *ja*?" He stared around the room, asserting his authority.

"The will continues, *If my son Dieter dies before me, I bequeath my property equally to his two sons, Ernst and Frank Veicht, with the stipulation that my wife, Heidi Veicht, be allowed to live out her days in peace in the house we built together.* It is signed Tomas Veicht and witnessed by two men."

In the stunned silence that followed, Ernst Veicht slowly stood. He stared at Adolphe, who was shaking his head back and forth.

"You are not my father?" he said incredulously. "My father is this Dieter Veicht? Why have I never heard of him?"

His gaze turned to the elders, to Norvald and Jan. "Is this so? *Herr* Thoresen? My grandmother affirms this?"

Norvald translated and Jan nodded. "*Ja*, she does. Dieter was born to Tomas and Heidi three years after they adopted Adolphe. Your father and your mother died when you were less than two years old and Frank was but a baby."

As Norvald translated Jan's words, the hush over the congregation melted away. Voices, both men's and women's, whispered, "Adopted? Adolphe was adopted?" and "I never knew Tomas and Heidi had another son!"

All said this except one wizened, elderly woman. Slowly she stood to her feet, leaning on her daughter. "Elders, I am a witness to these events. May I speak?"

Rikkert and Gunnar looked at each other and then Klaus. "*Ja, Frau* Tokker."

"I am ten years older than Heidi Veicht. My husband and I came here from Ohio when Tomas and Heidi did. I remember when Adolphe's parents died and Tomas and Heidi took him in. I remember well when Dieter was born, when he married, and when Ernst and Frank were born," her papery voice shook with age and emotion.

"Not many farmers lived in this community back then, but my husband and I did, God rest his soul. He is one of the witnesses to this will. I remember when Adolphe and Rakel took Ernst and Frank into their home and made them their own. But they required Tomas and Heidi never to speak of Dieter again. *This was wrong.*"

Frau Tokker pointed at Adolphe. "You threatened to take Ernst and Frank far away if Tomas and Heidi did not agree to keep quiet about Dieter.

"I remember, you see, because Heidi wept on my shoulder when Dieter and Gretchen died—when you took their boys and would not allow their grandparents to see them until they promised that you and Rakel could raise them as your own."

She shook her finger at Adolphe. "Now at last the truth comes out! Ernst and Frank are Dieter and Gretchen's *kinder* and Tomas' heirs. It is *they* who own this house and land, even this room our church has worshipped in all these years!"

With that, the elderly *Frau* Tokker, assisted by her daughter, sat down.

A sad silence settled on the room. Then Ernst faced Adolphe and raised an unsteady voice. "You have lied to us all of our lives. *All of our lives!*"

Adolphe stood up. "You will not speak to me with disrespect! I raised you; I am your father!"

Ernst shook his head. "No. You are *not* my father." He trembled with long-suppressed hurt and rage. "Have you ever treated us as a father should treat his sons? No!"

Rakel was also on her feet, pleading with Ernst. "Ernst! You do not know what you are saying! You must obey your father!"

Ernst looked at her sadly. "I am grown now. I will never obey this man again. And you and your husband will leave this house today. You, you . . . you are not welcome here."

He grabbed Frank and yanked him to his feet. "This is *our* home now, Frank."

He strode to the elders and took the Bible and Tomas' will from their hands. "These are our grandmother's, *ja*? We will return them to her." He pointed at Adolphe. "Please help this man to pack his belongings and leave our property. He has his own farm to go to."

Ernst paused and added, "Take the church's things, too—the benches and tables. There will be no church here again. When we return, I expect *them*—he pointed at Adolphe and Rakel—and all these things to be gone." With a confused Frank trailing behind him, Ernst stormed from the room.

Consternation and confusion reigned. Jan shook his head in anguish. *Lord! Confusion is not from you! This is now worse than before!*

But a still, small voice rumbled in his heart: *I cannot heal until what has been covered is uncovered and brought into the Light. I must do a deep work. Trust me.*

Sighing, Jan muttered, *Ja, Lord, you know I will.*

ؘ ✹ ৈ

CHAPTER 29

1874

Jan and Søren stood on the knoll above their old soddy and wiped the sweat and dust from their necks and faces. With grim faces they studied their fields to the east: acres of corn, shriveled and stunted, their stalks and tassels barely stirring in the dry breeze.

To the north, parched by the glaring sun, were their wheat fields. The Thoresen men, aided by Sigrün and to a lesser degree by Little Karl and Arnie, had already harvested the meager early wheat and oat crops. This second crop of wheat, when sent to Omaha, was to have meant dearly needed cash in the bank.

But they would send no crops this year.

On Thoresen land and all neighboring farms, the usually lush prairie browse was burned to dry stubble. What corn the Thoresens salvaged would have to feed their cattle, horses, goats, and sizable herd of pigs—not only through the cold winter months, but even now.

The drought that had broken briefly a year ago had reasserted itself; little rain had fallen this spring to water their fields. The few newspapers circulating through their community reported that the drought was widespread and severe, threatening the very survival of America's plains and prairie farmers.

And so, as distressing as this crop was, they would need every bit of it—the ears, the stalks, and the leaves—if they were to keep their animals alive another year.

Jan clapped Søren on the back and sighed. "Praise to God! We will at least have enough to get by another year."

Jan and Søren, now sixteen years old, strode between rows of corn and randomly selected a few ears to sample. They each stripped the husk from an ear and examined the corn within. Søren bit into his ear and uttered a grunt. "The kernels are not big, *Pappa*, but they are sweet."

"*Ja*," Jan replied, "but the ears will get no bigger. We should start the harvest tomorrow, eh?"

Søren agreed. Corn was the most labor-intensive and time consuming of their crops to harvest. Every Thoresen would work the harvest, from dawn to dusk, until the crop they so desperately needed was safe within their barn.

In the distance they heard the clanging of the bell signaling the midday meal. They walked in silence back to the farmhouse, both of them planning their afternoon tasks in preparation for tomorrow's start of the corn harvest.

As they strode into the farmyard, Little Karl, Arnie, and Kjell ran toward them, jumping with abandon into Jan and Søren's arms or grappling them around their legs.

"*Onkel! Onkel!* Is it time?" Little Karl shouted.

Arnie hollered, "*Søren!* Is it time?"

"Is it time to harvest the corn?" Little Karl yelled louder.

Kjell, only three and a half, raced around Jan and Søren, screaming, "Is it time? Is it time?" again and again, part of the general chaos that greeted Jan each day.

Heidi, smiling with happy abandon, waved from inside the screened door. She held tiny Uli by the hand. Uli, too, jumped up and down, shrieking her delight that *Onkel* and Søren were home for dinner.

"All right, all right," Jan said, pulling one little boy from his legs only to have another clamp on. "Let us all go to the pump and wash up, *ja*? Your *mamma* will not let any dirty hands or faces at her table, is that not so?"

Jan and Søren made their way to the pump, dragging the tribe of wild boys who protested against getting their hands and faces washed in the cold water, even on the sweltering August day.

During the large dinner served by the women, Jan and Søren made plans to sharpen the farm's scythes and look over the other tools they would use for the harvest. When Uli began to fuss for her nap, Jan took her on his knee. He gently bounced her until she leaned against his broad chest, yawned, and her eyes drooped.

Jan looked about the table, satisfied with what he saw. Heidi had cemented her place in their home with her love and care. To Amalie she was mother and confidante, one who understood Amalie's loss and grief. To the children she was their *bestemor*, the only grandmother they would know. To Jan, Heidi was strength of spirit. Her stability and joy comforted and encouraged him.

Her grandsons, Ernst and Frank, had, in the last year, retreated from the community and had little to do with anyone, including their grandmother. "God will heal their wounds someday," Heidi declared bravely. "I will pray for them until the Lord undertakes!"

Adolphe and Rakel had moved back to their own homestead, and the German church had not voted Adolphe as their lay minister. Instead they had called an older man whose gentleness was reminiscent of Tomas'. The church met in his barn, quite a distance from the Thoresen and Bruntrüllsen farms.

Soon after, Adolphe and Rakel sold their homestead and departed. No one knew where they had gone.

Norvald continued holding services in his barn for those who lived too far from where the German church met. The Thoresens, Andersons, and others gathered with them on Sundays.

"*Takk-takk.*" Amalie gestured for Jan to pass Uli to her. "She will go to her nap now that she has had a moment of her *Onkel* Jan's attention. Then Heidi and Sigrün and I can get back to our canning."

At least the green garden is doing well, Jan observed. As long as the well held out, they could pump and haul water to the garden, ensuring that their family would eat through the long winter months.

Jan gave Uli up reluctantly but acknowledged that he and Søren needed to get back to work. He pushed back from the table and frowned as the light from the kitchen window dimmed a bit.

"Are those rain clouds to the north and west?" Søren remarked. "I did not see rain on the almanac, did you?"

Jan went out the door and stood on the porch followed by Søren, Little Karl, and Arnie. The sun shone nearly straight overhead but the northwestern horizon was covered by a cloud that stretched from the heavens to the ground. Jan's heart thudded, and he did not understand why.

"It looks like . . . snow . . ." Søren said, puzzled. "Like a blizzard? How could that be?" True, they had suffered summer hailstorms many times, but a hail-producing thunderstorm came from dark, even black, thunderheads.

The cloud was miles wide and miles high. It covered every aspect to the northwest, blotting out their view of the distant prairie and all on it. And the cloud was advancing. Quickly.

Something landed on the porch. Jan glanced down just as something smacked him on his chest. Instinctively he swept it off, but something else struck his trousers. This time he grabbed it and looked closely.

A grasshopper of some kind. It was small and black, no larger than a penny, but . . .

Arnie shrieked and swatted at an insect on his shirt. Søren brushed another out of Arnie's hair.

The cloud was near, closing on them. And then the locusts were falling from the sky, millions upon millions of them, falling like living hail.

"*Pappa!*" Søren's shout conveyed terror.

"Get inside!" Jan bellowed. He and Søren grabbed up the boys and threw them into the house, following them and slamming the door.

"Close every window," Jan commanded, swatting the bugs that had fallen on them and been carried indoors. "Pull the shutters closed!"

A great sound beat the air, growing louder and louder. The children were crying and screaming. Amalie and Sigrün rushed about the house sliding up the windows so that they could reach the shutters and pull them in. Jan and Søren ran to help them, swatting at the insects that were hurtling through every crack.

The day darkened unnaturally but the noise of insect wings increased until it was a deafening pounding upon the house, drowning out all other sound.

They huddled in the kitchen, the little boys crowded onto Jan's lap sobbing in terror. No one spoke—*no one could be heard!*

They could do nothing but wait.

In the near dark Søren studied his father. Jan's face was set in sorrowful lines. Søren knew, without being told, that nothing would remain of their meager crops.

Hours later the din faded and the late afternoon sun came out. Jan's small nephews had cried themselves to sleep in his arms and began to stir. Jan set them down and gestured with his chin to Søren.

His *sønn* opened the kitchen door with caution. Then he opened the screened door. It swept a swath of insects from the porch. They were everywhere, all moving, all chewing. Jan and Søren walked toward the barn, by way of the green garden, their sturdy boots crunching insects with each step.

The garden was covered in inches of locusts. Where bush beans and tomatoes had stood several feet high, only a mound of insects remained.

Jan shuddered. The collective din of the insects' mandibles chewing and grinding away was all they could hear until they drew near the barn. Then the sounds of distressed animals reached their ears.

Jan and Søren ran the rest of the distance. The locusts had found their way inside the barn and sheds and were consuming grain, hay, and straw wherever they found it—in the stalls, in the feed boxes, in the pens, even beneath the animals now crazed by the insects climbing on them, clustering in their ears and eyes.

Under the hay shelter, Jan and Søren's meager stacks of baled grasses and hay crawled with grasshoppers. Jan grabbed heavy canvas tarpaulins. "Let us cover the bales as tightly as possible!" he shouted.

"But the locusts are already on them!" Søren yelled.

"Sweep off what you can," Jan replied, "But covering the bales might keep more locusts from getting to them—perhaps we will save some!"

Even as they worked, Jan's mind was trying to grasp the enormity of the swarm and calculate the damage to their farm.

If nothing is left, we will have nothing to feed the animals, his mind clamored. *Nothing!* He began to pray—not just for his family, but for every friend and neighbor. The Andersons! Norvald and Inge! The McKennies! He knew that for some of his neighbors, this would be the final straw.

O God, how will we survive this?

The insects ate their fill for two days, devouring anything containing moisture. They beat upon the windows, fought their way inside whenever a door was opened, and crept through cracks into the house.

When Jan and Søren ran to the well to fetch water or to tend the stock, the insects fell on them, chewing at their clothes. When they returned to the house Amalie and Heidi would pick the insects from them. By the second day even the children picked up the locusts and threw them into the fire without flinching.

On the third day, to the thrumming of millions of wings, the locusts took slowly to the air. Jan and Søren watched from a kitchen window as the swarm rose, again darkening the skies. Gradually the shadow of the swarm disappeared to the south and east.

"Where will they go, *Pappa*?" Søren asked, his voice low. "Will they be back?"

Jan shook his head. "I don't know."

Jan and Søren surveyed the damage: It was utter and complete.

The locusts had eaten every living plant to the ground. Jan could only compare the destruction to that of a fire—and yet, he had seen fires leave more behind.

The garden was bare dirt defiled with the husks of many dead locusts. On the slope where his apple trees had helped shade the graves, two sticks remained, their trunks and branches stripped and gnawed bare.

In the hay shelter, the canvases they had strapped over the hay bales lay flat on the ground—all but one. Søren lifted it and found three or four bales still intact. Dead locusts littered the ground as he picked up and folded the tarps.

"Look at this," Jan called. Søren followed his father's voice to the barn wall where the tools hung.

"See, they have chewed on the leather tack. They have even gnawed on the wooden handles of our tools," Jan pointed out.

They went about the business of filling the watering troughs of the livestock and removing the carcasses of those animals that, in their crazed states, had injured themselves.

"The chickens are glutted, *Pappa*," Søren noted. The chickens were the only animals that had fed well. The locusts had attacked the straw in the pens, but the chickens had seen them as bounty. They were the only animals not clamoring to be fed.

Jan thought for a moment. "We have no feed left for the chickens," he reported. "It is gone, too. The locusts chewed through the bags and ate it all."

He pointed to the dead grasshoppers on the hay shelter floor. "Let us get the children to sweep up as many grasshoppers as they can. We can feed the chickens on them for a few days."

Søren ran toward the house leaving Jan alone.

And then? After even the dead locusts are gone? Jan sat down on one of the remaining bales of hay and dropped his head in his hands.

We have no feed, no hay, no browse for any of our animals, and neither will anyone else. Jan rocked back and forth. *We will have to slaughter most of our animals, saving only breeding stock to rebuild our herds. But what will we feed even them? And what will I feed my family through the winter, Lord?*

He began to shake. *O God! This land! It has taken so much! My brother, my child, and my wife! Our crops! And now our animals!*

"Oh, God!" Jan cried aloud in agony. "This land! This land is breaking my heart! I have nothing left of my dreams but this dust and my tears."

CHAPTER 30

News trickled into the community. The swarm of locusts, the largest ever sighted in the Americas, had swept through Nebraska, Kansas, and the western edges of Missouri. Some said the swarm numbered *in the trillions*.

Jan could not comprehend a number that large, yet he had only to recall the cloud of insects that fell on them to believe the report to be true.

They also heard a rumor that, by tracking the swath of insects through telegraphed reports, the swarm had been measured at 1,800 miles in length and some 110 miles wide. And the locusts devoured every growing thing in its path.

The Thoresens, like other farmers in the community, slaughtered all the animals they could preserve and eat that winter. Jan, recognizing that some families had no stock to slaughter except a milk cow and plowing mule or ox, gave away many of their steers and pigs.

At least they will have meat this winter, Jan consoled himself.

Keeping back the stock they hoped to keep alive through the coming winter, they shipped the rest to Omaha for immediate slaughter or sale.

They received just pennies on the dollar.

With the last of their money, Jan bought seed wheat, corn, and oats. He and Søren tilled the fields closest to the house and planted a small crop of winter wheat.

"What will happen in the spring?" Søren asked quietly. "If the locusts laid eggs here, will they hatch and swarm again?" Søren knew, every bit as well as Jan did, that if the locusts returned and destroyed spring crops, outright famine would grip the prairie and plains farmers.

"I don't know," Jan answered. "Only God knows."

Winter set in. A more normal snowfall watered their fields through the winter. In March Jan and Søren watched, with cautious optimism, their winter wheat sprout and grow lush in the spring rains.

As the prairie came alive, they herded their few animals out to feed on newly green browse. The stock, near to starving, ate to the ground whatever they could find.

Jan or Søren moved them to new browse three times a day and brought them into the barn each evening. Prairie predators, too, were starving, and were a constant threat to Thoresen livestock.

Jan had kept two cows and their calves, two oxen, and breeding stock from their goats, chickens, and pigs. At the last minute he kept the bays, hoping that he could, somehow, keep them from starving. Now he hobbled the horses, with ribs outlined under their coats, alongside the cows and oxen and allowed them to eat their fill.

In April and May Jan and Søren plowed as many fields as they had seed. Then they prayed.

Spring rains watered the fields and the Thoresens rejoiced. Within two weeks the seeds were greening the prairie. Jan kept Little Karl, Arnie, Kjell, and the farm's dogs busy running off the prairie nibblers, who were also starving.

Alarming news of another great swarm of locusts spread through the farming community. This swarm, hatched from the rain-watered soils of Kansas and Missouri, was reported to be devouring all in its path, a swath northwards to Minnesota and south through Texas to the Gulf of Mexico.

The Thoresens prayed for mercy. The infestation of locusts stayed east of RiverBend and its neighboring lands. God willing, the drought was ending and they would harvest a crop!

1875

"You have changed, Jan," Amalie said quietly after the children had been excused from the table. "I was just remembering . . . when we came from our old country. You were a different man back then, joyous, full of mischief and fun. Not so . . . serious."

Jan didn't answer her right away. What was there to say? He shrugged.

"Jan, you should, perhaps, pray about taking a wife, *ja*? You could have your choice of several very eligible women, don't you know?"

"And you, Amalie? What of you?" Jan shot back.

She laughed, but without much mirth. "Ah, Jan. Who would marry a woman with five children, eh? A man might take me and my children to gain my land, but you know I will never give away what belongs to Karl's *sønns*."

And that was the excuse Jan used to push away suggestions that he marry again. He could barely manage his and Karl's land—320 acres— by himself. Yes, Søren was shouldering a man's load now, but how could he, Jan, take on a wife? He had Søren, Amalie, and her five children leaning on him already.

Of course he was a changed man!

Amalie spoke again. "Besides, I have prayed, and I am content to care for our families. It is what the Lord would have me do. But you, Jan. You are *not* content, eh?"

Jan put his head in his hands. "Enough, *Søster*. I thank you for your care and concern!" Sorry for his sharp tone he added, "Will you pray for me, then?"

"Ah, Jan. I am always praying for you," she whispered.

Jan thought of Elli every day. As he milked, his hands knew what to do, so he let his mind wander. When he plowed, he could make straight rows without conscious thought, so he dwelled on his memories of Elli.

For the first few weeks after she and Kristen had died, he had been tempted to blame the Beckers—but watching a very broken Maria Becker and her only remaining son leaving their homestead and returning to her father and mother had been chastisement enough on that count.

Then, although he avoided plumbing his feelings too deeply, he had also been tempted to blame Elli herself. *For her servant's heart.*

If only she had been content to stay home and not give of her time and care to others, she would never have been exposed to the sickness! Was not our family, our love enough for her? Jan found himself mulling over those and similar thoughts.

But he knew the truth of it. *Lord, you sent her to serve others. She heard you speaking to her! Yet what good did that do, if now she is dead? Why did you take her if she was doing your bidding?*

During this spring's work, he thought on how God had slowly transformed Elli, changing her mourning over their lost baby into the joy of serving others. Jan had not been blind to Elli's struggle—he had seen how, with stern determination, she had pressed in to what God had called her to do.

His eyes welling with tears, Jan swallowed the same medicine he gave to Elli now more than three years past. *It is so. I am wasting my life and joy pining over what I do not have—what I will never have again in this lifetime. Elli is gone. I must surrender her to you, once and for all, Lord.*

He pushed such recollections from his mind, but they always seemed to return. Gradually he began to wonder—to question whether the Lord was bringing Elli's choice to mind for a purpose.

Maybe I should take a lesson from Elli, eh, Lord? Jan pondered. *Perhaps Amalie is right and I have allowed these hardships to change me too much.*

But what can I do to serve others, Lord, that I am not already doing? Do you have something other than the strength of my back for me to give?

Jan, Søren, and the younger boys were hoeing weeds between the rows of corn. The stalks were growing tall and thick. Harvest would be on them soon!

Jan found himself humming an old song, a jaunty little tune, bringing his hoe down in rhythm to it. In the row to his left Søren picked up the tune, whistling it softly between his teeth. The chop of his hoe matched Jan's.

To Jan's right, Little Karl and Arnie started singing the words and Jan joined in. They sang louder. The hoes slashed through the weeds and the clods in time with their song. Søren harmonized and they picked up the pace.

Amalie, Sigrün, and Heidi, bending over laundry tubs in the yard, heard the song wafting toward them. Amalie paused, looking away toward the creek where the men and boys were working.

"They're singing," Kjell hollered. "*Onkel* and Søren are singing!"

"Singing," little Uli repeated, clapping her hands.

Heidi smiled joyously and Amalie grinned back. "*Ja*, they are singing! It is a happy sound, is it not?"

When Jan reached the bottom of the row he ended the song and the boys laughed for the sheer joy of it. Jan grabbed Little Karl and hugged him. Arnie, not willing to be left out, dropped his hoe for a hug, too.

Jan motioned to Søren and the four of them stood on the edge of the field, hugging and laughing. "Such good men I have," Jan praised them. "No man could ask for better, eh? It's a happy man you are looking at."

Søren grinned. He knew his *pappa* was speaking mainly for the young boys' benefit, but he appreciated Jan's words anyway. Karl and Arnie, now ages nine and seven, basked in Jan's embrace, their faces shining with pride and confidence.

Be a father to the fatherless, a voice spoke in Jan's ear.

The words were so clear, Jan nearly turned to see who spoke them. But he did not—for immediately he recognized their source.

The voice spoke once more: *Be a father to the fatherless.*

"What is it, *Pappa*?" Søren asked. Jan had gone from laughing to complete stillness.

"I have heard the Lord," Jan slowly answered, wonder in his eyes. "He has told me what I am to do." He sank to his knees. "Will you let me pray for you, boys?"

Søren, Little Karl, and Arnie dropped to their knees beside Jan. Jan placed his hands on Little Karl and Arnie's heads. "Lord, do you see these fine young men? I ask you to be as real to them as the earth upon which we kneel is real. Come close to them, Lord God. Show yourself to them and call them by name to surrender their lives to you."

He lifted a hand and placed it on Søren's shoulder. "Do you see my *sønn*, Lord? Ah, how I thank you for him and give him into your care— I ask you to call him by name to your side. And these nephews of mine, O God, I thank you for them. They are as dear to me as my own *sønn* is, Lord."

He drew the three boys to him. "Let us walk rightly before you all of our days, Lord God! Let us live for Jesus' sake and be his light in this dark world."

"Amen!" Søren, Karl, and Arnie said in unison.

That night Jan knelt next to his bed in the barn and prayed. "I know you were not speaking to me only of my brother's *sønns*, Lord. For I saw, for a mere second, a little picture in my mind of others . . ."

As Jan waited for the Lord to speak to him, he clearly saw Ernst and Frank Veicht. "*Ja*, Lord. I will be a father to these fatherless ones. They will be the first."

He prayed longer and assented to what he felt led to do. "Tomorrow I will begin, Lord. First thing!"

Jan laid his head down in peace. "Ah, Lord. Your peace is my comfort." And he slept.

The following morning Jan and Søren rode out on the bays. "We will be back midday," he had told his family at breakfast. As they rode to Tomas and Heidi Veicht's old property, Jan quietly explained his purpose to Søren.

It has been more than two years since I have been here, Jan realized. He stood in the saddle and searched for the young men. They were in the fields and came when they saw Jan and Søren.

The two young men greeted Jan warily. "*Herr* Thoresen. Søren. We did not expect you. Is our *großmutter* well?" Ernst asked. He was not as angry as when Jan had seen him last.

"*Ja*, she is well," Jan assured them. "I came to talk with you. Can you spare me a few minutes?"

"Of course, *Herr* Thoresen!" Frank nodded with a smile. He challenged Ernst with a glance. Ernst shrugged and led the way.

As they settled around the kitchen table, Jan appraised the two Veicht men and the condition of the house. "Heidi would be proud of you," he began. "You are growing into good farmers and responsible men."

They ducked their heads and thanked him, but Jan could tell his words meant a lot. He smiled and said softly, "Yesterday I believe the Lord spoke a word to my heart."

Their reaction was immediate. Ernst and Frank both looked down in what Jan thought was a combination of fear and anger.

"*Ja*, I know . . . how that sounds, but I am not like—" Jan did not want to say "I'm not like your stepfather, Adolphe," so instead he amended, "May I explain? I would like to ask you to join Søren and me one evening a week to study the Scriptures together."

Frank looked at Ernst who continued to look down at the table. His face was flushed, his mouth pulled into a tight line.

"Ernst," Jan gently probed. "This does not sound good to you, *ja*? I think you have had the Bible taught to you without . . . a father's love?"

Ernst's chin came up and he studied Jan. Jan did not flinch from the examination.

"I remember your grandfather, Tomas, teaching about the grace and goodness of God as well as his righteousness," Jan added. "I . . . propose that we study the Bible in such a balanced way as Tomas did, so that God's goodness can draw us to him."

He smiled at both Frank and Ernst. "That is what the Bible says, *ja*? It says God's *goodness* leads us to repentance? We will talk of many things and share our hearts together as men. What do you say? Will you try it?"

He looked from Ernst to Frank as they considered his words. In silence they looked at each other, and then Ernst answered, "*Ja*, we will try it."

"*Gud!* Good. Can you come this Wednesday evening? Bring your Bibles and we will search for God's goodness together."

They stood and Jan offered his hand. As Ernst took it, Jan gently pulled him into a hug. Ernst, confused and a little embarrassed, did not know how to respond. Jan embraced him, patted him firmly on the back, and let him go.

Then he turned to Frank, extending his hand in the same manner. But when he looked into Frank's eyes, he saw tears standing in them.

"*Ja*, Frank, I know. I know," was all Jan said as he enfolded the young man in a hug. Frank clung to Jan, weeping silently.

Søren cast his eyes to the floor, a witness to something both terrible and beautiful in its power. *Be a father to the fatherless*, his *pappa* had said.

I am so very blessed, Søren suddenly realized.

❧ ✳ ❧

CHAPTER 31

Through the remainder of the summer and into harvest, Jan, Søren, Ernst, and Frank met weekly. Mostly they read a chapter of Scripture and then Jan invited questions and discussion.

Heidi was beside herself with delight knowing she would see her grandsons on a weekly basis. Before long, Ernst and Frank were regulars at their dinner table on Wednesday evenings.

The commitment to meet weekly—especially during the harvest—was not an easy one, but it was a price Jan paid willingly. Søren, with no little awe, watched as his father drew Ernst and Frank into the fiber of their family.

As fall came on and time was a little more relaxed, Jan occasionally rode over to visit the two brothers by himself. Søren imagined he understood the once or twice when Jan returned heavy-hearted and closemouthed. Søren had witnessed Adolphe's treatment of his stepsons and could only imagine the painful things of which Ernst and Frank were unburdening their hearts to his father . . . so Søren understood when Jan declined to discuss those visits.

Lord, Søren prayed, *Please give my Pappa the ear that can hear and the words that can heal!*

The small church that met in Norvald's barn was surprised to see Ernst and Frank one frosty Sunday morning. Jan clapped both of them around their shoulders and introduced them to members who had not attended the German church.

Ivan sidled up to Søren. "What's this I hear? You and Ernst and Frank have Bible study with your father each week? Why have you not told me?"

Søren shrugged and grinned. "If you ask my father nicely, he *may* let you come."

The following Wednesday Ivan and another young Swedish man showed up. The study and discussion was lively and warm, the best Søren could recall.

"*Pappa*, this is a good thing, our study night. Can we open it to others?" he asked before the gathering disbanded that evening.

Jan looked around. "I think it is up to us, *ja*? I will only say that it should be for young men. This is the vision the Lord spoke to me. So that we will grow up into men together, *ja*?"

VIKKI KESTELL

The others nodded their heads in vigorous agreement.

"*Gud.* Then we are agreed."

By the time winter was spent, the group of young men had grown to nine. They had missed a few meetings when storms came through, but the study and fellowship was growing in importance to them all.

"You have changed, Jan," Amalie observed again one evening, but she was smiling. Heidi was smiling, too.

Jan chuckled. "So. A *gud* change this time, eh?"

"Yes! Very good!" Amalie laughed, something that was becoming more common.

"And you, too, *Søster*, eh?" Jan studied Amalie—the woman who had been nearly conquered by the hardships of their first months on the prairie and who had withstood the crushing loss of her husband. "You have changed, too."

Jan and Amalie smiled at each other, the bittersweet and knowing smile of those who have fought a battle and survived together.

Another spring and summer passed. The Thoresens gathered in good harvests and Jan was able to put money in the bank.

We have been in America ten years now, he mused. *And Elli, Kristen, and Karl have been gone four years.*

He was surprised that the pain that had accompanied such thoughts for so long did not stab quite as deeply as it had in the past.

And then another busy year passed.

Thank you, Lord, for your faithfulness, Jan prayed. *And thank you for the contentment and joy I have found again!*

The young men's study had become a community affair. Some evenings fifteen young men crowded into the Thoresen living room. Many of them were bachelors who had struck out on their own and who had no family in the community. On those nights the house resounded with good-natured ribbing, much laughter, earnest conversation, and heartfelt prayer.

"*Be a father to the fatherless*," Jan remembered on such a night. *Never, Lord, did I expect to render such a service to you! I thank you!*

Heidi surprised Jan and Amalie one evening by asking Søren to help her say something to them. "You are both as dear to me as my own children," she began, and she clutched Jan's hand in hers. "For what you have done for my Dieter's sons, I can never, never thank you."

Amalie paled and looked to Jan.

"But?" he asked softly, his eyes watching Heidi's face.

"*Ja*, but," she whispered. "But I have been praying and I feel the Lord has spoken to me. It is time I go back home. Neither one of my grandsons has yet found a wife, and they need me."

Amalie began weeping and shaking her head.

"*Nein, nein, Liebschen*," Heidi murmured patting her hand and shoulder. "There's no need to cry! We will see each other at church each week . . . and every Wednesday, if you will allow me to come with Ernst and Frank when the men have their Bible study?"

"Of course!" Amalie cried. "Whenever you wish! You will always be welcome here."

As she sobbed into her apron, Jan looked a question at Heidi.

"Jan, my dear son in the Lord, there will be no questions of propriety when I leave," Heidi answered through Søren. "The lives you and Amalie live are open books to our community."

"Still, I will stay in the barn, I think," Jan answered. "I am quite comfortable there and . . . and I wish to never give any room to gossip or suspicion. Søren, perhaps you would like the downstairs bedroom when Heidi leaves?"

Jan had no idea where that suggestion had come from, but Søren grasped it eagerly. "I would! Thank you, *Pappa*."

"*Ja*, maybe *you* will be bringing a wife home someday soon, eh?" Heidi asked, a tease lighting her eyes.

Søren blushed scarlet at the suggestion, but he also couldn't hold back a grin.

1878

"*Jan! Søren!* Please help!" Abigael's desperate cries reached across the creek and to the fields where Jan and Søren were working. They dropped what they were doing and ran down the slope, splashed across the creek, and up the other side. Abigael, seeing them coming, ran back toward their tiny barn.

Then Jan and Søren could hear Henrik's screams. Jan shuddered. No man would shriek like that unless in unbearable pain. Søren looked at his father, his face white with apprehension.

Just outside the small barn's door they saw Henrik's ox thrashing on the ground. Henrik was pinned beneath the massive beast. The traces of the plow were tangled about its feet; the sharp edge of the plowshare was digging into the ox's legs. The more the ox thrashed, the deeper the sharp edge cut.

Henrik and Abigael's boys had hold of their father's arms but could not budge him. Each time the ox thrashed, trying to free itself from the plow, Henrik's cries of pain pierced the air.

Jan moved around the deadly hooves until he was near the ox's head. The wild look in the animal's eyes increased when it saw Jan. Jan, speaking softly, reached out a hand and placed it on the ox's head, careful of the animal's horns. He stared the animal in the eyes and rubbed its knobby head.

While he tried to calm the ox, he reached around to the back of his trousers and pulled a sheathed knife from his waistband. Søren knew immediately his father needed him to cut the traces.

As the exhausted ox settled, Henrik's screams died to heartrending groans. Finally, Søren had cut the traces and was able to pull the plow away from the ox.

The ox struggled to his feet, eliciting fresh shrieks from Henrik. Jan slipped a rope through the ox's nose ring and led him to Henrik's corral.

When Jan returned to his friend's side, Abigael, desperate and scared, was trying to assess Henrik's injuries. The man lay panting in the dirt, his face gray, his body motionless. A small dribble of blood hung on the corner of his mouth.

Ah, Lord! Jan prayed. *Help us in our need!*

Abigael encouraged Henrik to climb to his feet, but Jan put a hand on her arm. "*Nei*, Abigael." Jan could tell that something inside Henrik was broken. "Søren and I will carry him, *ja*?"

Henrik's two boys, now thirteen and eleven years of age, showed Jan their scrap lumber. Jan and Søren cobbled some boards together into a makeshift stretcher. He and Søren lifted Henrik onto the stretcher with as much care as they could. Jan took pains with Henrik's left arm; he could tell by the bulge under the skin that it was broken. They carried him into the one-room house and laid him on the bed.

"Oh, Henrik!" Abigael moaned. "Where are you hurt?"

Henrik looked for and found Jan's eyes. "Send her outside," he mouthed.

Jan nodded. "Abigael, please take the boys outside and calm them. I will talk with Henrik, *ja*?"

Abigael looked at Jan and then at her husband. Jan knew that she saw through his request. Her shoulders slumped, but without another word she ushered her sons outside.

"Jan," Henrik groaned through gritted teeth, "I am done for."

Jan shook his head vehemently. "*Nei*, it is not your decision, friend. We will let God decide that, *ja*? Now tell me where it hurts."

"First fetch me a rag. There is blood in my mouth."

Jan found Abigael's rag bag and wiped the blood from inside Henrik's mouth. Henrik coughed and Jan wiped more away.

"Now tell me," Jan repeated.

Henrik stared at Jan. "My arm and my chest hurt. I think my arm is broken. Perhaps my ribs also."

"*Ja*, I can see that." Jan gingerly felt along Henrik's left forearm where the break was. "We will send for *Fraulein* Engel, eh? She knows how to set broken bones."

Henrik was quiet and avoided Jan's eyes. "You are not telling all. What are you not saying, Henrik?"

Henrik continued to avoid looking at Jan. Jan sat beside him and wiped more blood from the corner of his mouth. And waited.

When Henrik at last spoke, his words pierced Jan's heart. "When the ox fell on me, I felt something break in my back. At first it hurt. Now I cannot feel my legs."

Jan blinked. He reached over and touched Henrik's left foot. "Do you feel that?"

"No."

Jan touched his other foot. "And that?"

"I feel nothing."

"Try to move your foot, Henrik."

"I have been trying since you and Søren freed me from the ox," Henrik whispered.

Jan covered his eyes with his hand. *Ah, Lord!*

Fraulein Engel came and tended to Henrik's injuries as best she could. She set his arm and with a grave expression nodded when Søren translated Henrik's fears to her.

"You know what this means?" she asked Henrik softly.

Henrik looked away and nodded.

When she had done what she could, she called Abigael and asked her to sit next to Henrik. Seating herself, Fraulein Engel took Abigael's hand. Jan and Søren stood nearby so that Søren could tell Abigael and Henrik what Fraulein Engel was saying.

"Abigael," she began gently, "Henrik is injured inside. His back is likely broken. He cannot move his lower body."

Abigael's eyes skittered from Fraulein Engel to her husband and back. "What does that mean?"

Fraulein Engel squeezed Abigael's hand and recaptured her attention. "He will not leave this bed, dear sister. I know you will care for him as long as is needed." That was all Fraulein Engel said, but the sympathy in her eyes told Abigael everything.

That had been more than a week ago. Henrik had not improved.

Jan and Søren helped Henrik and Abigael's sons with the work. Jan encouraged and prayed with the two boys who, in the span of a day, were required to shoulder all their father's responsibilities.

Jan stared toward the Andersons' farm. Henrik would not see another spring, perhaps not even another month. The signs were certain. Then what would Abigael do?

Lord, please strengthen Abigael and Henrik for what is ahead.

In February they buried Henrik. At Abigael's request they laid him to rest within the Thoresens' cemetery.

"My sons do not wish to give up their father's land," Abigael told Amalie and Jan. "But Henrik told me before he died that they are too young for us to hold out here. I can already see that—but *my sons* do not see it . . . yet."

She looked from the graves toward their house. "I do not want them to give up their schooling forever either. In a year, I think, we will return to our families, mine and Henrik's, in Illinois. It would break my heart to leave Henrik buried on land that will someday belong to others."

Amalie put her arm around Abigael and wept with her. "It is good that you bury him here with our loved ones. We will tend his grave for you when you leave."

CHAPTER 32

1879

Abigael and her sons were leaving. The Thoresens and other neighbors helped them prepare for their journey back to Illinois. Abigael was taking little beyond their personal belongings; she sold their stock and gave away their household effects.

Amalie and Abigael embraced for a long moment. "I will miss you," Amalie sobbed. "I will never forget how you and your Henrik welcomed us when we first came here, how you helped us when we were in such need."

"I thank you for your friendship," Abigael choked on her words. "Please . . ."

Amalie knew the assurances Abigael needed to hear. "You will not worry, dear one. We will tend Henrik's grave as one of our own."

Jan and Søren drove Abigael and her boys into RiverBend to the train. When it arrived, Mr. Bailey helped them aboard. Jan, Søren, and the Baileys waved goodbye to Abigael and her sons as the train eased away from the station.

Later as Jan looked across the creek it grieved his heart to see their small house abandoned. "The bank will sell it for us," Abigael had told him.

Jan turned away. *I cannot believe I once coveted Henrik's homestead.*

1880

Norvald was the first to tell Jan. "A new minister and his wife have come to RiverBend! He intends to start a church there." He grinned. "You know none of us *Svenska* are preachers, so we asked him to come and bring the word next Sunday."

"*Gud!*" Jan agreed. "That is *gud*. I, too, am hungry for a real man of God's word."

Jan thought for a moment about another minister who had tried to plant a church in RiverBend. The man had not been prepared for the hardships he encountered and had become discouraged. He left after less than a year. "Does this new minister know that another tried to start a church in town three years ago?"

"*Ja,* he does. This minister, I think, is made of better stuff than the last one."

Jan tapped his chin. "If he *is* a good man and teaches the whole of God's *Skriften,* I will pray and get behind his efforts. We need an established church in town, *ja?* Our community needs it. And I do not wish to see another church fail here."

"I agree with you, Jan. I will pray also. If the Lord leads us to support the new minister, I will stop holding meetings in my barn and encourage our friends to pray about joining, too."

With Ivan translating English to Swedish, the young minister—Jacob Medford—preached in Norvald and Inge's barn that Sunday.

He is very young, Jan smiled to himself, *but, oh! I can feel his love for God. This is a man I can have real fellowship with.*

Ah. He is a newlywed, too, Jan noted, *and his wife is even younger than he is.* Tall, slender, with a sweet expression, the minister's wife shone with love and admiration as she listened to her husband teach on Philippians 1:3-6.

> *I thank my God*
> *upon every remembrance of you,*
> *Always in every prayer of mine for you all*
> *making request with joy,*
> *For your fellowship in the gospel*
> *from the first day until now;*
> *Being confident of this very thing,*
> *that he which hath begun a good work in you*
> *will perform it until the day of Jesus Christ.*

Jan felt his heart expand to receive the word. *Ah, Lord! I need this, ja?* He and Norvald exchanged approving glances, and Jan noted that Søren and Amalie were fully engrossed in the message.

After the meal, the men of the church invited Jacob Medford to visit privately with them. "We would know more about you," Norvald explained, "and more of what you believe and teach."

The young man smiled. "I would like that, too."

He spoke of himself, his walk with God, and the call he felt to pastor. For an hour or longer the men of the church asked him questions. Jan was impressed that the minister, inexperienced as he was, was humble but not insecure.

Norvald looked about the circle and received nods. "We would have you come and preach again, Mr. Medford," he said. "Are you willing to fill our pulpit while we pray about God's direction for our church?"

"I would be honored," Jacob answered. "I will seek the Lord for his direction, too. I should tell you this, though: It is in my heart to establish a church open to the whole community. If we find it is not the Lord's will that I remain with you, I pray our fellowship will remain unbroken and as sweet as it has been so far."

Ah, Lord, Jan marveled. *This is a good man you have brought us. As young as he is, he is already a mature man of yours.*

Over the next month Jacob and Vera Medford became fixtures in the Swedish church. As news of his preaching filtered through the little town and surrounding neighborhood, others came to worship in the Bruntrüllsen barn, including a few members of the German church.

They greeted Jan with unexpected warmth. Jan was touched that these families still thought highly of him after his conflicts with Adolphe Veicht.

On a Sunday in mid-November, Søren nudged his father. "Look, *Pappa!*"

There, just inside the doorway of the barn, stood Rikkert and Duna Kappel and their family.

Jan rushed to greet them. "My friends! I am so happy to see you." Jan shook Rikkert's hand and then—spontaneously—they embraced.

Rikkert, still holding Jan's forearms, studied him closely. "I have missed our fellowship, yours and mine, Jan Thoresen."

"As have I," Jan returned, his heart full. "So. Will you come and worship with us?"

The following Sunday the church formally invited Jacob Medford to pastor the church. Jacob, his expression solemn but filled with joy, spoke of his vision for a church open to all the community. As he talked, Matthias Comer, a farmer living close to town, stood up.

"I wish to give one acre of my land to the church for a meeting place," he declared. "The land I give is not far from the town. We can build a meeting place there, *ja?*"

A roar of approval was his answer.

PART 2

And I will restore to you the years
that the locust hath eaten,
. . . And ye shall eat in plenty, and be satisfied,
and praise the name of the LORD your God,
that hath dealt wondrously with you:
and my people shall never be ashamed.
(Joel 2:25a, 26)

CHAPTER 33

1881

Søren wiped his sun-bronzed face on his sleeve. He was in the cornfield west of their house and barn, turning row after row of dark soil. The ox harnessed to the plow plodded on patiently and Søren followed behind, keeping the plow's blade buried in the earth and the furrows straight and evenly spaced.

As he raised his face from his sleeve, movement across the creek caught his eye. Where the road wound from behind a low bluff, a horse and buggy emerged and climbed to the top of the rise. Was someone coming to visit?

Søren saw the driver gesture to the Andersons' abandoned house nestled in the hollow between the bluff and the briskly running creek bordering the Thoresen land.

The driver pointed to the Andersons' fields that spread out atop the bluff behind the house. Then he gestured toward the Thoresen farm. After a minute more the buggy turned onto the track that ran down to the house in the hollow.

Søren was intrigued and didn't realize, for many steps, that he had allowed the ox to wander. Blast! He would have to turn the ox and go back to where his plowing went awry.

By the time he had managed to plow over the crooked row, the driver and his passenger—a woman—had stepped from the buggy and were examining the house and outbuildings.

Must be that bank fellow, Morton, Søren figured. *He's supposed to be selling the property for Abigael.*

Søren placed his attention back on his work and plowed steadily for another hour. The next time he looked across the creek, the driver of the buggy and his passenger were sitting beneath one of the trees near the creek.

"Looked like they were having a picnic," Søren reported at supper a few hours later.

Jan shrugged his shoulders. "Just so. Mr. Morton took a lady friend on a drive, not a prospective buyer for the Andersons' farm. A woman without a man would not buy the land, *ja*? That would be foolish."

Søren nodded. "*Ja*, you are right."

The following morning involved the typical happy chaos of hurried chores, eating, dressing, and driving to the church house near town. Amalie and the children were, as usual, excited and anxious to arrive early and spend time with friends before the service.

Søren drove Amalie in their new buggy pulled by the bays; Jan drove the rest of the children in a wagon. Jan loved the drive on Sunday. He and the children, excepting Sigrün, would sing all the way to and from church. Anyone could start a song; as soon as they did, the rest of them would join in and finish it.

As they pulled into the churchyard, Jan raised his hand to greet his friends. He, too, looked forward to good conversations and the exchange of news. He waved to Norvald, Rikkert, and then Brian McKennie.

Fiona McKennie and her daughter Meg were engaged in an animated dialogue with someone Jan didn't recognize—a woman, and certainly not a woman from around here! Her clothing, what he could see of it, was stylish and expensive-looking.

Søren noticed her also. "*Pappa*, that is the woman! The woman who was at the Andersons' place with Mr. Morton," he said, sidling up to Jan.

Jan nodded. He was mildly curious, but did not get a good look at the woman's face before Norvald approached with a grin and a hearty handshake.

Brian McKennie left his fields toward the end of the week—in the middle of planting season, no less!—to pay a visit to Jan and Søren. "Th' woman who was visitin' our church Sunday, Mrs. Brownlee is bein' her name, has bought the Andersons' homestead!"

He pointed across the fields to the little house. "An' is already livin' there, she is, as ye can be seein'."

Jan stared with astonishment down his fields and across the creek. A thread of smoke issued from the stovepipe poking out of the roof. *How is it I did not notice this?* he asked himself. chagrined.

"She came on th' train all by her ownself last week an' was stayin' at th' boardin' house," Brian continued with raised brows. "Our Meg made her acquaintance and brung her t' Sunday supper."

"What? She traveled alone? She is *there*"—Jan jerked his chin toward the Anderson homestead—"*alone?*" he demanded.

"Aye. She thinks t' be makin' a home there." Brian nodded sagely. "My Fiona and I are that worried about her, we are."

Jan's thoughts were in a snarl. He could not fathom why any woman—and one as unprepared for country life as this one certainly seemed to be—would *choose* to live alone on a homestead.

And in the Andersons' house! Jan shuddered. Henrik had been hard-pressed to keep their clapboard house together before his accident. In the year after Henrik died, the condition of the dwelling had only declined.

Yes, Jan and Søren had helped Abigael and her *sønns* work their fields and lent a hand with chores many a time, but the house had now been sitting empty for more than a year. It was in a sorry state!

What could that woman be thinking? Abruptly he realized he was angry—angry and resentful.

"'Tis for God this woman be searchin'" Brian softly added. "Fiona and I are agreed on it; Mrs. Brownlee be hungerin' for truth. We pray God she be findin' him here."

Brian's words, repeated by Søren, found their way into Jan's annoyed thoughts. *She is hungry for God? Could she not find God where she came from?* His frown deepened.

Brian eyed Jan's furrowed brow. "Th' reason I'm visitin' would be Mrs. Brownlee wishin' t' hire carpenters. Sure, an' ye both know th' house is fallin' apart?"

"Hire?" Søren's eyes gleamed. "She wants to hire carpenters for cash money?" Opportunities to work for cash were rare.

"Aye. Not t' be passin' tales, boot Mrs. Brownlee is looking t' be good for it."

He explained that Mrs. Brownlee was anxious to have the work commence as soon as possible. Brian shuffled his feet and grinned. "Ye are bein' th' best carpenter near, Jan—and I was th' tellin' of it."

Jan rubbed the back of his neck and sighed. He had been relieved when Abigael and her sons moved back East! The responsibility of ensuring that Henrik's family survived had been heavy, what with farming Thoresen land and caring for his own family.

He caught himself shaking his head and, irritated, wondered again, *What could that woman be thinking?*

"*Pappa*, we have most of the early crops in," Søren urged him. "We can finish tomorrow. I would call it a blessing to make a few dollars of my own."

Jan thought a few minutes. What Søren said was so—the timing was good. And his *sønn* deserved the opportunity to earn some money.

"*Ja*," he said at last. "Tell her we come Saturday, eh?"

Søren let out a whoop and thumped his father on the arm.

❧ ❈ ❦

CHAPTER 34

Saturday morning Søren leapt from his bed and hustled to finish his morning chores. Amalie frowned and clucked over him as he wolfed down his breakfast.

In the same breath she reminded him, "Don't forget, Søren, I want you to tell me everything about our neighbor when you come home this afternoon, eh? Just think! Another woman nearby! Thank the good Lord!"

Søren promised and pushed away from the table the instant Jan finished their morning devotions. "I'll get the tools ready, *Pappa*."

"I would like to meet the new lady, *Onkel*," Uli said eagerly. "Could I come with you some time? I could help the lady!"

Jan touched Uli's cheek with affection. *Such a comfort she is to me, Lord!* "We don't even know her yet, little one. But I'm sure you'll meet her soon enough, eh?"

He sighed inwardly. Since Brian had visited, Jan had wrestled with his attitude about their foolish new neighbor until finally—as was usual—he had cast the care of the situation on the Lord.

You must not borrow trouble, eh, Jan Thoresen? he reminded himself.

He and Søren cut through their fields and crossed the creek where it was closest to the Andersons' old house. Søren carried the large tool caddy; Jan toted a saw across his left shoulder and the lunch pail in his right hand.

As they sloshed up the slope from the creek, the door to the house swung open and the woman stepped out. Søren, a shy smile plastered on his face, introduced himself and then his father. Jan shook the woman's hand and greeted her but remained mostly silent as she and Søren discussed what she wished done.

So this is Fru Brünlee, Jan thought. Keeping his face carefully neutral, he studied her.

What he saw was a woman in her thirties whose clothes hung upon her slender frame as though she had been ill. Her hair, a dusty ash-blonde, was coiled and neatly pinned at the back of her head, framing a face that, too, was unnaturally slender and wan.

Ah, Lord! It is worse than I imagined. This woman is so thin she will likely blow away in the first strong wind! She has no understanding of what living on the prairie will require of her.

Her hands, he'd observed when exchanging greetings, were soft, smooth, and gentle—not the hands of a woman acquainted with work.

But . . . something decidedly firm played in the set of her mouth. And her eyes were not blue, as he had first believed. They were gray—*and staring right back at him.*

Jan flinched but managed to return her scrutiny with detachment. After all, *he* had been caught studying *her.*

Mrs. Brownlee showed them around. Jan and Søren knocked on walls and doors, took measurements, and discussed the materials they would require.

They had finished their inspection and Jan and Søren were discussing the inadequacy of the front door and its frame when Mrs. Brownlee coughed politely, requesting their attention. She flushed as, from behind her back, she withdrew a few sheets of paper covered in pencil drawings.

"Excuse me. I, ah, I know it's important to make everything weatherproof, and I want that of course. But while you're working on the basics, I would like, that is, I have some ideas I would like incorporated. Right here . . . on these papers?"

Jan understood few of her words but he was interested in the drawings she laid on the table before them.

She had drawn a rectangle representing the house and had sketched in windows on the east and south walls and added an interior wall to divide the house into two areas. On the north wall where the stove sat, she had indicated cupboards and shelves. Off to the side she had drawn their details.

Engaged, Jan studied the outline of a covered porch that ran the front length and down the south side of the house. Jan pointed to the sketch, ready to give credit where it was due.

"She has done a fair job of this, eh?" he asked Søren. "We can improve on her cupboards and shelves, I think, but she has certainly given this some thought."

He and Søren discussed the windows and the interior wall, the roof, and then the porch. Jan rubbed his chin. "I would feel better if we do all of the necessary work first. Who knows when a storm will come? And does she know we can only spare about two weeks right now? This porch is nice but not necessary. Maybe we can build it by the end of summer, but not right away."

"*Ja*, I agree," Søren answered. Mrs. Brownlee watched their conversation with a keen eye. "But I think she will be disappointed, *Pappa*," he finished.

At last Søren told her, "These windows must be ordered. Mr. Bailey's company doesn't stock them this size, and he only keeps a few on hand anyway. If you are intent on this . . . veranda? My father says it should be built last, after the roof is replaced, the interior work done, doors rebuilt, and windows installed.

"We may not be able to get to the decorative part until late summer if we are to complete the essential repairs between plantings, that is, in the next two weeks."

"I see," Mrs. Brownlee replied, blinking.

Søren was right, Jan thought. *She is disappointed.*

She must have realized he was watching her, however, for she smiled brightly and, straightening her shoulders, added, "Well then, we will get the essentials done and not worry about the porch until later. But I would like it as soon as is convenient."

He and Søren got to work. They pulled off the front door and door frame. While Jan was measuring for a new frame and door, Søren busied himself nailing down loose boards.

That morning Jan built a solid, sturdy door and was engrossed in framing it in when he noticed what *Fru Brünlee* was doing. The woman, clearly unaccustomed to using tools, was hacking ineffectively at the weeds growing around the yard.

Out of the corner of his eye Jan noted her clumsy attempts to widen the swath of cleared ground in front of the house. *At least she has the sense to wear gloves*, Jan grumbled as he turned his attention back to the doorjambs. *But as she is unaccustomed to such labor, I have no doubt she will lose her ambition inside of an hour.*

At midmorning, Jan and Søren had drawn up a list of lumber and materials they needed and called for *Fru Brünlee* to come and approve it. The woman, grimy and clearly uncomfortable, assured them that they could order or purchase whatever was on the list.

"All the arrangements are made with Mr. Bailey and Mr. Schmidt— you may pick up whatever you need."

Mr. Thoresen spoke rapidly to Søren in Norwegian, who agreed. "My father suggests one of us take our wagon to town to get the lumber, so I will leave right away. There are several things to be done here in the meantime; my father will stay and work on them."

"That's fine." She hurried away to the pump and Jan saw her wash her hands in the cold water. Søren strode across the creek and toward their barn to hitch a wagon.

Leaving the finished door until Søren returned to help him mount it, Jan turned his attention to making repairs to the small barn and to the outhouse.

Surprising him, Mrs. Brownlee continued chopping and raking weeds. *I thought she would have given up by now,* he scoffed.

Jan noted the many times she went to the pump to bathe her face and hands. Then he saw that she was unsteady on her feet. He also recognized the determined set of her jaw. Sighing, he left his repairs and waited between her and the pile of weeds she was building.

Apparently, she hadn't realized he was there because she turned and walked right into him. She stood blinking, plainly exhausted.

Jan took the rake from her hand. "Too much," he said mildly. "Sit, please."

She sighed and stumbled to the pump to again rinse her hands and face and then, with weary footsteps, dragged herself into the house.

Jan did not see or hear the woman until Søren returned with the wagon of lumber. By then Jan had finished clearing the area around the house and set the piles of weeds to burn. He and Søren started unloading the wagon.

"Have you eaten lunch yet?" *Fru Brünlee* was squinting in the sunlight, wiping sleep from her face.

Ah! She has slept, Jan surmised, feeling his earlier misgivings justified. *No one on a farm sleeps during the day! Just as I thought . . . she will soon find she has no business out here on the prairie.*

Søren laughed. "No, but I'm sure hungry enough to. We brought ours in that pail, and I'm just getting back as you can see, so we're about ready now."

"Would you like some coffee with it?"

Jan understood *coffee* well enough! "*Ja!* Dat's gud."

Jan and Søren finished unloading and then settled in the shade of one of the trees. Jan heard Søren's stomach growl and grinned at him. Søren grinned back and unpacked their lunch pail.

As they waited for their neighbor to bring the coffee, Jan stared across the creek, seeing their farm with new eyes. He liked what he saw: well-maintained buildings; fields plowed in orderly rows; cows grazing in the distant pasture.

At last *Fru Brünlee* returned with hot coffee and her lunch. Jan blessed the food in Riksmaal and she echoed Søren's "amen."

Jan and Søren tucked napkins into their shirt collars and attacked their lunch with abandon. Jan had polished off a thick, open-faced sandwich and pickles, carrots, and turnip slices and was eyeing a slice of pie when he noticed what Mrs. Brownlee had prepared for her own lunch: a single slice of bread and bit of cheese!

Jan was amused and said to Søren, "Look what this woman is eating after all the work she did this morning. It is no wonder she is so thin—no one has ever fed her properly!" He chuckled and bit deep into his pie. Søren nodded and grinned as he inhaled a second sandwich.

"What did he say?" *Fru Brünlee* asked, smiling with them.

"Oh! He said that the reason you are so thin is that no one has ever fed you properly," Søren replied, not appreciating that passing on his father's comment was, perhaps, less than prudent.

A red swath spread up the woman's neck to her cheeks. Jan's eyebrows shot up and he glared at Søren. Søren apologized immediately.

"Mrs. Brownlee, I'm sorry—what I said—what he said wasn't meant to be rude. Our women eat quite a bit. Why, Sigrün eats nearly as much as I do when we are harvesting. I truly apologize if we've offended you." Søren glanced at his father who was still glaring at him.

She nodded and, after a moment, she offered, "It's true that I'm not used to working hard—or even being around men who work hard and eat as well, I mean as *much*, as you do. I'm sure my appetite will get better as I work out-of-doors."

She paused and bit her lip. "You see, I was sick a bit ago and haven't gotten my weight back yet. But I will."

As Søren translated, Jan nodded his understanding. He cut a small wedge from the wrapped cheese and offered it to her.

"*Gjetost*," he told her. "Gud, gud for you."

"Goat's cheese," Søren explained. "A specialty from Norway. It's very nutritious. We have five goats in addition to our cows."

She sniffed it dubiously. Then Jan noticed her do that thing again—that straightening of her shoulders—before she cautiously nibbled the dark brown cheese. She took another bite and then finished the piece.

"I like it. Thank you."

Jan gestured to Søren. "Ask her if she has any milk here."

"She wants to know if she could buy some from us."

Jan nodded. "Yes, tell her we will work something out."

Now into a serious lecture, Jan directed, "Tell her if she has been ill she should be careful and not overdo it by working outside too long *like she did today*! That is, until she rebuilds her strength."

Søren hesitated before repeating his father's advice to their new neighbor.

Jan frowned and added, "Tell her, too, that she is too pale! She should work outside sometimes without a hat. After all, sunshine is good for us! It will give her some color. She is as pale as milk. Of course, not too much at a time. And tell her to eat more, eh, *Sønn?*"

Jan watched and listened to the conversation between Søren and *Fru Brünlee*. Søren chuckled several times and—was he *apologizing?* Apologizing for what Jan had asked him to tell her?

But apparently *Fru Brünlee* thanked Søren for his advice. She ate everything on her plate, so Jan added more, *just a little more*—a second piece of gjetost, several pickles, and some cookies—and watched until she swallowed the last bite.

Jan nodded in approval. "Come," he said to Søren. "I want to get started inside. Henrik and Abigael's house has become as drafty as a barn."

Jan and Søren worked inside the house the rest of the afternoon. They moved Mrs. Brownlee's few things away from one wall so they could paper between the studs with black tar paper.

When *Fru Brünlee* saw what they were about, she pulled up a chair and watched them as though fascinated. After Jan and Søren finished tarring the entire wall, they cut long planks and nailed them lengthwise to the studding, butting the boards together with a few soft taps of a hammer on their sides. All the while, *Fru Brünlee* studied their work.

Then it was time for them to return home and do the evening chores. Jan and Søren put Mrs. Brownlee's things back where they had been.

"We don't work tomorrow, Mrs. Brownlee," Søren informed her, "because it's Sunday. But we'll be back Monday morning. We'll get a lot done since we have the lumber here now."

"Thank you! It's already looking better! And I'm sure I will see you at church tomorrow. Perhaps I could meet Mrs. Thoresen then."

"I would be happy to introduce you, Mrs. Brownlee," Søren answered.

Jan helped Søren gather their tools and lunch pail and they strode down the slope across the creek and fields to the waiting cows and other chores.

That evening Amalie asked question after question about their new neighbor. Jan quirked an eyebrow at Søren, turned his eyes toward his plate, and abandoned his *sønn* to trying to recall—and satisfactorily repeat—every detail of what *Fru Brünlee* was wearing, where she was from, what her plans were, whether she would be coming to church in the morning, and so on.

Søren glowered at his father, but Jan was paying careful attention to his potatoes, pretending he didn't see his *sønn*'s accusing looks. That is until, after several minutes, when he realized that the table had gone silent and an unanswered question hung in the air.

Jan glanced up. Amalie was leveling her own stony look at him and Søren wore a smug grin. The children giggled behind their hands.

"What?" Jan shrugged his shoulders. "What is it, Amalie?"

"I said I was hoping to ask *Fru Brünlee* to Sunday dinner tomorrow."

"Oh?"

"I asked if it would be all right with *you*, Jan Thoresen, but your potatoes seem to be of uncommon interest this evening."

The boys guffawed and Uli giggled aloud, not even trying to hide their glee. It wasn't often that *Mamma*'s ire was directed at *Onkel* Jan!

Jan flushed. "Of course, Amalie." He looked around the table. "Well? Is everyone finished? It is already time for us to clear away the food and read God's word, eh?"

The children quickly turned their attention to their plates.

CHAPTER 35

Fru Brünlee did come to Sunday dinner the next day. Søren introduced Amalie to their neighbor before church began and, at a nudge from Amalie, offered the dinner invitation, which the woman accepted. In spite of the language barrier, Amalie also, in her own inimitable way, appropriated their neighbor's company during the service.

As was their routine, Jan sat at one end of a pew with a row of Thoresen children between himself and Amalie. What was not usual was the presence of *Fru Brünlee* sandwiched between the children and Amalie. Even with the children as a buffer, he could hear her clear voice during the singing.

As it lifted sweetly, Jan paused and listened. Something hopeful and vibrant clung to her voice, but perhaps something sorrowful at the same time.

Jacob's message that morning was powerful, and Jan sensed the Holy Spirit working through it. His sermon ended with these words: "Pray with me now: *Lord Jesus, I ask you to forgive me and receive me as one of your lost sheep. I turn away from other gods, other desires, other paths. I will follow you. I will listen for your voice and live for you. Thank you for dying for my sins! Amen.*"

The Thoresens filed out, but *Fru Brünlee* remained seated, lost in prayer.

When she finally emerged from the church house, the Thoresens and McKennies gathered around her, hugging and exclaiming in joy.

"You're born-again now, Miss Rose! Praise God for his lovingkindness! We're seein' it all over your face. Sure an' it's like glory in your eyes!" Fiona said with tears.

Fru Brünlee didn't answer, but she hugged Fiona, she hugged Brian and Meg. Amalie squeezed her enthusiastically and Søren shook her hand. Sigrün simply smiled at her.

Jan stood a little to the side. His heart was happy for what had occurred, but he had no English words to convey his good will.

"I don't know what to say," Mrs. Brownlee finally managed. "I never knew God was so . . . so . . ."

Jan shook her hand. All he could manage in English was, "God is gud, *ja?*"

Sunday dinner was pleasant and, as on every Sunday, Jan led a discussion of the pastor's message. He was mildly surprised at how engrossed *Fru Brünlee* became as Søren translated the conversation.

So! She has a new heart, now, Lord. She will be hungry for your word, eh? Jan mused as he, Søren, and the boys left the table for their chores.

"I think it will rain soon, *Pappa*," Søren predicted. They both studied the dark clouds moving toward them.

"*Ja*, I agree. I will have the boys bring the cows in early." Jan stopped and turned back. "*Fru Brünlee* has never seen a real farm, eh? Do you think she would like to see the milking?"

Søren shrugged. "I don't know. I will ask her."

Søren returned shortly with their neighbor. That she was delighted and curious was evident: Her head swiveled back and forth and her eyes tried to take in everything—and she had *many* questions. Jan chuckled over her enthusiasm. She seemed to be particularly enthralled with the goats, so he milked one and offered her a cup of the warm, frothing milk.

And put his foot in his mouth.

"Make fat." Jan nodded at Mrs. Brownlee's thin waistline.

Her gray eyes narrowed. "Thank you for the milk," she replied politely. She rinsed and hung the cup on its hook and walked away.

Jan shrugged. "A temper that one has," he huffed to no one in particular.

An hour later he saw that the rain Søren predicted was not far off. He went in search of his *sønn*. "Please tell *Fru Brünlee* that you will drive her home so that she does not get soaked in the rain that is almost here, eh? We can keep her horse and buggy overnight."

Søren repeated Jan's words, but Mrs. Brownlee flatly refused. "Tell your father thank you, but I was just about to leave, and I can handle getting a little wet. I had better go and say goodbye to Mrs. Thoresen." Her annoyance was scarcely hidden.

Søren shrugged at his father and Jan shook his head.

She is stubborn, too! Jan added to his inventory of their neighbor. He and Søren followed her into the house.

After *Fru Brünlee* thanked Amalie for dinner—thanks that took many minutes and apparently had to include praise for their home, their kitchen, Amalie's dishes, and the fine meal—and after the exchange of embraces, she leveled her gray eyes on Søren and Jan. "Will I be seeing both of you tomorrow?"

"Yes, you can count on us," Søren answered.

Jan, convinced a wise man should keep his mouth closed, shook her hand silently.

He and Søren watched Mrs. Brownlee drive down the road. Within moments the rain was pouring, and her buggy was soon lost in the mist.

"Well, she is soaked now," Søren observed. He and Jan exchanged bemused looks and both of them shrugged their shoulders.

"I don't think I understand women," Søren muttered.

His father just snorted.

Jan and Søren, toting their tools and lunch pail, returned to work on Mrs. Brownlee's house Monday morning. The night's heavy rain had leaked through the roof, so they stripped off the old shingles and rotted boards, tossing them to the ground below.

Fru Brünlee did not waste her time while they labored, Jan observed as she heated water outside and scrubbed her clothes. *I doubt she has ever done her own laundry either*, he opined, recalling her soft handshake.

By the time her washing was on the line, the men were cutting and nailing down new lumber on the roof. At the end of the day Jan was satisfied with their accomplishments. Søren informed their neighbor that they would return to shingle the roof in the morning.

The list of improvements was shrinking, and Jan's concern was lessening. He and Søren were surprised to see Brian McKennie pull up in his wagon, his mule tied to the back.

"Good day t' ye!" Brian called. Brian and Jan shook hands. "'Tis plowin' Miss Rose's garden t'day I will," Brian informed them. "My Fiona will b' teaching her th' plantin' on the morrow."

Jan nodded and looked at Abigael's old garden. Neglected for going on two years, the plot was overgrown with prairie grass. While Jan and Søren worked inside, Brian would have his hands full plowing and clearing the garden by himself.

Jan and Søren worked steadily, finishing the walls and starting the shelves and cupboards for *Fru Brünlee's* cooking area. Søren ran in and out of the house fetching materials for Jan.

"She's following Brian, breaking up clods," Søren reported with a snicker.

"Eh?" Jan was engrossed in cabinetry making.

"And I bet she's never walked in dirt in her life!" Søren added, laughing.

At lunch time the four of them relaxed under the cottonwoods along the creek bank. At least the men did. *Fru Brünlee* sipped water. Jan could see she was already exhausted—and yet was eating nothing! He arched his brows at Brian but kept his opinions to himself.

I won't make that mistake again! he vowed. He still had a picture of her driving away, back ramrod straight, in the drenching rain.

Brian finished the plowing soon after lunch, loaded his plow into the wagon, and headed home. An hour later Jan felt compelled to check on his neighbor.

He discovered her curled on the prairie grass, sound asleep. Her hair, usually so tidy, had fallen out of its pins. Pieces of grass stuck out of her loose braid.

I wonder if she knows ants are crawling on her dress? Jan chuckled to himself.

He looked over the garden plot. Brian had plowed less than half of what Abigael usually planted, but what he had turned over would produce more than enough food for one person. *Fru Brünlee*, however, had cleared only about half of the plowed area.

Jan realized his neighbor had awakened and was trying discreetly to tidy her hair. He nodded but didn't say anything to her as she straightened her back, wincing in pain. Instead, Jan called to Søren in the house.

Jan pointed to the garden. "We should help her finish this, eh? Otherwise I don't think she will be ready tomorrow when *Fru* McKennie comes to help her plant it."

Søren smiled and called to her, "Well, Mrs. Brownlee, would you like some help 'bustin' sod'? The three of us can get it done before chore time."

Their neighbor looked relieved and thanked him. "I really would appreciate it—and I'll pay you, of course."

Jan shook his head emphatically. "No," Søren replied. "For the carpentry you can pay, but not for just being neighborly." Jan saw her thinking on Søren's words, her brows puckered.

Jan and Søren worked quickly, shaking and removing the clumps of prairie grass and leaving the dirt in the garden spot. They hoed, broke up the clods, and tossed out rocks.

"Take your rake now and level it out," Søren instructed. They were packing up to leave. "When Mrs. McKennie comes tomorrow, she'll help you get it planted."

"Thank you both so much again," *Fru Brünlee* responded in gratitude. She was smiling, so Jan and Søren smiled back.

She has a nice smile, Jan thought, *in spite of that temper!* He whistled as he and Søren hiked across the fields to their barn.

CHAPTER 36

Jan and Søren finished the repairs *Fru Brünlee* required with three days to spare. Jan had a never-ending list of tasks waiting for him at home—practical and needful tasks he should put his time and energy into. Yet as he recalled the porch drawings Fru Brünlee had made, he also recalled her disappointment. Disappointment she had quickly covered.

I can build that porch, Jan considered, tugging at his chin. *Three days will be long enough. Søren need not spend his time helping with it.*

So he built the veranda—just as his neighbor had sketched—across the front and down one side of her little house.

Well, she had her heart set on it, he rationalized later. *Now she can sit there watching the sun come up in the morning. In the evening the sun will paint color and shadows across the prairie. She will have much pleasure from that veranda!*

I liked building it for her.

He shrugged uncomfortably as he admitted to the pleasure building it for her gave him. He was turning those thoughts over in his mind when another thought distracted him—the watering system he and Søren had helped her build before they finished the repairs. It had been interesting watching her, novice that she was, planning it out, he and Søren following her instructions.

She played in the mud and water like a child—and tried hard not to like it.

He snorted a laugh. *Yes, I enjoyed that, too,* he mused, but most of all he had liked giving her *Snøfot* . . .

The inspiration had come to him the morning he was going to start on the veranda: *With her own goat, she can have fresh milk every day!* he'd realized, *and learn to make her own gjetost.* He'd shared the idea with Uli, and they had chosen *Snøfot* together, by far the prettiest of their goats.

His neighbor had been overwhelmed when Uli had presented the dainty goat to her. He'd seen that Rose—Jan frowned and corrected himself—*Fru Brünlee*—had been deeply touched by the gift.

She approached him with *Snøfot* dancing on the lead behind her. "Mr. Thoresen," she'd said seriously, "I want to thank you."

He hadn't lifted his eyes from his tape measure and scrawled notes. Perhaps he'd been afraid that she would say her thanks and then quickly excuse herself and go about her business. So he had kept his eyes on his work but inquired, nonchalantly, "You like?"

"Yes. Yes, I do. I don't have any idea how to take care of her, but she is the loveliest creature I've ever owned!"

Jan had struggled to understand as usual, but he'd caught part of it. "Uli teach." He gestured at the yard, still keeping his eyes on his work but in truth racking his brain to form intelligible words in English. "*Snøfot* eat grass, all here. Make gud milk."

And he had finally turned to her, letting her know that he expected her to keep her end of the unspoken "bargain." "You get fat, *ja?*"

A shadow had crossed her face and he realized he had—*again!*—used that offensive word. Apparently "fat" was *not* the proper word to convey health and wellbeing in English!

You are an ignorant fool, Jan Thoresen! he berated himself.

But *Fru Brünlee* had shaken off the offense. He watched the short struggle as she weighed his good will against his misspoken words.

She had responded with an honest, "I will try. Thank you, really." Then she had offered her hand.

He had nodded, shaken it, and turned back to building the veranda, the feel of her soft hand still tingling in his.

Not at all like Elli's firm, strong hand.

The thought—*the comparison*—startled Jan.

Almost as soon as *Fru Brünlee* accepted *Snøfot* as a gift, coyotes found and followed the goat's scent to her small stable. Jan and Søren heard about *Fru Brünlee's* newest problem from Brian the following Sunday.

"*Should I be getting a gun,*" she says t' me, with eyes *that big,*" Brian spoke out of the side of his mouth, shooting a backwards glance toward Rose Brownlee.

Brian had just repeated the tale "Miz" Brownlee had related to him: Coyotes had circled and tried to get into her little barn in the night. She had found their tracks in the morning.

"*Nay, tis a dog ye mus be havin,*" says I," Brian added, "boot she was nay likin' th' sound o' that, I tell ye!"

As Søren translated Brian's story, he and Jan couldn't help but turn and stare at their neighbor across the churchyard.

Fru Brünlee, correctly deducing that they were talking about her, glared back and then straightened, lifted her chin and, with what Jan was certain was a sniff, turned her back on them.

Ach! She is in a fine mood! Jan smothered a grin. He and Søren listened to Brian finish and they agreed with him.

"You are right. She needs a dog," Søren nodded. "Doesn't your Connie still have some pups?"

Now Brian chuckled. "Aye, surely. She is havin' two left that I would be givin' Miz Brownlee th' choice of, boot when I says so, her mouth was lookin' like she'd bit int' a persimmon!"

It was too vivid a picture. All three of them chuckled and Jan clapped a hand on Brian's shoulder, still grinning.

Ja, I can see that! he laughed to himself. Then he sobered. Something still had to be done.

"She must be made to see reason about a dog," he stated. Brian and Søren gaped at Jan, both conveying, "and who will be making her do that?"

Jan snorted. Apparently the task would fall to him. "You gif dog *Fru Brünlee?*"

Brian nodded. "Aye. That I will."

The next morning after chores, Jan saddled one of his bays. He didn't ride astride often, but it was a lovely day for a ride, and he thought Uli would enjoy the errand. They headed toward the McKennies', Uli chattering and bouncing behind him on the horse's broad back.

As they crossed the bridge and climbed the knoll, Jan spied his neighbor working in her garden. She did not see them.

On the return trip from Brian and Fiona's place he and Uli crested the rise and looked down toward *Fru Brünlee's* home. Sprawled across the horse in front of Jan was one of Brian's half-grown pups.

Jan shook his head. The young dog was going to be a handful. He wondered how his neighbor would react when she saw the pup.

This time, as they trotted down the track and into her yard, *Fru Brünlee* did notice them. She waited as they rode toward her.

"*God-dag, Fru Brünlee,*" Jan called. He swung Uli down and dismounted.

As Jan had hoped, Uli immediately ran to their neighbor. Jan could not understand all Uli was chattering to *Fru Brünlee*, but the woman always brightened when his little niece was around.

Ja, I'm counting on that, Lord! Jan prayed with a grimace.

Jan tied a rope to the dog's collar and set him on the ground. He tried to see the dog through his neighbor's eyes and was not encouraged: The pup was an ugly mongrel, all legs and huge paws, clearly with a great deal of growth ahead.

Jan led the dog to Mrs. Brownlee. The dog pulled at the rope and growled at him until Jan jerked firmly. Then the dog turned suspicious eyes on *Fru Brünlee*.

She eyed the dog with equal distaste, and Jan suddenly had to bite the inside of his cheek. He remained a silent but amused observer of Uli and *Fru Brünlee's* exchange.

"Put your hand out to let him smell you," Uli suggested.

"Will he bite me?" *Fru Brünlee* asked.

Uli looked surprised. "Why would he? He's only mad at *Onkel* for making him lie quietly on the horse."

She held out her hand to the dog. "See?"

The dog licked it.

"Ugh! I don't want him to lick me."

"Why, Mrs. Brownlee! Don't you like your dog?"

"I don't care for dogs, Uli, especially big ones."

Fru Brünlee made a face and Jan experienced an urgent need to clear his throat.

"But you don't want the coyotes to get Snowfoot, do you?" Uli persisted.

Jan listened and watched. He may not have understood every word, but he did recognize disgust—and a little fear—when he saw it. He spoke to Uli who nodded.

"*Onkel* says if you are afraid of the dog he will know it. You must be bold because you are his mistress, and he must learn to mind you."

Then Jan's neighbor stared at him, defiance in the firm set of her lips. He stared back, challenging her.

Somehow Jan managed to keep his face resolute. And he wasn't all that surprised when she squared her shoulders.

I think I would have been surprised if she'd done otherwise, he realized. He was coming to expect her to show grit in new and difficult situations.

Fru Brünlee held out her hand to the dog. He sniffed it and then her skirts. He looked up expectantly so she patted him. She looked a trifle relieved.

Jan handed the rope to her and asked Uli to pass on some instructions.

Uli nodded and told Mrs. Brownlee, "*Onkel* is going to drive a stake for you to tie him to; otherwise he may try to go home. You are to leave him tied up for two days and feed him. Then he will think this is his home and stay all by himself. Also, stake Snowfoot near him—not too near at first, though. Soon he will know Snowfoot lives here too and will protect her."

Jan sauntered down to the creek and broke off a low cottonwood branch. He cut it to a two-foot length, trimmed it, and whittled one end into a point. Using a hammer from the stable, he drove the stake into the ground and tied the pup's rope to it.

Uli fetched Snowfoot, tied him near the dog, and gave *Fru Brünlee* a few more suggestions. All the while, Jan watched the woman. He knew well enough that she didn't want the dog, but she was trying hard to adjust herself to what was necessary rather than what she wanted.

Jan found himself admiring her struggle to do the right thing. Then he shook his head. "Uli, come. We have work at home," he called. He pulled Uli up in front of him on the horse.

Trying valiantly to be gracious but not *quite* managing it, his neighbor addressed him. "Hm. Thank you very much, Mr. Thoresen."

Jan glanced from the dog back to her. It was all he could do to keep his expression neutral—when what he *really* wanted was to release the laughter bubbling just below the surface. *Maybe even tease her a little!*

"*Ja*, sure," he replied as calmly as he could muster. Then he had to chew the inside of his cheek.

At his answer, *Fru Brünlee's* eyes narrowed and Jan could tell his neighbor saw through him. In fact, she *knew* he was laughing inside.

If he didn't get out of the yard soon . . . He clucked to the bay. As they neared the bridge, Jan released a pent-up laugh.

That was the most fun I've had in a long time, he chuckled.

"What is funny, *Onkel*?" Uli demanded.

"Eh? It is nothing. What a glorious day the good God has given us, *ja*?" But he was glad Uli couldn't see his face, because he was grinning from ear to ear.

CHAPTER 37

"I heard Mrs. Brownlee had a bad encounter in town," Søren mentioned at the midday meal one afternoon. Jan's head snapped up. He waited for Søren to explain, but his *sønn*, with a look bordering on ecstasy, was biting into a piece of fried chicken.

"So? What bad encounter?" Jan snapped. He set his fork down and waited.

"Oh. With Mark Grader! He was in the Schmidt's store. Guess he was trying to get more credit, and *Herr* Schmidt wouldn't give him more. I heard Grader started smashing dishes—dropping them on the floor!—trying to pressure *Herr* Schmidt into changing his mind."

Mark Grader and his brother had been nothing but trouble in the little town for more than a year. They were known for starting fights, not paying their bills, and bullying RiverBend proprietors. Most of the community believed the worst of the problem had ended when Mark's brother, Orville, was sent to prison after badly injuring a man in a fight.

Apparently the problem had returned.

Amalie and Jan both looked concerned; the children looked between them and Søren.

"Ach! But someone must stop such wrong things!" Amalie remonstrated.

"I heard Mrs. Brownlee tried to stop it." Søren shook his head and grinned. "For being a little city lady, she has a lot of gumption!"

Jan's opinion of her at the moment was quite different. *What could she have been thinking!* he fumed. *RiverBend has no law enforcement! Does she not understand what some men might do to a woman who is alone, with no one to protect her?*

Jan's ire kept rising. *Has she not the brains God gave a goat?* he demanded within himself. Having lost his appetite, he stood up and cleared his plate from the table.

"Jan? Where are you going? Jan? You haven't finished your meal!"

But he left Amalie protesting and the children staring wide-eyed at his back. "What has gotten into him?" Amalie asked Søren.

Søren shrugged and grabbed another piece of chicken from the platter.

A few weeks later, Jan saw *Fru Brünlee* driving her little buggy up their road. *She has likely come to visit Amalie.* Jan's brows pulled together into an annoyed frown. He was still angry with her over her foolhardy confrontation with Mark Grader.

He thought no more of her visit until later when Amalie informed him, "*Fru Brünlee* wishes Little Karl to drive a wagon of her goods from the train to her house. I think you had better go too, Jan," Amalie added as she poured coffee in his cup. "I would feel more comfortable if you helped so nothing gets broken, *ja?*"

It would serve her right, Jan fumed.

"So? Will you go, *Bror?*"

"*Ja,* I will go," Jan drawled, feigning reluctance.

Ja, I will go! he snarled silently. *I would like a chance to give her a piece of my mind!*

He took a calming breath. Secretly, perhaps he was a *little* pleased to have another opportunity to study their neighbor.

Early Wednesday morning Little Karl drove a Thoresen wagon into their neighbor's yard. Jan rode beside him on the bench seat. They found *Fru Brünlee* ready and excited to leave for town. Jan helped her up where she sat on the bench behind him and Karl.

She tried several times to engage Karl in conversation and Jan had to grin at her frustration. Karl could speak the English well enough—but the boy was so tongue-tied around their neighbor that her efforts got her nowhere. After a bit, she just relaxed and enjoyed the drive.

She is not afraid to try new things and she adapts quickly in new situations, Jan admitted. *Even ill-advised situations,* he added. He tried to muster his irritation again, but it had abandoned him.

Jan realized his neighbor was becoming a little anxious as they drew near the train siding. When he helped her down she immediately sought out their friend, Mr. Bailey, who showed her where her freight was stacked.

"I b'lieve all the boxes what came fer ya will fit in that one wagon—cept'n that 'un." Bailey pointed to a crate stenciled liberally with the words "Fragile" and "Do Not Drop."

"Reckon you'll hafta take my wagon, too. My boy kin drive it back when it's empty. He's a mite small yet, but he kin handle th' horses okay. Over here, Mr. Thoresen. All these boxes here."

Jan was taken aback at how many boxes and crates were stacked in the shade of the freight office. Little Karl looked from the many crates to Jan, who shrugged.

And then something interesting happened. Apparently *Fru Brünlee* had not yet met Mary Bailey. She introduced herself and straightaway invited Mary to church.

Jan felt chastened. *The Baileys have been our good friends for many years, and I have never asked them to church?*

He thought of their first encounter with the Baileys when a younger Robert Bailey, rifle at the ready, had put a stop to the railroad workers carelessly tossing their things from the freight car. If it hadn't been for Bailey, their family would have suffered the loss or damage of many of their things.

And after the train had pulled away, it was Mary Bailey who had offered them a hot meal and agreed to trade one of their oxen for a milk cow!

How could I have not spoken of the Lord to them in all this time? Jan frowned. Even worse, he realized, *I did not know that a local pastor had forbidden the Baileys from attending his church because they had been raised Catholic.*

Jan grimaced. He could think of only one local pastor who would have done so. *Ach! Forgive us, dear Lord!*

Karl and eleven-year-old Jeremy Bailey rode in Bailey's wagon on the return trip. Jan helped his neighbor into his wagon. He paused; without a word he returned to his friend Bailey and put out his hand.

As they shook, Jan did his best to put into English words what his heart wanted to convey. "Mr. Bailey, you come church. God luffs you. God vants you."

He and Robert Bailey exchanged a look of mutual respect and friendship. His friend nodded and Jan returned to the wagon.

The drive back had been both good and bad for Jan. It surprised him how comfortable he felt in *Fru Brünlee's* company. *But.* But the conversation had quickly grown beyond his ability to follow. It grieved him to ask her to speak more slowly.

Nevertheless he *had* enjoyed the drive. Enjoyed it more than he was willing to own.

When they arrived at her house, Karl and Jeremy were almost dancing with excitement to help open the crates and boxes.

I am curious, too, Jan admitted. *It will be like Christmas to see what has been sent from a city far away!*

Fru Brünlee first selected the large crate whose boards were stenciled *Fragile* and *Do Not Drop*. Jan prized the lid from the crate that stood as tall as Fru Brünlee's shoulders, and then she, standing haphazardly on a box to reach inside, pulled out the packing.

"Now," she smiled at Jan, "you may pull the other boards off—but carefully, please."

Jan hefted a crowbar and glanced inside before fitting it to a corner of the crate. "Hah!" he muttered. What he glimpsed inside intrigued him.

He pulled the crate apart one board at a time, revealing a tiny, glossy piano. *Cherry wood,* Jan noted, admiring the grain.

"Oh, isn't it sweet?" *Fru Brünlee* crooned, caressing the glassy veneer. "Let's put it inside right away—out of the sun."

Jan, Karl, and Jeremy picked the piano up and placed it against the wall Jan and Søren had built halfway across the cabin. *Fru Brünlee* followed with a winding stool and set it in front of the spinet.

Jan examined the instrument closely, stroking the grain, studying the workmanship. "Play, please?" he requested.

"Oh! Well, maybe just to try it . . ." His neighbor ran her hands over the keys and played something . . . something wonderful.

Jeremy Bailey was thrilled. "Gosh, Miz Brownlee, that 'uz beautiful! Never heered nothin' like it afore."

Fru Brünlee was saying something about a concert, but Jan was fixated on what he'd just heard. *To make such music,* he stared at the keyboard, *to create melody and harmony with the hands . . .* He was entranced.

Karl poked him, jolting him from his thoughts. He and the boys went outside to open the rest of the freight.

Every new box was a fresh adventure! Linens, dishes, kitchen utensils, lamps, knick-knacks, sewing notions, clothes, wall hangings—even a myriad of seeds, seedlings, and cuttings!—emerged to the delight of *Fru Brünlee* and the boys.

"May I pay you all now?" she asked when all the crates were opened.

Jeremy and Karl blushed and nodded, both boys excited to earn cash money.

With a small frown, Jan refused. "*Nei,*" he stated, shaking his head. "*Venner.*"

"Pardon, Mr. Thoresen?"

"*Venner,*" he repeated. "Friends."

She seemed touched, he thought.

"Thank you! You've been so kind to me. I do thank you so much."

Jan felt words . . . and *feelings* bubbling up from inside, but they stuck in his throat like sand . . . so he just nodded.

"Come, Karl," he managed to choke out.

On an afternoon two weeks later, Amalie and Uli prepared to walk to their neighbor's home for what Amalie, in raptures, described as "a luncheon." Amalie and Sigrün first fixed the Thoresens' midday meal before Amalie and Uli departed, leaving Jan, Sigrün, and the boys at home.

Although Sigrün had also been invited and despite Amalie's persuasive attempts, his niece declined to join the little party. After they had eaten, Jan touched Sigrün's arm gently and she came to his arms, resting her head on his shoulder as she had so many times as a little girl.

As she had for months after the sickness had taken her pappa, her cousin, and tante. Jan knew she was afraid to go where she might be pressed to speak.

At the late evening meal, Amalie and Uli could not stop talking about the "luncheon." "Such lovely things *Fru Brünlee* has!" Amalie gushed. "A beautiful lace tablecloth, china, a silver tea service!"

"And chocolates!" Uli raved. "Every sort of chocolate candy! On such a beautiful plate! Fru Brünlee asked *me* to hold the pretty plate and pass the chocolates around!"

Up until now Karl, Arnie, and Kjell had scoffed at or ignored most of Amalie and Uli's recitation. However, when Uli crowed "chocolates!" the three boys became patently disgruntled.

"We never get chocolates," Kjell groused.

Jan, too, had paid only marginal attention to Amalie's description of the lunch and its conversation. He was, of course, happy for Amalie. His hard-working *søster* rarely received such a treat.

Then Amalie began chuckling. She crossed her arms and held herself while she laughed.

"Well? What is it?" Jan asked.

"*Fru Brünlee!*" Amalie chortled. Uli giggled with her.

Jan sighed. "So? What has our neighbor done now?"

"*Nei!* If you had seen her face!" Amalie and Uli laughed more.

Søren looked from his frowning father to his *tante*. "What is so funny?" Søren finally insisted.

"Ach!" Amalie wiped her eyes on the corner of her apron, and tried to compose herself. "*Fru Brünlee* said to Uli, in front of all the ladies, *Uli, please tell Amalie that Herr Thoresen did the most excellent work on my cupboards and porch. What a blessing it must be to have a husband so skilled.*"

Søren snickered, and the boys joined him. Amalie kept chuckling. "Oh, Jan! These many weeks she has thought you and I were married! Oh, if you could have seen her face, *Bror*!"

Jan blinked slowly and did not laugh.

She thought I was married?

It was breakfast at the Thoresen table. Early morning chores were over and five hungry men were shoveling fuel into their mouths as quickly as Sigrün or Amalie could set food before them.

"*Onkel*," Kjell said with his mouth full of fried potatoes. "*Onkel*, I took eggs and butter to *Fru Brünlee* this morning. Ach! She was *very* angry."

"Eh? Something was wrong with the butter?" Amalie asked, concerned.

"*Nei, Mamma. Nei.* She was angry with her dog. She said, 'Please tell Herr Thoresen that the dog he gave me is tearing up my yard and garden. Ask him what I should do, for heaven's sake!'"

Kjell, with one hand on his hip, delivered a more than passable imitation of *Fru Brünlee*, sending the boys and Uli into spasms of laughter. Amalie, her mouth twitching, fussed at their poor manners, but her brother-in-law was not helping: he was grinning with them!

Ja, I can see that, he thought, covering his mouth with a napkin.

"That is enough now, Kjell," Jan said when Amalie frowned at him. "I will talk with her." But he grinned through breakfast.

That night in his room in the barn, Jan laughed aloud. Several times during his long day he had recalled the pleasure of his visit with *Fru Brünlee*. He had cut a nice, supple switch, walked across the field and creek, and handed it to her.

"Kjell say dog bad. Here." And he had handed her the switch.

"What do I do with this?" *Fru Brünlee* had demanded, her words frosty with disdain.

Jan chuckled again. *So indignant!* At that moment he had nearly laughed in her face. When she pointed to the bush that her ugly, ill-mannered dog was dragging across the yard, Jan had promptly demonstrated the switch's use.

"Now, *Fru Brünlee*—must do if dog bad. *All* times." He had spoken firmly, perhaps too firmly, for she shrank from him.

So he gentled his voice and pointed. "See?" The gangly pup was baring his belly, a submissive sign.

After that Jan began to notice the many little improvements she had made to her yard—shrubs, bushes, and newly sprouted seedlings. He had studied her garden and was, he admitted, impressed.

Then he had seen her fruit saplings! He counted four of them. Grunting in approval he commented, "Four, five year, get fruit."

"Yes, I know. I . . . just wanted to start them, to see them grow." She was flushed with the pleasure of her first successes, but Jan sobered, doubting again that she would endure those four or five years to see them flourish.

She had talked on, saying something he could not follow, so he held up his hand. "Talk so slow, please, Mrs. *Brünlee*," he had asked. The "Mrs." did not come easily to his tongue, but he did his best.

Later she had offered him some cool tea and they had sat on the steps of the porch he had built, discussing the Bible as if it were the most natural thing in the world to do.

It had felt natural, Jan realized. Natural and comfortable. Satisfying.

When he had finished the last of his tea he stood. "Go now, Mrs. Brünlee. You make dog gud."

She grimaced but agreed.

Jan knew she had not the stomach to switch the dog when he needed it. "Proverbs 13:24," he quoted as he started away. Perhaps she would look it up and learn an important principle.

> *He that spareth his rod hateth his son;*
> *but he that loveth him chasteneth him betimes.*

Jan smiled again. His neighbor was becoming something of a fascination.

CHAPTER 38

The heat of midsummer hung heavy on the prairie. Jan lifted his hat and wiped his face with the kerchief he carried in his back pocket. He relished the breeze that cooled his damp head. He would be grateful to run his head under the pump and rinse the sweat and grime from it when it was time for the midday meal.

He studied the field before him, satisfied. Their corn stood high, topped with golden tassels, full of plump ears. The winter wheat crop had been a good one, too; soon the second sowing would reach maturity.

I thank you, Lord, for this bounty! he rejoiced. *So many years we did not know how we would get through, but you have always made a way. Thank you,* he again prayed.

He scanned the horizon. Thunderstorms began building this time of day, so he regularly turned an eye to the skies. To the west he noted a cloud and paused to study it.

Typically, thunderheads built vertically, growing from white to dark gray and black, until they towered, full of moisture, high in the sky. The cloud he was watching was moving . . . quickly, too quickly. It looked as though rain were sheeting from the cloud to the ground—

His body reacted before his mind grasped what he was seeing. Heart hammering, Jan began running toward the house and barn.

Nei Lord! Not again! his mind began to scream. He saw Arnie and hollered at him to ring the bell. "Keep it ringing!" Jan shouted.

As fast as he could move, Jan began hitching the bays to the wagon. *The cloud is moving from north to south. Perhaps two miles west?*

"McKennies'," Jan breathed. After that, Norvald and Inge's, and the Gardiners'!

Søren, Karl, and Kjell came running because the continued clanging of the bell signaled an emergency. "What is it, *Pappa*?" Søren shouted.

"Look to the west," Jan answered, his words grim. "Karl! Arnie! Kjell! Get our plows and all of our hoes, shovels, and picks. Bring gloves and every empty burlap bag! Bring kerosene!"

The boys scattered to do his bidding. Amalie and Sigrün stood on the porch, watching, wringing their hands, worried.

Søren turned to Jan, his face ashen. "Locusts?"

"*Ja*, get the mule and tie it to the wagon," Jan answered, grinding his teeth. "Please God, it is not as big a swarm as the last time—maybe several acres?" The boys returned, piling tools into the wagon.

"Get in," Jan instructed. "We must follow the swarm. If it lands, we will fight it."

They were not the only farmers in the neighborhood to recognize the swarm for what it was. As Jan turned at the road that led to the McKennies', he saw other wagons racing toward them.

Then the cloud was passing over their heads, going ahead of them, the chittering of thousands of wings chilling Jan's heart. As they watched, the swarm descended on McKennie corn.

Fiona saw the wagons coming and waved them on. Jan stood and urged the bays faster until he saw Brian, Norvald, and a few of their neighbors gathered at the edge of the field. He threw the reins to Arnie and jumped from the wagon.

His friends nodded to him but their eyes were on the field. The swarm crawled over much of Brian's cornfield and the collective tearing and chewing of locust mandibles was loud, familiar, and terrifying.

Jan studied the field. "Brian, the swarm has just landed, *ja*? We know they will be busy for a few hours. Let us plow a firebreak around them and set the field on fire. If we use kerosene and the field burns hot enough, will the swarm not choke in the smoke?"

They looked up as another wagon careened toward them. Others were close behind. Jan was surprised to see his neighbor's buggy pull into the yard. The gathering was growing in number.

Jan yanked his attention back to their problem. "We cannot wait," Jan warned. Søren quickly translated his advice.

"What Jan says will be workin'," Brian agreed. "Boot 'tis meanin' we've got t' break our backs in t' next hour or two, three at t' moost, or our chance will be goon. And if are we missing this chance, your fields may be next!"

Søren spoke up. "My father says if Brian McKennie is willing to sacrifice his corn, we should be grateful to take advantage of such an offer." There was a buzz of talk and Brian spoke again.

"Well, laddies, let's to it! Th' Lord be blessin' ye all. Even ye women what feel ye can help, we'll be needin' ye."

The group of men dispersed into action, hitching their plows and following Brian's shouted instructions even as he hitched his own. Søren and Karl hitched the bays to Thoresen plows; Jan hitched his mule to Brian's disc. Jan called Arnie, Kjell, and the McKennie boys to grab hoe, shovel, and pick, and pointed where they were to start.

The boys went after the corn, chopping and ripping it from the ground to clear a path before the plow. Jan shouted to the mule and it pulled, the tool biting into the soil. He forged ahead and Søren plowed to his side a few feet behind.

Together their swath was about two feet wide—not anywhere near wide enough. The boys ahead of them hacked at the cornstalks and tossed them into the field to burn and they plowed on.

An hour later, Jan and Søren met Brian and Norvald head-on as they plowed toward them. Jan and Søren drove around Brian and Norvald and continued on to widen the swath.

Perhaps fifty neighbors and their wives and children were now working furiously to complete a firebreak. Someone was distributing gunnysacks to beat the fire if it jumped the plowed break. Another neighbor and his son were constructing torches and dipping them in a bucket of kerosene.

Still the firebreak was unfinished; Jan drove his mule mercilessly. Behind them, others spread the turned dirt, tossing prairie grass and fallen cornstalks aside, hacking deeper into the field to widen the swath.

In the commotion someone shouted a warning—the cloud was lifting! Whether the break was ready or not, if the swarm lifted off, they had agreed to torch the field rather than let the swarm escape untouched. Those holding torches waited for the signal shot, but the mass of insects hovered and then descended not far from where it had first landed.

Up ahead, Jan could see another man plowing toward him. He swung his plow to the right, and they drove by each other, connecting the widened swath. It was enough! Shouting orders, the men unhitched the animals and had them led away to safety.

Brian and Jan's boys were handing lit torches to each person able to hold one; every man, woman, and child stood along the firebreak, waiting for the signal. Jan saw men pouring kerosene around the edges of the field.

Jan received a torch and saw one of Brian's sons light Fiona's and *Fru Brünlee's* torches. The acrid smoke burned Jan's already parched throat as they awaited signal! Through the haze he saw Rose Brownlee, her mouth set in a determined line.

The gunshot! Jan plunged his torch into the cornfield—there, there, and there. The kerosene-soaked edges of the field smoldered and then burned.

Thick, dense smoke billowed upwards, growing, spreading. A slight wind freshened, driving the fire on Jan's side of the field toward the infestation. On the other side of the field, he knew his friends and neighbors would be laboring to keep the fire from jumping the break.

The sound of thousands upon thousands of insect wings grew—the swarm was lifting! Jan grimly watched as the insects climbed away from the smoke, escaping.

Oh, God, how we need you now!

The breeze dropped, then backed; the wind shifted direction and blew! On the other side of the field, the fire roared up—engulfing the swarm! Frenzied buzzing grew louder as did the roar of flames.

Then it was raining locusts! Jan shouted; the men and women on either side of him surged forward. Swinging burlap bags, they beat the stunned insects as they fell from the air. Deeper into the field they pushed, over the hot ashes and smoldering stubble, beating the locusts.

They had won. The locusts were gone and the fire was out.

Jan, Søren, and the boys gathered their tools and trudged toward Brian's house. The boys made for the pump and rinsed streams of black grime from their heads and faces.

A few women were hauling buckets of water to the workers. Jan's throat ached; when he was offered a cup, he could scarcely swallow. He looked around, seeing the human toll of their efforts.

Faces and clothing were blackened. One of the Gardiner boys was coughing and retching from the smoke. He heard Fiona weeping over Brian's blistered hands. He saw his neighbor helping Fiona wrap Brian's hands.

Folks were leaving now, by ones and twos making their way in exhaustion to their wagons for the drive home. Jan positioned himself on the road where it left Brian's yard. Søren stood with him. As their friends and neighbors passed, he asked for a moment of their time and Søren translated his request.

Søren nodded when he saw Rose Brownlee—and they grinned at each other at the same time. Hearing Søren's chuckle, Jan turned. His usually impeccable neighbor was covered in soot, her hair a tangled mess.

Jan grinned. "So! Mrs. *Brünlee* like play dirt?"

"It does not appear that I am alone, does it?" she joked back. She sighed. "What a shame! We did get the locusts, didn't we? But Brian's corn is all gone."

"*Ja*. And help Brian now."

"How? How can we help? Can I help?"

Jan smiled again. "You help . . ." He asked Søren for a word. "You help already, Mrs. *Brünlee*. We . . ." He consulted Søren again.

"We share corn, all farmers . . ." He waved his hand to include those living in the area. "*All* safe now. We share for Brian."

Fru Brünlee smiled and nodded her approval; Jan nodded in return, their understanding perfect.

Those in the community who had survived the great locust infestation of seven years past knew what God and the neighbors' quick efforts had saved them from. Instead of disaster and near starvation, they rejoiced in an abundant harvest.

Jan released a sigh of weary relief when the train bearing their corn, wheat, and hogs left the station in Norvald's capable hands. He and his family had labored long and hard to bring in the crops and store up more than enough food for the winter. This year he would have money to put in the bank.

Amalie had taken their neighbor under her wing throughout the summer, teaching her how to store or can her garden's produce. When the Thoresens killed their hogs, *Fru Brünlee* had learned to make soap, cheeses, candles, and sausages at Amalie's side.

Jan shook his head. Every time he decided *Fru Brünlee* would certainly back down, give up, or turn up her nose at hard, messy work, she surprised him.

Maybe she would survive on the prairie after all, but only winter would determine that.

Jan heard Arnie and Kjell telling Amalie that the school would have a new teacher when the fall term began, a Mr. Letoire. Jan stood in the doorway, considering an idea.

"Ach! Jan, please close the door, *ja*? You're letting the flies in," Amalie scolded.

Jan grabbed a cup of coffee and headed for the living room, thinking hard. The schoolmaster usually boarded around the community during the school year, each family taking him for a few weeks. Now Jan was pondering the vow he'd made years ago.

I will not learn the English, he'd vowed in the heat of his pain and anger. *I have Søren; I do not need to learn.*

Today that vow was sounding foolish and pig-headed. *Yes, another example of my impulsive nature,* he chided himself. *Karl surely would have had words to say to me on that count, eh?*

He turned back to the kitchen. "Amalie, may I ask a favor of you?"

Amalie looked in surprise to see that Jan was serious. "*Bror,* I will do anything for you, do you not know that? What is it?"

"I was thinking that perhaps the new schoolmaster would board with us."

"Ach! Is that all? Sure, don't we usually have the teacher a few weeks each year?" Søren would give up the bedroom on the main floor and sleep with Little Karl when the teacher stayed with them.

"*Nei*, what I mean is . . . I wish him to stay with us the whole term."

Amalie studied him closely. "All right. But why, Jan?"

Jan cleared his throat. "Perhaps it is time that you and I learn the English, *ja*? If he is here, perhaps we can apply ourselves to it. But I know his staying all term will be more work for you."

Amalie blinked and said nothing. She stirred the pot on the stove for a moment. Then she shrugged. "As you wish, Jan."

"*Tusen takk, Søster*," Jan breathed. "*Mange tusen takk*."

CHAPTER 39

When the harvest ended, Jan had a new concern: *One Harold Kalbørg*. Jan pursed his lips as he thought on the problem.

At Sally Gardiner's wedding, Amalie had shown up at his side and nudged him. He'd looked down and seen apprehension in his *søster's* eyes. Then he'd followed her stare—and seen Sigrün on the dance floor with that young Kalbørg whelp.

Jan had kept a close eye on Kalbørg that day. No young man would be taking advantage of their Sigrün! But that evening Harold had approached Jan, his manner respectful and straightforward.

"Sir, I would like your permission to call on Sigrün."

Jan had said nothing at first. He had simply stared (with menace, he hoped) at Kalbørg, but the young man would not be deterred. He had waited for Jan's answer. Patiently.

"What do you have to recommend yourself?" The words had grated between Jan's clenched teeth.

"Yes, sir," Harold had answered, clearly prepared for the question. "I own my farm, half of my father's homestead. Someday—but not soon, I pray—I will inherit his half also. I have $200 in the bank, a house, a barn, two cows, a mule, a wagon, two horses, and a buggy." He cleared his throat. "I am a hard worker and a Christian man, sir."

At least he is Swedish. At least we can talk. Jan hemmed for another moment. "I will consider your request and give you an answer Sunday."

"Yes, sir. Thank you, sir."

That Sunday a somber Amalie had invited Harold Kalbørg home to dinner. It could not have been a pleasant experience for young Kalbørg, Jan admitted to himself later.

Jan had been aloof and vigilant during the meal. Sigrün had eaten little and blushed often. Her three brothers had stared at Harold and made faces.

And Uli had peered innocently into Harold's eyes and asked, "Are you going to marry my sister?"

Jan had been relieved when Søren had taken Harold off to the barn. Likely Harold had been, too.

Thanksgiving and Christmas passed in a blur. Amalie invited *Fru Brünlee* for Thanksgiving dinner, but as Amalie reported, their neighbor had also received invitations from the McKennies, Baileys, and Medfords!

Jan's less-than-tactful suggestion that Amalie had waited too late to invite *Fru Brünlee* was met with frigid silence.

In the end, their neighbor had hosted Thanksgiving dinner for the pastor and his wife. *And invited half the county for dessert*, Jan noted in wry surprise. The Thoresens crammed themselves into Mrs. Brownlee's tiny house along with the pastor and his wife, the Baileys, and Brian and Fiona's brood.

After the adults had found places to perch and the children were sprawled on the floor, *Fru Brünlee* and Mrs. Medford served a variety of desserts and coffee. Jan couldn't help notice how pleased and content his neighbor appeared that evening. He didn't mean to be studying her, but she noticed his prying stare.

Jan raised his coffee cup to her in a silent salute, contrite that he had again been rude. Unexpectedly, his neighbor smiled and raised her cup in friendly return.

Something warm washed through Jan. *What was that?* He blinked and took a hurried sip of coffee, scalding his mouth.

When Vera Medford sat down at Mrs. Brownlee's tiny piano, Jan forgot everything except the music. *Never have I heard such a thing!* he marveled. Even the children were still, suspended in the beauty of the moment.

Too soon she finished the piece but began another, eventually transitioning to gospel songs that had everyone tapping their feet, clapping their hands, and singing along with gusto.

Then they sang slower, more reverent songs. Jan's heart was already overflowing when the pastor's wife began to play

> *Amazing Grace! How sweet the sound,*
> *That saved a wretch like me!*
> *I once was lost, but now am found,*
> *Was blind, but now I see.*

Jan knew the words by rote; he repeated the lines silently: *I was lost, Lord, but you found me. I was so blind!*

"Blessed be your name," Jan breathed.

Temperatures dropped and they received their first hard freeze not long after Thanksgiving. Jan, Søren, and the boys left the house early to start the chores that morning. As the cold penetrated to his skin, Jan wrapped his arms around his chest and beat them to warm himself.

I wonder how our neighbor is faring in this freezing weather. He found himself worrying throughout the day, wondering again how she would survive the coming blizzards.

That evening he looked for a window in their house that would provide a view of the little house across the fields and creek. The kitchen offered an unobstructed view, but Amalie stared curiously at him as he peered through the glass.

Jan mumbled something unintelligible and wandered into the living room to warm his hands at the stove. He glanced at the two living room windows. A moment later he had pulled the curtain back and put his face to the glass. By cupping his hands around his eyes, he could see into the darkness.

There! He could make out a tiny light in *Fru Brünlee's* window, flaring through the frosty air. Smoke floated from the stovepipe. Everything seemed in order, and he nodded, satisfied.

It snowed that night, turning their fields into a wonderland. Jan found himself often pulled to the living room window, *just to check on their neighbor,* he told himself. *Ja, just to be neighborly.*

And yet his feelings were confusing and perhaps *not* merely neighborly. He pulled himself upright when he questioned where they were leading him. *You are but an old farmer and she is a rich, young woman, Jan Thoresen!* he scolded himself. *There is nothing there for you. Nothing.*

Christmas drew near and so did the end of the school's first term. The school recital was rare entertainment for their little community. The program was scheduled for the Saturday before Christmas Eve, and Amalie's children were wild to perform their parts well.

Jan looked around the simple schoolhouse—filled to capacity with the parents of school children and the children themselves that afternoon.

You are hoping your neighbor will come, is that it? he accused himself in a scorching tone. And then he saw she *had* come with the McKennie clan. Jan leaned against a wall where he had a good view of the platform—and of his neighbor.

Why are you doing this? his mind shouted. *Because I enjoy watching her,* he answered honestly. *I enjoy watching her experience new things and watching her learn to live again after . . .* After what? Yes, after receiving new life in Christ, but also after . . . something else. Something tragic?

What do you really know about her? he asked himself. Jan began to list what he knew of his neighbor and question what he did *not* know of her.

Ja, she has been married, he knew, *a widow.* A contrary thought struck him. Struck him hard.

She has money. What if, instead of a widow as we've assumed, she has fled a disastrous marriage? What if she is married still?

Jan swallowed, trying to moisten his suddenly dry throat. *Could she be married still?*

Why should that bother you, old man? he sneered. Nevertheless, he was disquieted. *How do I find out more?* he pondered. *Does she have children? If so, where are they? Where is her family—her parents and siblings?*

The recital concluded and Jan could remember nothing of it except Arnie's animated rendition of "The Charge of the Light Brigade." It had been well done—if not quite conventional—a poem immortalizing a recent war Jan had not heard of, in a place Jan did not know.

The following day was Christmas Eve. Amalie, Sigrün, and Uli were in a fever to finish the Christmas cooking and baking. Jan spent his free time in the barn working on secrets that would only be revealed Christmas morning.

They had invited *Fru Brünlee* to join them Christmas morning, but she had already accepted an invitation from the McKennies. Jan had to squelch the momentary annoyance—perhaps even resentment—he had felt toward Brian and Fiona when Amalie told him their neighbor had declined their invitation.

"Hrmph," He was using a fine rasp to smooth the wooden train set he had built for the younger boys.

He growled again as he glanced at the trivet sitting on his bench. He'd carved the design from solid wood and rubbed it until it glowed in the lamplight. Sigrün had been delighted when he'd asked her to paint colorful rosemaaling designs on it.

It was to be a gift from the Thoresen family. But when would they have an opportunity to give it to her?

"Hrmph!" He still wasn't feeling altogether charitable toward the McKennie clan.

That afternoon, Uli peered through the kitchen window toward their neighbor's house. "*Onkel,*" she said as he came in the door, preoccupied and slightly sullen. "Why can we not carol at Mrs. Brownlee's house this evening? I would like to be Saint Lucia and wear the crown of candles!"

Jan paused and considered her words. *Why not indeed?* He looked to Amalie.

"Ach! Why did we not think of this sooner?" she complained.

"Can we do it?" was all Jan wanted to know. Uli and the boys were clamoring for their mother to agree.

"*Ja*, sure we can," she smiled. "We will just give her some of *your* candy and cookies, eh?"

The boys were instantly crestfallen but Uli just laughed. "*Mamma!* We have been baking for days! We have plenty."

"*Ja*, we have plenty," Amalie laughed with her. "I am teasing. But Jan, we must take her lutefisk, too, don't you think?" The house was soaking in the pungent odor of the traditional Norwegian treat.

Lutefisk! Of course! Jan smiled. *A perfect gift!*

An hour after dark Jan and Søren hitched the bays to the Thoresens' sleigh. Amalie and the girls, their arms full of treats and gifts, climbed in with Søren, who would drive. Jan and the boys trudged through the snow alongside the sled.

The sleigh bells jingled merrily across the bridge and through their neighbor's yard. In front of her front door they piled out and organized themselves. Amalie placed the crown of candles on Uli's head and Jan lit each taper.

Søren had to keep shushing the boys who were giggling and cutting up. Each of them carried some small package of cookies or candy; Jan carried the still-warm lutefisk wrapped in brown paper. His nose crinkled with appreciation.

Then they were ready and trooped up the front steps to their neighbor's door. Jan led them in a traditional carol in Riksmaal and they sang with happy hearts.

When *Fru Brünlee* opened the door to their singing, she smiled her welcome. She was framed by the light behind her and for some reason Jan lost his breath. The carol ended well, but Jan had stopped singing.

"Oh, how lovely!" *Fru Brünlee* exclaimed.

The children pushed forward, eager to deliver their packages, and she waved them all inside. Amalie, Sigrün, and Jan came behind them.

"But what is this?" Rose demanded of the children. "Explain it to me."

"I'm Saint Lucia!" Uli bragged. "See my candles? We're looking for my new eyes but we found you instead!"

The boys laughed and hooted at Uli's description.

Søren added, "It is Norwegian tradition to visit one's neighbors between Saint Lucia's day—the thirteenth of December—and Christmas to bring candies and sweets. You are our only close neighbor so here we are—even if we are nearly late!"

Amalie and *Fru Brünlee* undid the packages; their neighbor exclaimed over each gift of cookies, candies, and cakes, and she promptly handed them around. Jan offered her the lutefisk and laughed as she wrinkled her nose.

"What is it?" She eyed it with suspicion.

"Lutefisk. Ver special," Jan explained. He cut the cord with his pocketknife and unwrapped the package. The Thoresens sniffed appreciatively.

"Ver special for Christmas," Jan explained, but he could not keep his eyes from twinkling. He could tell she *hated* the smell—and would die before she admitted so.

"Try, please?" The odor was having an unpleasant effect on *Fru Brünlee*. She forced herself to try the offered bite. He laughed—until he saw her nauseous expression.

Jan re-wrapped the fish. "Lutefisk not for ever'one. We take home and eat more, eh?"

"Thank you, anyway."

Then the children offered their present.

"I'm sure I didn't expect a gift," she protested.

"Open it! Open it!" they urged.

Jan could tell she liked it. She rubbed her fingers over the gleaming wood and gently touched the painting.

"Sigrün did the rosemaaling," Uli said proudly. "And *Onkel* carved the wood."

"It's truly beautiful—thank you all, very much!" Her pause was only the briefest. "Now I have a gift for all of you."

Jan was surprised, but the children clapped their enthusiasm. Their neighbor reached under her bed and pulled out a small box. She set it on the table and invited them to look.

Kjell lifted the lid. "Oh!"

The other boys and Uli crowded up to see. The box was lined with shells, starfish, coral, and sea horses—things the children had never seen.

"What are they?" Uli breathed.

"Let's take them out and see," *Fru Brünlee* suggested. Carefully they removed the items and laid them where they could be seen. They listened attentively as she described each piece, where it came from, and what it was like in the ocean before it died or washed up on a beach.

"However did you collect them all, Mrs. Brownlee?" Karl asked. He was holding a large red starfish.

She cleared her throat and answered calmly. "My son collected them over the last four years. It was a hobby of his, but I knew you had never seen anything like them so I asked my mother to send them to me for you. Do you like them?"

"Yes'm!"

Jan had listened intently to the conversation. *So, Lord, now I know a little more, eh? She has a mother and I think she has lost a son.*

When he watched her struggle and master her emotions, a kindred compassion surged in his breast. *Ah, I know. I know your pain, Fru Brünlee. I know.*

As the Thoresens took their leave, their neighbor gave each of the children a candy cane and a hug. She hugged Sigrün and Amalie and shook Søren's hand. Last of all she shook Jan's hand.

"Merry Christmas, Mr. Thoresen."

"*Ja*, and a ver Merry Christmas for you," Jan answered. Then he whispered. "And I denk you."

She did not understand.

"Denk you for special gift to children," he repeated. "Ver special." He pressed her hand and bowed. And then she did understand.

She ducked her head to hide the sudden moisture, but he saw it, just for an instant, gleaming on her lashes.

CHAPTER 40

Winter days were short and nights were long. In the evenings, Jan and Mr. Letoire now had time to work on Jan's English. Jan made an attempt to include Amalie in the beginning, but she had no real interest. Before long it was only Jan and the schoolmaster bending over books at the kitchen table.

English was not Jan's only preoccupation in the dark evenings.

Ach! What will Amalie think if I wear a hole in this carpet? Jan thought and grimaced. From the window in their living room he could see all of Mrs. Brownlee's house and yard. From there he could see her coming from and going to the house to her chores. And he'd found himself drawn to this window . . . regularly.

Like every morning. And every evening.

He shook his head. *I cannot be entertaining such thoughts*, he chided himself. He stared again at the little house across the fields and across the creek.

Such thoughts? What thoughts? What thoughts could he possibly be thinking?

He stared deeply into his heart and frowned. He only knew that the vague sense of responsibility for a neighboring woman alone on the prairie was growing . . . into something more.

He rubbed his face hard. A blizzard was coming soon. He could feel it in his bones.

He glanced at the house again and saw the woman, wrapped against the cold, heading for her little stable. *No doubt to feed and water her stock. She has taken to her responsibilities better than I expected.*

Jan cocked his head and listened. The wind was shifting. Picking up. He glanced back across the fields. She was at the pump now, filling a bucket. She glanced up and stared into the distance.

Søren unexpectedly joined him at the window. "Do you think she knows a blizzard is coming?" he asked. "I can see the cloud. It is southwest of us, coming fast. Surely she will see it, too."

Jan shook his head. "I don't know." He tore himself away from the window. "Are we ready for it?"

"Yes, *Pappa*. The boys and I have taken care of the stock. They have plenty of feed and water for now. The barn and sheds are closed up."

As Jan nodded his approval, a gust of wind slammed the farm house. He wanted to go back to the window and make sure their neighbor was safe in her house, but Søren was there, watching. Instead Jan made for the kitchen to wash up.

The season of blizzards was upon them. As inconspicuously as possible, Jan kept an eye out for Mrs. Brownlee from the window in the living room. Each time a storm screamed across the prairie and fell upon them, Jan felt an uneasy need to know that his neighbor was tucked, safe and secure, within her home. And he was glad after each storm that he and Søren had insisted on certain improvements to Abigael and Henrik's house—particularly the new roof and strong doors.

Many times as evening fell he saw the lamplight flare in her window. Jan imagined his neighbor reading or cooking in the tiny but snug house. The picture he drew in his mind made him smile.

The last Saturday in February another storm pummeled their community. As the family arose Sunday morning, there was no thought of going out in the blinding snow and wind for church. After the men and boys took care of the milking and the stock's needs, the family settled in for a day of quiet indoor activity.

Jan stared through the window but could see nothing of his neighbor's house. The winds had scoured a high drift of snow against the barn, and he could not even make out the shapes of their sheds through the swirling snow.

Jan frowned. *Lord, please help our neighbor, eh? She will be sorry to miss church today.*

The weather began to abate early Tuesday morning, but as soon as the Thoresens finished the milking, the bruising roar of another storm was upon them. The pounding of wind-blasted snow lasted until Friday afternoon.

By then Jan was surly and anxious for *Fru Brünlee*. Uli, unknowingly, offered a way to allay his worries.

"*Onkel*, look at the sunshine on the snow!" she shouted. "Can we go for a sleigh ride? Please?"

Jan opened his mouth to snap a crotchety "no" and caught himself. An audacious idea—*a perfect idea!*—had entered his mind.

"Bundle up, little one, *ja*? It may be bright, but it is very cold!" He pulled on a heavy wool sweater and buttoned his long coat over it. He twined a scarf around his neck and covered his head with a thick wool cap.

Then he had Little Karl help him carry the sleigh out of the barn and hitch it to the bays. He surreptitiously glanced across the fields but saw no activity at his neighbor's house other than a wisp of smoke curling from the stovepipe.

A few minutes later he and Uli were flying down the frosty track toward the bridge. The sleigh's bells rang brightly in the icy air. He pulled up in front of Mrs. Brownlee's house and was a bit disappointed when she did not step out to welcome them. Wouldn't she have been alerted by the happy, jingling sound of sleigh bells?

"Let us knock on her door, Uli, shall we?" Uli bounded up the steps and he followed behind her. She was already knocking on the door when Jan joined her.

They waited. After a few moments their neighbor answered the door and Uli bounded inside, announcing joyously, "Mrs. Brownlee! *Onkel* is taking me for a ride; do you want to come?"

Their neighbor said nothing, only nodded her response. Jan followed Uli inside and closed the door while their neighbor, wordlessly, went for her cloak, bonnet, and gloves.

Jan cocked his head. Something was not right with *Fru Brünlee*.

He studied her and saw dull, puffy eyes and a forced smile. Were those tears drying on her cheeks?

Their neighbor, as if she were swimming in thick fog, slowly dragged on her hat and gloves. Uli frowned and looked up at her *onkel*, concern on her young face.

Jan stepped forward to assist as *Fru Brünlee* fumbled with her cloak. Unconsciously she sniffed and rubbed her cheek with a gloved hand.

Jan looked from Uli to *Fru Brünlee*. Without warning he grabbed Uli and "whiskered" her cheek, sending her into a fit of laughter. The sound of Uli's cheerful laughter seemed to wake their neighbor from her stupor.

"Sun is ver shining today, Mrs. Brünlee," Jan said in a light tone. "Ver gud day drive, *ja*?"

He hustled Uli and *Fru Brünlee* outside and into the sleigh, wheeled the team around, and raced up the hill. From there they flew across the snow-crusted upper fields of her property.

Uli screamed in delight and Jan did not discourage her, noticing that his neighbor was waking and taking note of the scenery flying by. Jan drove for miles, letting Uli's chatter and the fresh air do their work.

His little niece sang "Jingle Bells"—many times—and *Fru Brünlee* joined in. Jan was relieved to see her smile and sniff the snowy air. Later when Uli fell asleep between them, Jan and his neighbor rode, at a more sedate pace, in companionable silence.

"Vinter most gone, now." Jan wanted her to know that the worst was over. "March haf many nice days; some storm too, but most getting nicer."

Fru Brünlee sighed. "I guess I don't care much for winter out here, but I can't say I wasn't warned."

Jan didn't care for the edge of defeat he heard in her response. He shrugged. "Vinter ver hard, *all*. Must busy. Must outside some and also vit' people."

"I know. I just haven't been able to see anyone recently. I guess I let it get me down."

"Not eat gud, also?"

"Hm? Oh. Food hasn't tasted good to me lately."

He knew he was risking a cold rebuff, but still he gently suggested, "Mrs. Brünlee, body belong God; must take care for him, *ja*? Take care mind, too."

"Your English is improving, Mr. Thoresen. Have you been working on it?"

Jan chuckled in silence. *How deftly she turned the subject! Now this was his neighbor!*

Glancing sideways at her Jan answered carefully, "*Ja*, am learn some."

The sun was low on the horizon when Jan and Uli returned *Fru Brünlee* to her home. The dog she had named "Baron" ran between them and jumped up on her skirts, refusing to be ignored.

Jan snorted. She had developed an affection for the ugly mongrel but had certainly not trained him well.

Over Baron's yips, she thanked him for the ride.

"I take Uli Monday," Jan mentioned quietly, staring out over the snow-laden fields. "You like come too?"

"Yes, I would. I would greatly enjoy it."

It was during the long winter and over the course of several sleigh rides that Jan began to pray . . . not just *for* his neighbor, but about her.

CHAPTER 41

Jan had given in completely. He *enjoyed* watching his neighbor— surreptitiously, of course—and was always glad when Amalie announced *Fru Brünlee* would be coming for Sunday dinner.

Perhaps even today, Jan hoped with an inward grin. *It has been a few weeks, after all!*

He saw Mary Bailey approach Rose and growled his frustration. Amalie hadn't been quick enough! Someone else was tendering an invite.

But no, Mrs. Bailey was handing *Fru Brünlee* a telegram.

Telegrams were always bad news.

Skirting the knots of people visiting in the churchyard, Jan found an unobstructed view as she tore open the paper. Her expression told him what he'd feared. Something bad had happened.

"Søren!" Jan called. His *sønn* waved to him. Jan gestured him over and glanced back toward *Fru Brünlee*. It could not be good—her face had crumpled.

He grabbed Søren by the arm and dragged him to their neighbor. "Ask what we can do," Jan directed.

Søren and *Fru Brünlee* spoke for just a moment before she turned away, covering her eyes with her hand. Søren whispered to his father, "*Pappa*, she has heard bad news. Her mother has died."

Jan thought for a moment. "Will she go? Ask her, please."

Søren approached their neighbor again and gently asked the question. He looked toward Jan and nodded. Jan drew near and instructed Søren, "Tell her we will take care of her home and animals and take her to the train. Ask her when she will leave."

"Tomorrow, *Pappa*."

Jan nodded. "Tell her we will come and take her in the morning."

The train, in a hail of cinders, steamed away from the RiverBend siding. Jan stared after it. *She has gone. Gone to mourn her mother. Gone back to her family.*

All he could think or imagine was how easy it would be for her to never return to her little house across the fields and creek from him. That single thought dug an ache in his chest he did not know how to address.

Nearly three weeks later, Jan, Amalie, and Uli were waiting and watching for the arrival of the train. Vera Medford had assured Jan that Rose was, indeed, returning. The train slowed and, with a release of steam, stopped.

Then Uli let out a whoop and raced down the siding. "Mrs. Brownlee! Mrs. Brownlee!"

Their neighbor scooped Uli up and smothered her round cheeks with kisses; Uli squeezed *Fru Brünlee's* neck and matched her kiss for kiss. Jan stood stock still, mesmerized, until Amalie dragged him along. She, too, wrapped her arms around their neighbor, talking all the while.

Jan stood back, calm enough, although he wondered, for the briefest moment, how it might feel *to wrap his arms around*—

Finally, when he had an opportunity to greet her, he took her hand and said, "Velcome home," something he'd practiced often in the last twenty-four hours.

Jan could not keep up with the chatter flowing among Amalie, Uli, and *Fru Brünlee*, so he focused only on *Fru Brünlee's* replies.

"And Baron? How is Baron?" she questioned.

Jan snorted and he told Uli, "Tell *Fru Brünlee* that her dog is fine— even if we did give up trying to keep him at our house."

Uli added, "He chewed through the ropes and went back home, so we just let him stay there. He's waiting for you right now."

Fru Brünlee smiled, and Jan clucked his tongue in mock disapproval. "Dog ver gud now, eh?" he commented wryly. She just smiled larger.

She has come back! She does not intend to leave but to stay!
Those words rang within him and, like a bellows fans an ember to life, her return blew fresh hope into his heart. A question burned in there, demanding an answer.

I must know the answer! his heart insisted.

So, Lord, he prayed, *I wish to test the water with Fru Brünlee. Will you help me?*

He practiced what he would do, what he would say, rehearsing the shape and sound of strange English words until he could not sleep without them intruding on his dreams.

He dressed himself with care and polished the leather of the buggy to a high shine, all as inconspicuously as possible. He did not want to draw Søren's or the boys' attention to what he was doing, and he *did not* want to field any questions!

Without a word he drove away from his farm.

"Mr. Thoresen, hello!"

Fru Brünlee seemed glad to see him.

Ja, god-dag," he greeted her. "You please to take ride?" He indicated his buggy in the yard.

"Yes, yes!" *Fru Brünlee* rushed away to gather her coat and mittens, and Jan took a deep breath, the first hurdle overcome. He fingered the dear object in his coat pocket.

They drove through the spring snow, a cool breeze whipping their cheeks. His neighbor sighed and closed her eyes in bliss.

"Day to ride—not to house, *ja?*" Jan offered, using his best conversation starter.

She nodded and smiled. "I'm glad you came."

She is glad I came!

Across the snow-clad plain on little-used roads and tracks the bays charged. After a while Jan spoke, loud enough to be heard over the swish of the wheels and the wind whistling by, "Ve go, look river. Ver big now. Ver *grand.*"

He pulled up on the team as they approached the brow of the overlook. He laid the buggy alongside the edge. Below, running from north to south, was the same creek that divided their properties.

It was wider and deeper here where it emptied into the river. Snow covered the banks of the creek and hung over the sides of the small torrent. Jan relished the view. From here they could see the creek pouring into the river—and beyond that the prairie stretched far into the distance, more beautiful than any winter portrait.

All was silent save for the shifting of the team . . . so he pulled the object from his pocket. In the palm of his hand he held the only image of Elli he owned, a tiny tintype set inside a hinged, leather-bound case. He snapped it open and looked at her face.

What would his neighbor see? Jan peered again at Elli's likeness, so familiar to him.

"*Fru Brünlee*, please to look at picture? Is mine vife. Name vas Elli. Vas gud, best, and kind woman."

Jan was not encouraged. His neighbor was staring at the river and had grown still. She seemed distant and disturbed. Then she stirred.

"Who . . .?" She looked up, inquiring, and Jan realized she had not heard what he'd said.

"Mine vife, Elli." He repeated patiently. With dogged determination he continued. "Fever, ver bad come. Our *datter* Kristen, mine brot'er Karl, and mine Elli die. Go to God. Many years now."

His neighbor took the picture into her hand and studied it. He saw tears spring to her eyes.

"I haf much luf for Elli. Ver hard life vit no Elli," Jan added slowly.

Oh, Lord, help me, Jan prayed. He had practiced these words so many times, and yet they were flying straight out of his head!

He swallowed. "You luf, too. Your man?" Softly he added, "He die, too, *ja?*"

She shivered and her voice shook. As though he had ripped a scab from a mortal wound, her answer bled pain rather than blood. "Yes, he died. And my children, my sweet little ones."

She gestured at the water. "Our carriage slid into a frozen river like this one. They all died. They all drowned. *Except for me.*"

And then she was weeping uncontrollably and Jan knew. He knew she was in much more pain than he had realized. She was not ready to hear such words from him.

He slapped the reins once and the buggy pulled away from the high bank. Making a wide circle, he turned in the direction of her home.

As he drove he prayed for her. *Ah, Lord. A husband! And her little ones! To lose one's children in icy water? No one can prepare for such a horror. What a brave soul this woman has. Please help her! Please give me words of comfort!*

As they flew over the crusty roads her weeping subsided. Soon Jan could feel that she was calmer. She was, he thought, about to speak, so Jan pulled on the reins and brought the team to a gradual stop. He turned and faced her in the seat.

She was embarrassed. "Mr. Thoresen, I'm very sorry for my behavior . . . I didn't mean . . ."

Jan shook his head. "*Nei. I* sorry! Not know for (he searched for the word) river?"

How could I have chosen a worse place to take you? his heart groaned.

She acknowledged this and he tentatively continued. "Mrs. *Brünlee,* vas Mr. *Brünlee* Christian?"

She nodded.

Jan was remembering staring into Elli's face after she passed. He could still recall, *vividly,* the peace that washed over him when he realized . . . her body no longer held her spirit.

How could he convey this great truth to her? He opened himself to her, speaking from deep within his soul. "Mrs. *Brünlee,* ven trust Jesus, not gone alvays, now only. I tell you trut', little woman, God *never* gone, alvays vit you. As Christian brot'er I promise you, God vill help."

The gratitude he saw in her eyes nearly undid him, and yet he required himself to face reality . . . *Ja, I have my answer, eh, Lord? She is not ready.* He called to the horses and neither spoke again until they reached her home.

Still silent, he helped her down and walked her to the front door. Of course *Fru Brünlee's* dog—*the one I insisted she have,* he sneered—jumped up in happy greeting, nearly overturning her, while alternately growling and baring his teeth to Jan.

Jan had had enough. "Down!" Thunder and frustration rolled in his voice. The dog dropped to the floor of the porch.

"Gud dog," Jan managed to say. He took a deep breath. "And denk you, Mrs. Brünlee. Ride vas ver nice." He opened the door, holding it for her and closing it after she passed through.

He did not return home right away. Instead he drove out onto the prairie, following a faint track. As he drove he worked to quell any hope he'd had. *Ja, I am just an old farmer. I must not wish for what cannot be mine. I must no longer think on these things. Ja, just so.*

These were the stern commands he issued to his heart and his head. These were the words he repeated to himself in the weeks following.

A tentative spring arrived. In typical prairie fashion, the weather could not be trusted: One day promised glorious sunshine and warming temperatures; the next day dashed those promises with freezing rain and late snows.

The second school term ended and so did Mr. Letoire's stay with the Thoresens. He departed the community for a visit back East until the next term began in late fall.

Harold Kalbørg had courted Sigrün through the winter, and Jan had watched as Sigrün's demeanor toward Harold grew from shy and blushing, to confident and hopeful, and finally to love-struck. Still, Jan needed to know how Harold would deal with Sigrün's inability to speak. Would he truly love her regardless?

As Jan observed them together, Harold behaved as though no impediment to their conversation existed: While he talked, the young man watched Sigrün's face and responded to a simple nod, smile, or shake of the head.

When the day arrived and Harold asked to speak privately with him, Jan had not been surprised. He had already discussed Harold's suit with Amalie.

"Søster," he said gently, "This man is in love with your *datter*, and she is in love with him, *nei*? But you have the final say. If he is not the best for her and you say no, then when he asks, I will say no."

But Amalie could not refuse Harold's suit. Harold was a fine man and it would be a good match. Even more, it was what Sigrün wanted. So when Harold had asked Jan for Sigrün's hand, Jan, grudgingly, had given his blessing.

Jan sighed. He could not believe Sigrün was marrying, that she would be leaving their home, never to live with them again. He knew Amalie was struggling with the same emotions. Amid all the happy preparations for the wedding, they occasionally caught sight of each other and recognized the grief the other was feeling.

My Kristen was two years older than Sigrün, Jan pondered with sad wonder. *Likely we would have already celebrated her marriage to some nice young man.*

Now that Sigrün and Harold were promised to each other, Jan would do all he could to give Sigrün the wedding she wanted—the wedding he knew Karl would have given her.

The morning of Harold and Sigrün's wedding, Jan, Søren, and the boys milked the cows, did their other chores, and then emptied the barn and swept its floor. They hauled in bales of sweet-smelling hay and arranged them in rows for seating down the length of the barn.

They lined one wall with tables for food. At one end of the barn Jan and Søren placed a table and laid a white cloth upon it; here Harold and Sigrün would say their vows.

The morning flew by; Jan changed into the new suit he had bought especially for Sigrün's wedding. All the while, like a soft melody playing in the background, Jan's heart chanted . . . *Fru Brünlee will be coming soon.*

When Amalie had told him that their neighbor would be cutting all of her beautiful roses for Sigrün's wedding Jan had been struck by the selflessness of the gesture. *But you must not think it means anything for you,* the voice of reason warned him.

Friends and neighbors arrived to decorate the barn. They hung evergreen boughs from the loft, twined flowers about the posts, and draped rugs and shawls over the hay bales. As the preparations progressed, Jan kept one eye on the road, watching for his neighbor's buggy.

Stop this! he chided himself. *You are done with such futile daydreams.*

When guests began to arrive, he found himself anxiously looking for her. *You must stop this nonsense,* he remonstrated, but he could not prevent his heart from looking toward her arrival.

There. He saw her climb down from the buggy, her face flushed with excitement and pleasure. She was wearing a dress he had not seen before, a gown the color of dusty pink roses trimmed in cream and burgundy. She lifted a box from the buggy and made her way toward the barn.

Jan's pulse quickened even as he pulled himself up. *Do not torment yourself,* his mind hissed. From a discreet distance he observed as she opened the box and arranged the roses she had brought with her, twisting and tying the strands of climber roses to the altar legs and placing a branch of blooms across the altar.

Then the ceremony began and Jan was walking Sigrün down the aisle toward the altar. As though drawn by a magnet, his eyes found Rose—*Fru Brünlee!* his conscience corrected—and she smiled at him.

A jolt ran down his spine as their eyes met.

After the ceremony, friends moved the bales of hay to the outside of the floor so the feasting and dancing could begin. Jan checked with Amalie.

"Everything is perfect, Jan," she said, grateful for his oversight. "I thank you for such a beautiful wedding for my *datter!*"

At last Jan felt he could relax. Immediately he looked for Rose—*Nei! Fru Brünlee!* his conscience jeered again. He caught sight of her leaving the barn; he followed her to her buggy, where she was removing a small guitar case.

"I carry for you," he stated, reaching for the case.

"Thank you," she answered, clearly surprised.

"I vant do," Jan replied.

They walked toward the barn, but when Rose tried to take back her guitar, Jan—shutting off the warning voices in his head—would not release it.

"Please, ve dance first?" At that moment he cared little what the voice of reason shouted.

"Oh, Mr. Thoresen, no, no, thank you. I don't, I mean I haven't danced in a long time. Thank you, no." But as she reached for her guitar, Jan held it away.

"No. Ve dance now, please." He smiled and his eyes sparkled with merriment.

"Mr. Thoresen! I really don't think . . ."

Jan teased her until she smiled and nodded. Taking her hand, he led her out to dance and, a moment later, they were whirling across the floor. When the song ended, Jan could not bear releasing her. He called loudly for another tune, and he twirled her away.

When he—reluctantly—released her, his neighbor collapsed, laughing, on a bale now pushed up against the barn wall. Jan loved watching her enjoy herself but Søren called him away at that moment. "Scuse, please," he said.

Jan took care of several decisions and stopped to thank friends for coming. He had been gone from Rose's side for more than half an hour when Søren, with Ivan at his shoulder, interrupted Jan's conversation with a guest.

"*Pappa.*" Something about the single clipped word caused Jan to excuse himself. He followed Søren and Ivan to the edge of the dance floor and saw *Rose Brownlee in Mark Grader's arms.*

Grader tightened his grip and pulled Rose closer, but she struggled against him. Jan could see her embarrassment—and fear.

I have never seen her afraid, Jan realized, and he did not like it.

With Søren and Ivan close behind him, he crossed the dance floor and tapped Grader on the shoulder. Grader stopped short and eyed Jan.

"Oh, thank you, God!" Jan heard *Fru Brünlee* breathe. Her anxious eyes begged for his help.

"What you want, Thoresen?" Grader snarled. "You're interruptin' our dance."

Jan's mouth curved in a slight smile. "'Scuse, Mr. Grader. Ve need talk now. Ver important. Out dere." He waved toward the barn door.

"I'm busy. Now get out of my way."

When Grader's hand came up to push Jan aside, Jan was ready. He grabbed and twisted Grader's arm behind his back. The man flinched, but Jan kept his hold.

"Out dere, please," he repeated softly.

He saw Grader's hold on Rose relax; Søren and Ivan each grabbed an arm and hustled Grader out. In the same moment, Jan stepped in and began dancing with his neighbor as though nothing out of the ordinary had happened.

Jan could feel *Fru Brünlee* trembling in his arms.

"Better, *ja?*" Jan asked, but tears threatened to spill from her eyes. Jan shook his head once and clucked his tongue, then spun her gently across the floor.

What would it be like? he asked himself. *What would it be like if this woman I am holding belonged to me?*

He smiled softly and glanced down. *Fru Brünlee's* color was settling. He could sense she was recovering from the unhappy incident. When the dancing ended and the singing commenced, he deposited her with Fiona McKennie and, bowing, left them.

Perhaps he was still in the thrall of saving Rose from Mark Grader; perhaps this happy day and its attending celebration overrode his doubts and fears, but later, when the singing was nearly over, Jan stood to sing the last song.

The song he sang was an old, traditional ballad, a love song. He sang it for Harold and Sigrün on this holy day, and he sang it for the hope reborn in his heart. He searched for and found Rose's eyes—and he sang it to her, past caring if his yearning for her showed through.

Do you hear me, little woman? Do you hear what my heart is singing to you?

He saw her look around, puzzled. Then she sat down, out of his view.

Jan finished the song. As he did, he noticed Søren, a strange expression on his face, staring at him, but Jan shrugged. He was no longer disheartened. He had crossed a line—*win or lose*, he would not draw back.

Harold and Sigrün were preparing to leave, and the guests were loading their gifts into Harold's wagon. Sigrün kissed her mother, each brother, Uli, Søren, Jan and, once again, her tearful *mamma*. Then Sigrün and Harold drove off to begin their lives together.

Jan, Søren, and the boys changed into their work clothes and began cleaning up. The milking and afternoon chores called to them.

Jan, Søren, and Ivan were moving bales of hay out of the barn when Jan saw Rose saying goodbye to Amalie. He watched her; as she prepared to leave, Jan left his work to hand her up to the seat. Jan could feel Søren and Ivan's eyes on him. Apparently, Rose could, too, for she coughed in a nervous manner.

"It was a lovely wedding, Mr. Thoresen," she remarked, and he could see she was anxious to get away. "Simply 'grand'!"

"*Ja*," he nodded.

Ja, I have set my course, little woman, he whispered to himself. *Soon. Soon I will make my heart known to you.*

Holding her gaze with his, he offered a cryptic remark. "Next vun better, too, *ja*? *God-dag*, Mrs. *Brünlee*."

❧ ❀ ❧

CHAPTER 42

Fickle spring! In the days following Harold and Sigrün's wedding, temperatures plummeted and the skies poured cold, stinging rain.

The Thoresen males, clad in rain gear, herded their stock into the barn. It was early in the day, but downpours had turned the pastures into a bog and more rain was coming. The cows and steers came willingly as they were called.

One of their milkers, however, refused to move. She stood in the pre-storm mist, bawling for her calf.

"Callie's calf has gone missing," Arnie informed Søren. "You want Kjell and me to go look for him?"

Normally Søren would have sent them, but not today. Their northern pastures ran along the creek of his *Onkel* Karl's land, and the creek was far over its banks. No, neither his father nor his *tante* would want the younger boys near the sodden, unpredictable banks of the creek.

"I will go, Arnie. Tell your *Onkel* Jan where I am, eh?"

Søren slogged through the mud toward Callie. The cow's eyes were wide and round, her demeanor agitated.

"*Ja*, we'll find your calf soon enough," Søren muttered. The mist was beginning to freeze, stinging his face as colder air pushed in ahead of the storm. He needed to hurry; he was losing the light.

Søren headed north and crossed the fence line into the pasture, assuming the calf had become mired where the pasture sloped toward the creek. Keeping a healthy distance from the water's edge, he walked farther from the house while scanning along the bank.

In the near-dark he saw a flash of something white. Where a young cottonwood stand usually marked the creek bank, a torrent now rushed.

Søren drew closer, mindful of his footing, until he came abreast of the white object. Shaking his head, he realized he was seeing the white flash on the calf's face. The poor creature floated, tangled in the roots of the tree. Drowned.

Søren burst through the back door of the farmhouse on a gust of wind that rattled the windows. His slicker streamed water onto the kitchen floor. Amalie, clucking and fussing, grabbed towels to mop it up.

He went to his room and changed into dry clothes and then found Jan in the living room, warming himself in front of the stove. "We are losing the corn along the creek," was Søren's quiet report.

Jan nodded. "*Ja*. Too much rain. Never have I seen so much at one time."

"I found Callie's calf drowned in the cottonwoods in the north pasture. The water is flowing pretty hard through the stand of cottonwoods."

Jan shook his head at the news.

"The bridge is almost underwater, too," Søren added. "We may have lost part of it." He shivered and held his hands in front of the stove. "Such an afternoon! It is so dark, I can hardly see a thing."

Jan nodded again and moved to the living room window. He cupped his hands around his eyes and placed his forehead on the window, but could not see past the sheeting rain.

"We made a good roof for Mrs. Brownlee," Søren commented. He figured his father was looking for a light in their neighbor's window. Impossible. Nothing would shine through this downpour.

Uli bounced into the living room. "Søren, *Onkel*! *Mamma* says it is time to eat."

"Thank you, little one," Jan said smiling. He lifted her up into a bear hug and then set her down again. Uli laughed and held his hand all the way to the table.

Jan woke in the night. He had gone to bed in Søren's room to spare himself the soaking walk to the barn; Søren was sleeping upstairs with Little Karl.

He listened. Something had disturbed his dreams, something concerning. Rain still battered the house; the wind still howled. The room was cold and he shivered.

And then he heard it again. Not the howl of the wind —a different sort of howl. He sat up in bed. There it was again.

Jan was scrambling into his clothes when he heard Søren hustling down the stairs. "What is it?" he asked his *sønn*.

"Sounds like an animal." Søren lifted a shotgun from the rack above the kitchen doorway.

After donning slickers, Jan and Søren opened the kitchen door and stepped into the storm. They heard the howl again, from the direction of the barn. Søren put his mouth close to Jan's ear. "Does that sound like a dog?"

Jan didn't answer. It *had* sounded like a dog.

It had sounded like Baron.

He ran, heedless of the rain-slick mud.

Near the chicken coops they saw a huddled form. Søren stood a ways off and leveled the gun at it. Then the form uttered a piteous yelp.

"*Nei!* Do not shoot!" Jan knelt next to him. "Baron! What is this?" The dog's tail thumped once but he did not move except to release another mournful howl that ended in a whine.

"Søren, it is Baron. He is hurt, I think. Get a blanket from the barn, *ja*?"

Søren returned; they wrapped the dog in the blanket and carried him into the house. A stream of rain and mud followed them.

"Aunt Amalie will have a fit," Søren muttered under his breath. And then he saw blood flowing in the trail of mud. "*Pappa*, look."

Jan's face creased into worried lines. "Get old blankets or towels. I am taking him to the living room by the stove."

Søren ran into Amalie coming down the stairs. "What is it? I heard horrible sounds!"

"It is Baron. He is hurt and bleeding. *Pappa* has taken him into the living room. I am getting more old towels and rags." He touched Amalie's arm. "*Tante*, I am worried about Mrs. Brownlee."

Amalie reached the bottom of the stairs and viewed the trail of mud and blood from the back door into the living room. Instead of wiping it up, she rushed to help Jan.

Jan was lighting lamps and bringing them close to where he had laid Baron. A look crossed between Jan and Amalie. She knelt down and opened the blanket while Jan held a lamp overhead.

As she tried to examine Baron, he whined and licked her hand. "Ach. You don't want to bite me, do you? You just wish me to be careful and not hurt you more, eh?"

Her face paled. "Jan? Look here, *ja*? Is this not a gunshot?"

Jan squatted down and looked where Amalie was holding Baron's fur apart. Blood seeped at a steady stream from a hole in his chest . . .

"*Søren!*" Jan's roar woke the house.

"*Pappa?*"

"Get Karl. Saddle the bays. We are crossing the creek."

Ten minutes later they were mounted. Søren, carrying the shotgun, and Jan, with Karl riding double behind him, were searching for the best place to ford the raging creek.

Jan elected to cross where the water had flooded farthest into their fields. He held the large Morgan steady and urged him into the water. Karl clung to his back like a burr as the horse stepped into the rushing stream.

The icy water stung like fire and rose until it was chest-high on the bay. The big horse snorted and side-stepped but forged ahead. Jan knew the bottom of the creek here was smooth and that his horse would keep his footing.

A little more than halfway across, the horse picked up his pace and plunged up the opposite slope in a burst of speed. Wet and relieved, Jan turned to signal Søren, but his *sønn* had followed as soon as Jan's horse was halfway across.

Søren's horse plodded up the slope to where Jan and Little Karl waited. Jan and Søren conferred briefly.

"In this weather you or I should be able to sneak up to the house and see what is happening," Jan spoke into Søren's ear.

Leaving the horses near the creek with Little Karl, the two men crept toward Rose's house. A single light glowed behind the curtains in the kitchen. Jan signaled to Søren and they made their way to the south side of the house and the steps that led up and onto the covered porch.

Because he weighed less than Jan, Søren stole up the steps. He stopped under the window where he spied a small gap in the curtains. For several minutes he peered into the house. Then he made his way back.

He did not speak and Jan's heart began to thunder in his chest.

"Well? What did you see?" he demanded.

Søren swallowed. "I saw a man sitting in a chair with his face and arms on the table. He looked to be sleeping."

Jan grew still. "What else?"

Søren swallowed again. "Another man, on the floor. He . . . he looks dead, *Pappa*." Søren looked at Jan. "A lot of blood there is. On the man and on the floor."

"And *Fru Brünlee*?" Jan steeled himself.

"I did not see her, *Pappa*. She is not in the house."

Jan turned away from Søren. *She is not there? How could that be? Where else would she be?*

He and Søren stole away from the house, back to where Karl held the horses. Jan boosted Karl onto the broad back of his bay and then looked up at his fifteen-year-old nephew. It was perhaps an odd time to notice, but Jan, looking up at "Little" Karl, realized how much like his father the boy was becoming.

"I'm sending you to fetch help," he told his nephew. "Bring back Brian McKennie, *ja*?"

"*Ja*, I will bring him, *Onkel*," Karl assured him and walked the horse toward the road, keeping as far from the house as possible until he was out of earshot.

Jan turned to Søren. "Let us go in. We will surprise the sleeping man, *ja*? I will take him. You make sure the other man is . . . really dead. If he is not, you take him, eh?"

Søren nodded. They crept to the front door—*The stout door I made strong and secure with my own hands!* Jan realized. Taking his time, he pressed down on the latch. It was locked. He shook his head at Søren.

Like silent shadows, they made their way around to the back door. Jan, knowing that the pantry and a second door stood between them and the men inside, inserted the flat blade of his knife between the door and the lock. The lock clicked open.

Jan slowly pushed open the door, only to find that the inside door stood slightly ajar. He cautioned Søren, and then they slipped inside.

The man at the table was indeed sleeping. His soft snores were regular, his mouth slack. Both of them recognized him: *Mark Grader*. Søren held the shotgun on him while Jan crept toward the man lying on the floor in a pool of blood.

It was Orville Grader, and Søren had been right. The man was dead, his throat torn.

Baron! Jan concluded. But there was no sign of Rose.

Jan nodded for Søren to wake Mark Grader.

"Where is Mrs. Brownlee!" Søren demanded again, his voice a frustrated snarl. "You say she ran out the back door, but we have looked everywhere for her! Where is she? What did you do to her?"

Jan and Søren had tied Grader to a kitchen chair. For the past hour they had been alternately questioning Grader and searching the yard.

"Her dog killed m' brother! It were her dog what done Orville in!" Grader blubbered. "But I ain't done nuthin to Miz Brownlee, I swear! Orville . . . He, he, he's the one who wanted t', you know—"

Mark Grader must have seen the disbelief and rage cross Jan and Søren's faces.

"I dunno where she went, I tell ya!" he protested in a whine. "I dunno!"

Then Jan leaned over Grader and Grader looked into Jan's eyes— eyes that had grown cold and merciless. Grader tried to draw back, licking his lips nervously.

"Mebbe, mebbe she tried to cross the creek, git up t' yer house," he suggested in a weak voice.

Jan blanched. In his mind he saw Rose fleeing these men, daring the rushing torrent she so feared, *but running to him for help!* He saw the creek soaking and swamping her skirts and saw her struggling as the weight of them pulled her down and swept her away. His heart twisted until he could not breathe.

Søren put his hand on his father's shoulder. "I think Karl is back."

Jan and Søren opened the front door. Karl and Brian climbed the steps and stood on the porch next to them, draining the rain from their hats and ponchos.

"Have ye found Rose?" Brian asked immediately.

"*Nei,*" Søren replied, slipping into Riksmaal. "Grader says she escaped out the back door last evening. We've looked everywhere. He just now said maybe Rose tried to cross—" Søren choked and couldn't finish his sentence.

A murderous rage, a hatred he had never known, smoldered in Jan's breast and ignited. For the first time in his life, he desired to kill a man. He itched to place his hands about Grader's neck and choke the life out of him. He wanted to pound his face to a bloody mass.

He threw open the door and strode back into Rose's house.

CHAPTER 43

As Jan curled his fists and started toward him, Grader shrank in terror.

"Jan!" Brian pulled at his arm. "*Jan!*"

He forcibly yanked Jan around. "Be sendin' your boys doon th' creek on horseback, Jan. Now."

Jan turned to Søren. His chest was heaving but he could not catch his breath. He could not wipe the image from his mind of the rushing torrent and Rose's skirts, heavy with water, pulling her under.

"*Pappa*," Søren said softly. "Little Karl and I should take the bays downstream, *ja?*"

Søren's eyes were haunted. He, too, had a vivid picture in his mind, but it was the image of the drowned calf tangled in the tree roots near the creek bank. He could not help it—when he looked into his heart, it was not the calf, but Rose's white face he saw floating in the roots of the cottonwoods.

Jan nodded. He could not think; he could not act. *He could only hate.*

He looked again at Grader who paled under Jan's icy disdain. The man, struggling wildly in his bonds, began to shriek and beg for his life.

Grader's shrieks startled Jan, and he saw himself mirrored in Grader's fear-filled eyes. What he saw stunned him—Jan saw his own hatred.

Dear Father in heaven, Jan gasped. *I am undone! I thought you had tamed my heart, but in its depths I am yet a murderer!*

Jan dropped his face to his hands. He stumbled out into the yard. Peering at the sky through the downpour, he cried aloud, "Father! I am sorry! I know you hear me . . . please forgive me."

A crack of thunder answered him. Jan dropped to his knees, sobbing.

Søren and Little Karl had been gone half an hour and early morning was changing the skies from black to a sodden gray when Fiona and Meg arrived. Jan shook his head at their questions and did not trust himself to speak.

Fiona was making coffee when Brian uttered an urgent exclamation, "Jan! 'Tis rememberin' something I am! Th' Andersons' old soddy! We showed it t' Rose! Coom! Help me t' be openin' it!"

Jan stared at Brian, not comprehending. Brian grabbed his arm and pulled him along.

The Andersons' dugout. Of course. Of course I remember it! Jan wrenched the shovel from Brian's hands and raced ahead of him. He reached the side of the knoll first but could not find the door—the rain had turned the hillside into a slurry of mud and grass. He drove the shovel into the hillside here! There! Again and again until—at last—it struck wood.

Jan scrabbled with his fingers for the edge of the door. He found it, jammed the shovel's tip into it, and leaned his considerable weight on the handle. The door began to give but Jan would not wait. He simply grasped it and, straining with all his might, ripped it from its hinges and flung it aside.

He paused. The soddy was as dark as the storm-swept night had been. Within, it was as still as a tomb.

She is not here! his heart screamed.

"I'll be fetchin' a torch!" Brian yelled above the now drizzling rain.

Jan dropped to his knees as his strength left him. He crept forward, feeling about him with his hands. Dry, pounded earth was all his hands found.

He crawled forward, sweeping his arms across the floor in an arc. Still his hands found only hard, dry dirt.

And then. And then his left hand encountered cloth. Damp, clammy cloth. He followed the cloth until he felt a hip and then an arm. He traced his way up the arm until he touched an icy cheek. He picked up her hand—as cold as death! He could not feel her heart beating in her fingers.

"Brian! Brian McKennie! Here—she is here!"

He scooped Rose into his arms. She was as light as a feather.

O Lord! Please don't let her spirit fly away to you!

"Rose!" Jan choked on his words and his love poured out. He could not stop—he babbled words of endearment in his native tongue, not knowing if she could hear them, knowing she could not understand them.

"Rose! Little Rose!" he called her urgently.

In his arms, her body shuddered. "Help me," she moaned.

Alive! O thank you, God, she is alive!

She moaned again and her head twisted against his chest. "Please! Don't let me fall in the river . . ."

"*Nei*, Rose, I not let you fall," he murmured and pressed her closer to his chest so his warmth would comfort her.

Forever, he cried to God. *This is what I want, Lord! To forever hold her and comfort her!*

Brian appeared with a torch. In the light Jan looked down on Rose's face to assure himself that she was truly alive. Her face was so cold that her cheekbones shone like polished white marble in the flickering light. Jan carried her across the yard and into the house, surrendering her to Fiona and Meg.

They were ready with towels, dry clothes, and hot bricks to tuck into the bed. Fiona, her face sober with worry, gently shooed him away.

Jan stepped into the other part of the house and saw Grader, his arms and legs still tied to a chair. The man watched Jan with anxious eyes.

Jan's chin dropped to his chest and he prayed. *O Lord, I surrender this unruly heart to you. Totally. I hold nothing back.*

He looked at Grader again. The man was terrified for his life.

Jan began to string halting words together in English. "I sorry," was his first quiet, awkward sentence.

He wanted to say, *I was wrong! It is not my place to condemn!* but "Please to forgiving me," was as close as he could manage.

Grader's mouth opened a little. He did not answer.

Jan licked his lips, searching and desperate for right words. "I forgiving it to you," he said, meeting Grader's gaze.

Jan swallowed hard. "You." He pointed at Grader, who flinched. "You asking da Lord Jesus. He forgiving it to you, too."

Grader stared at Jan, perplexed. Jan wasn't surprised—he knew how pathetic his attempt to tell him that Jesus would forgive him had been! But perhaps Grader would, somehow, understand.

And then . . . Grader's eyes misted over. He dropped his gaze to the floor and a sob caught in his throat.

Jan nodded and started toward the door. *Tusen takk, Lord.*

He closed the door behind him.

CHAPTER 44

Jan wandered through the barn and out into the acres of young, green cornstalks. *O Lord, how in the world did I get here? How did I manage to fall in love with this woman—and I cannot even have a conversation with her, let alone tell her all that is in my heart! I am a pathetic fool, Lord.*

It had been days since he had spoken to his neighbor. He stopped walking and stared across the corn and across the creek. *But, O Father, how I need her! She is like a cool, soaking rain on my dry, parched heart. She is like your grace when I am weak.*

A desire deeper than any he'd ever known gripped him. *O God, I need your wisdom. I need your help.*

He saw his son stride across the barnyard, his long legs eating up the distance, a youthful "bounce" in his walk. *Ah, to be young again with so much energy!* Jan chuckled.

No sooner had the thought passed through his mind than another obstacle raised its head. Jan grabbed his head with both hands. *Ach! And she is so much younger than me! What could she possibly see in me? I'm almost old and used up.*

He listed all the reasons Rose could not return his love: There were such vast differences in their backgrounds and language! She was wealthy and cultured; he was, well, *only a farmer!* She was young and lovely; *he was at least twenty years her senior!*

Jan wondered, not for the first time, how he could discover Rose's age. Was there ever any good way to ask a woman how old she was? Jan ran his hand through his hair in frustration—again.

I'm not getting any work done today, Lord, he groused. *How can I work when I feel that my future is in that little house over there and I cannot reach out and talk to her?*

Jan saw Søren take the steps to the kitchen two at a time. He smiled. *Oh, if I had only applied myself to learn English like Søren had years ago . . . If only I could speak it as naturally as he can! If only—*

No.

An implausible idea crept into his head. *A daring idea.* Jan turned it over and considered it from all sides.

But Søren would never . . . would he?

Jan heard the kitchen door slam all the way across the cornfield. Søren bounded down the steps toward the barn.

Jan's eyes narrowed. He was halfway to the barn before he realized he'd made up his mind. He didn't care what Søren felt! He would harden his heart against Søren's protests and his *sønn* would obey him in this.

"Søren!" Jan shouted the name. "*Søren!*"

"Yes, *Pappa*. What is it?" Søren was mucking out the milking stations. Karl, Arnie, and Kjell, each busy with their own chores, stuck their heads out curiously.

"Come. You and I will take a bath. Clean clothes."

Søren gaped as though his *far* had grown a second head. "*Pappa?* It is only Tuesday. We bathed already this week, *ja?*" Karl, Arnie, and Kjell, hearing the word *bath*, scattered.

"We will bathe again. Now. In one hour we will be clean and ready." Jan turned away without further explanation.

"But *Pappa*? Where are we going?" Søren was talking to Jan's back—his father was already halfway to the house.

Amalie! Jan nearly panicked. *Amalie will want to know what I am doing!*

Then Jan remembered. *Ah, yes! Amalie and Uli are at a quilting. Good!* His sister-in-law would not be asking any questions.

Jan put two large pans on the stove, filled them with water, and built up the fire. He was hauling out the heavy hip bath when Søren, still baffled, dragged himself through the back door.

"Go. Fetch clean clothes," Jan said, ignoring Søren's questions. While Søren was in his room, Jan ran to his room in the barn to lay out his own clothes but halted, caught momentarily in a conundrum.

Should he wear his suit? Wouldn't that be most appropriate? Jan's hands trembled as he reached for it. Sweat was already beading on his forehead. He was suddenly anxious!

This is madness! he thought, almost talking himself out of the whole thing. Then he thought of Rose and he could not bear another night of wondering, of aching.

He looked again at the suit. No. He was already nervous enough. Just ordinary clothes, but clean and fresh smelling.

Forty-five minutes later, with both of them clean and dressed, Jan sat Søren down at the kitchen table and told him. There would be no turning back now.

"*Sønn*, in a few minutes we are going to *Fru Brünlee's*. I will ask her . . . to marry me."

Jan couldn't believe the words had come from his mouth, but Søren jumped out of his chair. "I knew it! I *knew* it! I knew there was something going on!" He grinned at his father and punched him in the arm. "She's great, *Pappa*. I am so happy for you!"

Jan stared steadily at Søren. He would not allow his nervousness to show. "Just so. I am glad you approve."

"So what do you need me for? You don't want me there, messing up your big moment!" Søren, still grinning, babbled on. "You know, Ivan and I thought something was up at Sigrün and Harold's wedding, especially when you were singing and—" He frowned. "Say, why did *I* need to take a bath and clean up, anyway?"

"Sit down, *Sønn*," Jan commanded. When Søren sank onto his chair, Jan leaned over the table and looked him in the eye.

"I do not speak the English well, do I?"

Søren shook his head. "No, but I'm sure you and Mrs. Brownlee will—"

"—And I have not the way of flowery speech, have I?" Jan pressed, waving him off.

"Yes, but—"

"—And you speak the English just like an American, eh? Even just as well as *Fru Brünlee, ja?*" Jan's eyes bored into Søren's.

"Well, of course, but I—" Søren stopped. He stared back at his father, the worst possible thought popping into his head. His eyes widened.

"No, *nei, nei, nei, Pappa!* You could not want me to, you don't mean—"

"—Søren, you will help me in this, *ja?* I need you to do this important thing for me."

Søren was shaking his head. "*But Pappa!*" He was almost whining.

Jan ignored him. "Søren, you will tell her, *Fru Brünlee, I am speaking for my father*. You will say, *Please do not think of me; only listen to my words as the words my father says to you*. You will say exactly what I say to her and tell me exactly what she tells me back. You will do this for me."

Søren, his mouth an incredulous "o," wagged his head back and forth in protest. Jan skewered him with relentless eyes. "You will do this for me," he repeated.

When Jan could be put off no more, he and Søren set out across the young cornfield toward the creek. Søren dragged his feet and muttered dark things under his breath.

Jan ignored him. He was giddy—no; flushed with fear! Then almost sick with worry—then elated. His hands felt clammy, his throat tight, closed off.

Rose was watering her flowers and saw them coming; Jan's breath caught as she raised her hand in happy greeting.

Rose! You are so beautiful! he marveled.

She welcomed them, and Søren managed a choked "hello," but Jan could not squeeze a sound out. *O Lord, I am a pathetic man!* he moaned within himself.

Neither Jan nor Søren offered a reason for their visit, and Søren looked everywhere but at their neighbor. Eventually she invited them inside and put on a pot of coffee.

Jan sat down and folded his arms—to keep her from seeing his hands shake! He schooled his face. Søren, growing more distressed as the coffee perked, said as little as possible.

Rose cleared her throat. "Amalie is fine?"

"Yes, ma'am," Søren managed.

"Has anyone seen Harold and Sigrün recently?"

Søren nodded, choking on something unintelligible. Rose gave him a sharp look.

She asked a few more questions; Jan caught just two or three words every sentence. When she turned her back for a second, Søren sent a pleading glance toward Jan. Jan frowned back and jerked his chin in Rose's direction. She was saying something . . .

". . . sometimes watch the calves playing in the morning. They are so frisky . . ." Her hands trembled as she placed cups and saucers on the table.

Søren stared at his feet and Jan stared at Rose. *Ach! I have made her nervous! Is she frightened?* He frowned. *Lord, that is not my intention! O Father! I need your help!*

Jan could not move. He was frozen. Then Rose glanced from Søren to Jan and Jan watched her, hoping for a sign. She set out the cream and sugar, poured the coffee, and pulled her chair up to the table.

With as much calm as he could muster, Jan sugared his coffee. Sugar, no cream. When he finished stirring it he spoke to his son. "Please begin, *Sønn.*"

Søren sat up straight and ran his hand through his hair in distraction. Rose smiled fondly at Søren.

Ja, she likes my family well enough, doesn't she, Lord? Jan thought.

But Søren looked like his stomach hurt, and Jan saw Rose shoot him a quizzical look.

"Ah, Mrs. Brownlee, I, ah . . ." He turned pleading eyes on Jan who stared back.

"As we discussed, Søren," Jan insisted. He took a sip of his coffee.

"Mrs. Brownlee," Søren began again, "I am here as my father's, ah, spokesperson. He wants to talk to you and is making me, I mean *using* me to translate." He sighed again. "I'm sorry—this isn't very comfortable for me, but, well anyway . . . you understand."

But Jan saw that Rose did *not* understand!

"*Sønn*, you are confusing *Fru Brünlee*!" Jan hissed. "Sit up straight as we discussed, *ja*?"

Søren straightened and repeated formally, "From now on, please disregard me. I'll be saying what my father says, and you may answer him through me."

Fru Brünlee nodded, but she was obviously perplexed.

"Mrs. Brownlee, (this is my father speaking), the first time I saw you in church, I realized you were different from other women I knew. You had a hunger for God on your face. You were searching for him with all your heart."

Rose startled and she shifted her gaze to Jan. Their eyes locked and Jan, for the first time, spoke his heart directly to her as Søren translated his words.

"You were also grieving. I knew that because I, too, have grieved for loved ones. I saw it in you and I prayed for you. When we came to work on your house I saw you had character, determination, and a dream. You worked hard for your aspirations. You wanted to be the whole woman God created you to be, and I admired you for that. I tried to help you any way I could. I wanted to be your friend."

Jan paused. Søren paused. His neighbor, her face inscrutable, waited.

"Are we friends?" Jan asked, daring to hope for more.

"Why, yes. Yes, of course," she stammered.

"Gud," Jan replied.

Søren continued for him. "Mrs. Brownlee, I have been alone for a long time now. The Bible says it is not good for a man to be alone—" Jan frowned as Søren choked on the translation of his father's words. "I think it is not good for a woman either."

Are you hearing my heart, dear woman? Can you see my love for you? Jan could scarcely breathe as his eyes sought hers again.

"Once before I tried to speak of what is in my heart, the day at the river. But I blundered and you were still hurting and couldn't hear. Then when we couldn't find you the night Baron came to us for help, I knew, I knew then that we must come to an understanding.

"I am your friend, but now—" Again Søren stumbled as he translated the intimate words. "But now I want to have you as my most precious friend. I must know if you could find that possible."

Unflinching, Jan's gaze held hers. And he waited, hoping against hope. Several minutes passed during which Jan died a thousand deaths.

And then *Fru Brünlee* frowned and looked away.

Jan swallowed. *She does not feel the same as I do! O Lord, please help me if I must live without her!*

Still turned away, Rose sighed, and Jan hardened himself against the rejection he knew was coming. With his last vestige of self-control, he held himself still, impassive.

She frowned again and whispered, "Søren. Would you please leave us? And thank you."

Søren fled the house without a backwards glance. Rose got up and went to the stove, lifted down another cup, and filled it with fresh coffee. And still she did not speak, did not look at him!

Jan waited. She seated herself and stirred cream into it, but she would not look at him. As though ignoring him, she quietly sipped it.

Minutes passed; her coffee was gone. Still she sat, waiting.

Could she be waiting for him? Waiting for him to speak . . . directly to her?

His throat was closed and his tongue stuck to the roof of his mouth. He could not even swallow!

"Rose," he breathed. *Rose! Oh, how I love the sound of your name on my lips!*

She glanced up, looking for . . . something? Then her eyes dropped again to her hands, *her sweet hands!* folded around her cup.

The silence lengthened.

Dear Lord, what am I to do? What am I to say?

Somehow he managed to speak her name once more. "Rose."

Her eyes were focused on the table, but a single tear dropped onto the tablecloth. Another hung on her cheek.

Have I hurt you, my love? Jan's heart twisted at the thought. He lifted his work-rough hand slowly toward her face and touched the tiny droplet.

And he finally found the words. "I luf you, Rose."

She lifted her head and looked for . . . confirmation? Assurance?

Knowing he was risking everything, Jan relaxed his vigilance and allowed his eyes to echo his heart.

Rose and Jan stared, heart to heart. What he saw made him tremble. And hope!

He pushed back his chair and stood to his feet, hand outstretched. Still she hesitated.

Finally, he whispered, "Rose. Vill you come . . . to me?" He held his hands steady, outstretched to her.

She touched his offered hand, and he drew her up, into his embrace. Once she was in his arms, the dam in his soul burst and he was stroking her cheek and her hair, saying everything he felt but could not put into English. Jan shuddered and closed his eyes against the emotions that rushed into his heart.

She looked up; he bent down to her.

What will she answer, Lord?

"I will," she whispered back.

Jan's heart soared and he could breathe again. He kissed her, tentatively, and kissed her again. *O Lord, I thank you!* Jan prayed and rejoiced.

Jan wrapped her small hand in his and led her outside where they sat together on her front steps.

"Rose."

"Yes, Jan?"

He kissed her hand and held it close. "My Rose."

"Yes, Jan."

CHAPTER 45

Sunday before service, Jan steered Pastor Medford away from the others. "Pastor, haf gud news."

Jacob Medford smiled. "Tell me!"

In spite of his clumsy words, Jan was able to convey his happy announcement. He watched, impassive but secretly delighted, as Jacob's expression slid from blank surprise . . . to dumbfounded . . . to astonished joy.

The next thing Jan knew, his friend and pastor was pounding him on the back and shaking his hand. Jan grinned like a schoolboy.

Still grinning, he looked for Rose. She was watching and hid a giggle behind her hand.

My Rose! was all Jan could think as he saw his love reflected in her eyes.

As the service began, Rose took a seat next to Amalie as she often did. Today, however, instead of the children between them, Jan took the seat on her other side. Harold and Sigrün were seated in the pew in front of them; Søren sat on Harold's other side.

My rightful place! Jan's heart thrilled. *From now on we will share all things!* And he could see the same acknowledgment on her sweet face. It was all he could do not to take her hand and hold it possessively in his!

Then she was struggling not to laugh and, leaning toward the children on his other side, she put a warning finger to her lips. Jan glanced at the four smirking faces down the row from him. Eyes bright with excitement, Little Karl, Arnie, Kjell, and Uli were trying their best to restrain themselves.

Be a father to the fatherless.

Yes, Lord, Jan nodded. *These are mine. I am their father.*

At the end of the service, Jacob shook his head, still shocked and bemused. "Folks, I've been asked to make an announcement. There's going to be another wedding soon."

Jan could not stand the suspense. His hand reached for Rose's and she gave it willingly even as speculative eyes glanced everywhere but at them.

"Hrmm! Since I've only just been informed myself, I know you'll be as surprised and certainly as delighted as I am. Folks, I am happy to announce the upcoming marriage of Mrs. Rose Brownlee and Mr. Jan Thoresen!"

Congratulations burst all around them, and Sigrün, her face aglow, turned and embraced Rose—until Rose pulled away, amazed.

"What did you say?" Rose grasped Sigrün's shoulders. "Sigrün! You talked!"

A silence fell. Sigrün, unaccustomed to being the center of attention, shifted from one foot to the other. All eyes were on her.

"I'm so happy, Rose," she whispered again. "For you, for *Onkel*."

A roar of approval rang through the building, but Jan could not speak. He was reliving those dark days, seeing Sigrün as a little girl, ill and reeling from the loss of her *pappa* and beloved cousin. He was remembering her clinging to him in grief and fear, traumatized and saying nothing. Speaking no words for all these long years!

Ah, Lord! he prayed, humbled and grateful, *Surely nothing is too difficult for you! You have healed her brokenness . . . and your mercy has tamed my wild heart.*

No, Lord. Nothing is too difficult for you.

$\mathcal{P}$OSTSCRIPT

And it shall come to pass in the last days, saith God,
I will pour out of my Spirit upon all flesh:
and your sons and your daughters shall prophesy,
and your young men shall see visions,
and your old men shall dream dreams:
And on my servants and on my handmaidens
I will pour out in those days of my Spirit;
and they shall prophesy

Jan sat up, fully awake, his mind clear. The night was calm and silent, lit by moonlight, but his heart drummed within his chest. He could still sense the holy hush attending his dream. He half expected to see a sacred messenger within the moonbeams slanting through the window.

He looked to the other side of the bed and saw . . . *his bride*. His Rose! Her soft, even breathing told him that all was well.

Jan climbed from the bed and padded to the window. *O Lord! Such a dream I have never had!* He closed his eyes and could see it all again—hear it all again . . .

A young girl raced through the prairie grass. The echoes of her laughter floated on the air. She stopped and looked Jan full in the face.

"Hello, Pappa!"

Kristen? No, not Kristen . . .

Jan reached out and touched the long braid, as white as spun silver, trailing over the girl's shoulder. He stared into her bright eyes, deep and clear, blue as a summer sky.

His eyes!

She took him by the hand and they walked. As they walked, the girl grew and matured. When they stopped, they stood on the road running through Thoresen land, the track that led east and then northward, deeper into the prairie. The girl was now a young woman, tall and stately, her wheat-blonde hair fell gracefully to her waist. She smiled at him, her lips gently firm but sweet.

Rose's mouth! O dear Lord!

"Pappa," the young woman said. "Look." She gestured. "See your heritage, dear Pappa."

Down the road from the east trod a long line of people. The young woman released Jan's hand and went to greet them.

She embraced and stood among several who were, clearly, her children—his grandchildren! Behind them the line extended beyond view, men and women, boys and girls, light-haired and dark. They gazed at Jan and nodded . . . with love and honor.

Jan reached his hand toward the young woman, to call her back, not wishing her to leave him. She smiled again and her face glowed with great happiness.

"Bless us, Pappa! We are your heritage, Pappa, your heritage in the Lord. We will carry your faith—the Good News of Jesus, our Lord—forward into many generations!" And she and those with her bowed their heads.

As if it were the most natural thing in the world to do, Jan lifted his hand as she requested and, in a clear voice, pronounced a father's blessing. "I bless you my daughter! And your children . . . the children the Lord will give you. Be fruitful. And go with Him."

The many with bowed heads then lifted them and looked up into the heavens. Faces shone with elation. Some stretched up their arms.

They faded from view.

Only the woman remained. She did not return to him but, solemnly, she spoke a soft parting word, a haunting refrain.

"What I lose, Pappa, is not lost to God. In him the lost are found."

She was gone. Jan whispered her final words. "The lost are found. The lost . . . are found."

He heard Rose stirring. "Jan?"

"*Ja*, my Rose. I come." He crawled under the covers and sank into the welcoming warmth of her arms. As Rose nestled into the crook of his neck, she sought his lips and they kissed.

Only yesterday had they married! And only mere hours ago they had, for the first time, given themselves to each other.

Jan opened his eyes in the dark of the room and could still see the little girl with trailing white braids.

Your heritage, Pappa.

She had seemed—and still seemed!—so real.

Could it be? At their time of life? He and Rose had not spoken of children, but . . .

With a great sigh of peace, Jan tucked the dream into a corner of his heart—a precious place where he would remember it and keep it safe.

Ja, Lord, as you will. I and mine are yours.

ം ✸ ം

The End

Buy Book 3, *Joy on This Mountain*,
in print or eBook format from most online retailers.

ABOUT THE AUTHOR

Vikki Kestell's passion for people and their stories is evident in her readers' affection for her characters and unusual plotlines. Two often-repeated sentiments are, "I feel like I know these people" and "I'm right there, in the book, experiencing what the characters experience."

Vikki holds a Ph.D. in Organizational Learning and Instructional Technologies. She left a career of twenty-plus years in government, academia, and corporate life to pursue writing full time. "Writing is the best job ever," she admits, "and the most demanding."

Also an accomplished speaker and teacher, Vikki and her husband Conrad Smith make their home in Albuquerque, New Mexico.

To keep abreast of new book releases, sign up for her newsletter on her website at **http://www.vikkikestell.com/** or connect with her on Facebook at **http://www.facebook.com/TheWritingOfVikkiKestell**.

Faith-Filled
Fiction™

Made in the USA
San Bernardino, CA
12 August 2016